It was either a hush-hush government project gone wrong or . . .

I finished off the beer. "Well, it sure beats the alternative."

"What do you mean?" said Monaghan.

"Well, let's see. The alternate scenario is that a man-sized, or larger, flying carnivorous doglike creature flew in the open window of the suite, attacked and dismembered the man, then flew out again with nobody seeing any trace of it." When he didn't immediately respond, I got curious. "There *wasn't* any trace of such a beast, was there, Lieutenant?"

The old cop sighed. "I think that's enough for now, Mr. Vallone. If you get any more information, if this man sent you something or whatever and you receive it later, you *will* call and tell me about it, won't you?"

"You didn't answer my question."

"And you didn't answer mine."

THE
MOREAU
FACTOR

Jack L. Chalker

A Del Rey® Book
THE BALLANTINE PUBLISHING GROUP
NEW YORK

A Del Rey® Book
Published by The Ballantine Publishing Group
Copyright © 2000 by Jack L. Chalker

All rights reserved under International and Pan-American Copyright Conventions. Published in the United States by The Ballantine Publishing Group, a division of Random House, Inc., New York, and simultaneously in Canada by Random House of Canada Limited, Toronto.

Del Rey is a registered trademark and the Del Rey colophon is a trademark of Random House, Inc.

www.randomhouse.com/delrey/

Library of Congress Catalog Card Number: 99-91722

ISBN 0-345-40296-0

Manufactured in the United States of America

First Edition: February 2000

10   9   8   7   6   5   4   3   2   1

For Eva, as always,
and most specially now

ONE

When the matter of the flying werewolf first surfaced in Washington, D.C., I never once thought of the dinosaurs.

It was midautumn, a time I hate worse than any other in the year. Yeah, I know there are folks who rhapsodize over the colorful leaves and lots of people crowd the rural highways and parks to see these bursts of color, but, let's face it, autumn is the season of dying, of death, of the end of hope. It's when those leaves change color that they die, and then they fall in big heaps that somebody has to deal with or they clog drainage and begin to rot. Autumn is when the days grow progressively shorter and the nights take over, when the cold blasts of the north come down and drive happy people inside. Death and decay, that's autumn. Even winter is better; everything's already dead, snow sometimes covers up the evidence, and the days grow longer, giving promise every morning that something better is coming.

The question, after this day, would be whether or not what was coming truly *was* better, or just . . . different.

It was a gloomy, gray day in Washington, and the light, cold rain that went through you to the bone had slacked off just a bit, allowing me to turn off the wipers for once and get rid of the dancing dead leaves that had wedged under the wiper and caused nothing but a massive smear. I was headed up Connecticut Avenue to the Wardman, to meet somebody I'd never heard of before that morning, in hopes that his claim on my voice mail that he had the "story of the century" was even a slight bit true. Everybody always had the story of the century, but it was a long century and most of it hadn't happened yet.

Even the old nation's capital had seen better days. Oh, it kind of looked okay, but if you stared close you could see the occasional gap in buildings where there shouldn't be gaps, and the peeling paint on the signs. You'd notice that all those formerly quaint little shops lining the avenue were now imported junk shops run by people who'd come here from someplace far away in hopes of realizing the American Dream and were discovering that a 7-Eleven was the same the world around.

We old-timers and natives still thought of the Wardman as the old Sheraton Park, a weird hotel built by a madman of geometry driven nuts with government regulations, but it had long ago passed into the hands of other chains. The old hotel used to sit between the National Zoo and Rock Creek Park, built right into the side of a hill; you could enter on the bottom level, go up seven floors, walk down a corridor, and find yourself in the basement of a different but related seven-story hotel. You still did that, but some genius had figured out how to disguise that fact when they redid the hotel back in the late seventies and it wasn't as obvious anymore. Even so, I never felt that I was going where the button on the elevator said I was going in that building until the doors actually opened. There was always this weird, crazy feeling that I'd step out on another planet or a parallel world or something. It was often said that half the people you passed in the halls were old guests trapped there for decades, still trying to find the way out.

Development had long ago moved downtown and the Wardman and its twin, the Shoreham, were now kind of isolated out in the middle of nowhere. Nobody went into Rock Creek Park after dark these days, and the zoo wasn't great company after closing.

As I turned to go toward the upper parking lot I saw all the flashing red and blue lights, and I had this sinking feeling even though there was no reason for me to think that it had anything to do with me. Well, hell, maybe it was a better story than the one I was there to get, I thought. Might as well see what's what.

The cop had been there a little while; he looked wet and miserable and in a *very* rotten mood. I put the window down and he bent down a bit to examine me. "Sir, are you a guest in the hotel?"

"No," I responded. "I'm here for a business appointment with a guest, though."

"Sorry, sir. The main entrance and lobby are blocked off and probably will be for a few more hours. If you turn around, though, and go to the lower level, you can enter through there and there's access from the convention level to the main hotel elevators."

I nodded wearily. "What's the problem?"

"Nothing that need concern you, sir."

I reached down and stuck the press card on the dash, then tried to get my wallet out from where the seat belt secured my pocket. "After many years, son, I find that whenever a cop says that to me it's *exactly* something I should be concerned with."

He looked at the card and my press pass. "*Baltimore Sun,* huh? A little far from Baltimore, aren't you?"

"Forty minutes up I-Ninety-five," I told him, careful not to say how fast I *really* took it. "I'm with the Washington bureau anyway, though. *Times Mirror* syndicate. *L.A. Times*, *Sun*, lots of others. Do I get a parking spot now?"

"You couldn't get in there with a tank," the cop responded. "But it should be good enough to get you into the lobby. The rest of them have set up there."

"The rest of who?"

"You know—Channel Seven, Channel Four, Channel Nine, Channel Five . . ."

"Mere TV, no depth. What about the *Post*?"

"Not yet, although there's a half dozen from the *Times* in there and even the *National Enquirer*. The way this one's going, I wouldn't be surprised to see Oprah and Geraldo."

That was a lot of media, even without the *Post*, which so far had probably decided it was a local story unworthy of the nation's paper. You always could find out more about the president of Albania than the D.C. City Council by reading the *Post*. "Somebody dead?" I asked him.

"Yes, sir. You'll have to move along now, find a place to park it, and come in like I said. I have to keep this street clear."

Good luck, I thought, noting that they still allowed parking along here and you could barely move in the best of times.

Going forward rather than turning around, though, I saw that there was a whole side of the street just beyond the hotel that was clear. Sure, it was labeled "No Parking," but that was what a press pass was for, wasn't it?

Actually, the last time I'd thought that I'd been towed the boss made me pay the pickup. Still, I wasn't about to play round and round under these conditions, and if they'd blocked off the parking up here, there wasn't a chance in hell that you could find anything below either in the lower entrance or over at the Shoreham. I picked up my recorder and my cell phone and was off to work.

The first thing I noticed as I walked to the upper entrance was the lack of any ambulances. You usually had several, even for one stiff, at this stage of the game. I *did* spot the medical examiner's car, but that was strictly for carrying around his or her equipment and evidence bags detached from the corpse. It sure wasn't a hearse, of which there wasn't one, either.

The cop hadn't acted like they'd taken the body away, so was I just on the wrong side of the hotel or was there something odd here?

No, I couldn't be on the wrong side; the cop had directed me to the other side. Okay, so there was something odd, and that made it all the more interesting. Dr. Samuel Wasserman would have to wait.

They were having a bad time of it in the vast lobby, particularly with a hotel that, even in the off season, had several hundred guests, maybe more, and was nearing the evening hour when people were either returning to the hotel or going out to dinner. They'd managed to seal off the area and elevator to the right while keeping traffic elsewhere okay, but clearly guests were being encouraged to walk a bit and go down to the grand entrance far below. I couldn't help but notice that they had used hotel ropes and stanchions rather than police tape for this, which made the whole thing look like a janitorial decision.

The TV people had all their little setups going. Whatever happened had been quite nice to them, allowing at least brief stand-ups during the last part of the evening news. I didn't spot anybody on the print side who looked familiar—local crime stories weren't my normal beat—but I got near where Jan Carleton was about to give her last stand-up before they went to national news over on Nine and that would at least give me a summary as a starting point.

"Police have not yet released the name of the dead man, although he is said to be a biologist with the National Institutes of Health, in town for the American Association for the Advancement of Science convention and symposiums that start this weekend at the convention center. At the moment, all the police will say is that the death was extremely violent and that there are no suspects. We hope to have more details on this brutal slaying at eleven. Back to you, Gordon."

The moment the little earpiece told her she was off and the red light on the camera died she was looking around, frowning. "Anybody seen Jennene? Has she gotten the name and details yet?"

The new age of pseudojournalism, I thought, not for the first time. The poor little anonymous producers go and dig out the facts and get the stories for them, then they write them up in real big letters using words even an ex–beauty queen like Jan could understand, or at least read, and then the photogenic "reporter" would be the mouthpiece of the producer for maybe twenty times the producer's salary.

"They ain't lettin' nobody up there yet, Jan," Harry Lapisky shouted over to her. Harry was one of the few good guys still doing general reporting for TV; he sometimes even dug out his own stories, but he really loved that camera.

"Yeah, well, they're either gonna give us something or we're gonna make everybody who goes in and out of there famous," she snapped back, looking anything but amused.

"*Jennene!* Where the fuck are you, you incompetent little bitch? We're on again in twelve minutes and I haven't even got a goddamn script yet!"

Yeah, that's right, baby. Tear the ass out of that poor little producer for not giving you the words to say.

Harry spotted me and came over. "Well! Hello, stranger! Don't usually see you out on the geek patrol anymore. The body isn't some big shot politician, is it?"

I shrugged. "Hi, Harry. No, beats me. I'm not even here for this, whatever it is. I had a meeting with a source set up, but it doesn't look like it's gonna happen, at least not today." I looked around. "So what's going on to bring out the stand-up troupe?"

"Jeez! You didn't even have your scanner on? Oh, yeah—I forgot. You don't do that kind of shit anymore. Well, the word from the initial call-in was that some guy had been torn to pieces screaming horribly the whole way, and they got a couple of witnesses squirreled away who were down the hall waitin' for the elevator and who swear that nobody went in or out of the room or up and down the hall. One of 'em used a house phone to call the hotel dick, and when they got to the door, they said, the chain was actually on. They had to break it down. Got in, and found the window open and the guy in the room in a condition that'll require blotters to get up the remains. We all got that much. Anything more I can't pass on until after my stand-up. You understand. I got to give the public some reason to keep tuning in to a guy like me when Miss October is over on Channel Seven."

I nodded, but I didn't think he had to worry much. In *this* town they tended to keep the old folks around. Hell, just between Channels Four and Nine the combined age of the two main anchors was a hundred and forty if it was a day. To Jan, this was just a stopover to *Good Morning, America.*

"Harry!" somebody called from across the lobby, and Lapisky turned and gave him a wave. "Got to go! Nice seeing you! Let me know if we can work something together sometime!"

I just gave him a smile and nodded, but I appreciated the respect. These days I'd be lucky to come up with anything dramatic; I was coasting and I knew it, but it wasn't really fun anymore. It was just that I didn't know how to do anything else.

The cops were keeping a rigid guard behind the roped-off gateway to the elevator, but I noticed that a couple of uniforms had been pulled and replaced by officers who really looked the part. They knew that the scene was going to be all over local TV in about five minutes and even if the D.C. police couldn't catch flies they always managed to look good for the cameras.

There was, however, clearly more than just the locals involved. Lots of nice dark suits around, kind of FBI Standard, and there were a couple of obvious Feds I couldn't peg just from looking at them.

Most of the bystanders were probably AAAS attendees themselves. The guy I was supposed to meet was here for it, too, but God knew where he was at this point. Well, he had my cell phone and pager numbers if he wasn't spooked by this.

I didn't know how good the absent Jennene was at digging out facts, but I figured Harry and his producer had huddled, so maybe he had something. I made my way over close to him to listen to his sixty seconds of fame for today.

"Mememememe . . . Youyouyouyou!" Harry sang into the mike. "That a good enough sound check for you, Tom?" He looked back down at a paper in his hand and muttered, "In case you think *The X-Files* and *The Twilight Zone* are just fairy tales, D.C. police tonight have one for the Sci Fi Channel right here at the Wardman . . ."

Now *that* lead got my attention, and I waited for him to go on, feeling impatient. If this thing lived up to its billing I might get on this story myself after all.

They cued Harry, the lights went on, and he began, barely glancing at the paper. It was a nice contrast with Jan over there, who was waiting for her producer to finish her extra-large-print cue cards.

Harry, though, was on. "In case you think *The X-Files* and *The Twilight Zone* are just fairy tales, D.C. police tonight have one for the Sci Fi Channel right here at the Wardman. Shortly after six this evening hotel guests waiting for an elevator heard what they described as 'horrible screams' from a room down the hall. Frightened, they did not investigate but called hotel security, who reportedly had to break in the locked and chained door.

"Witnesses off the record called what they saw inside a 'charnel house,'—the body of a man variously described as 'torn to shreds' or 'splattered all over the hotel room.' Shaken police call it the most violent murder they have ever seen, but there was no one—and no *thing*, either—in the room, other than the victim's remains and an open window with a sheer six-story drop to a concrete patio below. People who were on the patio at the time report that they heard the screams but saw nothing. Pending positive identification of the body and notification of next of kin, the identity of the victim is not yet being released. We'll stay on the scene as developments in this bizarre case warrant. Jim?"

I couldn't hear the follow-up question that was transmitted from the studio to Harry's earpiece, but he looked serious and nodded. "Yes, there's some sort of government secrecy involved, although they can hardly hush this one up. There are representatives here from at least five agencies, including the FBI, CIA, Secret Service, and one or two of those agents for places you can't find, as well as the D.C. police. In fact, it's so crowded with various cops and agents up there, I wouldn't be surprised if Smokey Bear came out of the elevator wearing a big yellow marshal's badge. Until and unless they release more on the victim, however, it is impossible to say if he was with NIH or just associated with them. He certainly wasn't local; locals don't take two-hundred-a-night hotel rooms."

Well, it was beginning to sound more and more interesting. Not that I thought I could outdo the major media crowd here; there were even some network types nosing around, or at least their producers, and they had a hell of a lot more people and money to go digging than I did, but there might be something here, some angle my old contacts might help uncover that these folks might miss.

My claim to fame was that, years ago, I got a Pulitzer. Or, at least, I got half of one, for a series now long forgotten that unmasked some pretty nasty dealings between a couple of unlamented now ex-senators, a House committee chairman, and some pretty ugly foreign government types. Much of it was what we used to call the Sieg Heil Brigade, those politicians who'd get in bed with Hitler Jr. if he said he hated commies, but some of it was also bribery and blackmail. It was big news back in the days of the cold war, but it was just about as forgotten now as the names of those dirty politicians.

Most of us old-timers thought of the cold war period as the good old days, really, when scandals *meant* something and weren't just who was sneaking into bed or on or under desks with who or what. The nation hadn't been the same since it no longer had a common enemy to battle. Hell, these days you run into a few crazy terrorists here and there, a bunch of shady drug types, and you just know it's a non-story until they kill a bunch of people, and then it's good for a week or two tops. When my dad grew up, way back in the Dark Ages, or the idealized fifties, they had duck-and-cover A-bomb drills. You had to know where your nearest fallout shelter was at all times, and you expected Armageddon on twenty minutes' notice. I always get a kick out of these young wimps who think it was Ozzie and Harriet and the Beaver back then. I knew from the stories, the pictures, and some of Dad's old gang who stopped by, that they grew up in the New York tenaments dodging zip-gun bullets from guys in leather jackets whose territories were marked out on concrete jungles. Dad still had scars from switchblades, but, never mind. Always made me wonder about this "power of the media" crap. Grow up in Blackboard Jungle one step from nuclear destruction and the kids say, "Gee, they didn't have any worries back in those peaceful days." I guess that's why I grew up so cynical myself. Heck, the running gag in *Father Knows Best* was that the dumb schmuck didn't know anything at all . . .

I remember when the people who were now in the lobby trying for angles on their two and a half hours of afternoon and early evening news actually had to be *reporters* and go get the news and dig out the information. You know, Woodward and Bernstein, two kids on the D.C. crime beat, bring down a president when the White House Press Corps hadn't a clue, that kind of thing. Now *everybody's* the WHPC, waiting for handouts and vamping in between while checking their makeup, but so long as you had that reddish blond hair and pouty lips like Jan there, people were going to watch anyway.

I was jolted back to the twenty-first century by my own Buck Rogers gadgets both going off at the same time. It drew nasty looks from the sound men even though it was a Tower of Babel in there anyway.

I checked the pager, which had a number to call and a name, "LT MONAGHAN," a name I recognized as being one of D.C.'s finest. I clicked it off and looked at the cell phone, and it said the same damned number was calling, so, what the hell.

"Chuck Vallone," I said. "Speak to me."

"Vallone? This is Lieutenant Monaghan, D.C. Homicide. Where are you right now?"

"In the lobby of the Wardman," I told him. "What's up?"

"Christ! You're already here, then! I want you to go to the elevator and tell the patrolman there who you are. He'll want a picture ID. Give me a couple of minutes to radio your clearance. Then come through and take the elevator to six. I'll have somebody bring you in from there."

Now *this* I wasn't used to. Inviting the press to a sealed-off scene? Something was fishy here. For the first time, I got the sinking feeling that maybe I wasn't going to be able to do the background interview after all under *any* circumstances.

"Okay, Lieutenant. Be up as soon as your boys will let me."

I pushed "End" and then ambled over toward the guard, who looked very much like he used to be the nose tackle for the Washington Redskins. You know—three-hundred-plus pounds, mostly muscle, face like African chiseled stone, hands about the size of cantaloupes. Trouble is, he was looking at me like I was the opposition quarterback.

I stalled for a moment and then heard his walkie-talkie squawk. He picked it up, said something into it, it said something that, at this distance, was more distortion than voice, and then he reclipped it on his belt. I figured that had to be the clearance, so I proceeded, hoping that none of these Boys in Blue or Men in Black knew or remembered me. It had been a long time since I'd done anything local, so there was a chance that none of them even realized I was a newspaperman. At least I hoped that was the case.

I pulled out my wallet, ignored the press card, and pulled my Maryland driver's license and approached the cop. "I'm Vallone. Lieutenant Monaghan said to show you ID and come on up to him."

The big cop was impassive for a moment, then reached over and took my license and looked at it, then at me. I wasn't sure if he was reading the stats or comparing features, but he finally seemed satisfied.

"Okay, go on up, but no walking around by yourself up there," the cop warned me. "Go where you're not supposed to be and you might wind up stepping on evidence or having evidence step on you."

I got the message, and couldn't help but feel an inward smirk as all of my colleagues back there were watching me go under the ropes, pass by the guardians of law and order, and punch the "Up" button on the elevator.

It was a quick ride; they had a cop in each elevator with a key override. They couldn't exactly seal off the whole wing of the hotel for this, not with it basically full, but they could ensure that you had to go up by one of the banks in the other wing and walk over to your room, and that you showed a key to go up to your floor, and down was the only way you could go if you left your room.

There were the usual goings-on on six; lab boys dusting practically the whole hall, various forensic equipment here and there, and a human gate blocking off the room in question and the elevator bank. I could just imagine what these folks were going through who had expensive rooms up here.

Well, at least they could feel safe that their rooms weren't going to be robbed.

"Mr. Vallone? I'm Agent Chomsky, FBI," a fellow in a gray suit and perfectly correct tie said to me as I stepped into the hallway. He put out his hand and I took it, even though it seemed pretty silly. As I suspected, he had a handshake like a dead fish.

I looked around. "Pretty crowded and noisy here. Should we go someplace?"

"We have a room over here that we can use, if you like," the agent said, gesturing away from the direction I wanted to go in. "You can wait there until Lieutenant Monaghan and a few other law enforcement people get the chance to speak to you."

This I didn't much care for. "Agent Chomsky, I was downstairs, in the bar, crowded as it was with reporter types, nicely munching nuts and enjoying a beer when I got mysteriously summoned up here. Now, I don't want to be uncooperative, but unless you're ready for me, I'd much rather go back to the bar."

It threw him. It really did. I was amazed, but, then, he *was* a little young for the big time. He probably had a hundred patters for folks who wanted to be elsewhere but not for somebody who wanted to wait it out in the bar. As expected, he froze for a bit, did a *Stepford Wives*–type *click-whirr*, then reset.

"I'm sorry, sir, but you'll have to wait in the room. I'm sure it won't be long."

"Sonny, I'm sorry, but unless I'm under arrest or being held for some reason, I want to wait in someplace comfortable. I'm not going anywhere. Or, we can go see the nice lieutenant now. Maybe *he* needs a drink, too. I bet he does, by the looks of this."

The young man swallowed, then said, "Wait right here. I'll go get him."

I wasn't used to seeing an FBI man doing legwork for the local cops. Either this homicide cop was a double dipper with a secondary job or the kid was vamping for a much higher superior who was way beyond Monaghan. Looking around and seeing guards keeping people from using the elevators or stairwell but none of them preventing movement of the technicians and cops who were inside the barriers, as I was, I simply followed the young agent down the hall and right into the hotel room, looking like it was what I should do.

It had been a really nice business suite before this. Now, it looked like they were going to have to strip the thing to bare walls and start all over again.

Even with forensics guys all over, it was a mess. I knew the human body had a lot more blood than you'd think, but this was giant sized. It was all over the place. Walls, ceiling, rug, furniture, you name it.

At least whoever did this wasn't a vampire.

Even if master cleaners could get out the blood, which I doubted, they also had to contend with the smell. Not just the smell of death, but an odd, acrid, unpleasant, yet somewhat familiar odor, like, well, like that of a kennel. No, not a kennel. The dog pound during a heavy rain.

They had removed the body, or at least what parts of it they could reassemble, but the marks on the rug and furniture showed that he'd not merely been killed, he'd been literally ripped to pieces. *Jesus!* I thought, and for a change I wasn't being the least bit sacrilegious. *What kind of monster could do this?*

And not leave a sign of its own self.

The young agent was speaking with an older guy in a much cheaper blue suit, whom I took to be the lieutenant. I assumed from his look that he was years beyond getting sick of the black Irish jokes. Dark brown, very weathered features, with short gray hair and bushy, snow white eyebrows. It gave him a look of world-weariness that matched his baggy clothes.

If this guy was also something higher up, he sure didn't do it for the money.

The young man nodded back, turned, started walking toward the door, and then stopped dead in his tracks as he saw me standing there.

"You can't be here, sir!" he protested, shocked.

"But I *am* here, son. Quite a mess."

"But—but you've got to *leave*! Please!"

By this time Monaghan had noticed me and with one of those sighs he wandered over to us.

"That's all right, son. I'll take it from here. Go notify Inspector Barnes." He looked straight at me then. "And you must be Charles Vallone? Sounds familiar, somehow. Why is that, Mr. Vallone?"

I shrugged. "I'm a writer, Lieutenant. You might have seen something of mine someplace." I decided to hold back the fact that I wrote for a semilocal newspaper as long as possible.

"Maybe. Don't get a chance to read much these days. I see that gruesome scenes don't put you off."

"No, not really. I've been in my share of combat zones over the years. Never saw or smelled anything quite like *this*, though."

"Yeah. Well, neither have I, and I thought I'd seen 'em all. Let's step outside in the hall, anyway, though. I'm through here and these people still have a lot of work to do."

I complied, and we wandered down toward the elevator

once more. "I told the eager young agent that I'd just as soon wait at the bar downstairs. Want to join me?"

The old cop chuckled. "Wish I could. It's not the drink that would get me, though, it's that wall of reporters downstairs. Let's go in this room over here and I'll see if I can requisition the minibar."

The room, which I assumed was the one I was originally supposed to have gone to, was a mirror image of the murder scene, only this one hadn't had much exciting happen in it.

I sank into one of the padded chairs and Monaghan produced one of those all-purpose police key rings, selected a particular small probe, and stuck it in the minibar lock. He turned, it turned, and he asked, "What's your pleasure?"

"You missed your calling, Lieutenant," I told him. "They got any decent beer in there?"

"Heineken, Sam Adams, the usual."

"Give me the Heineken. I never did see much difference in Sam Adams and a dozen other beers."

He handed me the beer after opening it, then got a Bud for himself. "I'm a working man. Working man's tastes," he commented.

I took a swig, then asked him, "So, Lieutenant, are all the rumors swirling on the *Five O'Clock News* true? I mean, locked room and everything?"

"Yeah, but you probably saw for yourself. They broke it in and found that. Victim was Dr. Samuel Wasserman. Know him?"

"Never met him, but I figured it was him. I was supposed to meet him for dinner. When they said sixth floor, NIH, and then I saw the room number, it didn't take a lot of imagination."

"We found his notebook computer with your name and numbers and a notation that you'd be meeting," he told me.

"That's why both my phone and pager went off. You called both."

"Had no idea which was which. Like the usual brainy type,

he was a mess in his files." He paused a moment, taking a long draw on his beer. "So, when was your appointment?"

"We were supposed to meet here, in the bar, at six," I told him. "Funny—I guess that would have been right about now, huh?"

"Yeah, well, he won't make it. And you were here strictly for that? You didn't know anything about the murder?"

"Not a bit until I pulled up and couldn't get in to park. I *still* didn't really know it was him until I began to listen to the TV people downstairs and then confirmed it up here."

"What did the two of you intend to talk about?"

"I really don't know. I wish I did, particularly now. He apparently knew me through my writings or something—it was one of those things I meant to ask him—and called me and said he had information that was so frightening and incredible that he didn't know what to do and that he had to tell somebody, somebody *they* wouldn't necessarily have covered but who might be able to act on it. That's not the kind of thing you can ignore, even if it does sound paranoid as all hell. I checked him out, of course. Found that he was a leading man in his field, that he'd been nominated for a Nobel in biology but didn't win, and he'd been a big shot academic and researcher. That was enough for me. I mean, hell, what did I have to lose? And, at my age, it seemed like one last big potential for a payoff. I mean, what a book if it lived up to its billing, right?"

"Yes, I see. And what exactly was his field?"

"He was a geneticist. Worked for years on the Human Genome gene-mapping project right here, then when that was pretty well done he'd gone into some kind of high-tech computer project with Carnegie Mellon that nobody seems to know much about or wants to know much about, if you know what I mean, and then he pretty much vanished. Hadn't been seen or heard of in the past two or three years, although he would pop up now and then at some big-shot conferences. Never gave papers there, but seemed to be conferring or recruiting. That was kind of consistent with this meeting here. I figured he had to be on some kind of government hush-hush project, probably not the initiator or boss, and from the looks of the Fed presence lurking around here I'd say that was true."

"It pretty much checks with what we know," the cop admitted. "If he had other scientists in mind, though, he didn't record any names in his notebook."

"Kind of falls into 'conspiracy theory heaven,' doesn't it, Lieutenant?" I commented. "I mean, he's murdered just before he can talk to a writer about something that obviously scared him and was top secret."

Monaghan chuckled. "That may be great for one of your books, but it's not the way things happen around here. It's tough to keep anything secret, let alone conspiratorial, in this town. Besides, if it was a government job, why be so showy? He could have just vanished, or have taken ill—there's a lot of ways to kill someone without drawing the news media of the world to it."

"Not if you wanted to advertise his death," I speculated.

"Huh?"

"Well, let's say you have a big black job. Let's say you're reverse engineering the Roswell flying saucer, taking for a moment that they really do have one. Tons of people, many major brains in science and engineering, even technicians, heavy equipment operators, guards, you name it. A ton of people, enough for a small Air Force base. And if one of them talks and has anything to back it up, you're stuck. That's why I never thought there was anything to that Roswell stuff. All those people and not one piece of evidence in all those years. Not only against human nature, it's against history. But, let's say it's true. And one guy decides to talk. Not to the news— for one thing, he just sounds like another nut and the reporter would have the weight of counterpropaganda dropped on him to make sure he *stays* a nut. So you call somebody like me instead. Give me the leads, hope I can turn up some money to follow his information and break the story without having an eleven o'clock deadline. He's been in public before, there was no reason to think he'd crack, but when you did it was

late and he was already here and already had an appointment
with me. So what do you do?"

"Take him out, or make him vanish and put him on ice,
maybe, but not this sort of thing."

"Or, maybe you go the other way. Not knowing how many
folks he's contacted, or what else he's said, you're faced with
the fact that there are hundreds of people, maybe thousands,
who might also be tempted. If he just vanishes, well, you
never know, and he's a blip on the local news. Take him out in
spectacular fashion, super gory and in public, and you get
maximum publicity. If you're sure that they can't trace him
back to you, then let him go out in the most awful way possible. Headlines. All that. You've got a really nasty object
lesson there that everybody who knows anything is gonna
find impossible to miss, but what have you lost? In the end,
he's still just the four hundredth or so unsolved murder in the
District of Columbia."

"So you think it's the government-conspiracy-type equivalent of a mob hit, huh? Broad daylight, messy, send a message. If I really believed in those kind of conspiracies, and
that they could hold up for a long period of time, I might
agree with you, but I just don't believe it."

I finished off the beer. "Well, it sure beats the alternative."

"What do you mean?"

"Well, let's see. The alternate scenario is that a man-sized,
or larger, flying carnivorous doglike creature flew in the open
window of the suite, attacked and dismembered the man,
then flew out again with nobody seeing any trace of it." When
he didn't immediately respond, I got curious. "There *wasn't*
any trace of such a beast, was there, Lieutenant?"

The old cop sighed. "I think that's enough for now, Mr.
Vallone. If you get any more information, if this man sent you
something or whatever and you receive it later, you will call
and tell me about it, won't you?"

"You didn't answer my question."

"And you didn't answer mine."

I got up, stretched, and went over to the windows, pulling

back the curtains and seeing right away that something else hadn't been mentioned. "Well, then, I guess that makes us even."

Monaghan didn't think that was funny. "Listen, Mister Writer. We've got a dead man here and the kind of death that makes people paranoid. And you've got no special status here. For all I know you're a suspect. Right now you're the only name I can link to him closer than three to four years ago. And what the hell are you looking at?"

"The window wasn't open," I commented, looking out into the darkness. "These windows are the kind that are made to not open, the better to keep the climate control in. So, tell me, Lieutenant. Was it kicked *in*? It sure as hell wasn't kicked *out*, since there were people below."

"You're a little too smart for your own good, aren't you? I can see why he might have called you." It was grudging respect from a pro, and I appreciated it. "Still," he continued, "you're not immune, you know. Whoever or whatever did this might well think that you know more than you're telling. They might not stop to figure out why you and not somebody else. You think about that?"

"Not until now," I responded seriously. "I *don't* know any more than you do, probably less. But now that I'm up to my waist in this, I intend to try and find out. Want to trade information as we get it, Lieutenant?"

"No deals, Vallone. I won't write your book for you. But you *better* clue us in on anything you find and tread very, very softly on this. You have no idea how high up this has gone."

"Oh, I think I'm beginning to figure that out on my own," I told him. It was pretty easy to figure that there were lipstick cameras all over this room and mikes that could probably measure my blood pressure. I'd already spotted a couple, and they were either being redundant or there was a turf battle going on between agencies.

"You need me anymore, Lieutenant?"

The cop took out an old-fashioned notepad and handed it

to me with a pencil. "Name, address, all your phone numbers, and where they reach," he told me. "We'll be in touch."

I gave him what he wanted. "Can I go now? If I don't have an appointment, then I'm going to have to figure out some-place else for dinner, and I'm starving."

"Smart-ass. It's amazing to me somebody hasn't gotten to you by now with that kind of attitude. Okay, though. Go."

"What's the secret back way out?" I asked him. "Anybody who comes out of that elevator down there and doesn't imme-diately go to a cop car is gonna be mobbed by media."

"Ask Brown at the desk station on the right as you go out. He'll get you an escort to the back service elevators. Where are you parked?"

"On the street, a couple of blocks away off Rock Creek."

"Well, we'll get you outside. After that, it's your problem."

I wondered if he would find out what the folks on the other end of those cameras and mikes undoubtedly already knew from just looking me up in their own databases, and, if so, when.

It was really hard to keep that calm-and-steady routine going when all I wanted was to get to my laptop in the car, type out the specifics, and get it to the City Desk in Balti-more. And, by God, this *better* be a front-page byline!

TWO

To tell you the truth, I really didn't have time to get spooked about the facts in this story until after I'd filed the whole thing and really was looking for a place to eat.

Okay, a lot of that conspiracy stuff was just the kind of crap everybody thinks—otherwise, I'd either be dead long ago, or a town that can't keep two secrets for a week can keep the big ones for decades, something history denies. Since you can't disprove a negative, though, it sure makes money and it sure sells papers and pumps up ratings. It's why being in the media is kind of scary: you have no sense of the power you might wield and there's only your peers to keep you honest. And, heck, most people *believe* that stuff. More people believe in flying saucers, I saw in one poll, than believe that anybody ever walked on the moon. Go figure.

Not that there weren't black projects. Oh, there were always plenty of those. They got all that lovely money, almost nobody to be accountable to, and so long as you spread the pork around a little bit they will ask no questions. Sometimes something comes out of it. The ultimate black project was the Manhattan Project, of course, and it was also the ultimate example of what I mean.

The project was enormous, the most expensive black project ever in terms of real money, and the head of the Senate Intelligence Committee was a good old boy from Knoxville who could make or break the project. The story goes that Roosevelt and his aides spent a good hour or so on the hard sell, and the senator just sat there, impassive. Finally, when they were done and all looking at him as the man who could get that much money for national security through Congress on his word alone, he suddenly brightened up, smiled, and said, "Hell, Franklin, that sounds great! Now where in hell in Tennessee are we gonna put it?"

Stealth bombers, laser-guided smart bombs, you name it, they come from a long tradition. What's also traditional is the flip side nobody ever talks about: the hundreds of total, complete and utter idiotic flops and disasters that were also funded as black projects and died leaving mostly holes in the budget. Those were the ones that could get you a great story, either on TV or on the front pages, and those were mostly buriable, as it were, only because so many projects that were done in the light of day were so awesomely wasteful that nobody had to work to dig out the really secret flops.

Technology was the key, of course. Ever since the industrial revolution mucked things up we've been increasing our knowledge in all fields exponentially every decade, and by the end of the twentieth century it was accelerating out of control. Hell, we were already arguing by then, not *whether* we could clone people, but only if it was right and proper to do so. Sliding into the twenty-first century headlong made me happy sometimes that I never had kids, at least none that I knew of. What kind of world would theirs be?

Nuclear, chemical, and biological weapons, that's what everybody worried about, and they should, but they were old stuff, passé, and besides, everybody knew about them and worried about them. Dog bites man. They were a big story only when they went off when they shouldn't, or went off when they were aimed at lots of innocent people. Otherwise, they were back in the technology section.

I'd started off in this business covering local politics, then graduated to covering national politics, all the backroom deals and dealings, and it finally became like shooting fish in a barrel. Besides, I was getting old, out of touch, or so they said, and there was more than one move to ease me out, but I'd been careful not to price myself out of a job and, I thought, resourceful enough to find a new niche. I don't know how I eased into science and technology, but it seemed a way to keep up and maybe prove that I was still young. Nobody else wanted to take the beat unless it was to uncover some vast new conspiracy to turn us all into the Pillsbury Doughboy or something like that. Nobody much cared about space, unless somebody died, and everybody already thought they knew computers, so let the old boy have his fun.

I'd been on this beat for some time, zeroing in on the Beltway Bandits, those huge corporations ringing the D.C. beltway and the interstates that fed into it, that had wonderful names nobody had ever heard of and did God knew what. It proved to be a really interesting time. They were evenly divided between companies that specialized in figuring out what various branches of government wanted and providing it, even if they had to invent it to do it, and those who figured out what kinds of research they could continue to own, and someday profit from, that the government would mostly pay for them to develop. It was both highly speculative and cutting edge. It had a lot of failures, and some spectacular successes. Advances in everything from biotechnology to robotics were getting scary even to me. And if these were the ones I *could* get interviews on, I could just imagine, and occasionally lucked out and discovered, what might be going on in some of the black projects.

I'd gotten interested during the days of the Human Genome Project. That's old news and old hat now, but back in the nineties two companies, one pretty much universities-and-government and the other private-industry-and-government, started off to map every single gene in the human body. What it was, what it did, how it got turned on and off, and so on. They were already curing at the genetic level diseases that nobody dreamed could ever be cured, and they were already facing lots of opposition from scared groups, activists, Luddites, and congressmen in particular, who were convinced that Doc Frankenstein was alive and well and working in Rockville, Maryland.

Of course, that fear was also the only reason any of us could still buy life and health insurance anymore, too, since the insurance companies needed only a throat culture to be able to tell just what diseases you were most likely to die from and exclude those from your policies. And who said we didn't need government?

I guess it was those same guys who told us for a decade that the stock market simply couldn't crash again. I just wish those guys would do the proper thing when they screw up: go up to the top floor of their fancy office buildings and take a flying leap. It was those folks who ensured I'd still be working into old age.

I went over to Sixteenth Street and ran out toward Silver Spring, figuring I'd find some little hole in the wall to eat at. I'd just settled on Eddie's, an unfancy steak and burger joint, when the phone rang again.

"Yeah?"

"Chuck? Adam Hall. We've had some surprising pressure on us in the past hour to keep most of the details out of your story. In other words, to edit out the descriptives and make it look like the rest of the handout stuff. They even called the big man out in L.A. Said we were going to give out details they had deliberately suppressed in order to nail the killer, that sort of thing."

"Yeah, I expected that and warned you about it, Adam," I replied, knowing that he'd understand I was using the collective "you" in this case. I usually didn't hear from Adam unless it was to discuss things like salaries, bonuses, and whether or not the editorial board really liked me. "Still, there's not a lot there. Wonder what they don't like? I mean, I fingered a couple of agencies, I guess, and I gave a firsthand description of the murder scene, but that's about it."

"Apparently that's enough. At least the firsthand description. You have to admit it's pretty weird."

"Weird? You oughta *been* there if you think what I turned in was weird. I don't know what this is, Adam, but something kicked in a sixth-floor window where there's no balcony or ledge, did it in broad daylight, and ripped a guy to shreds, then left the same way he got in. Sherlock Holmes may have some ideas on it, but I'm just a poor dumb reporter. Besides, they can't sit on anything over there. If we don't get it in the early edition it's gonna leak all over the morning news anyway."

"Okay, just wanted to hear that you had no second thoughts."

"Why the hell should I have any second thoughts?"

"Well, maybe because if the cops knew about his appointment with you, then maybe whoever killed him knew it, too. And has no idea that you don't know anything about what he was going to talk about." He paused for a moment. "You *don't* know, do you?"

"Not a clue, but I'm sure gonna be working on it."

"Fair enough, but, for the time being, watch your back."

I chuckled. "Hey, if this thing can fly through windows and do *that*, then if it wants me it can get me. Not much I can do about it. Can I go eat now?"

"Yeah, sure. But keep us informed of what you're doing so if anything does come up we can follow up on you. Coordinate with—oh, how about Karen Reedy on the City Desk?"

"Karen? Okay, will do. Again I ask, can I go eat now?"

"Yeah, sure. Talk to you soon." And the line went dead.

Hell, we're already anachronisms, I thought. Print news in the era of the nonreader whose concept of news is what rock star overdosed on what this morning. With the dozens of cable TV news operations, the big nets, and even the computer nets, what were we, anyway, except something many people still felt essential in the morning because otherwise they'd have to talk to their husbands or wives over breakfast. Nobody read a newspaper for *news* anymore. In fact, if they didn't trim it, my story was already on the Internet edition just as I finally found a parking place and locked up and headed for Eddie's.

The trouble is, I couldn't enjoy my food. Damn it, I never spooked easily, and I didn't get grossed out by scenes like the one I'd seen that evening, but when your own boss is worried enough to call and do a pro forma warning, then you feel like there's something to it, almost like he knew more than the poor reporter he was jerking around.

I mean, reporters didn't get whacked very often except maybe in combat zones, but it did come with some of the territory. Calls like Adam's to me just about *never* took place, not in that kind of context. Sure, giving me a handler was one method of operation—they expected an expense account, and some investment in me as well, to develop a story that would take time, and they wanted to be sure that they weren't getting conned. It didn't happen often, but the fact that it did only signalled that they thought this story had real potential. But the warning . . .

Well, I'd been totally honest with him on that score, anyway. Anybody who could bring off the scene that had killed poor Dr. Wasserman was beyond my ability to stop. On the other hand, there were so many Feds up there that I was surely being watched, followed, monitored, and who knew what else. I only hoped they'd be there to intervene if need be and wouldn't be too busy taking pictures of whatever it was.

That whole line of depressing thought gave me a bit of heartburn that went way beyond what Eddie's usually did, and I decided it might be time to go home, get online, find some promising new directions, and hope that nobody flew through my window. On the other hand, a visit the next day to my old friend down at the Spy Shop in downtown might be in order. If they were going to be bugging me, I wanted to know it, and, most important, I wanted to know when they *weren't*.

I had a small condo not far off I-95 just north of Laurel, Maryland. It was reasonable, the association tolerated a slob like me if I wasn't *too* cruddy, and it was about equal distance in drive time between the Sunpapers in Baltimore and Capitol Hill, allowing me to be most places in an hour or less. It wasn't much, but I didn't really need much. Not much to show for a guy looking backwards at fifty. Hell, I even had the awards, most of the prestige photos, that kind of thing, in the small office I had in the *Sun* building, an office I was only in once or twice a week for a few hours. It was my showplace; this was my hideout.

I'd parked in the same space a thousand times, and walked up the same walk, went into the same main door, and then up to the same front door I'd always used, but this time it felt different. *Damn it! If you're gonna be paranoid at least get more information and really scare yourself!* I scolded my inner psyche.

Jeez! I'd gotten myself so spooked I kept feeling like I was Ebenezer Scrooge coming home on Christmas Eve to be haunted.

I opened the door and nothing leaped out at me from the darkness. I put down my briefcase, which included the memory module from my car's computer, and the lights came on as movement was sensed in the entry hall.

I stopped and looked around. Maybe I hadn't been so dumb after all to be paranoid.

Somebody had been here. Oh, they hadn't wanted the same kind of example as with the good doctor, and maybe they hoped I wouldn't even notice, but a lot of stuff had been taken out, examined, and then put back without a lot of rehearsal on how it had originally been arranged.

The place was essentially a two-bedroom apartment with a living room, kitchenette, and bathroom, all on one level. It was also supposed to be guarded by a gate guard at the entrance, then by a central alarm system for the building, and then again by motion sensors I'd installed inside the apartment. If any of that had gone off, nobody had bothered to tell me about it, not even a note.

So, that meant pros, and probably not burglars, but what kind of pros would be so messy but not *that* messy?

"I told the association I should be allowed to have a dog," I grumbled, then did a thorough check of all the rooms. There was also a patio door that led out to a small balcony, but since I was on the second floor it wasn't a place I'd felt needed a full alarm system. Silly me. The alarm still should have gone off in the guard's shack and in the central system's headquarters when they opened the patio door. There was no sign of forced entry on it, no broken glass, nothing. Since, allegedly, there were only two magic keys that could silence the alarm without one of the system techs coming here and the second key was in the hands of the alarm company, I had to figure that whoever this was had the clout to pick up that key and use it. Hell, even I couldn't get in without making an incredible racket if I lost my key. I knew that by embarrassing experience. And yet, here somebody had just waltzed in. I had *my* key, so . . .

Scratch thirty bucks a month for my share of this alarm system, that's for sure.

Nothing had been taken, I was sure of that. At least, nothing I'd notice. One of the bedrooms was my bedroom, of course, and the other was a kind of home office with my computer and such. Since I took the sensitive stuff with me when I left each day, I assumed they'd enjoy my attempts at the great American novel and all those sexy holograms. I had no doubt that they had copies of everything, and I hoped it took them forever to break the superencrypted paranoia disk I always kept around as a joke in case this happened but never really figuring it would. It used encryption systems that I'd been assured were used by banks and spy agencies and it would be hell to crack, and I'd had it made up for me by one of the top criminal hackers in the business as payment for not identifying him directly in a column. Nothing was uncrackable, and I suspected that these types had the best National Security Agency computers and techs at their disposal— NSA was just a few exits down the highway, after all—but the hacker had assured me that it would do damage as well and would contain some wonderful bombs for the system that opened it.

Of course, all that would lead ultimately only to my mother's old recipe book, but that was part of the fun of it. At least I could sleep tonight dreaming of all those guys over at the NSA battling the Neptunian Deathstalker's wonderful traps and tricks and finally winding up with the best spaghetti sauce you couldn't buy.

Still, it was worth calling in again on the cell phone—I assumed my regular phone was tapped and this one probably was, too, but what the hell—and got a worried editor.

"Jeez, Chuck! You want to stay at a hotel or something for now? We'll pick it up."

I thought about what I'd seen and where I'd been. "Um, no, I don't think a hotel would make me feel any safer, Adam, thanks anyway."

"You call the cops?"

"No, I don't think that would make much difference, either. There's no forcible entry and as far as I know nothing's missing. Be nice to know what they thought I had that was worth this, though. I mean, the guy never said more than 'Let's get together for dinner and I'll give you the story of your life,' and he was dead when I got there, so I don't know what he was going to tell me and I don't have anything from him. Go figure."

If anybody *was* doing an intercept, that ought to at least buy me a little time. The fact that it happened to be true also helped, but paranoids didn't always take truth for what it was.

I signed off fairly quickly and decided to get some sleep. I mean, what the hell could I do if they came in? I half expected to wake up in some cell in deepest Washington with some guys shining bright lights on me, but I also knew that this would bring down the whole press corps on whatever this was about in a way nothing else could. I might not have any privacy from now on, but I was pretty damned sure they would watch rather than touch, at least for now, if only in hope that I'd lead them to whatever it was they were looking for.

In the meantime, staying awake all night and staring into the darkness in fear and trepidation would only make me miserable without doing anything at all to advance the problem.

I do admit that, after I turned out the last of the lights, I went over to my patio doors and peered out at the parking lot.

It was stupid, I knew—if they wanted me they could get me easily and if it was the kind of folks who tore the doc limb from limb then being in front of these patio doors was an open invitation. Still, it was just something I had to do before nodding off.

All quiet, of course. But, then, maybe not . . . What was that, way the hell over at the far end of the lot, keeping just out of the streetlights? It looked kind of like a man, average height, in some kind of trench coat. How . . . *obvious*, I thought. Like they *wanted* to advertise.

Still, something looked a little off, even though I couldn't put my finger on it. Something in the way the guy was standing, or in the way he moved a bit. And then he came close enough that the light shined down and partly illuminated him, and I drew back. That *face*—like some weird animal's face, not really human at all . . .

I drew back instinctively, but then had to look again.

Nothing. Nobody there.

Either I was letting my imagination get the best of me or I'd seen whoever or whatever it was who'd visited the doc at the Wardman.

Stupid me. No matter which explanation was right, I lay there in the darkness and had a really tough time nodding off, half expecting those patio doors to burst open at any moment and some monstrous man-sized creature to burst in . . .

In the morning's light, I had to admit that my imagination was most likely the villain. The distance to that lamppost was a lot farther than it had seemed, maybe too far to really have seen any details in a face, and it was most likely one of the neighbors in a robe or housecoat putting out the garbage. Still, it was hard to get that face, that *presence*, out of my mind.

I checked with some of the neighbors but as usual nobody saw or heard a thing. I didn't want to make them paranoid, but I didn't like somebody just walking in and throwing stuff all around. I mean, if they're going to really search a place they ought to at least be decent enough to put stuff back.

The mail was the usual bills and junk, but just as I was working the phones trying to find out some lead that would at least point me in the right direction—hell, even the wrong direction, the way things were going—the bell rang and it was the FedEx man with a parcel that required a signature. I took it, not expecting anything, and when I noted that the airbill's return address was the Wardman Hotel Business Center I got very interested very fast.

It was a pretty small package inside one of the courier envelopes, and when I took off the lid I saw, first and foremost, a computer disk, and, under it, some tiny glassine envelopes containing God knew what.

I decided to take a look at the computer disk on my laptop; *this* I have with me at all times so it was unlikely to have been compromised, and, with its satellite cellular link, I could upload anything interesting to places it would be tough to track.

What it was, was a compiled program that, when I activated it, produced a bizarre video display that made no sense at all unless maybe you were on some really strong drugs, and below that, tons and tons of letters and numerical sequences with no obvious key. I had no idea what the hell I was looking at, but, at the same time, I had every expectation that I was looking directly at what everybody was searching for. It was upload time—and to several dozen places. I wanted to make sure that nobody was going to be able to deduce all the locations of the copies, even if the doc had neglected to include the secret decoder ring.

While that was running, I took a look at the envelopes. Weird looking stuff, but, then again, every medical sample I ever saw was of something I could never identify, even if it had come from me. They looked like dried hair and skin samples, but from what? At least one of the short tufts of hair was dark green.

I wasn't sure I liked where this might be leading. Did little green men have little green hairs?

A tiny card with the lot, written in obvious haste with a simple hotel ballpoint, said, "Mr. Vallone—have the samples checked by a good DNA lab. I think it will interest you if we cannot meet." The signature was the simple initials "S.W."

Okay, Doc, I'll bite. You got killed over some hair and skin samples?

Still, somebody went to a lot of trouble to look for something in my place, and the doc was dead, so if it was some kind of lead then I'd follow it. Besides, if I was being watched, then it was a sure thing that they saw the delivery, and since they didn't get what they were looking for the night before, well, the assumption would be pretty clear. I had to move before they decided to come and take it from me.

Wasserman wrote like the kind of geek he'd been. Have it checked by a good DNA lab indeed. Okay, so the Human Genome Project had been based in the Maryland suburbs of D.C., and one of the biggest private DNA crime labs was over in Gaithersburg, but it wasn't like you could look up DNA labs in the Yellow Pages or just walk in off the street.

"Hey, fellows, I got this weird material in the mail. Can you tell me if it's Martian skin?" Yeah, sure. Well, okay, not Martian. We knew better than that now, but maybe from farther out?

And did they masquerade as us and walk among us in the dark, wearing trench coats, able to disguise all about themselves except maybe their weird ratlike faces?

Great. Maybe I *was* getting caught up in a real-life version of *The X-Files* or something like that, but everybody knew what happened to people like me who found out too much, right?

Hell, I didn't mind a war or a nest of spies or something, but I was too damned old for this shit.

Well, I had it, whether I wanted it or not, and I knew deep down that I couldn't drop it at this point if I wanted to. The dear departed doctor had seen to that. They'd never believe that I didn't know more than the zero I did, and they'd never believe I gave 'em all the copies. Nope, it wasn't a great choice but it was the only one open to me: I had to go for another Pulitzer.

Funny thing was, so few people read the few remaining daily papers these days that if they'd done nothing, nobody would have noticed, and everybody, including me, would have gone on to other things in a day or two. Now that it was my ass, I was going to get to the bottom of it if I could.

The real problem was, how the hell could I get these samples analyzed? Those who were looking for them would naturally cover any DNA testing labs, and they didn't sell Test Your Own DNA Junior Science Kits at the nearest Toys "R" Us, or even at the National Science Foundation, so I'd have to go to one anyway. The trick would be to keep my involvement at least one step removed, at least for now.

I called D.C. Homicide. "Lieutenant Monaghan, please."

I was mildly surprised that he was actually in the office. Detectives usually weren't, but I guess he was still doing reports from the day before.

"Lieutenant? Chuck Vallone. Looks like I'm more sucked into this than I figured."

Briefly, I told him of my break-in and home search and even mentioned my sense of a creepy shadow of a figure outside that night. Finally, I told him about the package.

"Samples of something, you say?"

"Yes, and a note to get it to a DNA lab. I'm sure you sent samples of various splotches, hair, and whatever from the murder room to a lab. Any chance of piggybacking on yours with these so that it's not so obvious that they're mine?"

He considered it. "Very irregular, and pretty expensive."

"Aw, com'on, Monaghan. You know this dovetails your own investigation, and it may be the only chance you'll have to guarantee that you'll get the same results I do at the same time. Besides, I have a pretty good budget on this story. We can cover the added expenses."

I knew from the start that he would do it, if only to get his hands on the added samples. "All right, here's what you do. Use a reputable courier company, pick it at random and phone it from a secure phone. Have them pick it up from you and then deliver it to Dr. Sandra McCall at Genetique in Gaithersburg. Include a note that this is in reference to and additional evidence for D.C. Homicide case number nine-seven-three-S-six-stroke-S-W-stroke-M. Got that?"

"Yeah, I got it. And the results?"

"I'll call you. They generally take a week to ten days on this sort of stuff, but I have a rush on some really bizarre tufts of hair we found under Wasserman's nails. Say, Friday for my stuff, Monday most likely for yours."

It was worth playing the game to get what was necessary.

Genetique was one of the top DNA forensic labs in the entire world, and one of the first. It had the top equipment and top brainpower to break down and read almost any decent sample, and it did a lot of work for the government in this region. I didn't like that; I had to figure that the boys who went through the house probably knew the folks up there really well. Still, what the hell. I sent one tuft of brown hair and one slice of mean-looking gray skin to McCall as instructed; then I used a second courier to take the three other samples, in three different packages, to three different overnight services and then off to three different DNA testing labs I'd pulled up off the net, billing to Karen at the *Sun* and reporting to a blind box at the paper. One of the labs was in London. I had to figure that even if they intercepted the Genetique stuff they wouldn't catch them all, and, if I was lucky, they might figure that the two samples were all there were. I hadn't even told Monaghan how many little envelopes I had, and it was quite possible that my shadows didn't know how many there might be, either.

That done, and all through the satellite phone, I felt there wasn't much more that could be done except find some folks who might be able to tell me what the hell was on the data disk. I made several copies, then sent the data to a few really brilliant hackers I knew, one of whom, Fleet Admiral Coli of the Fecal Fleet (no kidding) was fifteen years old, had never been tracked down by anybody official, and had hacked areas of the government for me—just for the challenge—that I'd have sworn nobody could get into.

After that, it was time for me to track down some folks in the open, not only because it was something to do that might pay off, but also because, hell, anybody watching would get suspicious if I *didn't* do anything to follow up.

So my first stop was to go over to the AAAS convention downtown and see if I could find out anything about the departed doc and also maybe somebody who could figure out the weird stuff on the disk. While I knew that I was opening a can of worms the first time I displayed that disk, it was the only way to get any idea of what the hell I was dealing with. Besides, at this point I had copies, both here and all over the place, to spare.

Now, the AAAS convention was where I was supposed to be all along, covering the more interesting things going on right now and doing a series of features for both the online and printed newspaper. I was, after all, allegedly the science and technology reporter, even if my education wasn't as full as maybe it should have been.

There was a lot going on. They were putting the finishing touches on the first manned flight to Mars in spite of a concerted effort by both the left and right in Congress to kill it, as usual (the capacity to dream tends to be the first thing you lose when you run for office, apparently, unless it's dreaming of being president), and there were the usual science geeks there who also wanted to kill it because they thought it was stealing money from their pet projects. This had been going on since the first manned spaceflight program way back in the sixties, as if those guys had a prayer of getting their funding if there wasn't an accompanying manned spaceflight effort involved. It was kind of like when they'd almost killed the space station by showing how much the money would mean to world hunger or tax cuts (never mind the whole ten-year price was less than the American public spent during that same period on either pizza or cosmetics, it *sounds* big) even though there was virtually no chance that the money, if "saved," would go for anything except more pork.

I'd been doing that whole series and focusing on it because the public was fired up by the idea, even if all the unmanned probes and the rock samples that came back had been inconclusive, but pessimistic, on life there. There was something about Mars that touched the romance in the human soul, something only politicians could not feel.

In fact, a lot of the fun in an AAAS convention was finding the small talks and seminars by those guys who acted like we already had Mars down pat and were exploring the "Now what?" questions of what came later. I'd been covering some spirited debates on whether or not Mars could really be colonized, and, if so, if it could be terraformed so that people might live there without having to wear space suits and live in sealed domes. There hadn't been as much water as hoped but there was barely enough, they thought, and certainly the soil was mineral rich for agriculture if enough CO_2 could somehow be found for the plants to breathe. It would be not only an expensive process but, unlike all the glorious hopes and science fiction dreams, a very long process as well. Politicians weren't too good at investing in next year; investing in something that might take centuries was a sure funding loser.

I was seeking out one of several people in the last seminar I'd attended before getting the dinner invitation. There had been this panel of exobiologists who were arguing that the cost-effective way to colonize another world in both time and money would be parallel physical and biological modification programs. You'd terraform Mars slowly in one direction, while "marsforming" human beings genetically so that they would be able to exist in an environment that wouldn't exactly be the Land of Milk and Honey to the likes of you or me, but would be a happy medium between the partial change in the physical environment and the partial change in the biological forms. I remembered asking the panel if they could really do this with human beings, and they basically dismissed this as a nonissue, like we could do it easily and possibly even cheaply with existing technology. That was kind of scary, but considering the revolution this field of genetics had already wrought in medicine, it was certainly believable.

I remembered one of the panel members, a woman, responded that there had been serious proposals as far back as twenty years ago, just after we had decoded the last of DNA, to start just such a research program, but that everybody from religious groups to medical and biological ethicists and even TV had risen up with visions of Frankensteins and pretty well killed the idea politically. She seemed almost sorry about that. I wasn't so sure, but she did present a good starting place for this new stuff. I searched through my program and found her name. Kathryn A. Marshall, Ph.D., lecturer at Stanford, fellow at the Lawrence Livermore Labs.

She was easy to identify; the other three panelists had been men.

The telescreens in the lobby of the convention center were very handy for cross-referencing and finding anything and anybody. I stood at one of the kiosks and said, "Dr. Kathryn Marshall, biology. Locate today."

The screen did nothing for a moment, then said, "No match for today. Tomorrow, eleven hundred, Bioethics, CC Room 340. Only match."

So she was on one more thing than most of the folks here, but that was for tomorrow. Of course, it did mean that she wasn't one of those one-day wonders; she was actually still around someplace. Finding anybody in the convention halls would be next to impossible, but it might well be possible to find her hotel and leave a message. I reached for my handy sat phone.

"Karen? Chuck. I need a quick rundown of the downtown D.C. hotel guests. Kathryn Marshall, from somewhere in the Bay Area. No, not Chesapeake Bay—San Francisco Bay. You're getting much too parochial."

"I went to public school," she retorted, but added, "Okay, I'll see. I'm running queries now."

Hotel registers were, of course, confidential and not for

public use, but anybody in the press knew how to get at them, as did anybody in the government. It took only a few seconds. "Grand Hyatt, Chuck," she responded. "They encrypt the room and other details."

"Good girl! Remind me to give you an extra gold chocolate."

"Yeah, thanks a lot."

The Grand Hyatt was within walking distance of the convention center, and I figured I had little to lose. I went out and walked over to the big hotel. Once inside, I went to the video/voice mail phones and picked one up.

"Room number?" the v-phone asked.

"Unknown. This is for guest Kathryn A. Marshall. Please convey."

"Guest rooms cannot be given, nor may I connect you without a room number. You may leave v-mail as an option."

"That's what I wanted all along, you talking rulebook."

"I do not understand your wish. Please rephrase."

"V-mail to Dr. Kathryn A. Marshall from Chuck Vallone, science and technology reporter, *Baltimore Sun*. Doctor, I attended your panel on exobiology yesterday and I would like to follow up with some questions and answers on that subject if I may, at your convenience, of course. You may call me anytime at this number and I will answer." I gave her the sat phone number, said the usual thanks, and terminated.

"Message stored," the v-phone assured me.

I walked away and was suddenly hit with a horrible thought.

The *last* biologist I set out to interview was spread out over an entire sixth floor hotel room . . .

THREE

I wasn't idle while I waited for the possible callback from Dr. Marshall. Although it was tough to zero in and talk with specific scientists at AAAS, there were some great computerized reference works in the Exhibition Hall and even some print books that were handy, and I was able to talk with a few people, almost by accident, just looking around at name tags and also searching out particular exhibitors, one of which, interestingly, was Genetique, of Gaithersburg, Maryland. In spite of the mobbed aisles and countless booths and displays, or maybe because of them, I began to consider a possible way to advance things quickly.

I went over to Genetique's booth and introduced myself to a smiling, middle-aged guy, who turned out to be one of the marketing directors for the company, named Dr. "Call me Al" Hall. I introduced myself and told him that I had some things out at his labs at that very moment.

"Connected to that bizarre murder case? Yes, it's the talk of the whole meeting here. Terrible thing. Just terrible."

"Did you know the victim?"

"No, not at all, but I understand he'd done work around here and with some of the people in our labs—before they worked for us, of course. Years ago. They were all working on the Human Genome Project then; it was the leading edge in both science and computing. For all the revolutionary stuff coming from it now, it's still going to be decades before we can even sort it out enough to really use it all, and there are, of course, all those political and religious groups blocking funding and demanding that the wheel be un-invented, as it were. I'm sure I don't have to tell *you* about *them*."

"Yes, Senator Dilford and the Reverend Dr. Hopewell, among others," I responded sympathetically. "I'm afraid that they're still trying to stop any advancements in the space program because those rockets might poke holes in Heaven or at least let the rain back in."

"Ha ha! Very good, sir!"

"Tell me, Al—are you a geneticist, too?"

"Well, I have advanced degrees in biology, if that's what you mean. Couldn't sell our services without a strong background. But it's the M.B.A. in marketing that's most important in my present job. I was just never happy with pure research and lab work. Four years undergraduate work, three more in grad school, and it turns out I should have been an insurance salesman. Oh, well . . ."

"I kind of figured you'd have to be pretty up on things just to be fronting the company out here, considering the type of people who come up to you and ask questions." Now I had to spring it. "I see one of your promotional shows over there is being driven by a stock portable pretty much like mine. If it wouldn't be too much trouble, you think you could take a look at something and tell me what I've got? It's on disk, and I have one here."

Hall seemed hesitant, then shrugged. "Why not? Not too many folks beating down the doors and it's getting a little boring. Give it to me and I'll do a reset and we'll have a look."

I handed over one of the copies and he shut down the presentation computer's looping program and the huge one-hundred-and-fifty-centimeter high-resolution wall screen went dark, then came up with the familiar operating system interface. He put the disk in, clicked on "Run"—there was no way you could use voice commands with this kind of din in the cavernous hall—and after a moment the mysterious split-screen effect came on, with the nearly psychedelic color display throbbing and changing on the top while the lines and groups of letters and of numbers started scrolling past.

Al stared at it for a moment, frowning, then turned to me. "Where'd you get this?"

"Wasserman. He sent it to me before he was killed, but with no instructions or user guide. You know what it is?"

"Well, part of it, certainly. The groups of letters are clearly DNA sequences. The numbers are the mathematical series in which the individual sequences must be switched on and off in order to get a result. It's not enough to know the DNA of something—otherwise we'd have no problems recreating dinosaurs or repopulating the jungles with tigers and elephants and all the rest. You have to know the ordering of the sequences as well, and that usually means you need a living subject. Clearly they had one here. What the display represents on the left I have no idea, but I'd bet it's related to the sequences. It's not DNA strands the way I'd expect from this setup, though. It's something else."

Several other people had stopped to look at the scrolling display when we'd set it up, most probably thinking it was part of the corporate sell, but a couple seemed fascinated by it. One rather good-looking fellow with a slight beard and bushy eyebrows over deep blue eyes asked, "Have you sequenced it out to find out what it might be?"

I turned to him. "I wouldn't have the slightest idea how to do it, frankly. You mean that there are programs around that can take this code and show what it's building?"

He nodded. "But I think you already have that built into this. I suspect that the graphics on the left are close-ups of molecular models taken from the scroll. Too bad you can't zoom out and see the whole organism."

"No way to tell from the letters, huh?" I was kind of disappointed.

He laughed. "Hardly! The DNA of even very basic lifeforms is extremely complex, and when you think that the entire genetic code of a chimpanzee is less than two percent different from your DNA or mine, well, *nobody's* mind is *that* good! Still, if you had enough computing power, a computer set up for genetic sequence interpretation, and a couple of good techies, I think you could probably get some idea of whatever that represents. Might take time, though, considering that from the start the only thing you can be reasonably sure of is that it's animal or vegetable and not mineral. But the info's there."

I turned back to Al, who, I discovered, was taking advantage of the new small crowd of the curious my disk was drawing and was passing out company literature. When he was satisfied that he'd covered everybody, he came back over to me. "That's quite a disk. Useful, too."

"Tell you what—keep it," I told him. "If your people can figure out what it builds, then my paper will definitely pay for the service. If not, it'll make a good challenge for your folks and it looks like it'll really draw customers even in this place."

He seemed surprised. "You're sure?" Then he suddenly figured it out. "Oh, of course! This is a copy!"

"Of a copy of a copy and so on," I confirmed. "I don't want anybody buttoning this up, so I'm Genetic Santa, spreading the Wasserman gift to all and sundry, which is what I think he wanted. I just wish I knew what he wanted to tell me. I'm pretty sure I wouldn't have had to guess on this thing if we'd been allowed to meet and have dinner."

"All right, well . . . you have your card?"

I gave him one, and scribbled Karen's name and toll free direct line on the back as well. I thought it best not to remind him that whoever or whatever killed Wasserman would likely not be too keen on us decoding this disk. Hell, so much for public demonstrations to put fear into the hearts of those who might be tempted to look further into Wasserman's work. In a town where everybody was always yelling and posturing and where there were always protest marchers and demonstrators, subtlety was the key to actually getting something done.

I was perfectly willing to give more copies of the thing away, but I didn't want copies getting into the hands of the competition, by which I mean anybody from the *Post* to *Scientific American*, so there were some limits. Genetique already had the samples; hell, this thing might actually help. Maybe the disk was the DNA sequences for one of the whatevers those samples were from.

The meeting and thus the convention center was closing for the day and I still hadn't heard from Marshall. I would have left messages for the other three on that panel as well, even though they wouldn't be as nice to look at, but none of them showed up on the schedule for the rest of the conference and the odds were that they were already home or packing. Marshall was the best hope for at least some background and thought on it.

Well, she was going to miss a good dinner on my expense account, that was for sure.

I headed back toward the Grand Hyatt with the idea of at least checking to see if my message had been picked up. If not, I figured I'd go over to Travalina's for dinner and then head over to Baltimore to check in and see if anything had come up that might be a good idea to talk about on the telephone. In point of fact, the better restaurants had been in Baltimore for years, but ever since they moved the paper out of downtown it was a pain in the ass to get to them.

I also wanted to personally see how my dispatches on the AAAS and the murder were being distributed. Congress was not in session, which was a blessing, although these days they seemed to work only about ten three-day weeks a year for their executive-sized salaries and incredible perks. The president, too, was off raising money in southern California, which wasn't a bad place to be this time of year, so that left me with a science angle and no political follow-ups to cover. It meant I might actually get space on the lower part of the front page rather than as part of the "Today" section. It also meant a home/headline page headline and link online, too.

There may not have been many newspapers left in the country, and too many online news sources, but bylines still counted, not only for prizes and bonuses but also because of the calls it got you from all the talking heads programs every time they needed an alleged "expert."

I was almost to the Hyatt entrance when I could feel my sat phone vibrating. I stopped, thinking I might have a business dinner after all, and took the call. "Vallone."

"Mr. Vallone," came a really weird, barely male-sounding voice that was the kind that put the same sort of chill in your backbone as squeaky chalk on a blackboard. "That was an unwise thing to do back at the Exhibition Hall."

Truth was, it sounded like the voice was being electronically distorted. God, I hoped it was. It wasn't pleasant to think of somebody who really spoke like this. Still, the only way to go at it was head on.

"So what do I get for it? Splattered all over my apartment like Dr. Wasserman? Boy, *that* will keep 'em from putting an all-out effort into finding you, buster."

"I considered doing such a thing last night, but was more or less talked out of it," the voice responded, and I felt a sinking feeling in the pit of my stomach. "Now I see I was a fool not to have done it, but it is too late now."

"Listen, pal! Was that you under the lamppost in the parking lot last night?"

"Ah! You *did* see me, then. And yet you went ahead. Very foolish, Mr. Vallone. Still, it is of little consequence in the end, I suppose. Without Wasserman you have only that information, and when they decode it and plot it they will dismiss it as a great job of biology humor. See if I'm not right. Otherwise, consider that things have been kept out of public view for a very long time in and around a government and city that can't keep a secret for fifteen seconds. Take care where you tread from this point, Mr. Vallone. So long as you get nowhere, I think we will speak no more. But, if you get lucky, if you become a danger, rest assured we will meet each other face-to-face." Before I could respond there was a *click* and I knew the connection was over.

The caller ID said "BLOCKED," so I pushed the code to call back the last number that called me. There were a lot more beeps than I thought there might be, and finally there was a ringing sound. After a dozen or so, somebody actually picked up.

"Yeah?"

"I'm calling back a number that just called me," I told him. "Who is this?"

"Name's Joe. This is a pay phone in the entry of the Anacostia Towers. Ain't nobody here but me now."

I sighed. "Okay, thanks. You saw nobody around using the phone?"

"Nope. Just walked in. Nobody else around. Kinda dark here anyways."

"All right. Thanks anyway," I told him, and hung up.

Anacostia Towers. A new, improved project to replace the old, disreputable projects and just as bad as the old ones. A curious choice for somebody like my killer to use, but, then again, maybe he had a relative over there. Great hideout. And it was for damned sure that nobody in the area would help the cops if they came looking.

Still, I'd half expected it to be from one of the government buildings or agencies around. They all tended to block automatically, and, hell, it wasn't all that easy to get my sat phone number.

Or was it? Hadn't I left it in a lot of places, including today?

I had a hunch about what he meant about biology humor and the disk, though. Ten to one it was going to be a perfectly valid full sequence but for something out of a monster movie or maybe a comic book or V.R. game. Anybody with reasonable skills and a lot of computing power could do it, but only in the computer. Actually making the thing was more than a little bit harder, I suspected.

And that, of course, explained some of it. With Wasserman, it might have been possible to show that the sequence really could be created, given the right labs and computers and the like. Without him, it was fantasy. Maybe they could build the Creature That Ate Cincinnati, but unless you could produce it, or them, then all you had was a lot of Hollywood fantasy.

My phone went off just as soon as I'd put it back in my coat pocket. I took it out, flipped it open, half expecting to hear old electro-voice again, but instead a woman's professional tones were heard.

"Mr. Vallone? Kathryn Marshall. I got your intriguing message on my hotel voice mail. I'm sorry for taking so long but I just got in from doing some sightseeing."

"That's all right. In fact, I happen to be in the Grand Hyatt's lobby at this moment. If it wouldn't be an inconvenience or foul up any evening plans, we could discuss this matter over dinner if you like, on my paper."

She thought a moment. "Well, we didn't have any dinner plans, as such, and while we were going to the Folger tonight I'd just decided I was too worn out to do anything but come back here and relax. So, if we don't have to go very far, you have a dinner guest."

"Fine. You said 'we,' though. Is there somebody else who might be coming along?"

"No, no. I'm doubling up with an old friend but they're still going to the theater, so this works out quite well. What time?"

"Anytime at all," I told her. "It's, um, six-fifteen now, so it could be now or it could be at seven, seven-thirty, whatever."

"I'd like to take a shower and change. Shall we say in the bar here in, oh, one hour?"

"Seven-fifteen in the lobby bar it is."

I hung up, hoping that *this* time the scientist who told me they were going to shower and change and meet me in the hotel bar would make it.

The trouble was, sitting there for an hour with little to do but drink a couple of beers and think, I tried to put together this crazy puzzle that had started only a little over twenty-four hours previous and see if it made any sense at all.

A Ph.D. and researcher in genetic science sees me at an AAAS panel, apparently is impressed with a question or two of mine, and leaves me voice mail to meet him, with promises of "the story of the century." Well, it's still a pretty young century, but it'll do to have the story of it at least once, so I head over there at the appointed time, call him to make sure all is okay, and he tells me he's going to take a shower and change and then he'll meet me in the Wardman bar. Instead, he gets pasted all over the room even though it's locked from the inside, is six floors up, and witnesses outside the room see nobody leave, all this apparently before I even leave the meeting after filing my daily story, and I find it out when I get there. Now he sends me a disk with what is surely going to be some monster DNA sequences, and I don't mean just in terms of size, and some clippings of God knows what to analyze, while somebody with clout who's a real pro ransacks my town house and somebody else who looks like a freak-show Bogart stalks me.

For what? It just didn't make any sense.

Even the phone call, I suppose, was designed to scare me. It did, but not any more than some of the threats I'd gotten in my career from other very dangerous characters.

How did they get in to kill Wasserman? Or, more importantly, how did they get out? How did the killer make such an incredible mess in so short a time? Some new kind of really ugly top secret weapon that made you explode?

It felt like a government agency was involved. These folks had wiretaps and sources of information and influence that came much too easy to them. I mean, how the hell did they even know Wasserman was meeting me?

That was suddenly obvious. They had his phone tapped. If I hadn't called him for confirmation, then they well might not have known until I had met with him.

Trouble is, that probably would have guaranteed that both of us would have blown up that night, so maybe it wasn't so unlucky or as dumb a break or move as I'd thought.

But what could they have been afraid that Wasserman would tell me? Afraid enough to move like that?

It was pretty clear that finding out what the hell Wasserman had been doing, and where, and for whom, since he'd left the Human Genome Project, was the first priority here. I went over to a corner of the noisy and crowded bar and called in to Karen at the City Desk.

"City Desk."

"Don't you have a life, doll? You're always home!"

"Hello, Mr. Vallone. Try calling at ten in the morning and you'll find me home and sound asleep, and if you try me on Sunday or Monday, not you or anybody else is gonna find me."

"I'm a professional. I can find anybody. Any news on the various leads? Anybody calling asking nasty questions?"

"Well, this Dr. Wasserman is a real mystery. He's no big shakes as a scientist, just one of those guys who toils in obscurity in the labs, and then suddenly he ups and quits and puts his house on the market and just vanishes. Not a sign of him in any of our employment databases. Odds are he was either working for some government black project or he was working for a non–North American company. We're trying, but this becomes needle-in-a-haystack time."

"Yeah, I know. Can't win 'em all. But there's got to be something, even if it's just a subscription to *Science News*. Nobody can just disappear these days, even if they want to. I'm still getting mail for my mom and she died in ninety-nine. We're all immortal now, once we're in the computers."

"Yeah, that's why it's probably government black project. They're about the only ones who can create a black hole these days. Oh—and some guy called and said he had a lead on the Wasserman thing but he'd speak only to you. I figured you'd want to talk to him so—"

"So you gave him my sat phone number, right?"

"Yeah, sure. It's not like it tells him where you are."

"I have a suspicion that it might. This guy—real spooky voice? Like he was disguising something?"

"Nope. Sounded normal to me. Real classy-like, too. Either had voice lessons or he's a Brit who's been over here a while. You know the sound."

I did know what she was talking about, at least the type. So he wasn't using his electronic voice changer with them. Why? Because he felt they'd be too much on alert, or not give out the number? Then why do it with me? Were they afraid I'd recognize the voice? Was this guy somebody I knew?

No, that was unlikely. But it was not only possible but very likely that he was somebody who I might run into, maybe at AAAS or around here.

"You recorded the call?"

"Yeah. Blocked number, trace was to a phone booth, but we have it. Want me to play it for you?"

"Not now. Put it on my voice mail and I'll listen to it when I get a chance this evening."

"Will do."

"The phone booth in Anacostia?"

"Huh? Nope. Definitely not Anacostia. It was a Seven-Eleven in East Baltimore, actually."

That was a little bit of geography there, even if enough time had physically elapsed to make the moves. Well, Spooky Voice said he'd been talked out of killing me. Maybe this was the guy who talked him out of it, in which case I owed him one.

Okay, so there were at least two of them, both male, one in Anacostia and one in Baltimore, which probably indicated that Smoothie was doing some investigation on me or others at the paper or whatever, although there were some major science and research facilities over there as well. Johns Hopkins Hospital was in East Baltimore, and there were a lot of other medical-technical companies around there. More needles in a haystack, but it was another piece of the puzzle, nonetheless.

The key remained Wasserman. If I could find out where he'd been all those years, and why after all that time he suddenly decided to become a whistle-blower, then I'd know who had the motive.

And every news organization in the country, if not the Western world, was trying to find that out. If any of them had, at least so far, we'd have known it, though, so it was deep undercover or Third World time. There were lots of Near Eastern and Asian regimes that would run any potentially nasty experiments with no controls or ethical qualms if they were to counter Satanic America. Lots of them fooling with germ warfare stuff, too, since it was cheap, easy to hide, and really mean. I remember one in particular from not long ago where that nasty little virus would have totally sterilized all males who came in contact with it. They were *that* close to an immunization they could have given to their own, and only their own, people as part of routine shots and then they'd have loosed that thing on the rest of the world.

So far genetic research in this country has been kept in the hands of the medical establishment and overseen by ethicists, but it wouldn't be a big shift if technology elsewhere went into the designer-gene market. I remember a DEA man commenting once on breaking a ring that hadn't quite gotten it right but was close. Just two shots and some reinforcement from pills or stuff dissolved in juice and you were almost to the point of having a potion that would turn any woman under forty into a willing sex bomb while making her dumb and docile, every teenager's fantasy drug. "Trouble is, if they'd actually perfected it, there'd be thousands of women lining up to take it, even at that mental and behavioral price," he noted cynically. "Hell, instant beauty, thinness, sexuality—pretty sad commentary on life, but that's the truth. With so many of 'em anorexic or bulimic now, this would be worth the price to them."

I suspected that he was right. I kind of wondered what a male equivalent of that might be—that is, something that would cost you horribly yet be so seductive you'd take it anyway. I was stumped until that same agent noted that I'd just done a fair job of describing heroin.

I guess that, so long as each of us, deep down, thinks we're immune from what gets everybody else, we'll always be susceptible to what gets us individually.

The only reason the designer gene thing hadn't happened yet was the enormous level of technology and expertise necessary to do it. It wasn't like growing poppies or coca leaves and doing some processing in the jungle; there was very little tolerance for error, and it was tough finding a formula where one gene sequence fit all. Still, I had to wonder if that wasn't part of this. Suppose somebody was doing it and creating monsters? Suppose Wasserman had been hired to set up things, but after he saw the product he chickened out?

Not the drug lords, though; the thing was, they didn't have the patience to wait years for a return, no matter how big the potential profits down the line.

Governments did.

Particularly governments that didn't have to justify their budgets in public debates.

Still, unless I got a lucky break, I was unlikely to be the one to find out that piece of information, not with the combined weight of all the nets going after it. My best chance, I suspected, was to go the long way around, going by deduction or by informant to find out just what the hell was worth a man's life in this case. That was the hard way, but that was usually the way it was in this business. Good investigative reporting was pretty much like police work; you dug and asked until you either stumbled over something or, more usually, some informant came forward and gave you what you needed.

Dr. Kathryn Marshall probably wasn't that informant, but it was almost a shame that she wasn't. She walked into the bar and looked around, and I couldn't help thinking that she was much too good looking to be a lab biologist. Her bio said she was pushing forty, but she easily looked ten years younger, and if she was informally dressed in a stylish pantsuit she looked good enough to go to fancier restaurants than *I* was used to eating in.

Realizing that she wouldn't know what I looked like, I got

up and walked over to her, feeling every bit the middle-aged dumpy guy I was. Beauty and the Beast indeed.

"Doctor? I'm Chuck Vallone."

She smiled. "Oh! I wondered which one you were. Yes, I remember you from the panel. You asked some very good questions."

I sincerely doubted that she did remember, but at least she didn't look disappointed.

"Would you like a drink, or should we proceed to a quieter restaurant?" I asked her.

"Oh, I think we should go and eat. Too much noise in here to do anything."

"Do you have a preference?"

"No, anything you choose. I'm not a heavy eater but I have a wide range of likes and very few dislikes."

"Travalina's is only two blocks over and it's very good," I told her. "That is, if you like Italian."

"Italian is fine."

We went out and began walking down the street. It was dark and chilly, but there was no rain and there was the usual traffic that often irritated me but now seemed rather comforting. There is a certain safety and security in just being in the middle of things.

"I heard that you made something of a stir inside Exhibition Hall this afternoon," she commented as we walked.

"Oh, yeah? You heard about that, then? I was just trying to identify the one piece of data Wasserman sent me and it seemed like a good idea at the time."

"And did you get a reaction from anybody?"

"Well, yeah. Among other things, his killer called me and told me I was acting very dangerously."

She looked genuinely alarmed. "He *didn't*!"

"Yes, I'm afraid he did. Weird-sounding voice, too, like somebody with an electronic muzzle. Either that or he likes inhaling helium."

"And you're not frightened?"

"Actually, I was more scared yesterday than now. They

won't come after me unless I dig up something so incriminating that they have no choice. To do that to me now like they did to Wasserman would be to put every agency and agent in the world on this and they're much too heavy-handed for anyone to withstand that kind of pressure. No, the cat's out of the bag now, at least in terms of the data disk. The samples, now—they're another thing. We'll have to see who comes up with what on those."

"Samples?"

I told her of the parcel, but not how many or how scattered they really were. No use in telling more than you have to. I was in the information *gathering* business; what I chose to disseminate was called good reporting.

"Dark green hair, you say?"

I nodded. "And gray matter, kind of rubbery. Not brains, though—skin or blubber or something like that. Hard to say. They were dried out and actually prepared, I think, with some kind of fixative."

"I'd love to have one of them to analyze, once I got back to my lab in California," she noted. "I suppose that's out of the question, though."

"At this stage, maybe. We'll see what happens to them, though. If anything's left maybe I can send you one for a second opinion."

By this time we'd reached Travalina's, and while there was a small crowd there, Paul was not just an old friend but a distant cousin of mine, and we had no problems with a table for two. The press, Congress, and relatives—they all could miraculously come up with reservations, even if they had just now decided on the place. And I was two out of three.

After we'd ordered and were waiting for the wine and appetizers, she asked, "So just what do you think I can contribute, Mr. Vallone?"

I sighed. "You can tell me about Project Chameleon for starters."

She seemed startled, then said, "You've been doing your homework."

"Well, you did mention it on the panel."

"But not by name. I got my Ph.D. working for the planning sessions on Chameleon, but, of course, they never came to anything once Congress discovered what it was and the moral high horses were mounted."

Shortly after the turn of the century NASA had begun a series of think tanks on Mars colonization. Not the ones that had been there for years, but assemblies of specialists from all parts of business and academia, split into teams, looking at the best ways, not to send people to Mars or just live on it in domed clusters, but to really *colonize* the place.

All the computer crunching in the world said that even if Mars could somehow be terraformed, and the amount of water available was only about eighty percent of what had been hoped, and maybe was too little to do it, colonizing would take a couple of centuries and, much more to the point, several *trillion* dollars, with a few hundred billion right up front. That alone was enough to make a lot of folks stop, and politicians have never been fond of the space program anyway, let alone schemes like that one, and often have had to be led kicking and screaming to do much of anything. Every single advance in space, just like most major advances in science that hadn't been the product of war, had been virulently opposed by the establishment of the time.

The trouble with this one was: no benefit for a very long term and outlays on a scale so massive that they would sap a quarter of the gross national product of the entire world.

In other words, it wasn't going to be done.

And NASA, knowing the facts and always having to be half-scientific and half-political entity, wanted somebody to come up with an alternative that might well be possible and doable.

Project Chameleon had been the result. The name was deliberately ambiguous; it could mean converting Mars, or converting other factors instead. In point of fact it was basically a wide-ranging think tank so broad and covering so many teams with different objectives and points of view that most didn't even know the others existed. It depended on coordination by NASA, both at their Jet Propulsion Lab in L.A. and in a special section set up at Goddard just outside Washington, D.C.

The political branch had eventually come up with a figure that they believed would be the maximum realistic ten- or twenty-year budget such a project could manage to get through Congress; it was a massive amount, but only a drop in the bucket of what would ultimately be needed. After all, we were talking about a whole planet, when it had been estimated back around the turn of the century that simply reclaiming the Sahara and turning it again into the forests and grasslands it had been before man screwed it up would cost trillions. That was true terraforming; this was infinitely more complex.

While the JPL coordinators concentrated on what could be done with Mars given the money, the Goddard folks concentrated on what could be done elsewhere to make the minimum acceptable. The answer wasn't in physics and chemistry and those allied fields, but in the most controversial part of biology, the part that terrified the public, the news, and the politicians equally.

The concept was to engineer humans genetically so that they could live, grow, reproduce, even thrive, on the stuff that the JPL folks could give them.

I stared at the pretty doctor, but this time not out of male sexual interest. "You mean they proposed *creating Martians*?"

She nodded. "That is one way of putting it, yes."

"We could do that?"

She shrugged. "We couldn't have done it back then, no. I mean, the whole Human Genome Project had only just been completed, and companies like H.G. in Gaithersburg were concentrating on developing and patenting single genes that could give you frost-free tomatoes, or, hopefully inject a gene into a heart muscle that would strengthen it, things like that."

"Things like that have made several corporations multibillion-dollar conglomerates," I pointed out.

"Yes, but as incredibly difficult as those gene therapy projects were and are, they involve only a very few genes, and even then it was tricky, since you were never sure until you did long-term trials if those genes wouldn't have a negative effect elsewhere in the organism or mutate in unstable and unpredictable ways. Now, if *that's* still a tough thing to do, even if we think of it as routine today, consider what was being proposed for Mars. Whole complex organisms, human beings essentially, who would be designed to breathe a mixture poisonous or too thin for us, to eat things that could grow in such an environment, to withstand without elaborate space suits and domes conditions that are literally alien to us, yet still have the intellectual capacity and education and skills to work and build there. That's not a few genes, that's redesigning *us*. I'm not sure even now that we have the computing power necessary, nor could we have any way of testing such things in the lab. And, of course, there is the question, if we somehow did leap over all those hurdles, of what we would have created. Would it truly be human, or a monster? Would it think like us? Would it hate us? Would *we* hate *it*?"

I could see the scene from the ancient Frankenstein movies of the mob moving in with torches. The answer to the hypothetical was easy for anybody, particularly an old cynic like me. Hell, we could support a small colony on the moon, snap close-ups of Pluto, and support complex mining operations under the oceans, but we couldn't, to this day, get along with one another. People in many countries who were genetically only slightly less related than cousins still shot each other over what god they worshipped or something one group did to the other's ancestors. We had lesser-scale versions of that here even now. But Martians, even human-made Martians—no, *especially* human-made Martians—they would scare the living shit out of people.

"What would they look like? Anything like us?" I asked her. She shrugged. "Who knows? We had a lot of theories coming in, but nobody had a clear idea. It was at that point all so much theoretical science. None of us believed that we'd ever do it, or that we'd ever be allowed to do it, and, of course, we were right."

"Stopped it dead, did they?"

She nodded. "Of course. And even though we had a lot of passionate advocates for the idea, ninety percent of us never did think it was anything more than an intellectual game, a way of seeing what might be possible, but just a contingency plan, a scenario. As soon as some of the ethical types began leaking it, the project was quietly but completely dropped, becoming nothing more than a documentary on the Sci Fi Channel and a Smithsonian special program some years back."

My little old conspiratorial mind began to wonder. "What about the darker side of the government, though? The ones with budgets they don't have to account for and where ethics is considered a job liability? Might they not pick some folks who were similarly challenged and keep going?"

She smiled, and I almost felt my armor melting. "No, hardly! Think of what we are speaking of here. Vast computing power on a still-unimaginable scale. There are four trillion cells in the human brain alone, and that's only a small part of the body. How many molecules and atoms beyond that? What could do it, and what would be the cost and expertise involved in it? Then, of course, you'd need expert biologists, many specializing in theoretical alien life-forms—it is a discipline, but a small one—and a massive supporting staff, you name it."

"They did it for the Manhattan Project in World War Two," I noted.

"True, but that was ages ago, ancient history. My parents weren't even born then, and science and communications were in the Dark Ages relative to what we do today. And the whole nation was at war and under wartime security. If you'd lived back then and discovered the atomic bomb project, your story wouldn't have passed a single censor, and you'd find yourself a soldier at the battle front very fast, or tucked away in some military reservation for the duration. No, I know that lots of folks think that flying saucers and water-fueled engines and you name it are for real, but if those things are out there I've never found them, and I bet neither have you. The bottom line was, they only had to keep that secret for, what? Four, five years? This would be *twenty plus* years and counting, and it would cost more. Do you really think they could keep something that big under wraps for that long? I don't think they could have done it back then with all that."

It was a good point, although I had lots of very smart, fully grown men and women on my lists who weren't even born until the century turned, who nonetheless were convinced that aliens crashed at Roswell, and that not only were we still keeping the secret of the *last* assassination, ancient history though it be, they didn't think we'd been told the truth about Lincoln, Garfield, or McKinley, either.

She was right, though. We'd even had those unpleasant six years when the Christian Crusade dominated Congress and almost turned us into a theocracy of sorts. If one of *those* guys hadn't unearthed a project like this, then it probably wasn't there.

Still, the fact that we might not manage it didn't mean somebody else might not try it. What went for us went for the European Union, of course, but a number of the oil and gas countries were under rigid dictators and one-party quasi-military rule, and there was Pan Asia and maybe a couple of others, too.

As quickly as I'd thought that, though, I dismissed it as so much silliness. If any of them had embarked on something this huge, then our own intelligence people would have picked up on it.

I was about to go into other areas more directly related to the events at the Wardman when my sat phone rang. " 'Scuse me," I told her apologetically. "There is no longer any escape from the office." I punched it on and said, "Yes?"

"Mr. Vallone. This is Monaghan, D.C. Homicide."

"Yes, Lieutenant? You got the results back?"

He paused for a moment. "Well, yes, sort of. But only because they make lots of backups."

"I beg your pardon?"

"I'm with the Montgomery County and Maryland State Police right now over on Route Ninety-one just north of Gaithersburg. You know it?"

"Yes? What happened?"

"You might want to come out here and see for yourself. It'll be a couple of hours before the scene's been gone over enough to take anything away, and we probably will just keep things pretty well blocked off until morning when we can see more of what we're looking at, although you can never be sure if the boys in fatigues or the folks in the black suits might show up and overrule the locals."

I sighed. "All right, Lieutenant. What happened?"

"Harry Jensen and Marcia Thomas were called up to Genetique to pick up the samples and analysis. Your stuff as well as mine. Of course, we'd been getting fed the stuff to our computers, but this is the hard evidence, the kind you keep for court, if and when."

"Yes?"

"Somebody, or something, tore the roof off their Chevy police cruiser like it was one of those old-fashioned cans of sardines. And it's still not fully clear if whatever did it didn't think of the two people inside very much the same way."

"I'm on my way. Other press is there, I assume?"

"We've been keeping them away, but eventually they'll see the car. I called 'em in, to tell you the truth, just so it would be harder for the Feds or military to show up."

"I appreciate the call."

"Well, they had your stuff, too, remember. And I'd stick to well-lighted roads if I were you." He paused a moment. "Tell you what. Go down to the Municipal Building and I'll have one of our patrol helicopters bring you out and back."

"Great. And when we meet this thing in the air you can investigate what slammed a chopper down, too, right?"

"I didn't say it would be any safer. But it's one hell of a lot faster."

I looked over at my beautiful science adviser with genuine regret. "I'm afraid I've got to break our date," I told her, explaining the basics of what I'd just been told.

Far from being unnerved, she seemed fascinated. "I'm done here. How many people does a helicopter like that hold?"

"You're serious?"

"I'd like to get a look at one of these sites, and this might be my only chance. At least, I *hope* it's my only chance."

She had *that* right.

"Well, I can't guarantee anything, since they're mostly flying over and back on me, I've never actually been in one of the local choppers, but it couldn't hurt to come along and try."

Hell, maybe I had a date after all.

FOUR

As it happened, while the choppers weren't normally for more than two people, you could cram a smaller third person in a kind of sideways jump seat behind the first two, and when I had the dispatcher call Monaghan and explain who I was bringing with me and why, the lieutenant readily agreed.

"Of course," the pilot commented, "we have no jurisdiction over in Maryland, so the locals and state will be in charge and make the final decisions on both of you."

"Nice of you to add more gloom to a massacre," I retorted. "Let's go!"

They say that there was once a time in the long past when every news organization in the world didn't have a helicopter, but that was before my time. But by my time the authorities had worked out some solutions to the problem, even if it was a little bit of a technological war between the newschoppers and the cops and firemen and such on the ground.

Maryland has been a wealthy state since at least the Civil War and Montgomery County's been one of the two or three wealthiest counties in the country since they decided to build the nation's capital just across the river from it. Oh, there were other counties around D.C. and most of the regular folks who were in government lived in them, but Montgomery was one of the two in the region where the millionaire politicians, the patricians, the Beltway Bandit executives, big-shot lawyers and lobbyists, and the like lived. Heck, the natives had been forced out by the property taxes ages ago.

Thus it wasn't a big surprise to come in on the scene of the crime and see vast numbers of flashing red and blue and yellow lights—fire, two police departments, maybe two and a half counting the D.C. people—going on and on.

"It looks like an airport," Kathryn Marshall commented, and it did indeed. But, right at the center, where lights were set up that made it bright as day, there was just about nothing to see but a big blurry region shining a little greenish yellow.

"What *is* that?" she asked. "Some sort of distortion field?"

"Too sophisticated," I shouted back over the noise of our own helicopter. "Distortion fields can be overcome by clever and highly paid engineers. *That* is a supertarp."

The supertarp was nothing more high-tech than a kind of old-fashioned circus tent put up by just a couple of people in a very high-tech way. Just about the diameter of a garbage can lid when compact, it could rise forty feet if it had to, and while it was said that there were certain kinds of cameras sitting in orbit that might be able to look through such things, those were still a bit top secret for us mere mortals of the press.

This one had been set up quickly and a bit hastily, but it covered the accident scene and managed to get above the trees without being in danger of collapsing on all and sundry beneath it.

"Think of it as a high-tech umbrella," I told her.

We had to maneuver to avoid hitting a few helicopters trying to get a peek under the thing, hoping they'd get lucky, but when our pilot turned on the "Police" flasher they deferred to us, not knowing which police we might be.

If they were anything like decent newspeople instead of the kind that read their scripts and passed the Buffy and Skip test, they'd have had their people on the ground and somehow slipped under that tent, or at least be interviewing somebody who had been under and who was more starstruck than in fear of his boss.

We landed inside the police blockade, but a block or so from the tent so as not to blow it down or mess up whatever it was covering.

It was cold, damp, and a slight wind was picking up, making it extremely uncomfortable, but that was autumn in the nation's capital, after all. I offered a hand to Marshall as she tried to negotiate, not really dressed for being out in the boonies like this, and she seemed to welcome being steadied.

"If I'd known I was coming out here I'd have worn my athletic sneakers or maybe boots," she said, thankful to be on a road surface and out of the cold and wet mud. The pumps were only one-inch heels but overall they were built for a nice Italian dinner and maybe a bit of dancing after, not wandering out in the burbs.

Nobody paid much attention to us until we got very close to the tent, but then several official types seemed to move in to intercept us, all wearing different uniforms.

"I'm Chuck Vallone and this is Dr. Marshall," I told them. "Monaghan of the D.C. police sent for us. There was something of mine in the car."

They insisted on checking IDs, but didn't seem too troubled otherwise. I suspected that few of them ever read a newspaper, let alone an out-of-town one, and when I said "doctor" they'd gotten the idea that I was a cop bringing in a forensic expert or something. Happened all the time, and obeyed several early rules of penetrating closed sites: Don't volunteer information, and always act toward everybody as if you really belonged there.

We had to duck to get under the supertarp, but once we did, it was a clear field of vision to the car, which was on its side in a ditch, the roof facing us. We both stopped dead and just stared. Monaghan hadn't been kidding about the sardine tin. The roof of what I always thought of as a very solid full-sized car had been peeled back using a kind of rolling action. I half expected to see a giant key-shaped device lying nearby.

There were folks from all sorts of police departments taking photos of it from every conceivable angle. I decided to push my luck and take a digital photo of the scene before me just as was. If they didn't notice and let me get out with it, it was a great page one and probably wire-service photo lead as well.

It would be a great high-resolution 3-D color shot, but was taken from far enough away that it wouldn't require much lab work to slightly obscure the contents of the front seat.

Monaghan wasn't immediately visible, but as we approached the car and I palmed the camera and slid it into a nice but not obvious compartment in my coat I heard his voice call. "Vallone!"

I turned and saw him ducking under and then walking toward us. Marshall just seemed to stand there, staring at the car, almost like she was in shock. I hoped that bringing her along wasn't a major mistake for her sake.

"What the hell is going on here, Lieutenant?" I asked him. "I mean, first the Wardman Werewolf, then—*this*."

"Yeah, I know. As for this one, at least I can give you a little scenario. They left Genetique, which is only about a half mile up that way, at about eight or a little later. At some point after pulling onto this part of the road that's dark and undeveloped—because it follows the ridgeline, see—something the driver saw coming straight at them made her swerve and momentarily lose control of the car on the shoulder. At that point something struck the car a major blow to the front and side, pushing it into this ditch pretty much as you see it. After that, whatever it was didn't bother with the door, it just peeled back the roof, bent the roll bars out of the way, probably removed the samples and case, and then it tried to pull the two occupants out of their seats. Modern seat belts being what they are, whatever it was beheaded them by pulling straight up and out on both heads. We don't think it meant to do that, since it was apparently bent on searching them and the front seat and glove-box area. At about that time two cars approached, one from each direction, and whatever it was panicked—God knows why, since it has this kind of power and strength—and took off with the sample case."

"My God! Did the occupants of either car see anything?"

"Just a vague shape in the darkness and off the headlight

beams. They both swore it was man-sized or bigger, but no monster, and that it just kind of up and vanished on them. Neither one got much of a look—it was pitch dark here and the headlights weren't fixed on the spot. One of them, a computer salesman from Damascus on his way home, got out with his flashlight, thinking there'd been an accident, but when he saw the roof back like that and the two decapitations in the front he ran back to his car, shouting to the other guy not to approach it, and called nine-one-one on his car phone. County officer doing a security check at the high school got the call and was here in maybe two, three minutes; the first state cop was maybe two minutes more."

"Did I hear you right? Two to three minutes? And two cars with live witnesses on the scene, so there's no time to hide maybe construction equipment from the highway extension just over there?"

"We saw that and thought of it, too, but nothing from the site's been touched. In fact, there are guys on the regular crew working over there right now. They start shutting down lanes and going to work for real at about eight, since that's after the rush is completely clear. None of them saw or heard a thing, and they all check out."

I shook my head as if to clear it. "What about helicopters or similar things?"

"We got enough here now, don't we? No, it's unlikely. Neither car's occupants heard any sound of a motor or rotors overhead, so unless this guy has the proverbial and impossible antigravity belt, he didn't go that way."

"Or wings," Kathryn Marshall said suddenly, not taking her eyes off the scene.

"Oh, sorry, Lieutenant. This is Dr. Marshall, biologist and genetics expert from Stanford. I told you about her."

"Yes. Good to meet you, Doctor. Did you say 'wings'?"

"Unlikely, but it's a thought," she responded, and I could see in her face that she was once more replaying Project Chameleon in her mind, just as I was. Unless this was one hell of a scam, the most logical explanation for all this was some creature with enormous, inhuman strength, that none-theless could fly. But how could something be built to fly and yet have the mass, and therefore the strength, of two bull elephants? And did I really want that Pulitzer on my own badly enough to find out?

The lieutenant sighed. "We're getting into Spook City here, aren't we? Monsters from the Tokyo skies?"

"Spook City, yeah," I responded, since it was pretty obvious that any explanation these events could have would be something way out of the ordinary no matter what. "Hell, Lieutenant, even if it's some kind of elaborate hoax to cover up some murders or worse, just finding a totally conventional explanation for this and the one at the Wardman would be enough to generate video specials. Worse, it makes no sense either way. Why go into this elaborately gruesome business in either event? I mean, if it's really some kind of monster stuff, the *last* thing you want is to advertise it to every government agency and news organization in the known universe, which doing this in Washington guarantees. And if it isn't, then it's a great way to get everybody digging into the darkest corners. Can't you just imagine the hearings at the Joint Intelligence Committee's next meeting in a few weeks? And if every spook outfit in the government isn't busy both burying anything—and I mean *anything*—they don't want examined while at the same time moving heaven and earth to find out themselves what this is, then I'm too old for this job."

Monaghan sighed and shook his head. "You got that right."

At just about that moment somebody with the Maryland State Police shouted, "Suits! Black Ford alert! Anything you want to keep get moving out *now*!"

Dr. Marshall turned to me and frowned. "What is that all about?"

"I think it's our cue to exit as well, Doctor. It means that the Feds are finally here to rescue the world from truth in the name of justice and the American Way."

It was probably a joint task force thrown together as quickly as the Feds could move, but who was in charge and what agency was really represented by which suit you could never tell. Oh, I might have a good idea if I could see a couple of leaders close up; in this town you get to know the bosses and pretty much who they work for or you wind up being screwed six ways from Sunday. The problem was, that meant that *they* knew *you* on sight, too. I'd been lucky the other day at the Wardman; those guys had been mostly young, and whether it was the traffic or the time of day, nobody there had recognized me. But by now this case was the kind of thing reputations and promotions ride on. Even if whoever had drawn the werewolf case had been good and on the ball, they'd have been aced out on this call for just that reason.

In fact, as Marshall got out from under the tent and walked with me and the lieutenant into the shadows of the overhead lights I could see that this time my instincts were dead on.

"Well, well . . ." I muttered aloud. "Here come the Black Bag Twins and the Black Squad."

"Huh?" She seemed more puzzled than concerned.

"That fairly good-looking fellow there is John Singleton Syzmanski," I told her, pointing. "He's supposedly with the National Security Council Office of Security but he's really with something we're not supposed to know about even though everybody knows it's there and has been there. Everything but the name, anyway. His father was the former director of the CIA, his uncle was secretary of defense, and he's got a line of relatives serving in high posts going back a hundred years in this country. All powers behind the throne; the Syzmanskis don't run for office, they seize it."

She stared at me. "You're serious."

"Never more so. The Dragon Lady next to him is never far from his side even though he's married to a proper Washington hostess. She's Myra Ling Kelly, native true-blue American but her lineage is only known to be Eurasian; her family tree just about stops with her parents, one of whom was a college professor of foreign affairs at American University and speaks with a very mild French accent, her mother's overseas Chinese via Singapore but nobody in Singapore ever heard of her. Rumor is they were both spies who met while in debriefing somewhere in Virginia. Daughter Myra's done well, if a bit on the morbid side—she's a medical doctor but her specialty is in forensic medicine."

"She's a coroner?"

"Something like that. More a detective than a doctor, I think. She supposedly is an FBI agent, but if she is I don't think anybody at the FBI could recognize a photo of her and she's not even listed in the building's phone directory. While she can be quite charming, her innate personality matches her medical specialty. I'm surprised she wasn't at the Wardman the other day; I sure expected her there. The only reason I can think of is that they were on another case or just weren't quick enough."

"I gather you know these people?"

"Syzmanski I know—it's hard to be in the Washington press corps for very long without knowing the family, and his uncle's a good man. Kelly—well, *she* knows *me*, but it's not like we're friends. I don't think she has any friends, really. Not any live ones, anyway."

"And the others?"

"They change, but that's only because there are a lot of them. The nickname for the teams inside the intelligence community are Black Squads, after the old government term for a project so secret that if you know about it they have to kill you. No, not quite literally, so stop looking at me like that!"

"Never heard of them. Oh, I know the rumors of mysterious government creeps and all that, but I never took that seriously."

"Well, take them seriously, then. They're not the supermen of the cartoons and wild movies, though; they're mostly highly educated and totally psychotic trained specialists who would cheerfully kill, or whatever, in the name of God, motherhood, and the Constitution, even though they almost certainly don't believe in God, probably killed their own mothers, and if they ever read the Constitution they did it for comic relief. That's really part of *my* job. A free press helps keep them from becoming our century's version of Hitler's SS."

I looked around, then over at Monaghan. "Hey, Lieutenant! Any chance of a lift back to headquarters? I'd rather not go through the suits right now. We weren't that cordial at our last meeting."

"I'm with you. They'll be checking the choppers, but my car's over there. Come on."

The car was unmarked but had police tags; it wasn't intended to be undercover, just not panic-inducing on the beltway. We got in the backseat, and Monaghan started up and put a flasher on the dash as we pulled out.

"If these people are as powerful and paranoid as you say, I'm surprised that they're letting us go," Marshall commented.

"Oh, they don't have enough manpower to block off this level without calling in the army," the lieutenant replied. "And if you think this place is crawling with reporters, video crews, news helicopters, you name it, now, you ought to see what would happen if they did pull them in. No, we got the drill pretty well down pat, as you probably heard from the state cop's warning. They'll eventually get the car and what's left of the occupants and they'll be there when the area's surveyed in daylight, but any evidence we *really* needed is already in the hands of competent authority in the county, the state, and the District. The days when they could block it all off are over; modern technology made that nearly impossible. But that's what makes this mauling so incomprehensible."

"Oh?"

"Whoever was trying to get the evidence had to know that the data's in a ton of places, including many secure ones, and not even we know where everything is. We've got enough to analyze all over again and use as solid evidence if we caught them. So why do it? What was such a big deal that they needed to secure the actual physical samples? Two people's lives—*good* people. One just married, the other had a husband and two kids. Even if this guy's somehow one hundred percent human and looks like you or me, he's still a monster where it counts."

"That's what makes no sense in all this," I agreed. "This is like putting up billboards. You'd have to be totally insane to do it like this."

Dr. Marshall said nothing, less traumatized than seemingly in deep thought. I decided to let her work through it and see what she could come up with.

It may sound callous, but after thirty years you get immune to all the dead and all the mess after a while, kind of like a soldier in war I guess. You have to, or you'll never sleep at night and nobody will do the job. But you never get immune to the puzzle and the chase. That's what good investigative reporting is: puzzle solving. Monaghan was the same. Oh, sure, it was mostly dead druggies and domestic disputes that exploded, but now and then there was the puzzle, and if you let the bodies get to you, you'd never solve the thing.

Any local could use the back roads to get into D.C. a hundred ways, particularly if armed with a police radio that told where the blockages were and the best ways in.

Monaghan dropped the two of us right in front of the Hyatt. "Where are you going now, Vallone?" he asked me.

"Baltimore. I want to take a good solid look at that analysis with my editors there and see where we go from here," I told him. "Doctor?"

She gave a weak smile. "This is more thrills than I usually get in a year," she told me. "Still, I have a panel tomorrow and I'd like to check in with some people now that I know a bit more of what we're dealing with. Is there any way I can get a copy of that analysis?"

"I'll have to okay it with the bosses, but if you give me your portable's fax code I'll get it to you if and when I can," I told her. "When are you going back?"

"Not until Sunday morning," she told me. "I have some grant work to push with our people here so we don't get cut off at the knees on funding come the new Congress. And, I admit, I have a few old friends to look up that I haven't seen in years."

"Well, Doctor, you have my sat phone number and my priority codes," I told her. "You can reach me anytime, day or night."

She gave me a genuine smile. "It's 'Kate.' "

"Beg pardon?"

"Kate. My friends call me Kate. *Never* Kathy."

"All right, Kate. I'm Chuck. *Always* Chuck. Never Charles or Charlie. Okay?

"All right, Chuck. And thank you. I may yet be of help on this."

"Anytime, Kate. Anytime . . ."

I didn't wait for the car to warm up before transmitting what I had back to the *Sun.* The pictures alone made me feel pretty good; the backup story including a bit about government security teams moving in would add just the right touch, and it might well blindside any attempt at getting to the publisher before we went to press. The clock said elevenfourteen so I'd missed the early edition and the home delivery one as well, but if it made the bulldog it would be enough, and it would then go to our sister papers out West and online. By morning the networks would have stolen my story, but they would have to pay for, and give credit for, the photos.

Driving out over old I-95 I considered the day well spent. The story was current, we had more exclusives, which a paper shouldn't have in this electronic age, which would earn me money, respect, and increase my living-legend status. I didn't know why Monaghan was being so good to me, but I suspected that he thought I knew more than I was telling and that I was going to do half his work for him. I'd have loved to, but I prayed he didn't find out how ignorant I still was.

It boiled down more than anything to the motive of the acts themselves, which was unusual. I mean, okay, some nut wanted something and took it and didn't care who he killed.

People died in dark alleys for a few bucks, always had, so why not for something bigger even if no more meaningful? You could even sort of see the Wardman stuff if you were confident nobody could figure out how you did it. Make it gruesome enough and anybody else who knows stuff, particularly other scientists at the AAAS, would be panicked into shutting up and maybe even taking off.

Hmmm . . . *That* was an angle. Anybody who had been scheduled for something at the conference or locally who was a vet in the genetic or biological sciences suddenly take a powder after Wasserman hit the news? Interesting point.

But this second one, *this* made no sense at all. The cops knew nothing, and what they were carrying was of no value to anybody now. It would have been of value *before* it got to the labs, but not after.

Either there was something they were being far too clever with for us to see it in all this, or perhaps they had let loose some kind of maniac or even maniac-creature to do Wasserman, and then couldn't control it or regain it.

"I considered doing such a thing last night, but was more or less talked out of it."

"Now I see I was a fool not to have done it, but it is too late now."

If he, she, or it was now overruling the bosses with brute force, I was in really big trouble. If not, then maybe I was still in trouble, but there was something even darker afoot, and not insane in the sense that we were using it at all. Is a well-trained guard dog insane when it maniacally attacks any threat to its master? If the well-spoken man was still holding this—this *thing* on a leash, then there was something less primal and perhaps even darker going on here.

And if I found it, would the master then let loose his mad dog on me after all?

It was entirely possible that my life was going to depend not only on solving this, but on my ability to get the story out there and in public view before the other side knew it.

Normally, like all those who work for the few remaining

newspapers in the country, I'm a total throwback and something of a technophobe, but right now high technology was my lifeline. Satellite phones and faxes from anywhere and instant posting to all six net levels made it very hard to suppress information, particularly when a person's name or employer had credibility as mine did.

I must have driven the parkway to Baltimore a thousand times, but somehow, even with all the traffic around me, I couldn't help feeling more than a little paranoid, like something was flying just above the treetops, pacing my car, ready to pounce . . .

Newspapers were nothing like they had been in my dad's time; now we were primarily electronic, with competing editions and instant revisions and such, but in one way we differed from everybody else in the news and entertainment business: there was, somewhere, deep within the organization, still a small group of dedicated folks who actually *printed* the newspaper for the shrinking number of people who could read and were interested more in analysis than talking heads. It was the one link, always threatened with closure, that kept us old farts astrally connected to Hildy Johnson and the universe of *The Front Page* from the Broadway of a century ago.

There was and remains a certain permanence to a newspaper, even if it's now a tabloid digest on high-quality paper your dog couldn't tear on a bet. Anybody with a computer could alter almost anything in the electronic records; hell, you no longer even had to know how to draw to paint, just how to describe it and adjust it a little. A shift here, a nudge there, and not only could your photos turn into something else but your text as well, and in any languages you wanted. I was one of the rare ones who actually still typed in my stories; I didn't like the idea that when I called rewrite for the dictation I wasn't even sure if I was ever dealing with a human being.

Still, by the time I turned into the parking garage in Baltimore and took a spot near the elevator, my sardine-can car wreck photos were already all over the place and probably

giving the likes of Johnny Syzmanski and his crew heartburn.
I had no idea what story they'd pegged it to, though; no real
time. I'd just sent the recording of the briefing we got, which
the camera also obligingly picked up and associated with the
pictures.

Because of the electronic editions, feeds to the satellite
channels, international editions, and the like, the paper never
closed even though it officially produced only a single morning paper, but after two in the morning things were decidedly
uncrowded. I didn't know who would be on, but I did want to
see the results of the night's work as well as the full Genetique report on my samples. Checking my mail, I found it
runneth over with small packages and stuff, and noted that
these were parcel service deliveries from places I wanted to
hear from.

I walked back to the City Desk and was surprised to see
Karen Reedy there going through somebody's copy.

Karen was one of those types who was just always there.
She wasn't pretty, she wasn't ugly, she was just, well, ordinary. Late twenties, brown eyes, sandy red hair cut short and
combed straight back, lots of genuine freckles, or so we assumed at least. She had one of those androgynous faces that
could be either a young woman's or a teenage boy's face, and
the fact that she never wore any makeup or even jewelry gave
few clues, while the watch she used was one of those mini-
computers, certainly not something that came in both men's
and women's sizes. Even her voice, while fairly high-pitched,
had a raspy quality kind of like a young teen in the process
of a voice change, although she was many years beyond that.
There were always rumors about her sexual orientation but
I knew that she'd lived with a succession of guys, mostly
nerds and academic types, and she seemed to change them,
and addresses, every six months or so. You could always tell
when a breakup was imminent; she tended to live at the office, like now.

One eye looked up and saw me coming. "Well, well!

The Invisible Man returns!" she commented, putting down the copy and sitting up straight.

"No wisecracks. It's been a rough couple of days. The photos and sound track come in okay?"

She nodded, shuffled through a mound of papers on her desk, then drew out some proofs and handed them to me. I took them, commenting, "I thought the electronic age was supposed to be the savior of paper."

"More forests have died since the invention of the computer than died in the first five hundred years of the printing press," she retorted.

I looked at the proofs. Pretty straightforward, but the effect was good. The roll-up of the car roof was quite astounding, even as a 3-D still shot.

"They didn't like the fact that whoever's talking wasn't identified on the track," she told me. "At least it's not clear who's who."

"Well, it seemed obvious to me," I told her. "I didn't have much time to spell it out, not with Syzmanski and his squad walking in like that."

"Yeah, we already heard from him, and he wasn't happy. Didn't threaten or anything, but Sammy Glicksohn called me a couple minutes ago and said that there's a lot of rumors online that the photo's a fake."

"Yeah, well, they always try that, but we could put a *true* fake of a little green man with two antennae emerging from a flying saucer in front of the Lincoln Memorial and more people would believe it than not. That's why credibility is everything here."

She sighed. "Yeah, well, you might have some problems in a different area there." This time it was an envelope in a drawer. "I figured you'd want to see this quick."

It was the report from Genetique, and it wasn't anything I expected at all.

"Clydesdale horse fur? Dolphin skin? Marek's toad? What the hell is this?"

"It's what your samples turned out to be. Nothing much exciting. You can find that shit in any high-school biology lab. I even looked up the toad. It's a common swamp toad from south Florida. Chuck, they're *nothing*. If they make any sense at all that sense died with your doctor."

I looked over the reports and kept having the feeling that what I was seeing just couldn't be right. Oh, they were keyed to the delivery I sent Genetique, and each was signed off by "SMcC," who I assumed was their Dr. McCall, but . . .

The fourth one, the one that concerned the sample sent in by Monaghan, was also included, although I didn't expect it. *That* was what tore it.

"Wasserman's own hair and skin? Impossible!"

"Yeah, well, they say it matches his old genetic code taken when he got his original security clearance."

"There was a lot of hair, Karen, all over that place, and an animal smell like you couldn't believe. But while I never met Wasserman—whole, that is—I sure did see his photo. Looked him up in the files when I got contacted. The bastard was bald as a cue ball."

"Kinky!"

"Sez you. Just because they can grow hair on said billiard ball doesn't mean everybody does it. It's a look. Wasserman was bald. Unless he grew hair since his last official photo, and I got mine from State, then he suddenly sprouted hair all over his body. Possible, but unlikely. Werewolves don't dismember and devour themselves."

"Yeah? You know that for a fact? What's your source on that, Doc?"

"Don't be a smart-ass. These reports are what's bogus."

"Well, if so, do you think the D.C. cops got the same report?"

"Most likely. This is more than just acing out the press." I took a seat at a nearby desk and put the bag of office mail on it, then removed a box. "Now let's see how thorough they were."

"What'cha got?"

"Eggs from other baskets," I told her, and opened the first one, from a lab out in California.

It was a decidedly different report, and one that instantly put some chills up my spine.

"The sample sent is genetically consistent with a single unified organism," it said, "but must be a computer generated or laboratory-grown sample for the purposes of research. It would take weeks, perhaps months, to deduce what the organism might look like were this its true genetic pattern, but the combined elements suggest an incredibly powerful computer on a scale reserved for national defense grids and worldwide monitoring, if even those would be sufficient. We could actually test the mathematical patterns only down to 10^{100} within the amount of time we've been given, but we have not found one single flaw, nor even an *implied* flaw, in the patterns so far. The nearest matches to the sample are a human female, age approximately late teens, and that of a common female of some species of Delphinidae closely akin to, but not identical to, the fully mature Pacific bottle-nosed dolphin . . ."

I sighed, and handed Karen the paper. She seemed to see in my face that this wasn't a time for wisecracks and so she just read it. "Jesus Christ!"

"I'm not sure Jesus had anything to do with this."

"You think these were real?"

"Hard to say. But I'll bet you our so-called dolphin sample at Genetique was more likely that one. Here, let me see what the rest of the relief packages have to say."

They had intercepted one of the others, and it came back generic, or innocuous, but two others were just as troubling. They, too, were of females, but what kind of females? Late teens human again, but one had code that was most closely matched to, but not identical to, sections from some unknown animal of the genus *Bos*—Karen quickly pegged that as in the cow, buffalo, or ox family—and some from an unknown branch of the family Suidae, and that was in just *one* of the samples.

"Jesus H. Christ! A young woman, a cow, and a *pig*? What kind of creature would that *be*? Ugh!"

"I don't know, but it does seem to me that if you were trying to make something new you wouldn't reinvent creation. You'd use proven patterns from existing creatures. At least, that's what I'd do."

"Don't be too smart. You flunked sex education," she retorted. "What's the last one?"

"Well, it includes the family Blattidae."

She looked down at her screen, having switched it to audio input. "I hope you're mispronouncing that."

"Probably. What's it say?"

She took a deep breath. "Cockroach."

I stared at Karen for a moment and she stared at me, almost like two thinking as one and not wanting to think that at all. Then we both tore into action.

"Laboratory tests from reputable genetic labs around the nation and in Europe reported on the genetic makeup of samples sent to Chuck Vallone at *Sun* Science and Technology, by the late Dr. Samuel Wasserman, who was mysteriously and explosively murdered at the Hotel Wardman in Washington, D.C., on November fifth. Samples were sent to laboratories within the capital area and to those outside. The results differed wildly . . ."

We went on and on, including both the full text of the report, the compressed genetic data that was returned, and so on. Both of us knew that it was more than just journalism to get it out there; there would be a sledgehammer to suppress the information as soon as it was discovered.

I also needed to get the ampules containing the remains of the actual samples into someplace very, very secure and buried very, very deep. Now at least I knew why two good people had died. I wonder what Dr. McCall *really* found in her tests and what she filed? It didn't matter. Somebody had wanted it covered up. Somebody who could intercept the electronic mail and substitute it without batting an eyelash, and who had been *very* slow, incompetently slow, in picking this up and moving to cover-up so that it all had to move messily and violently at the last minute.

Those two had died simply to prevent those samples from contradicting her damned phony report.

And the only person I knew involved in this who would go to those lengths without batting an eyelash just to cover his tail was John Singleton Syzmanski.

If they knew about it all now but very late in the game, then was the good Dr. McCall, who'd obviously done a professional job here, still alive?

I hit a copy of my latest dispatch to land directly on Monaghan's desk, another to Kate Marshall's sat fax, and then, in addition to filing the story all over the online world, Karen and I also filed everything we had, from the story to the reports, in so many places, including places we didn't tell each other about, that it was unlikely even *we* could get them all erased.

Karen looked over at me. "Chuck—don't go home tonight. Take a company car, not yours, and sleep someplace random. You hear me?"

"What about you?"

"No big deal. My fingerprints aren't on any of this, and if they came calling there would be little they could find out. I'm just the go-between. You've got the samples."

I shook my head sadly. "Those people in the car were just go-betweens, too. How far are you from home?"

She shrugged. "At this time of the morning, it's taxi city from here. Twenty minutes."

I sighed. "I don't like that. Twenty minutes in a random taxi can be a lifetime at the moment."

"Oh, quit worrying! We've already blown this thing wide open!"

"Maybe. I just have the feeling that we haven't done any such thing."

At that moment the phone rang and she answered it. "City

Desk." Almost immediately I could see her go a bit chalky white and tense up considerably. She turned to me almost woodenly, looking a little scared, and said, "It's John Singleton Syzmanski for you. On line three. And he knows you're here."

FIVE

I picked up the phone and touched the extension. "Hello, John. It's been a while," I said as calmly as I could.

"You ran out on me before we could talk earlier this evening," he responded, his all-American Yale tones sounding their usual old-school-tie self. Still, I knew him well enough to feel that he wasn't as comfortable as usual even on his end, an impression reinforced as we continued talking.

"Yeah, well, you know how this business is. I had to file the story before the rest of them beat me to it."

"Um, yes. That's quite a story, too. Sorry I haven't had a chance to look it over myself as yet, but I've just gotten the condensed version in rather colorful terms. I positively *hate* those kinds of surprises, Chuck, and I've had more than enough of them lately."

Karen was already hitting record and trace, but I knew it was futile. Syzmanski had access to all the latest NSA gear, and if he didn't want you to record him, it wouldn't record, and as for tracing—well, not only could he block the best but he could even have it as coming from your own phone if he wanted to make you think it did.

"Don't blame me for that, John," I replied, playing it his way. "I didn't have a guy torn apart just in time for the six o'clock news or peel a car like it was a can of anchovies. Hell, John, if you folks want free billboards then who am I not to read them?"

There was a nervous cough at the other end. "Well, yes, that's quite true, but as you may have surmised from my team's rather slow reaction to all this, it didn't start with us, either. None of this was supposed to happen. It's really fate, in a sense. There was an early ice storm in Denver, so Wasserman wasn't intercepted where he should have been but instead was rerouted via Phoenix. Then—*someone*, let us say, panicked. They didn't call us, they didn't report the mess, they tried to take care of it themselves, and the result was the disaster we are faced with. Nobody was supposed to die, Chuck, and now we have a *situation*, as it were. We've got a ham-handed killer out there afraid of us and afraid that he won't be able to clean up his own mess, and when you get a nonprofessional in a panic, well, you see what's happened so far. Until we get him, there's a potential for it to get even worse. In the meantime, we're busy hunting him and cleaning up his messes."

"Is that what this is all about now, John? Cleaning up the mess? Like me, for example?"

"Oh, heavens, no, old boy! What you filed will be momentarily sensationalized, but we'll be able to damp it down, explain it, or foist it on the crazies. My grandfather used to have one of those jokes when he was heading the NSA. The good news, he said, was that we could now listen in on and intercept and understand every single piece of communication going on in the world every moment of every day. The bad news was that there was so much coming in that it drowned itself out and you could only find what you were looking for after it was no longer needed. Now everybody's got that kind of ability, at least as much as my grandfather's era could do it with big iron. And the result is that nobody can tell the good from the bad, the wheat from the chaff, and everything gets more or less equal weight. What do you *really* have, anyway? Nothing!"

I took a deep breath, then asked him, "John, what kind of a creature is part human, part cow, and part pig?"

He was silent for a moment, then gave what sounded like a forced chuckle. "Those samples. That's why you should just turn them in, Chuck. They're just small pieces of tissue grown in a lab as part of a learning process, then frozen until Dr. Wasserman got the idea that he was on some black list or something and got scared that this meant we were going to lock him away and lose the key. But that's all they are, Chuck. There are millions of combinations, but no true organisms. They got scared, lost their funding and political protection, and it was shut down *years* ago. I mean, just think about it. That's a pretty silly combination for anything useful, but it's a clever theoretical exercise to prove a system. That's all it was."

It *sounded* logical, and certainly would play well, but there were now three people dead and if Johnny Boy had only just come into the case today who or what the hell burglarized my place? And, of course, there was the *other* question.

"Okay, then, John, tell me what mass of lab tissue can peel the top of a plastic-and-reinforced-steel car top from above?"

"It's not a flying monster, if that's what you think. It is a sort of weapon, and a classified one at the moment, and it's in the hands of the one we seek, along with a few other things nobody should have, but it's no Frankenstein. Let's just call it a kind of revolutionary infantry combat armor with some of the abilities of a tank, and let it go at that. It'll eventually be public, but not until some bugs are worked out. Right now the bug is the fellow inside one of those things."

I wasn't sure I liked that picture any better than I liked the specter of a giant humanoid wolf-bat, but it did seem to make more sense.

"Great. So you're telling me there's a guy out there who's nuts, has killed three people, is scared to death, and has a gadget that makes him Superman?"

"Now you've got the picture. Not a pretty one, but the real one. And, of course, we'll continue to encourage Frankenstein to keep it from coming out, and you have no proof that it exists and thus no grounds for a story that will pass muster on your editorial scanners. That leaves only those samples."

"If they're not of real things, why do you even care about them?" I asked him.

"Oh, Chuck! Chuck! That's all we need. To have Congressional oversight committees demand to know why we saved all that and where it is and how we can destroy it all and all that."

"Why *did* it all get saved, John?"

"Because you can't stuff genies back in bottles, old man! When something's due to be invented, it's invented, from gunpowder and star-shaped fortresses to electricity and atomic physics. There are a lot of crazies with lots of money and power running countries here and there, John. We had to keep the research, as far as it went, and the samples, just in case. So far, thank God, we've not needed to go there."

"So why was Wasserman there?"

"Strictly second tier! That's the kind you want when you need knowledgeable scientists to oversee simply mothballing a program. And, it was worth a lot to him in, shall we say, material ways."

"So what do you want me to do, John?"

"Just give me the samples you have. Drop the story, or we'll give you just enough for a credible wrap."

"And if I don't?"

"Well, remember earlier this evening. There's someone out there that none of us have been able to stop, who also believes that it's his duty to recover those samples now that you've so kindly told him you have them. And he's a lot cruder and crazier than we are."

"So what happens if I do give them to you? He's still going to think I have them," I pointed out.

"Well, of course, we'll protect you—"

"As bait, you mean."

"Well, it's a story, and you've taken risks. But, relax. He won't come all the way at you because he has sm—*sensors* that will tell him if you have or haven't got them. He won't bother with you until and unless you lead him to what he's looking for."

"Yeah, well, thanks, John. So where would I give these remaining samples to you?"

"I could run over and pick them up right now," he suggested helpfully. "In fact, I'm on my way as we're speaking."

I sighed. "All right, John. I'll be waiting." I clicked off and looked over at Karen, first putting a finger to my lips to show that she shouldn't talk and then pointing to her coat over on the rack. She frowned and looked a bit confused, but there was something in my look, I guess, that made her go along.

There were a dozen or so other people in the large room at that moment, none paying any attention to us, and I was pretty sure that those familiar faces were so trustworthy they probably hadn't noticed that either Karen or I existed.

I grabbed the samples and the real printouts, my laptop, and almost pulled Karen along toward the parking lot exit. She was smart enough not to say a word until we were inside the stairwell.

"What are you *doing*?" she demanded as soon as the door closed with a heavy *clunk*.

"He's got you bugged. Not the phone lines—you. Probably not personally, but they've got mikes in the city room and almost certainly at your desk. Karen, they know you just uploaded a ton of this shit and they don't know where anymore than I do. They are not going to leave you alone once they get here."

"But—"

"No 'buts.' Sorry to drag you into this, but until Adam or his bosses can get you off the hook, you're on it, and there's nothing at all you can do about it tonight. The only thing I can be sure of is that he was telling the truth that he's not here yet and doesn't have anybody local on us."

"Huh? How do you know that?" she asked, starting to sound almost as out of breath as I was as we headed for level four and the company cars.

"Because if he or his squad were here, then we wouldn't be doing this now, that's how. He was in D.C. and only when they picked me up at your desk did they dispatch him. That doesn't mean they won't have some Feds watching my car and all the exits, but they won't know why and won't be too thrilled about it."

"But what can they do to me? I'm just doing my job!"

"And they're doing theirs. If they can't find me or they find me without the samples, then they're going to come for everybody I came in contact with and they're not gonna be nice about it. And forget that 'freedom of the press' crap. All that means is that there's more than one way to grab a 'Reporter Killed by Robbers in Botched Holdup Attempt' headline. And there's worse."

"Worse? Than *that*?"

I nodded as we looked over the board and picked out a small propane model that looked like four thousand others on either beltway. "The thing is, to a point, I think he was telling me the truth."

"You mean about a guy out there in a Superman suit?"

"Could be, but there's more to it than that. I'm pretty sure that our killer Superman *is* a rogue, an amateur, and now at least a three-time murderer, and he's got a buddy who helps him set things up. You haven't seen how this guy kills, and he doesn't care one bit if you're male, female, young, old, innocent bystander, or paid agent. He rips heads off people and he tears other people apart. Now, let's get out of here!"

I let Karen take out the car on her ID, but without concealing me sitting in the other seat. Lot manager Charlie Mossbacker knew both of us, and just pretty much waved us through with a signature on the form stating that, yes, we knew that if we were killed in a wreck we were still liable for the car.

We pulled out into the darkness and turned a corner to go out along the middle branch toward the interstate grid and the beltway. There was very little traffic, so the three identical black cars screaming by were easy to spot.

"Hello, John," I sighed. "I think I'll be getting a call soon. I don't think I'm gonna answer it, though."

"Where are we going?" Karen asked me.

I hadn't thought of that. I looked at my watch and saw that

it was now almost four in the morning. Just the worst possible time to wake anybody up.

"Well, we need to kill some time, and keep out of sight. Are you hungry?"

"Am I *what*? After all this—?"

"Well, *I'm* hungry. Go out Seventy toward Frederick. There's a Pancake Palace near the Damascus cutoff that's twenty-four hours."

"Why, that's the craziest thing I could imagine!"

She was new to this, and, I could tell, even more scared than I was. "Look, first and foremost it's off the beaten path, but not much. We can cut over to D.C. via Damascus or go up to Frederick and around and down I-Two-seventy if need be. Second, just in case the other guy's around, there are lots of people, bright lights, security cameras, things like that there. It's even a minor truck stop, so there's always some kind of action and movement and people waiting around. It's a very good place to kill a few hours as safely as possible."

She was biting her lip out of tension, I could see that, but she also headed in the right direction.

"Then what?" she asked after a long silence.

"What? You mean when daylight comes? Dr. Marshall has a panel at AAAS. It's the last day, and I doubt if they're going to move on her, at least not until she's no longer on an official schedule. They've had far too much publicity on this already. She's the ideal one to read these reports and she'll know who'll make the best use of the samples. I'd also love to talk to McCall at Genetique if she's there tomorrow—or anywhere, for that matter, at this point."

"Tell me that doesn't mean what I think it means."

"It means I'm going to make every attempt as a middle-aged sexist male pig to surround myself with women, all of whom are probably smarter than I am."

She sighed. "Two out of three ain't bad, I guess."

"Two out of three? Don't put yourself down."

"Hey, I'm the one who ran out of the building with you, probably the safest place I could have stayed, even if I might have to have started living there. Hell, they deliver there. Pizza, Chinese, even crab cakes. Instead I'm riding toward the boonies with you, and, even more stupidly, I'm the one doing the driving!"

"That's why you're smart," I told her. "I haven't had but maybe two hours' sleep in the last two days. If I were driving I'd probably kill us both."

Even as I was eating my eggs, pancakes, sausages, and bacon, billed on the menu as the "Chloresterol Special" but really *much* worse for you than that, I was on the phone. Karen, sipping a cup of coffee and nibbling on a piece of toast, watched me with evident disgust as I consumed the mountain while also working the phone. She did, however, know better than to criticize my cuisine.

"Aren't you afraid they can find you using the sat phone?" she asked me instead.

"Not the way I'm doing it here," I told her. "Contacts, my dear, contacts are everything in the reporting biz. The number I'm using goes to all sorts of other numbers all over the known universe and it switches them, even as I speak, in a constant and random pattern, and they and this little phone know the crypto codes as well that allow things to seem like a normal conversation. The government uses similar methods to keep its communications relatively secure; just about all governments and big industries do."

"Yeah, but how did *you* get plugged into that? Did you expect to be on the run?"

I shrugged. "You never know. But, truthfully, I was given a dozen or so such numbers and my crypto keys by some people who thought I had the proper attitude toward government and authority, which means I hate it, at least in a theoretical way. You see, sometimes it's useful *not* to break a story, like the one about the crypto-anarchist hackers who have been inside the NSA in ways even that agency can't imagine."

"Not *really*!"

"Yeah. Really. Oh, they can't do anything, because the moment they did the NSA would be on them like an elephant stomping on fleas, but they can eavesdrop on certain less-than-totally-secure lines and occasionally they feed me bits and pieces of information. In this case, though, it's simply to make local calls."

When my father was still a teenager he went to what historians would later call the last of the great world's fairs, one of the New York ones. At that time they were demonstrating picturephones, the wave of the future. And every ten or twenty years thereafter, picturephones were *still* the wave of the future, even though they got lighter and cheaper and simple to use.

They never did catch on in people's homes. Who the hell wants to remain dressed up and looking good to get an eyeball-to-eyeball pitch from an aluminum siding salesman? People were all in favor of picturephones that showed the *other* end of the line, but they wanted to continue to talk in anonymity wearing curlers and underwear or maybe nothing at all. There are some technological advances whose time never came. Thus, my handy sat phone could call any number in the entire world, had infinite lookups, could pick up and relay my voice mail, electronic mail, you name it, and squirt it to the printer of my choice even if the printer was in a different country, but they still couldn't see me and I still couldn't see them and that was just fine.

I flipped open the back and ran the bar along the documents slowly until they were all gathered together, then I punched in a code and the truck stop's electronic fax shot them right to Kate Marshall along with my attached voice message that I'd see her after her panel, and a double-blind message box she could use if she couldn't make it. Because it was printed to her own portable's memory, not kept in some accessible box, I was pretty sure that nobody would get it but her.

I then began calling and leaving messages for Adam, for the Newspaper Guild, for the lawyers, you name it, so that if anybody wondered why I disappeared they'd know just who to ask.

Karen went to the john, then came back. "You know they have motel rooms here?"

"Yeah, sure. A few. Truck stops usually do. By the hour, too. So they can shower and get a nap without having to keep a hotel schedule. Why?"

"I saw you had a company cash card. Why not use it and get a little sleep? You can't do much else until morning and you're gonna be no use to me at all when the adrenaline wears off."

I tried to look disappointed. "Damn! And I thought I was getting a proposition."

"Yeah, well, maybe when I'm hard up, Pops."

"Ouch!" I said in mock pain, but it was a good idea.

It was a basic utilitarian unit, exited so you could see if anybody was coming, and it had a double bed, bath and shower, comlink, and wall screen. Even the Gideon Bible was a button on the comlink.

I stripped down to my underwear but no further and pretty much flopped on the bed. I normally had problems sleeping and when I was like this I had *real* problems getting to sleep through my exhaustion, but this time I just went out like a light, unconscious, no dreams. I was like the dead.

Which is why it took Karen a lot of time and effort to wake me up, even using ice cold wash cloths when all else failed.

"All right, all right," I mumbled, for a moment not even remembering where I was, or why, or who I was with.

"Get up, Chuck! You *have* to see this!"

I felt like I'd fallen into the gorilla cage and they'd used me as a punching bag, but I managed to groan, roll over, and open my eyes, even though everything was about as blurry as could be. I was now remembering, and I heard the comlink on, but for a moment nothing registered.

"What time is it?"

"Nine-thirty in the morning. You had almost five hours."

I picked up one of the cloths and used it to force myself

awake. Karen was relaxed in a T-shirt and panties but little else, and she was looking at the screen on the wall. She really was thin, and no tits at all.

I turned to the screen only to see the end of something.

"You see it?" she asked me.

"No. What is it?"

She punched it up again. LIST NEWS STORIES. GOVERNMENT AGENTS RAID NEWSPAPER.

I sat up.

She touched the headline and it began to roll. Since this was the second-level net I knew it was probably something that went out with everybody's cornflakes.

"What was described as a rogue squad of government agents burst through security at the *Baltimore Sun*, one of the fewer than two hundred remaining morning print newspapers, as they were preparing for their final edition today. They had blocked standard security with high-tech police jammers, but the paper has a continuous level-one feed covering all its offices on a proprietary channel. Thus, we have dramatic pictures of this unprecedented and illegal action."

There was the city room, pretty much as we'd left it, and then, suddenly, the doors burst open at the far end with a loud bang and there was John the S.S., as we sometimes lovingly called him, in full performance mode, his Black Squad from the previous night filing in behind him like military commandos.

Some guy came running toward them, sports shirt, brown hair, about my age, yelling, "Hey! Who the hell are you? You can't—"

"Shut up, asshole!" the charming Mr. Syzmanski responded with the kind of tone that one used for killing cockroaches. "Shut up and sit down!"

"Who the hell are you?" somebody else yelled.

"Mac Cohn, that's the first guy," Karen said. "There's Joe Lombardi, and Terry Santiago just behind, all yelling. And by now they've pushed every alarm in the building except the fire alarm."

With that a loud clang started and the fire alarm went off. Syzmanski cursed and grabbed Mac Cohn. "Turn that damned thing off!"

"Can't! Only the fire department has the keys!" Mac yelled. "Now get out of my city room!"

Syzmanski looked madder than hell. Yelling over the alarms, he screamed, "I'm with the U.S. government and this is a national security case. I want to know where Karen Reedy's desk is! And Chuck Vallone's office when he's here! I also want both of them and I want them *now*!"

"You got no authority coming in here!" Lombardi shouted at him. "You got no warrant or you'd show it, and you got no constitutional rights to do it, either!"

"Aw, *fuck* the Constitution! And here's my warrant!" Syzmanski screamed, pulling out a very nasty-looking gun. He fired it at the far wall, and a tracer of sharp laser light hit it and smoldered there.

That was another mistake. The discharge and the heat on the wall triggered all the sprinklers. Way in the background you could hear half the sirens in Baltimore arriving.

Syzmanski took the gun by the barrel and in his fury struck Mac a hard blow with the handle, but it was clear Mac wasn't hurt all that badly. The man in the now-very-wet suit and topcoat then whirled and shouted for the team to go down the stairs and meet him at the cars below.

"Identified as the leader of this alleged government squad was John Singleton Syzmanski, son of former CIA director George Syzmanski and nephew of the former secretary of defense. Computer analysis has verified this identification, although not the identities of the men and women with him, and the FBI motor pool in Washington has confirmed that all three cars carrying the assailants came from there and were checked out under his name. The bureau, however, says categorically that neither he nor any of the others work for the FBI and that they were loaned the cars out of interagency courtesy as a routine matter. Nobody so far seems to know what agency he and his people represent, nor have we been able to contact the deputy attorney general or any other close members of the family."

I had mixed feelings about seeing it. On the one hand, it was really wonderful to see the bastard get pasted, probably beyond repair. Even if they could prove that he was actually Ignatz, an alien from the planet Arcturus who could simulate human form, there would always be some who would doubt, and nobody was going to trust him again. Even his own side—no, *particularly* his bosses—would have to cut him loose, although the family and family money would probably get him out of the country and away from awkward questions.

Still, he had to be desperate, frantic, to do a stupid thing like that. Since he'd never be scared of his superiors, not with his connections, on that kind of level, something a lot scarier had come up.

"Still wish you'd stayed at your desk?" I asked Karen.

She shook her head. "No, Pops, you were right on that one. But we're not gonna have to sweat *him* anymore."

"No, maybe not, but his girlfriend was nowhere to be seen there, and I was always more scared of her than of him. The question is, what panicked a guy like that? Over *these*? Hell, he gave us an explanation that was more than credible last night. No, there's still a lot here we aren't getting, damn it."

"You gonna call in?"

"Yeah, but they got the story that tops any of ours for the moment. I need some coffee. Intravenous if possible, double espresso, quadruple the caffeine. I need a clear head."

"I can get you some while you wash up. You *are* gonna wash up, right?"

"Sure. What do you take me for?"

"A guy with pizza stains on his boxer shorts." She pulled on her jeans and put on her jacket and boots. "Be right back."

And with that she was gone. I looked down and discovered that not only was she right about the pizza, she hadn't bothered to mention a few other distinguishing marks. I made a mental note to pick up a change of clothes if I could, even if we had to stop somewhere and buy them.

By the time she got back I was dressed, more or less, mostly awake, and I'd checked my messages and I'd checked in with the boss.

"Glad you got Karen out of there," Adam told me. "I'll let her boyfriend know."

"Yeah, okay. I doubt if she's all that concerned about him, though. She never once mentioned him all night. Look, I'm going to follow up here, and she'd be very useful sticking with me, at least through today. Can we charge some clean clothes to the card?"

"Yeah, sure. Just so long as they don't cost more than what you're wearing now. I don't want to explain why you're suddenly wearing a five-thousand-dollar suit and she's got the Hope diamond around her neck."

"Adam, we'll have to be higher than that. This suit was outdated ten years ago. I keep waiting for it to come back into style."

"If you burn it, I'll go double."

I decided not to answer that, but Adam was a happy man with that video.

"How's Mac?"

"Bump on the head, no broken skin, very mild concussion. I might give him a day off after his celebrity wears off. The big mess is water damage from the damned sprinklers, but we'll cope. The security system firewalled the computers and heavy machinery and all the electronics otherwise are waterproofed, so we're still in business. Going to switch city to the old location on the fifth floor until they get this cleaned up, though."

"Adam—any word on Syzmanski? That man was scared shitless."

"I know. I could feel it, too. No, no sign, but that's to be expected. The Syzmanski Trust has a mere thirty or forty billion bucks to fool with, and I suspect he's halfway to Fiji on a family jet by now."

"Maybe." I sighed. I couldn't get the uncharacteristic behavior out of my mind, though. "Still, if whatever scared him is still out there, he may not be as far as we think."

"Yeah, well, if his own people get him he'll disappear in a whole different way, and if anybody else gets him he's going to be very hard to ignore."

"Anything on the rest of the team?"

"You know the Black Squads. They're all officially dead guys with dead people's identities while theirs have been erased. Hell, they'll be debriefed, transferred to Asia or someplace, and put back in the field."

I wasn't so sure about that, either. Still, there was little more I could do or say.

"Okay, I'm going to do some follow-up today. Maybe I'll get lucky. This thing keeps twisting like mad every time you feel like you found the handle."

Just as I switched off, Karen came back with no less than four giant cups of coffee. "All that time in college and what do I wind up doing? Fetching coffee for the reporters."

I clued her in on the situation back home. "You want to call home and reassure him?"

"Oh, I think Dwight and I have come to the end of our relationship. I'm just trying to figure out a way to get that through to him at this point."

"*Dwight?* Your boyfriend's name is *Dwight?*"

"Hey, that was some president's name sometime, you know. Besides, he's a geek. That fits him very well."

"You okay with staying out in the field with me for a little while?"

She grinned. "Sure. Why not? I mean, this is what I got into the business to do, right? And I've been sitting at a desk or out doing geek stories and coming back for a stint at rewrite. Big deal."

"Well, if you shack up with geeks, shouldn't you expect to draw the geek stories?"

"Yeah, but Dwight's only an engineer-type geek. They send me out to *really* find a guy biting the heads off chickens."

"Yeah? Ever find one?"

· "Nope, but I found a lot worse, let me tell you."

And as she consumed one of the coffees and I three, she proceeded to tell me about them.

It was chilly and overcast when we left the motel, but it didn't look like we were going to be facing any ice or snow. November was still too early for that, or at least for that to have any real presence, at least in the Baltowash area—or, if you were a confirmed Washingtonian or a government statistician, Washtimore.

The first order of business was a mall, and that proved easy in this neighborhood.

Once the area around Mount Airy toward Frederick was the country, and Damascus was likewise the wilderness, but now you could hardly tell that at one time the region had its own print newspaper. With a combined total population of over ten million, D.C.–Baltimore was the fourth largest metro area in the nation, stretching over ninety miles and containing both major cities and a lot of crowded smaller ones.

Knowing the kind of guys Karen moved in with, I deliberately did not allow her to pick out any fresh clothing for me, but I went with a casual outfit this time, and picked up an off-the-rack suit that almost fit if I needed to be fancy. Karen bought a fur-lined leather jacket, another of those jeans-type outfits she always wore, clean undies, and, I noted, some new shiny boots. At that, her bill came out higher than mine, but, what the hell, Adam was paying.

There used to be hues and cries about leather and fur, but since they could grow the stuff these days without bothering to grow the animal, things had pretty well died down in that department. Even the most fanatical animal rights advocate hadn't gone as far as the Molecular Liberation Front, at least not yet.

As we pulled out of the mall lot and got onto the expressway toward Washington I wondered about that angle.

"You know, Syzmanski said that these samples were nothing but test freezings of an old mothballed program," I reminded her.

"Yeah, so?"

"Well, if they're growing leather and fur and all sorts of exotic skins now using molecular genetics, why bother to keep these monstrosities? I mean, not that you'd *want* them, but if you ever did absolutely require a complex genetic code that involved a woman, a cow, and a pig, you could make it anew."

"Maybe. Maybe it's more complicated than growing just skin. I suspect it is. But, I think you're right, too. Why keep experimental formulas and samples for monsters? Too much money just to keep them, and far too much of an investment to actually create or sustain them even if you had the proverbial mad scientist."

"What about Wasserman? I asked you to trace him if you could, but I never had a chance to get your report."

"Well, we had a bunch of kids on it and they did a pretty fair job. Seems his passport expired while he was out of the country and he had to get it renewed to get back in. That implies that for most of that time he was living in one place, but out of the country, since he didn't need the passport."

"Where'd he renew it?"

"That's the interesting part. Majuro."

"Where the hell is that?"

"Capital of the Republic of the Marshall Islands. We have some links with it—some kind of defense stuff—and in history it was where they did a lot of things like hydrogen bomb tests."

"Jeez! This is beginning to sound like an old monster movie! Radiation, maybe mutants . . ."

"Well, it's the kind of area that nobody would look twice at. They have islands they haven't even counted yet, and it's kind of independent but kind of United States and kind of New Zealand, too, so you can see how it would be easy to use Acme Rent An Island for anything you wanted there."

"Well, at least we now know the rough area where our alleged storage and containment facility is."

"Yeah, plus or minus, like, thirteen hundred kilometers square, maybe more. That's a huge area!"

I thought a moment. "Anybody else connected to both the Marshall Islands in any way and our little investigation?"

"Not yet. But at about the same time Wasserman quit and vanished, a bunch of other specialists in various fields vanished as well. Not disappeared, they just resigned from where they were, sold their houses and cars, and left."

That was interesting. "What kind of people?"

"Neurophysicists, geneticists, psychopharmacologists— some of those with really *interesting* records—that kind of thing. Also lots of folks involved in artificial intelligence, big and unorthodox computer systems, like that. Not the kinds that make headlines, though. Middle of the road types. Not a Nobel in the bunch."

I nodded. "Makes sense if you're assembling people to build and maintain rather than do pure research. What did you mean by 'interesting' records, though?"

"Most of the psychopharmacologists had criminal records. A lot of them came straight out of prisons, were even sprung early."

"Illegal drugs, you mean."

"Yeah, sort of. Remember the big scare over the pinks and the blues? The super sex pills that turned people into nymphos and satyrs?"

"Yeah, I do. It wasn't my story but you couldn't help but see it. It was pervasive. We almost lost a generation there. The thing is, it not only made you oversexed, it also tuned the body. Made you look years younger, better looking, better developed. But if you later got the urge to stop once the physical effects kicked in, you turned into an old wreck very quickly, usually with a machine-gun burst of ministrokes. You mean those guys were among this group?"

"You bet. And others like them. Designer drugs and power trips."

That was scary, because it went beyond the samples and the worst fears of genetic mutation, deliberate or not. To a large extent we are controlled, or not, by chemicals in the brain and where they lie, how much is there, and so on. Genetic bombs in pill or injected form could alter not only your personality and behavior but your very brain makeup.

How easy would it be to make up such a cocktail that would create the kind of rage I'd seen at the Wardman? Not a Superman suit, but just a few little pills. And, of course, there were the psychological lessons of that pink and blue business. Even after they knew what it did, thousands of people still willingly sought it out and took it, women in particular. Scary stuff that intelligent people would voluntarily choose to be younger, oversexed bimbo addicts. It said something about our culture.

"You don't build that kind of stuff without heavy scientific hitters behind it, as well as government and corporate," I noted. "Any links *to* the Nobel types?"

"Give me a break! We were only working on it for like thirty-six hours! Still, if I were doing it, I wouldn't assemble any big teams. I'd put a ton of grant money out there and spread it around the Nobel types. Each of them working on their own specialty, well funded, good teams at top institutes and universities—hell, they wouldn't even have to know that they were working for something or somebody bigger. Never saw one of them who wouldn't kill his or her own grandmother for unlimited grant money for their pet project. And with all those private and corporate foundations out there, you might be hard-pressed to link them together yourself. And all that stuff would go to the second-tier folks—the technicians and engineers you hired and squirreled away who weren't particularly missed. Jesus! It's *perfect*!"

We were coming into the city and heading toward the new convention center complex now.

"Yeah, it's perfect. It's so perfect, how the hell are we going to prove it?" I asked her.

SIX

I hadn't gotten a reply from Kate Marshall. This didn't particularly worry me, since if she was anything like me or a million other people she didn't check all those messages and stuff until she was through her schedule for the day. Still, I was relieved when she showed up for her panel, looking still stunning and none the worse for wear.

Karen was less than impressed with the crush, the crowds, and all the rest. "This place is an anachronism. All these scientific big brains and they couldn't do all this with holograms and not have to stand these crowds or the expense of showing up?"

"You just don't think things through enough, youngster," I responded in my best grandpa voice. "There *are* some speakers and panelists who show up only as holograms or the like. Those who can't get away or who genuinely hate crowds, crushing, long trips, or who are trying to dodge process servers and ex-spouses. For most of these fine men and women of science, though, what this *really* translates out to is an all-expense-paid or deductible trip to Washington, D.C., for a vacation and some shop talk far away from bosses, spouses, and project deadlines. It also makes for bizarre bar scenes. I saw a group of engineers get almost to the point of trading punches the other day and what they were shouting at each other was equations!"

She shrugged. When you live around here the attraction of a free trip to Washington somehow pales in its allure.

"That's your geneticist up there? Pretty," Karen commented.

"No fair. I saw her first. Besides, her IQ is probably both of ours to the tenth power."

The panel was actually fairly interesting, with members being questioned by spectral holograms of researchers in several other countries who, presumably, couldn't get their own bosses or governments to give them a free ticket or who maybe weren't allowed to come so close in person to the source of evil in the world.

It was on scientific ethics, the old bugaboo that went back far beyond Mary Shelley, even if she had put it in the most dramatic of terms. The real question was, if we *can* do something, does that mean we *should*? And if there are things we shouldn't do, then who decides?

This had been a raging topic since before I first got into this business, and there were enough bad examples to make you really nervous. Everybody knew that in an isolated compound in the Far East, Wallid Shamanituk had a whole village of himself being "properly" raised, and that was scary enough. Everybody also knew that for every practitioner now in jail in the West for illegal and unethical cloning, there were probably a hundred out there doing it. The whole history of mankind from at least as far back as the start of the industrial revolution, or maybe the invention of gunpowder, was that we kept finding bottles with magic genies in them and we kept uncorking them, having people and governments misuse them, scare us silly, and then we try and shove the damned things back in their bottles. Didn't work. Kate's take on it wasn't that reassuring, either.

"Look," she said to one of the remote questioners, "right now we have computers designing and building other computers. Everything in our lives is wired, or electronic but wireless, and we're utterly dependent on them. We are speaking to one another here through an electronic medium that is astonishing even though we use it all the time in our work, and we take it for granted, just as we take for granted that all of us can understand one another, unambiguously, even if we are all speaking our native languages. I submit that there is probably no single agency, scientific or governmental organization, international body, *anything*, that really understands and can detail every single electronic happening and ability going on. There is no controlling authority for any of this save our employers, the funding groups, and our own individual ethics. Nor can there be such a controlling body without a near totalitarian oversight of everything we say and do. In the end, we must be pragmatic and use consensus among those of us who truly can influence the direction of new discovery. Nothing else will work."

Sounded good to me, but it set off a whole big debate among the others as to whether we could be trusted, whether we were still going to wipe ourselves out, if not by the atomics of the last century then by the chemical and biological revolutions of the twenty-first. And, yeah, there were even some political types and boss types arguing that there should be international treaties and rigid laws and secret technology police to save us from ourselves.

That was an interesting take, though. What were the Black Squads of our own government and those of other governments but secret technology police? People who were very smart and well grounded in cutting-edge technology who went around suppressing, secreting, stealing, and maybe even using the new stuff to save us all from ourselves.

I knew their own take on themselves, and they really did feel that they were the saviors of humanity. A little poisoning of the genetic well at Clonetown and maybe some other dictators and rich nuts get cold feet at trying it themselves.

One Black Squad member told me once that the greatest unknown and unpublished story of the past century was how and why we never had nuclear missiles fired in anger after the end of World War II. That's what bred the Black Squads, that and the resulting cold war and its tensions and the concurrent explosion of technology. The old stories of secret desert bases, men in black, all sorts of stuff like that, came from glimpses of the Black Squads at work. The argument that you only knew about their failures was valid, to a point.

But I always would ask one of them who they worked for. Oh, they'd point to a John Singleton Syzmanski or a similar man or woman, but they knew that wasn't what I meant. Who picked up the phone and called them in on that wreck? Who was so powerful and so scary that they could push Johnny Boy over the edge like that? Who gave the order for the "accidental" explosion of a small home-grown nuke that vaporized a quarter of a million people in Tripoli and which scared the rest of the Third World shitless as a result? Ditto the accidental escape from an Afghani underground lab of that supervirus that quickly made several ancient area conflicts moot over there before a defector miraculously got to India with the formula for the cure? All that blood, all probably spilled in the name of saving humanity—who gave the order? It was my one reporter's dream to find that out before I died or they got me. Frustrating as all hell.

And what were they doing with the technology they'd managed to suppress from us? What genies were strictly in their hands, as long as they could hold on to them? And what would happen if they ultimately got one they couldn't contain themselves?

Those questions were in many ways more relevant than the academic ethics being argued here. It was conspiracy stuff, nutso stuff, wild thrillers, that's all. It was kind of laughable, really. Make yourself a cartoon menace and sooner or later nobody but the nuts will take you seriously.

Me, I knew them firsthand, and I had absolutely nothing solid enough after all these years that I could take it to an editor. *That,* I suspected, was really why I was still alive.

And it made that scene in the city room absolutely astonishing.

The only time I ever had any liking for or understanding of Syzmanski was when I asked him once, years back, why he stuck with such a relatively low job like field agent when he could be another government or corporate big shot like the rest of his family.

"Because I couldn't stand not to know," he'd responded, and it was the one great insight I had.

Well, Johnny, you're out of the business now, I thought, with curiously little emotion one way or the other.

As we waited for the seminar to wind down, I couldn't help but notice that Kate was in some minor distress. It appeared she had some sort of rash or bite that wouldn't let go of her hip or thigh, and she was struggling mightily to scratch it without being obvious or embarrassing in front of such an audience. I could sympathize; I did occasional talking-head stints on the weekend political shows, which showed just how desperate they were for fresh faces, and it always seemed like I came on national broadcasts with a booger on my nose or some embarrassing stain on my shirt.

When it finally did end, I tried to catch her eye but I didn't think she saw me in the evacuating throngs. I had a hunch that if that spot was still bothering her she'd head first for the rest rooms.

"Want to intercept her and tell her who you are and that I'm here?" I asked Karen. "I think she's headed just over there to the left, to the room where, if I followed, it would *be* the story."

"Yeah, sure. Meet me outside there."

She was small and thin, but she could thread her way through a crowd, I gave her that. I was much slower getting out into the main entry hall, but I was just in time to see Kate, quickly followed by Karen, go into the women's just where I thought.

I waited around outside, wishing *(a)* that I had a cigar and *(b)* that it would be legal to smoke it anywhere in the area, but settling for the water fountain. After ten minutes or so I began to get worried, although, of course, when things let out everybody heads for the johns and the women's rooms are always much slower even if the number of stalls is the same or greater. Still, it was almost fifteen minutes before Karen came back out—alone, to my distress.

"What's the problem?" I asked her. "She's in there, isn't she?"

"Yeah, but it's the damnedest thing I ever saw. Perfectly round rash—and I mean computer-engineering-type perfect round—made up of jillions of little bumps. About the size of a golfball. She's kinda freaked and I don't blame her."

I didn't like that. "Well, what's she gonna do? I'm gonna have to go over to the men's myself here and let at least the first installment of all that coffee out."

"Go. I'll stick with her, and we'll play it by ear when you get back. I think she should see a doctor."

That sounded like a good idea to me, but not nearly so good as it felt reaching the urinal across the way in my part of the relief section. They were both standing out in the hall when I emerged, it being a lot quicker for me. Kate looked at me with a worried expression.

"When did this start?" I asked her. "Do you even know?"

"In the crowd, right around here," she told us. "I mean, I was in a crush of people trying to get over to the back door of the conference room and I felt a burning sensation. When I got into the room I couldn't examine much, but I half expected to see some kind of stain or rip in my pants but there was only a very tiny tear. See? You can see it."

I tried not to look like I was looking at a woman's ass and thigh too closely but I could just barely see it. She wore expensive clothes, and the red pants had a satiny look and feel to them, and I saw a slight stain. "A little darker around there, like it was slightly wet," I noted. "Karen said it was a perfectly round rash?"

"Yes. I wish I could show it to you, but not here and not where it is, at least for the moment."

"Have you ever seen anything like it before?"

"I sure haven't," Karen put in.

Kate was a little less sure. "Something *like* it, maybe. In emergency squad mobile units, where they pretty much put you inside a diagnostic robotic shell. Smaller versions, like the size of a dime or maybe up to a quarter, might show up in the injectors the robotic diagnostic equipment uses, either to administer stuff quick to the bloodstream or to attach monitors. But nothing this big, and no rash that looks like that." She paused for a moment. "My God! You don't think somebody injected me with something, do you?"

I looked at Karen, who nodded. "We think we ought to get you looked at by a doctor and find out," I told her.

I called in a favor from an internist working at George Washington and we took her over there in a cab. Dr. Joe Smeltzer met us in the emergency room and took us right past everybody else sitting there looking miserable and more deserving than Kate. Of course, this was a different kind of case and Joe wasn't an emergency room physician, and he had enough clout there to have a nurse run the paperwork as he had Kate sit in a wheelchair and then be moved by another nurse into an examining room in a part of the hospital I was unfamiliar with.

The nurse took Kate off to get in one of those godawful gowns, the one hangover from the early days of medicine that they never bothered to fix. You'd think that a hospital system that could analyze everything inside you in an hour and spit out tons of results could at least provide Velcro-strapped hospital gowns that form-fitted, but, no . . .

As usual, Karen and I were left sitting around and waiting. After a half hour or so, Joe reappeared.

"You know, Chuck, I had this sudden idea when you called that your life of excess had caught up with you and you were now in my power," he said lightly.

"Do you have anything yet on Kate?"

"She's quite good looking, if that's what you mean. No, nothing much yet. We're done running a full tox, and if she was poisoned it was no known agent. Blood, urine, so on looks normal, but she's right. That's no rash and that's no accident. Somebody injected her with something. We just haven't found what it was yet."

"How long before you'll know anything?"

He shrugged. "Maybe a few minutes. Maybe hours or longer.

Maybe days. Thing is, we've taken samples and we've completely scanned her, and all this data has been fed into the master diagnostic computers, which means it's being analyzed and puzzled over virtually worldwide."

"So what happens if it comes up zero after all that?" Karen asked him.

"Well, it could be a lot of things. It could be that it's a natural substance in just such quantities that it wouldn't show up when compared to her last stored physical. They can be little 'gotchas' if well designed and placed. Or, it could be something that would never show up, like distilled water."

"Why would anybody shoot distilled water into somebody else?" she asked him.

"To create a mark like that, concern like this. As a threat or warning. Or, it may have been that she backed into a charged and armed display somebody was carrying for some demonstration, which would be another reason for it to be water. Thing is, I can keep her overnight to see what symptoms develop, or she can go and I'll give her a topical that at least will get rid of that itching and burning."

"What would you recommend?"

"Well, I'd like to keep her overnight for observation, but unless something concrete turns up fast it's up to her. The one other thing it might be would take a couple of days to show up in any tests anyway."

"What other thing?" I asked him.

"Well, it's not the best way to administer it, but there are gene-therapy technologies that could be administered that way, and since she's had some nanosurgery in the past it's impossible to tell what's residual or what's been introduced on that front. If either of those is a possibility, and I'd bet on the first over the second since gene therapy is still not that universal and needs customizing to each patient, then I'd say forty-eight to seventy-two hours would tell us something."

"Yes?"

"Your medicard has your genetic basics on it. That and the finger scrape are how we can make sure the visit is charged to the correct patient. We have that and we have a full scan from her last employee physical sixty-three days ago. If there are any noticeable changes in either, we'll know what we're dealing with."

"Oh, my God!" Karen breathed, and I could tell that she was thinking the same uncharitable thing I was thinking.

If they could do it to Kate that easily, then they could do it to us.

I didn't know about Karen, but I, for one, was now even happier that I hadn't waited around for dear old Johnny Boy. On the other hand, I was beginning to see what kind of threat could scare or spook him into acting that stupid. *Here, John. Have Uncle Walter try and get you out of slowly turning into a warthog.*

Or, considering how much he knew and could spill, maybe I had it backwards. Maybe John and his Black Squad turned into warthogs unless they got their regular doses of something. Now *that* would keep you on the straight and narrow . . .

"Joe, if it is some kind of genetic or nano-type stuff, just what could it do? I mean, there are easier and faster and less detectable ways to kill somebody," I said worriedly.

"Oh, hell, this *has* to be generic, Chuck. Can't be anything else. If it's generic, it's strictly limited. That doesn't mean it can't do great harm, but turning you into a toadstool or like that—couldn't do it. Subtle adjustments in brain chemistry or triggering some latent stuff might occur, but it would be obvious and to no particular purpose. It takes seven years to replace all your cells naturally, and even speeded up it takes quite some time. Besides, if it wasn't specifically tailored to you and was overly elaborate it would probably simply kill you. Even if it were some attempt at an induced mutation for some sick reason, one dose is not a treatment. I doubt if I'd be really worried about this in the long run. The magic word is *pleiotropy*."

"I beg your pardon?"

"Well, you are an incredibly complex organism built by

your genetic code and modified by it and reactions to external factors. Okay. First, nobody can predict the changes those external factors will have, so that makes it much harder. Now add the fact that you don't have enough unique genes to make a 'you.' Genes do multiple duty. You change one, you don't just change the sequence you want to change, you change the same gene when it's used in *other* sequences, countless numbers of them. That's pleiotropy. It's why, even after so many years, the genetic treatments and therapies we have are still pretty direct and basic. Go for too much and you'll cause malfunctions that will be fatal, period."

I wasn't all that convinced by a big term, even if the logic did seem to work "I remember somebody saying that there was only two percent or so difference in the genetic code of a chimpanzee and us," I responded. "That doesn't seem like a lot of distance for a lot of change."

"But it's a vast distance, Chuck. Don't let them kid you. Consider that water is two parts hydrogen and one part oxygen. Not much. But add just one extra oxygen atom so you get H_2O_2 and you've got hydrogen peroxide, which you can use as a mild antiseptic or maybe to turn yourself into a blond. Not much difference? Don't drink the peroxide. No, this is an odd one."

"Because it's so large and not obvious?" Karen asked him.

"No. Because it's so large and she's still alive and testing normal. Here, let me go back and check. This is outside my field, really, but you're lucky, I had a man here today who owed *me* one who specializes in genetic analysis. If he hasn't found anything by now, then the odds are very good that it's all a big bluff." He gave us a wry grin and whispered, "Pleiotropy," and he was off.

But you'll want to see her back in two or three days just to make sure, I thought glumly.

Joe was certainly right that simple injections instantly changing you into some kind of monster were the stuff of bad mad scientist movies, but because of the medical therapies now routinely used, there were a lot of things you could speed up and there was a lot of generic stuff you could do that might not be fatal but would cause some pretty mean things, of that I was sure. And nobody would be able to bull Kate Marshall on that, either. That was her field, really. I suspected that Joe was going to walk back and find Kate and his big-shot genetics specialist talking shop at a level well over my old friend's head.

Karen looked at me and asked, "Do you know *everybody*?"

"Sure. All you have to do is stay in one place and grow old."

But both of us were really trying not to talk about the issue at hand. Just like before, it came down to *motive*. A demonstration for fear made sense, but somehow I didn't think these people really could be all that subtle, whoever they were. If it was some kind of attempt to induce a change, no matter what Joe said, maybe using a technology a bit more advanced than they had on the legitimate medical circuit, then what would be its purpose?

We were just about to send a message in to Kate that we were going to go our own way and check in on her, and that she should call me when ready, when, to our surprise, she showed up, fully dressed and looking a bit worse for wear but still not at all bad.

"So, how'd it go?" I asked her.

"Not good, as you undoubtedly know. They were trying to snow me but I knew as much or more than they did, particularly when all the tests came back. I don't know what whoever it was did to me, but I think I'm going to find out in a few days. What I want to know in the meantime is *why*."

I shrugged and gave a soft helpless sigh. There wasn't anything more I could say or do. "So, what now?"

"I want to go back to the hotel, take a shower, and change into something comfortable. Then, if you like, I'll buy *you* dinner."

"Okay with me," I told her. "Hell, it doesn't seem to make any difference at this point. If we're in a crowd, they got us. If we're alone on a dark road, they got us. If we're in the city room of a major paper or on TV, they got us. The hell with it, then. Let's stop running from them and see if we can find out who *they* are. Maybe we can stalk one of *them* for a change!"

"Just how are you gonna do that?" Karen asked me.

"We're going to start with the only address we've got. Kate, didn't you say you wanted to visit Genetique?"

They've been there almost since there was a Washington, D.C., I suppose, and they are still no more visible. Locals have called them the Beltway Bandits for years, even though virtually none are located on the ring road that circles the capital. Some are along the feeder highways leading in and out, but many are back off small roads and in country towns where nobody much knows they're there except for the amount they spend.

People who see their bright buildings and ultramodern fronts with those fancy high-tech names generally assume that they are branches of huge corporations that are head-quartered elsewhere; in fact, many of these companies exist to do the work of the government and have no other reality. Who thinks all those departments and bureaus do all that work themselves? Even agencies that do a ton of research, like the National Institutes of Health, tend to do just a fraction of the work assigned to them. The Beltway Bandits do the rest, for our tax dollars, and often have only one client.

Genetique was one of the older companies still existing and thriving; others its age tended to fold when the work was done, their facades and names changing and new Bandit companies, often with familiar boards of directors, taking their place. In almost all cases, you could find former senators, cabinet secretaries, even an ex-president or two at the top, their names and influence and contacts keeping the thing fueled. It was the cozy way things always have gone on in this city—those guys who retired or got defeated didn't just move back home to their districts and set up storefronts.

Genetique had 'em all, and more. Its board included ex-senators, a former head of the NIH, a former Speaker, two former ambassadors, and three Nobel Prize winners who'd won theirs toiling in university obscurity but were sure rich and famous now.

It was one of a half-dozen start-ups when they broke the whole human genome code and started reading out who and what everything and everybody was. Now you put your finger on a little disk, it took a few cells you didn't notice, and ten minutes later you could ask the computer virtually anything about yourself. It was great for security and even greater that you could now find and fix a zillion genetic flaws, even if they were always uncovering new ones when they fixed the old ones. Kind of like when they cured all the diseases of ancient times only to uncover even nastier stuff that killed you uglier. Still, it was pretty comfortable to live in a world where you could look like me and still not be worried about a host of potential genetic side effects, and, never mind ALS and all those other rotten killers, a process that also put ninety-five percent of cosmetic surgeons out of business had to be a good thing.

Of course, perfection still cost money, which was why I looked like I did and why, I suppose, the much lower paid Karen Reedy looked like she did. Or maybe, like me with my own self, she just liked herself that way.

At any rate, many of those great breakthroughs had come from Genetique, who'd developed almost twenty percent of the really miracle cures for the ugliest of genetic diseases—I think they were the first to patent a genetic-based treatment of Tay-Sachs, if I recall, and that was minor compared to the biggies that came later—and had exclusive patents on those gene therapies for many years. They'd found a gene-based treatment that could essentially dewrinkle skin and restore its moisture and luster, at least for a few years. Now *that* one had made all its stockholders billionaires.

Of course, it wasn't important that you found a way to tell skin to go back to where it was; it was important to develop it in such a way that you required repeated and increasingly expensive treatments. Genetique didn't do or sell such things themselves; they were a *research* outfit. No, they just took a ten percent commission on all that stuff.

The only reason most of us didn't look like all the ads, I guess, was how much money it cost, as usual. On the other hand, it was nice to think that a lot of us still looked like our ancestors, dimples and freckles and big noses and all, because we didn't give a damn about other people's standards of perfection. And, hey, they still dropped dead of the same stuff that would get me or anybody else sooner or later. But, to the end, they made great looking corpses.

There wasn't much of Maryland wilderness left between the beltways of Washington and Baltimore anymore, but Montgomery County had enough rich people to preserve their farms and horse-country stuff. Even so, going through the suburban sprawl and then past the big houses and the drives leading to the masked mansions, there was the occasional industrial surprise. Nothing that spewed smoke or fumes or attracted too many workers with lunch boxes, but going up a two-lane country road you suddenly came to a road going back into the woods that had one of those fancy pseudocarved signs saying "Genetique," with this really fancy holographic double helix trademark. Rumor was that it was created from the DNA of the founder's favorite foxhound, but nobody really knew for sure.

To get here we'd passed a spot where the road curved before splitting to go to Damascus and Germantown, and where there'd been a bizarre headline-grabbing "accident" that was already old news. I pointed it out to Kate, but aside from some bits of glass and a piece of twisted highway barrier, you couldn't tell anything unusual had ever happened there. They were generally quick and clean, that was for sure.

It was another fifteen minutes to the sign you might almost miss, and then I turned in and proceeded up the lane. The trees were an effective barrier from the local roads, but once you were out of them you approached a military-style gatehouse. There wasn't any barrier there, but there was a redgreen stoplight and a young man in a kind of mock marine uniform. If you didn't look closely you'd think he was military instead of, as it said on his sleeves, "Schickle Security Systems." I looked at the guy and wondered just how old he really was. Did one of the perks of the job include a full anti-aging treatment?

Some of the folks going to and fro in the parking lot sure made you think that it was. I never saw a younger, better looking group of near clones in my life. No, they weren't really clones, but they sure looked like the graduating class of some modeling school.

"Pleiotropy," I muttered, looking for a parking space.

Kate heard me from the backseat. "What was that?"

"My word of the day. The reason, I was informed, that you can't turn people into Martians all that easily. Then I look around this parking lot and they might as well be Martians as far as I'm concerned. Where's this pleiotropy here?"

She managed a slight laugh, although she was in an understandably depressed mood and had been all the way out here. "You're right—this is advertising for a gene-therapy company. Can't have the employees looking *normal*, now, can you? But it's a collection of simple things. Skin refreshment, wrinkle removal, adjustment of set points to burn fat and turn more tissue into muscle, hair regrowth, that sort of thing. It's a cocktail of individual and very limited cosmetic approaches. Only the weight control really does them much good, healthwise, but they *look* fabulous. I've had some of it done myself and I can tell you that it's great in the mirror but it doesn't help you much getting up in the morning and going to work."

Odd, I thought. As obvious as it was, it never occurred to me that some of those drop-dead looks were from a little application of her business. Probably didn't cost her much, either.

It was kind of sad, in a way. She had to have a great mind to get a doctorate in that kind of field, let alone be a leading researcher in one small branch of it, yet she still wanted to look like a fashion model. No, I take that back. None of us would mind that, but you'd think that, at her intellectual level, it shouldn't matter.

Well, I suppose it beat those damned pinks, with their cost of mental acuity. Still, you had to wonder. If it was promoted like hell to the people who could afford it, what kind of message did it send to the people that couldn't? And wouldn't a pink be a poor girl's route to drop-dead looks, and hang the price? There was a story in this, and a good one, maybe even a book and documentary. It wasn't the main story, but this began to have profitable possibilities.

I finally found a space by waiting for somebody else to back out. While making the rounds I'd gone past the reserved section twice and they had the names on little signs just in case you forgot. Dr. Sandra McCall's fancy sports car was there.

"It's absurd that all these people still drive to work out here," Kate Marshall commented. "In the Bay Area you take dedicated trams to the mass transit centers. If you have to drive at all, it's from your place in the suburbs to a transit station."

"That's true here, too," I told her. "The thing is, in *this* town having your own car is an essential status symbol, and using it all the more so, even if you spend half your life in jams. One person, one car on this lot, mostly. There's a regular articulated parking shuttle that'll take you to the transit mall, but not everybody will use it."

I was already a throwback, a newspaper man in a post-literate age, and I knew from my studies of the Good Old Days that people changed a lot less than they thought they did.

Entering the main Genetique building was almost like entering a Cabinet building or one of the Smithsonian's latest museums. The design was ultramodern, there were as many plants inside as out, or so it seemed, and the desks, aisles, and electronic directional signs made it feel like the main terminal at Dulles.

I glanced at Kate. "You better do the lead stuff in here.

They decide I'm here for an exposé and we'll get a Disney World ride on the wonders of genetics."

She nodded, and we went up to the central desk, where there was a railing between it and where you should stand. The moment Kate was within a half meter of the bar, a realistic hologram of a *very* nice looking young fellow came in with the usual sound effects and sparkling, as if he wasn't a computer construct but somebody beaming down from Space Station Titov. It was a neat if totally unnecessary effect, but it would awe the awe-able.

"Yes, how may I help you?" he/it asked, in a *very* pleasant voice.

Karen leaned over and whispered, "They make a lovely couple, don't they?"

"Why don't you move up and see what it decides is sympathetic for *you*?" I taunted her.

"Dr. Marshall to see Dr. McCall. I called ahead."

"I'm sorry, but Dr. McCall is not in today. Surely there was a mistake?"

"No, there is no mistake. And you should know not to tell fibs. Her car is in the lot."

"Her car is often left here when she is out of town. It is safer than leaving it at the airport or in her complex's lot."

Boy, that was one smooth computer!

"Well, can I speak to her supervisor, then? I'm from Stanford and Livermore Labs and this is a professional, not a social, call."

"I will see if anyone can help you, Doctor," the hologram responded, then did the shimmering act just so you'd know it was doing something.

The shimmering stopped. "Dr. Marshall, Dr. Stern will see you if you like. He is Dr. McCall's supervisor and the head of Genetique forensics. Will that do?"

She shrugged. "Yes, I suppose so."

"If you'll follow the guide it will take you back." A ribbon of yellow light exactly Kate Marshall's height appeared next to her, and you could read "Marshall" printed on it. It was a hologram, too, but clearly in this simple way it would be a very effective leader through the maze without bothering anyone else. Kind of neat, really. I hadn't seen anything like it outside of the Pentagon before.

Karen whispered, "Doctor, I think I need a doctor, Doctor, because Doctor me and Mrs. Doctor went to Doctor Smith."

I looked at her sternly. "Stop that! You are much too young to turn into me this quickly!"

Kate moved toward the guide and it began to slowly precede her, and we started to follow her, but a voice said, *"Stop!"* in the kind of Invocation By God authority that you did not ignore.

We all stopped, and turned and saw what I hoped was a hologram for either a very large African American guard or the chief defensive back of the Washington Redskins.

"Only Dr. Marshall has permission to go back. You two have not checked in or been identified, and do not have authorization."

"My name is Charles Vallone, and I am here with Dr. Marshall because I, too, have to discuss some related business with Dr. McCall or someone else in forensics. I received an invalid report on samples sent up here. What was sent back and what was analyzed is not what was sent to your labs. This young lady here is my associate, Karen Reedy, who is here primarily because I am."

"You two will have to wait. Dr. Marshall should proceed if she wishes to speak to anyone. We are on a tight schedule here and are already overworked. The two of you will be able to follow her later if someone will accept responsibility back there."

I looked at Kate. "Your move."

"I'll go back. You two follow as soon as you can."

"Okay," I replied, but I didn't like it.

When several minutes passed without any action, and I couldn't stir anything out of the apparition but a warning, Karen and I went over and sat down on one of the waiting area couches. I pulled out the sat phone.

"Who are you calling?" Karen asked me.

"Just a hunch." I spoke low into the phone, knowing I could be overheard by this level of security but deliberately egging them on a bit. "McCall, Sandra Tobin, Brunswick Court, Brunswick," I said.

There was a pause, and then a computer voice came back. "I'm sorry, but the only listing for McCall, Sandra Tobin in Brunswick has been disconnected."

I kind of figured that. "When was it disconnected?"

"October ninth this year."

That was not expected. That was a few weeks ago, long before this mess started.

"No forwarding?"

"Nothing left by the account holder. All accounts in that name closed."

"Cross-check. Any listing of that name in any location on the system?"

"There are one hundred and twenty-four Sandra McCalls listed, but none with middle name or any cross-reference matching, none initiated within the past year. The only number that is a match is an extension at Genetique Corporation in—"

"Never mind. Cancel." I hung up and put it away.

"So?"

"So Dr. McCall moved weeks ago, dropped her car here, and went someplace where she doesn't even show up on a cross-check." Karen knew that that meant she didn't even show up under that name on any hotel or motel register, rental car statement, cruise ship or airline tickets, you name it, that our database could tap into. She'd moved out, driven here, parked her car, then vanished.

And yet she'd signed my sample reports just a few days ago.

"Karen, go up and ask the magic genie what's with our approval," I told her. "I'm going to call the D.C. bureau and get somebody on tracing McCall's furniture, checking relatives, that kind of thing. Nobody vanishes without a trace these days."

She nodded and walked up to the bar around the central desk. There was no sign of the genie of Schickle Security Systems, either. In fact, when I saw what materialized in front of Karen I had to chuckle.

It was a young but exceedingly well-developed young woman about Karen's age, with an unmistakable Irish cast to her looks and speech.

Karen didn't miss a beat, although she didn't seem all that pleased when she headed back.

"Hey, Chuck, guess what? The thing says it never heard of us! Says it never heard of Doc Marshall, either. When I told it that we'd sent our associate back with a guide, I was told, with sweet politeness of course, that I had to be mistaken, because there was no record of it and it had a record of everything and everybody!"

I didn't like this. I walked up to the desk and suddenly the Fullback of God was there again. "Yes?"

"I believe it is time for us to meet a human being with either the corporation or your service," I told it. "We appear to have a problem with your system. An associate of mine that I brought here has vanished and you claim ignorance. Now, I'm with a newspaper and I'm working with the D.C. police on a case, so a lot of serious publicity can be brought down on this place if we have to deal with what is now appearing to be a kidnapping in broad daylight."

That did indeed bring some human attention. They came from all over the place, suddenly threw us to the ground, handcuffed us, and then literally dragged us out of the building and into the cold rain. It was useless to try and fight them, because they were, frankly, bigger, meaner, and stronger than either of us, and they basically dragged us all the way to where the car was parked. They then searched my pockets, got the key card, unlocked Karen's cuffs, and handed the card to her.

"You will both get in your car and drive off the lot *now*," one of the men said in a very menacing tone. "You will be completely off Genetique property and you will not return. If you do, at any time, for any reason, you may find yourself tripping and falling down a very big concrete stairway or have some equally tragic accident. Period. You've been gene-coded and noted. I am going to unlock the cuffs and you will get in the car and drive off, just like I said. And if you vary in any way we will stop you and we will break your legs. Understood?"

"Yeah, understood."

"Understand this, Mr. Vallone. We know exactly who you are and who you work for and more about you than you remember yourself. We have come up against the power of the press before. Good-bye, Mr. Vallone."

They threw me in the backseat, which still smelled a bit of Kate Marshall's perfume, and Karen immediately backed up, almost running over two of the men, who were not pleased. Then she went forward, almost knocking down two more, and headed for the exit.

"What should I do?" she asked me.

"Just what you're doing. Follow their instructions! This isn't the time to get them!"

"But what about Kate Marshall?"

"There's nothing we can do until we can call in our own army," I told her. "We're gonna have to talk to Adam, and maybe higher, and maybe some cops as well. And even with two of us as witnesses, I have a feeling this one's going to be mighty tough. Our best bet is to find out what this is all about and expose it."

All I could think about was how guilty I felt for bringing Kate into the lion's den, but who would have imagined this kind of bold and brazen stuff?

And these guys weren't scared. They knew just what they were doing.

SEVEN

When something like this gets pulled on you, it's usually the government, and, frankly, it's usually not *our* government, but you act fast and you know the drill. Fortunately, the bosses at the *Sun* and higher up the syndicate were still totally pissed off at Syzmanski's raid on the city room and ready to believe almost anything at this point. And that was something whoever it was at Genetique who'd ordered this brazen grab hadn't figured on. The scene of the city room invasion and Johnny Boy's "Fuck the Constitution" proclamation was still not very old news, and it could be easily refreshed as needed. Now we put some genetic horror stuff together with that and this, and we could create a very ugly public environment for almost anybody right up to the president, Congress, and even executives and stockholders at Genetique.

Oh, they were ready for us, complete with nicely edited security camera shots of us driving in, of just Karen and me getting out and walking up to the entrance, just us inside, and so on, and even one showing me taking a bar or something from my coat and hitting on the rail that was supposed to be what triggered their response, but it did them very little good. Our people showed an equally convincing tape of us walking up with Lady Godiva and the guards jumping all over her that made such "evidence" publicly suspect.

Even nastier was that I got the go-ahead to do the spook bit on them, and I loved every minute of it. Even Karen came up with some new touches. Not only did it feel good to hit back and make *them* uncomfortable, but damn it, it was fun.

Was Genetique creating killer monsters to silence whistle-blowers? Unnamed sources linked personnel in Schickle Security Systems to being on the sixth floor of the Wardman and below on the courtyard just before and shortly after the horrible mutilation and murder of Dr. Samuel Wasserman. Was a killer creature, created in Genetique's labs, responsible?

Two cops were killed by another creature after visiting Genetique. What did they find out? Rumors were that personnel from Schickle Security Systems and Genetique initially delayed reports of the murders, tried to take witnesses aside, and were only thwarted by the fact that the motorists had already called it in. Did Genetique unloose its murderous monster slaves once more? Pictures of orphaned kids and grieving spouses optional . . .

Heck, the *Post* got into it as bad as or worse than we were playing it, and when you went to the nets and the news channels, wow . . .

Genetique and/or the increasingly less mysterious Schickle Security Systems had made a lot of enemies of the press, it seemed, long before us.

Schickle was privately held, but did a lot of contract security for really high-tech intensive security systems around the area. It had started as a small African American–owned rent-a-cop agency years ago in D.C., but had been bought up by some consortium and then just started expanding like mad, suddenly showing a lot of money and a lot of technological access. The ownership was really concealed, but for security clearance purposes, which it needed to get the kind of jobs it excelled at, there had to be a series of stated responsible officers that could lead security people and make sure everything worked just so. And among the usual former politicians and former NSA and CIA directors there was one name that just jumped out at everybody because it was at the heart of Schickle getting so many high-security contracts.

Syzmanski. Casimir, in fact, patriarch of the clan and former National Security Advisor, CIA, DIA, you name it. Not in government for years and officially retired, but the oldest brother of former CIA director—he'd resigned the day after the Incident—George, who was the father of Guess Who?

Okay, Uncle. So now we link your rogue nephew and his fascist thugs to Genetique and its fascist private police, and there you are at the scene of one of these monster murders and later invading a newspaper demanding genetic samples and reports from—Genetique. Hmmm . . .

In addition to the fun, there was also always deep satisfaction at running one of these campaigns, no holds barred, at such a powerful and arrogant opponent. No matter how long they'd been around, no matter how many times they'd seen other people get ground up by a voracious press, they always thought that they were too powerful, too almighty to have anybody like dirty old Pizza Chuck nail their fancy-dressed hides. But with the gloves off, thanks to a pissed-off set of bosses, man, even *killing* me wouldn't do them any good. After getting Monaghan's boys to quickly secure Kate Marshall's hotel room and post her picture all over, and interviews with the doctors and such to establish that she'd been with us all the way, well, the resultant "Where Is Kathryn Marshall?" press blitz was The Story. And that meant politicians demanding Genetique execs show up and explain all this, and a national press staking out just about everybody and everything.

The competition was actually doing our work for us after this. We wanted bigger fish, so we weren't annoyed; in fact, I'd counted on it.

Karen, too, was having a ball with this. Not only did it feed her revenge urges and power fantasies but it fascinated her to see just how this all worked. A quarter of a millennium ago, Thomas Jefferson had said that a free press was the fourth branch of government whose primary function was to keep the other three honest. This was how you did it.

And the ship started to take on water very fast, too. Genetique stock started to tremble the first day we began the campaign, just because it was a negative; now you could almost watch it fall as the worldwide twenty-four-hour, seven-days-a-week stock market tracked and evaluated, and then shifted its money from that company to others. Naturally, they started trying to trot out their board people, the familiar political show-types, including, I'm embarrassed to say, one highly respected but now retired network news anchor. But pretty soon things were piling up to a degree that the rich and famous were far too nervous about their own reputations and other holdings to stand up for Genetique without being told by the company just what the hell was going on—and the truth.

Schickle Security Systems, being privately held, was faring even worse. Nervous political types had pulled the plug on its government security contracts and revoked its Class A security clearance for sensitive nonmilitary security. That was the kiss of death in this town.

At this point things were taking on such a life of their own that I got my car and actually moved back into my apartment, throwing out ninety percent of what was in the refrigerator and replacing it, and performing the last rites on a couple of pet plants.

And having been able to get home herself, Karen cleaned out her part of the shared apartment in Baltimore and moved in with me.

It wasn't a suggestion or a come-on or anything; it just sort of happened. It was also basically platonic, although deep down in male genetics there's never such a thing as a permanent platonic relationship, just frustrated ones.

Still, I'd been around a long time, and while I sensed that she'd go to bed with me if it meant keeping her active and in the field, I never wanted to use that kind of leverage in that way, particularly against somebody I liked.

Besides, she'd spent the last few years, maybe all her sexually active years so far, shacking up with guys and then dumping them. I was too old for that kind of thing; sex was available elsewhere and didn't require waiting for the boulder to drop.

At the end of a week the story was still alive, and whoever was behind all this at Genetique tried something else. I half expected it, had almost been waiting for it, but it wasn't going to be pleasant, I knew that.

The phone rang in the apartment one night, I picked it up after noting it had shown no person, place, or number of origin, and I heard a familiar voice say something entirely wrong.

"Chuck?" the voice of Kate Marshall came to me. "This is Kathy Marshall."

I knew at once that it was a fake call, of course. *"Kate. Never Kathy."* Either this was someone else using a synthesizer to impersonate her or she was sending me a signal. Either way, I knew that Genetique was still playing games rather than breaking.

I gestured for Karen to go to "Monitor and Record" on her office unit, and she did so immediately.

"Yes, Kathy. Good to hear your voice again. We were beginning to wonder about you," I responded rather coolly.

"I—I thought you'd be a bit happier to hear from me than that." She actually sounded disappointed.

"Well, you *have* been missing without a word for eight days now. You've been the subject of an international manhunt with no results, and even now, instead of calling the authorities to say where you are and where they can talk to you, you're calling me at home, from a secure phone that could be anywhere in the world or in orbit around it," I pointed out. "That's not the way people call in these circumstances. People call like you're calling now when they're making ransom calls."

That seemed to stop her, or whoever was on the line pretending to be her, for a few moments. Finally she said, "Look, I know it's all gotten nasty and confused and out of hand, but I can't do what you want. If you could see me you'd understand."

"That shot turning you into a warthog after all?" I was sorry for the tone, but I didn't for a second believe that this call was legit, no matter if she was there and taking dictation or nowhere near the phone.

"Well, it—it was the injection, yes. It had a fast-acting but completely unique carrier mechanism that doesn't show up for days in normal tests even though it acts very similar to a retrovirus carrier. When I met some people in whom it already had developed, I realized what was going to happen and that I didn't have the available medical technology to prevent it. Only Genetique did. I knew I couldn't leave. You really would understand if you were here. But I never thought they were going to rough you up or threaten you or anything. They had me actually work out a cover story and then return to you in the lobby so that I would stay and you would go, and it would have worked fine, but somebody in their damned security section overruled it and went for thuggery instead."

Thuggery. I liked that. It was an appropriate word.

"Well, I think they know better now, don't they?" I asked her, sounding a bit smug.

"Yes, I'm afraid that they do. But all you've done is ruin the company, at least for a while. You have no idea what is really going on here."

She was right about that. "So why don't you tell me?"

"I can't. Not now. Too many people's lives and families and maybe a lot more than that is at stake. But you've got to cool it down, Chuck. If you don't, these people will have no choice but to completely shut down and cover, and that will mean an awful lot of innocent people will suffer needlessly."

"A threat? They made you call to *threaten* me? After all *this*?"

"No, no! It's nothing to do with you being harmed. It's other people. And that's the truth!"

"Sorry, Kathy. I'm afraid this is going to take a lot more convincing than a phone call like this. I want to hear it from you face-to-face. No electronics, no holograms, no manipulations in the way, and no mysterious strangers standing guard. Then you have a *chance* at convincing me. But not like this.

You, and particularly those listening in here, must know it won't be that easy."

There was no response on the line and for a moment I thought she'd hung up, in spite of the call panel on the phone staying lit, but then she said, "Tell you what. We may be able to arrange something. I'll get back to you, hopefully later on tonight." And, before I could say another word, the connection went dead.

"Damn!" Karen swore. "Nothing! Nada! Whoever these people are, they're good at this!"

"What do you mean, 'Nothing'?" I asked her.

"I mean we couldn't get any sort of trace, and I was unable to do a recording monitor of the call even though I could listen in fine on the direct extension. They fed in some kind of tone or computer subcarrier and her end just wouldn't record! I have all your side of the conversation but hers is a total blank! We got nothing!"

I shook my head. "No, I don't think it's as bad as all that. That was very close to a white flag, that call."

"Huh?"

"I don't know if it was Kate or not, but she wasn't saying what she would have said had she not been surrounded by a lot of company. 'Kathy' indeed. The fact that they are seriously considering a meet—that's one hell of a concession."

"Yeah? They're not gonna meet anyplace where you can get a good look and be unobserved. You know that."

"Sure, but if I can see her I'll know at least what that shot was, and I may even find out more. She kept saying that if I could see her I'd understand. I've called their bluff on it."

"Maybe. And maybe you'll meet their pet monster again one last time, before they destroy it and move on."

"That was always a possibility," I admitted, "but consider that it's just as much a possibility that this monster's outside right now. I'm sure we've been watched constantly ever since we resurfaced at the Triple A-S convention." I went around and started turning off lights until we were down to just a nightlight and the lights on the equipment we had set up in my living room. I then walked over to the French doors to my minuscule patio and slowly opened the drapes.

Karen gave a slight shriek and I just froze.

Somebody, or some*thing*, was standing on the patio not two meters from the doors, looking straight back at us.

It was a curious figure, yet one I'd seen before from a much greater length. Short, maybe a hundred and sixty-five centimeters, no more, and stocky, apparently wearing a dark trench coat and an odd pullover hat. It was the face that got you, even in the dark, like a sense of folds upon folds, a sock puppet's face, not a real one.

And then it turned and launched itself into the air, and it was instantly clear that it had no trench coat, that what looked almost normal in the darkness was, in fact, giant furry wing-like membranes, almost like a giant bat's, and that this impossibly large "bat" could indeed fly, rattling the French doors as it took off into the darkness.

Karen kept staring at the now empty patio, but, after a moment, she swallowed hard and came over close to me.

"That—that was *it*, wasn't it? That was your monster."

I put my arm around her and held her, and felt her trembling slightly. "Yes, I think it was."

"I—I never really believed in it," she admitted to me. "I thought this was some kind of high-tech hoax. But it's not. We've seen it. And it's seen us."

"Probably repeatedly, although maybe not much in the daytime. I think it sleeps in the daytime atop some old projects over in Anacostia. Probably ones slated to be torn down this year or next. Not many people living in and around them at the moment."

She seemed to almost be trying to merge with me, and I looked down at her and suddenly realized just how small, and how very young, she was.

"What does it want? Why didn't it just kill us?" she asked me.

"I have no idea. I'm not even a hundred percent sure that it's working with or at the direction of the Genetique or

Schickle people. I do think at least one of those samples was from that thing, but I think the powers that be are looking for it. Don't believe the lines we've been feeding people. There are more than two sides here."

"You don't mean to tell me that you think that—that—*whatever* is a thinking being? It was a *creature*. Horrible . . ."

"Maybe, maybe not. I think I've spoken with it on the phone, in fact."

"But—where did it come from? How is such a creature even possible?"

I had been thinking about that, too. "I think somebody made it. Maybe years ago. Pleiotropy be damned. I doubt if they were trying to make what came out, and that may be why it's so monstrous, but it's close, damned close. Closer than we're supposed to be able to come to designer creatures now, and I'd say our monster is a grown-up, so we're talking fifteen, maybe twenty years ago."

"You think that thing came out of a lab? And that long ago? And nobody's found out about it or leaked it until now?"

"I didn't say it came out of a lab. Most likely, it came out of the same place you and I did. A woman's womb. If my theories are right, and I've been heading this way since the beginning, I think that creature is one of the early attempts at eventually building a Martian."

"A *what*?"

"Oh, no, not what it became. It was simply a learning exercise. Probably wasn't supposed to grow up, but for some reason they didn't kill it. It's entirely possible that it isn't even unique."

"You mean there are *more* of them like that out there?"

"Probably not like that," I reassured her. "Different. Different kinds of monsters." I closed the drapes. "Look, you know you're not going to sleep much tonight after this . . ."

"The master of understatement!"

"Okay, you can sketch; I can't do a convincing Mister Smiley Face. Use the sketchboard and whatever you need and see if you can give me a digital picture of what we saw that we can both agree on. I'll kibbitz after you're well along. Then we'll try and get the computer to fine-tune it. Let's see if we can re-create the creature's appearance. After that, we can start trying to figure out why it wanted us to see it."

It took a lot of the night to get there, and I hadn't realized how totally spooked Karen was until I got up to get some coffee in the kitchen and she immediately followed me in. I began to understand that, for a while at least, after dark we were going to be somewhat inseparable.

The trouble with computer graphics software is that, even after all this time, you still had to have at least some rudimentary artistic talent to get anywhere with it. The day when you could simply see an image and it would be immediately drawn for you in three dimensions was still, let's say, quite a ways down the road.

Even so, starting with Karen's effective sketch and my suggestions, computer voice-command tweaks, and the two of us arguing over this feature and that, we finally wound up with what both of us considered a fair and nearly photographic representation of what we'd seen on the patio. But it didn't calm her paranoia.

"You're sure that thing grew up that way?" Karen asked me as we worked on it.

"Yeah, I think so. Flying isn't something you'd pick up easily, and it was removed enough from humans to be at least at the chimp's two percent difference in DNA, even if Mommy was 'normal.' Why? You think Genetique can just shoot you in the ass and you turn into one of those?"

"Something like that. I'll believe anything after this."

"No, I think the experts were all correct on this one. It would take years to change you drastically, but it would be much easier to develop new strains in the lab using human eggs and then manipulating. Most, maybe almost all, would die, but occasionally one would take. Maybe one in a million. Who knows? That's our friend. Kind of artificial evolution. You do this in-vitro time after time and in all sorts of numbers and any ones that chance decides can live you implant."

"You mean they were just rolling the dice and *that* turned up?"

"Pretty much. Oh, I think they were probably going for the characteristics of muscle-powered flight, but that was it. It was the kind of complex ability involving an entire redesign of the human body that they would have to know if they were to eventually build a new race of beings that could survive, and thrive, on the surface of another world. If they could do even that creature back then, then an awful lot of technological breakthroughs were being hidden from the public, from much of the scientific community, probably even from most of the government. They were dreamers who were being shut down by fear and panic, or so it seemed to them. I'm sure that enough of them took the breakthroughs they normally would have published, but now felt they had to hide from the Luddites and witch-burners of state and church, and tried to find other patrons, other sponsors. It looks like they found them."

"This is crazy! Where could you build such a complex and get what you needed without being discovered in this day and age?"

I had thought about that myself.

"I don't know. But I'll bet at least one installation, maybe the main one, is not far from the Republic of the Marshall Islands in the South Pacific. Whether or not there are others I don't know, but I'd love to follow *that* trail, particularly on an expense account."

"Yeah, well, count me in, too. But wouldn't this have to be secret from the start? I mean, where's the animal studies, all that stuff they do before even the mad scientists try it on people?"

"It's there, somewhere," I replied confidently. "It's just not listed as such, or it's listed as discontinued, a dead end, or shut down. This is where a Kate Marshall would be most helpful. I bet we could find those answers, if only we knew which questions to ask."

By the wee hours we'd put our consensus flying monster

in net storage and it was getting pretty late to hear back from Kate or Kathy or whoever that was. If they really wanted a meet for some reason, they were having trouble agreeing to it or figuring out how to pull it off. For myself, I doubted that they would even try it, since I didn't think that that was Kate.

There wasn't much to do but check the security system, take one last peek out the windows and see nothing unusual, and then try and get some sleep.

For the first time, Karen didn't want to sleep on her mattress on the living-room floor. She was still shaken up, and I figured, what the hell, she didn't take up much space and I had an overlarge bed anyway.

She snuggled close to me, which is, let's face it, something of a turn-on for an old male fart like me, and, after a while realizing that neither of us had really gone to sleep, she whispered, "You want to screw? I really could use it right now."

I shifted a bit. "I wouldn't mind, but I won't. Not here, not now, not with you."

"Huh? Why not?"

"Because I like you and I work with you," I told her.

"Yeah, but . . ."

"If we did it, then before long we'd be a couple, for a while, and then it'd get to be a while and I'd be the next in line after Dwight. The next in a line of several that I know about, anyway. And then you'd get antsy and eventually move out and because of the past we wouldn't be working together anymore, and I've had enough loss and rejection in my life, I don't need any more."

She seemed quite surprised at this. "You mean that?"

"I do. And now I'm going to try and get some sleep and you should, too. I have a feeling we're in for a long day tomorrow."

For a while she was quiet, and I hoped that maybe that had taken care of it, at least for now. I really was getting close to drifting off by this point.

"Chuck?"

"Hmph?"

"Is that really how I am? I mean, is that the way I come off?"

"I'm a reporter. I report what I see and what I can deduce from said observations. I don't investigate everybody I meet, though. Only the ones who deserve it. You've worked for the *Sun* for almost four years, and you were an intern I think before that, and I can tell you that you have a pattern. I choose not to be a part of that pattern. I don't judge you for it, I don't care if it's right or wrong for you, I don't say that it's good or bad or indifferent. I only say it's not what I wish to be a part of. Period. Now go to sleep."

"It's not just 'cause I have small tits?"

"My dear, you have *no* tits. *I* have bigger tits than you have. But you do not build a relationship on stuff like that. If I am having casual sex and it's costing me anything from real money to expensive dinners and wines, then I want it all. Big tits, oversized ruby lips, big sad eyes, great ass, no waist, you name it. But none of that means shit in the end. It goes. Even with cosmetic therapy it goes. And even if it doesn't, if there's nothing underneath the glitz, it doesn't matter in the long run. Some of the best fucks I ever had were with people who were only physical, nothing at all inside 'em. No brains, no soul. People just *think* looks are everything. If they were, the human race would be a lot smaller."

She sighed. "That's sweet and profound all at once. You ever married?"

"Twice. And one other long-term relationship in my life. They all walked, sooner or later. They found guys who were better looking, more publicly connected, able to give them stuff that they didn't get being married to an anachronism. My curse has always been good contacts. One of 'em later married a senator, another married the executive editor of the *Post*. The third—God, I don't know where Laverne is now. Probably with a cult in the mountains somewhere waiting for Jesus to call her up to meet Him in the air. Funny, too. I never thought of any of them the way they turned out. I always thought they'd want to *be* a senator or *edit* the *Post*, not just get the social perks and money and influence by marrying it. You're dredging up some things I really don't want to think about most of the time. If you don't stop that and get some sleep, I'm going to kick you out of bed."

"I—I'm sorry. I really didn't want to hurt your feelings. I don't want to be the editor of the *Sun*, or even marry the editor—"

"Good thing, too. I gather she doesn't swing that way."

"Jeez! I'm trying to be contrite and you're making wisecracks!"

"I'm trying to go to sleep. How about we make an agreement? You go to sleep, or try to, and I'll go to sleep, for sure, and when we're making our rounds tomorrow you can tell me your life story and I'll fill in the rest of mine. But not now."

She sighed and did ease off a bit. "So what *are* we doing this morning?"

"If we ever sleep enough to wake up in time to do anything? Well, I want to go into high gear turning over new rocks. There has to be a trail on this, lasting fifteen or twenty years minimum. There have to be studies, and experts, and big labs and bigger universities and/or corporations involved. Nobody could cover up something this big so thoroughly."

"Yeah? What about all those assassinations?"

"Don't be absurd! All assassinated presidents were killed by conspiracy buffs who deliberately introduced just enough inconsistencies that they could make millions of dollars and retire young, writing books and movies and documentaries on how all those deaths were conspiracies."

Getting hit by a pillow effectively ended the sexual discussions.

Even though it was close to eleven o'clock before we got up, I immediately started on the phone and nets, going after longtime sources deep within the various agencies of government, while Karen went after the more public databases, cross-checking to find anything that might match what we were looking for.

As I expected, once you asked the right questions, the answers really were there, really did fall into place, although, admittedly, it was like starting a thousand-piece jigsaw puzzle and having only two or three hundred pieces, many not touching one another, out on the coffee table.

The government set up the Human Genome Project in suburban Maryland in the late twentieth century as a kind of mini–Manhattan Project where all the heavy industry wasn't required. Subject to budget cuts and all sorts of political wrangling, it plodded along, certain that its unglamorous mission of mapping every gene in the human body was going along just fine.

What they didn't figure on was suddenly being in a race with a lot of private companies, many of whom hired off the best and brightest from the government and also brought in whole new areas of computing. What set it off was first the decision by the Supreme Court, and later international courts, that you really could patent a gene. Gene therapy to produce disease-free and drought-resistant fruits and veggies started paying off almost immediately, and things began exploding. It wasn't long before they had mapped the first complete living organism. It was just a worm, but it was a start, and it was incredibly impressive coming in just a few years.

With so much money to be made from gene patents and new gene therapies, the number of companies became legion, the new millionaires in that area merged with the new billionaires in computers, and the government even helped by paying for a bunch of research in the area of retrovirus and nanotechnology with the hopes of curing some complex diseases like AIDS, Ebola, and other, later nasties. If you could develop a way to change their genetic structure to something harmless to humans, you were on your way to billions more bucks.

Of course, the religious coalitions and frightened politicians and public, egged on by tabloid-style journalism, got scared of where this might be headed and passed a ton of laws that vastly restricted research and development. There were also laws requiring anything consumable to be labeled as a genetic manipulation, and horror stories delivered to all the homes in the West about what could happen if you fed your kid doctored tomatoes. There were boycotts, protests, and even outright rioting in some areas, which caused a lot of folks to back off. That was about the time when Project Chameleon was killed.

It soon became clear that, around that period, a lot of work had been going on that went way beyond what made it even in the tabloid stuff, and some of the tabloid stuff might, in retrospect, have been true. Tales of water-breathing cats with gills who could really catch their own fish, and flying rabbits and the like. All allegedly destroyed, of course, after being recorded and tested.

It was during that period, too, that some animal rights folks went totally round the bend into terrorism. Killing a bunny was the same as killing a baby to them; some of them were so nuts they didn't even want inoculations against diseases. Labs started getting blown up, top researchers were stalked and shot. Much animal research had gone way underground, and when you looked at it that way you next started to find out what university departments were suddenly scaled back, what top geneticists, biotechnicians, and the like slowly went missing. You began to notice a pattern throughout the nations where this sort of research had gone on—it suddenly, well, vanished. Not only that, some formerly top biotech universities had interesting programs where grad students seemed to vanish completely from their campuses, never appear on any social lists such as season ticket holders for football or basketball, and then suddenly materialize again to claim their Masters and Ph.D.s. For what? Two copies of each dissertation were allegedly deposited, and then these dissertations became public and could be accessed by anybody with a computer.

Only these didn't seem to be there.

Oh, a few of them were there, but when you matched the specialties and even the dissertation titles on the graduation records with what was available, you discovered that there wasn't much of a "there" there.

Black project money from the government, well disguised but substantial grants from leading biotech and computer corporations, and, just as telling, high sales of massive amounts of very specialized equipment from the few firms that could make it, yielding record profits but no sign of where the stuff went—it was broken up so much you could never put Humpty Dumpty together. Pieces of experimental computers, kinds I'd never seen or heard of before, and with names that matched nothing ever recorded in public or even reasonably classified databases, went to totally different companies at totally different ends of the earth.

It was like discovering that Company A in Seattle ordered fifty thousand new high-speed needleless syringes but never ordered anything to put in them, even a decent amount of distilled water. But Company B in Miami ordered exactly fifty thousand doses of the base fluid but never any syringes or other materials, Company C in Austin ordered prototype cell-based programmable nanomachines that might fit into the rest, and so on. The twain never met, but you could assemble tens of billions in orders and deliveries that made no sense until you got your computer to put them all together and ignore who ordered them and where they allegedly went.

Suddenly we came up with enough computer geniuses, genetics geniuses, laboratory technicians of the highest order, and sufficient hardware of all sorts, to build and test and maintain *five* Project Chameleons. Starting slowly, but reaching full speed about . . . eighteen years ago.

When it came to nailing down various links, some other interesting patterns appeared. None of this was something you could yet take to a top editor, let alone to court or the bank, but it was a great start.

We began, of course, by cross-checking the data we could pull out of the available records with the name Syzmanski, and we came up a winner right from the start.

"Even more interesting," Karen noted, pointing to her screen, "look at the correlation. The ones who aren't in government at any particular time are on the boards of several of these companies. When big orders start coming in, certain congressmen and senators are backed with big money and leadership posts, and a Syzmanski becomes a deputy defense secretary in some area where it's not clear what their duties are, or one of their in-laws shows up in Treasury, or Standards, and so on, and when there's some investigations started in Justice, one of the family tree, not necessarily a Syzmanski in name, shows up in Justice. There's even big contributions to right-wing religious groups who start getting restless or curious. Wild. And that's only the Syzmanski family and the twenty other family names related to them. I bet when we start running down some of the other moneyed families on these boards and in government we'll find similar patterns."

"Good guess, probably. We're taking a snapshot here of what we often call the First Families Corporation. It's informal, but it's been around for at least a hundred years, maybe more. Mostly immigrant types who made it super big but still couldn't get in the Mayflower Club."

"Huh. Not many Jews, though. Or Irish, either. Or Italians, or . . ."

"That was the early wave of immigrants. They're so establishment now they spend half their time keeping the newbies out. This is the first wave of new billionaire families from the East—Poles, Czechs, Slovaks, Serbians, Ukrainians, Russians, Kazakhs, Persians, and so on. It's the story of America, kid."

"God! You really are a deep-down cynic!"

"You didn't grow up covering them. Still and all, it's beginning to fit. I wonder if they have visions of *Brave New World*. Praise Syzmanski! Hallelujah! Amen! Alphas, Betas, all the rest. Even better than Huxley's nightmare. You would be not only born and bred to a social level, but to a specific task level. Water breathers, great strength, flyers, night vision, God knows what else. All designed to deploy and operate the latest stuff for the super-Alphas of the world, themselves and their children. Develop Mars, mine the asteroids and the moons of Jupiter, maybe more. Maybe I'm not imaginative enough. God! It's beginning to make me sick!"

"Alphas and Betas? You mean they're run by Greeks?"

"Nope. Scary predictive novel written a century or so ago by a British writer who foresaw cloning and genetic engineering and all the rest and found them horrors. Name was Huxley."

"No Huxleys here that I can see, but there's at least one French guy."

"Huh? That's odd. Who?"

"Just a last name. Keeps popping up in various order statements, things like that. Over the whole period, in fact."

"Yeah? What's the name."

"Moreau. Signs for a lot of shit, even things that aren't supposed to be together."

I sat back in my chair and sighed. "My God! Maybe I was going after the wrong damned book!"

"And here's something else you might find even more interesting," she said, ignoring my comment. "There's a place down near where the Potomac widens out to meet the bay. It's a former embassy retreat, real palatial, used to be run by the Kazakhs until the oil boom collapsed. They sold it ten years ago to a new area company that apparently needed a retreat for its employees. You're gonna love it!"

"Yeah?"

"Company called Genetique. Ever heard of it?"

EIGHT

The place was called Chathams Court and it apparently had been Chathams Court when everybody from George Washington to the Union Army had come through there. In fact, it was only a few miles south of where Washington had been born. What the original building had been like it was hard to say, but it couldn't have approached the palace that had been built there back in the boom years of the late nineties by some very rich folks who turned traditional little isolated towns like Kinsale into "retreats."

It being where it was, of course, it looked like a high-tech and well-heeled complement to Williamsburg, but it was some kind of place. We looked it up in the old real estate listings. Thirty-six rooms, the smallest of which was bigger than any apartment I'd ever lived in, and including a grand living room with twin spiral staircases and a heated indoor pool in the center, not to mention riding stables, what was called a polo field (although I never remembered the Kazakhs playing polo), a nine-hole golf course designed by the best (come to think of it, I didn't remember golf being a big feature of Kazakhstani culture, either, but nobody said they weren't great sellers of goods). Boathouse, maintained minibeach . . . and a *yacht slip*? I looked at the beautiful three-dimensional color photo of the place and rotated it toward the Potomac. Sure enough, on one side of the waterfront property there was something that looked a lot like where they dock the cruise ships in San Juan, complete with a fully enclosed wharf leading down to a parking lot and delivery area. You probably couldn't repair a big ship there, but you sure could land it and resupply it, which left me with some questions. Ships that size can't move without being registered and checked out by the Coast Guard and marine police, and, if under foreign flag, inspected by Customs and Immigration. That would be done at sea on the way in, but there would be records.

Genetique did, in fact, have a yacht, U.S. registry, but it wasn't what I was looking for. In fact, it was much too small even if it was one I'd give my pension to own—only my pension wouldn't have covered the fuel bill. You entertained important people on one like that, you took them up and down the river and bay, you used it to isolate folks doing deals or for superprivate conferences, and you even might use it for one heck of a fishing expedition, but while you might risk going to the Caribbean on it, you wouldn't really want to cross the Atlantic or Pacific on it. Besides, it wouldn't take up half that moorage. No, we were looking for something bigger.

And we found it, in the navigation reports for the past year. It was called what translated out to be *The Songs of Sunset*, and so it was recorded along with its unpronounceable name in the Arabic alphabet. It was, however, registered in Panama, and its owners were listed as Chin Pharmaceuticals Pty. Ltd., Singapore.

It stopped regularly at this nice little retreat on the Potomac, maybe twice every year or so. On a hunch, Karen checked the Panama Canal toll records and found that it passed through coinciding with reasonable sailing times from here, and that it often put in at one or another small Pacific island after that.

"Let me guess. It winds up at Majuro, capital of the Republic of the Marshall Islands."

"Pretty good guess," she said. "But it also stops a number of other isolated places. Want to bet that it's almost a map of the main installations for this group, whatever it's doing?"

"No bet. When's it due back at this retreat?"

She looked. "Holy smoke! It's there now! It's been there

for like the last two weeks. It's due to sail . . . high tide Saturday. That's twenty-one seventeen. Destination is given as a private island under nominal Dutch sovereignty. Small private resort, not even an airstrip, it says. In fact, it says 'uninhabited since eruption.' Sounds yummy."

I sighed and looked over at her. "Get dressed. We're going for a helicopter ride."

Every news organization doing local stuff had helicopters; these were sleek, incredibly fast, incredibly quiet, and very fuel efficient. We were in the one for our local media outlets that the ad folks called the *Sunburst*, for which somebody should strangle them. Alex Montoya was our pilot, an old vet who could push this thing almost to the breaking point in speed if he had to. Now he was sitting still on a cold, crisp, but very clear, sunny afternoon at thirty-five hundred meters, and we were looking at Chathams Court on our virtual monitors like we were at fifty feet and right over it.

I never liked the virtual monitor stuff; I made Karen give up her personal V.R.D.—visual retinal display—while at the apartment because I couldn't peer at it over her shoulder, but this was the best way to handle it for these sky-vision things. Kind of like the old Ben Franklin bifocals, only if you focused straight ahead you saw what the camera was seeing almost like you could reach out and touch it. Glance all the way at the bottom and you saw "real" view, which barely had the place show up.

It was handy, though, because you didn't have to crane your neck and you weren't dependent on monitors in potentially windy conditions. You didn't even need a window, so Karen could be relaxed in a backseat wearing glasses and seeing exactly what I was seeing and even guiding the cameras. Me, I wouldn't guide 'em on a bet; the whole thing made me dizzy. I was still unnerved at sitting next to a pilot who didn't have any controls but appeared to fly the damned thing with head movements and a few flicks of his hands.

"Not much action outside," I commented.

"Jeez, Chuck! It's like *freezing* down there!" Karen reminded me. "Not much for outdoor sports or swimming. Bunch of cars in the lot there, though, and around that neat-looking inner courtyard road. Lots of trucks down by the water, too."

"Let's see the boats," I told her.

"Ships. Boats are held up by displaced air. These suckers need *ballast*."

"Boats, ships, let's see 'em!"

"Aye, aye, Cap'n!" The view shifted, a bit too abruptly for me, and there was clearly activity down there, with some guy taking stuff off a parked truck and then running it into the wharf building on a forklift.

Both boats, or ships, or whatever, were in. The little old forty-meter owned by the corporation was dwarfed by the super-streamlined white and gold vessel on the other side. It was a hundred meters easy, maybe more, and it might make the deep channel in the bay up to Baltimore but it probably was almost at its limit here on the D.C. channel, even though the Potomac was around fifty kilometers wide right where it dumped into Chesapeake Bay.

It was sure a United Nations of a ship, though. Singapore Chinese owned, registered in Panama, with all its names in Arabic. Somebody was really trying to be a bit confusing, I suspected.

"I've sailed on ships smaller than that for a week's tour of the Mediterranean," I commented. "How many people do you think she'll carry?"

"Depends on what else she's designed to carry," Karen replied. "I mean, we know how she was initially built from the plans, but not how and who and what modifications were made. She's certainly one of the fastest big ships currently running. State of the art, all computer run, no human beings required except by maritime law. One guy sits up on that bridge and tells it what to do and that's it. Fusion powered, top speed even with that weight easily in the forty knot range, although it probably cruises at thirty to thirty-five. Stabilizers, real smooth ride. You got that much money to have one of those, though, you have people waiting on you and doing all the basics. Machines are for the masses. That's why it lists a crew of fifty-six. Now, figure, big bedrooms, luxury dining, spas, all that stuff, as well as lots of cargo space, and you can see the heliport on the stern there, and I bet the ratio's about one to one, passengers to crew. Even so, you got to figure they could carry however many they wanted."

And, unlike on the way in, there wasn't much in terms of searching and the like on the way *out* of the country. They *would* need a pilot, though, at least for part of the way, with that kind of size and speed potential, but he'd be up on the bridge and all he'd do is make sure that his navigational software was performing properly and that he then retrieved it at the end.

Even so, if we called in an anonymous smuggling report or somesuch and got the thing searched, the odds were they could hide whatever aboard the smaller yacht without anybody finding it. And, just in case, that smaller yacht was a U.S. flag vessel, so it could tag along with *no* particular inspection and transfer to the big one at sea any persons or things they wanted. With other smaller vessels also able to do that, and a chopper landing on the stern, they could take anybody or anything in or out and it would be nearly impossible to nail them. Add to that their usual corporate and political friends, even if they were currently not answering your calls, and you had a license for an open border.

"So what are they smuggling, if anything, Chuck?" Karen asked me after a while.

And just like that it hit me. "People! And, of course, shipments of needed things that would be assembled with other shipments dropped by other boats at the destination. But, in this case, it's people."

"Huh? Illegal immigration?"

"No, no! That's what at least part of this was about. They were here for Triple A-S. It was probably Wasserman's job this trip, since they'd use different people, or even teams, as needed. They were on a *recruitment* trip! They're recruiting new blood and replacements. A small number who meet key educational and experience requirements. Where can you find them? All over, of course, but then you have to run a headhunter-type operation, leave all sorts of tracks, and you have to dance around the ethical issues and all that secrecy. So, instead, you do a preliminary search on the computer, matching people to your vacancies, then you match that list up with attendees at functions like Triple A-S. You may even use influence to give incentives so that the right people will show up in person. How many people did we have who went to the convention and then didn't return when they were supposed to?"

"Huh? Thirty-one, mostly minor- or middle-level people, but it was a startling number."

"Uh-huh. And, like Kate, they were brought here with other reasons reinforcing a personal trip. They didn't even know they were auditioning. And none of those thirty-one were married, currently living in a long-term relationship with others, had children, all those things that would bring a hue and cry too soon. Even so, they're pushing it, what with Genetique in hot water and us on the trail. Wonder who or what's so vital they'll risk a few more days this week rather than take them out of all this political and press heat as soon as possible?"

Karen thought about my theory. "But, Chuck—you don't mean like they offered Kate Marshall a job and she took it? Not after all that?"

"Nope. Something went wrong. Wasserman was killed, some third party or wild card was introduced. That didn't stop them, though. The arrogance of the rich and powerful. They went right ahead. And, yeah, they probably *did* offer her a position in her field, only under conditions she couldn't turn down. Trouble is, she's been so well plastered over creation as missing that they couldn't do the airport switch or other things. In fact, I doubt if they could do it with most of them, since sooner or later they'd have to get on a major international flight and those are now being very carefully monitored."

"They could hold 'em until things blew over."

"I think not. To get a highly paid and satisfied scientist to suddenly quit, drop everything, even friends and associates, not to mention ongoing pet projects, and vanish, takes some real incentives."

"You don't mean Kate Marshall would go through this with these bastards for money . . ."

"Not money. A shot in the ass. A shot that actually has to *do* something to you that would be the ultimate incentive. It doesn't work fast enough, of course, for us to see what it is, but if Kate went back there and then was told what it was and perhaps was introduced to someone already 'recruited,' the incentive might be irresistible, particularly since you're talking to someone who can understand your jargon and procedure when you show them just what you did to them."

"Holy Mary Mother of God!" As an old Italian lapsed Catholic I didn't have to see, I could actually *feel*, a lapsed Irish Catholic crossing herself. Finally she asked, "So what does it do?"

"I'm good, but I'm not that good," I told her.

"Besides, he's only guessing to impress you. He doesn't really know any of this," Montoya commented.

"I'm already stuck with one smart-ass," I snapped at him. "I don't need another."

He shrugged but couldn't wipe the smirk off his face.

What the hell, he was only a pilot. He didn't have to believe any of us.

"He's right, you know," Karen added not at all helpfully. "Even if you're one hundred percent correct, and she and a bunch of others are right down there waiting for horns to grow or something and going out on the evening tide on Saturday, we've got nothing but speculation. You're good, and the bosses wanted Genetique and particularly the Syzmanskis taken down a peg for their own sake, but *this* will never float, any more than they'd print our monster."

I knew that she was right. On Saturday our evidence and witnesses would be off to the Bahamas and later, probably not staying aboard, would be flown off that airstrip to private connections on one of the other islands around, to one of their project bases, or maybe all the way to ground zero in the Marshalls. And by next week they'd have Genetique cleaned up; its accounts were already in chapter 11 and trading had stopped on Wall Street, and as a shell they'd be bought up by somebody else, possibly even another one of the corporations involved in this, and for a while they'd be purer than the driven snow. In the meantime, like some organized crime figures of old, a long-term campaign to isolate the Syzmanski criminal involvement to just two or three people would be under way, the rest would be whitewashed, and within a few years it would be business as usual once again.

Sweet indeed.

"There are only two things we can do at this point, faithful companion," I said to her, only half-mockingly. "We can drop it and find us another story, or we can try and get somebody down there to get some hard evidence before they leave. Either that or capture our bat-man. The first is easy, the second is probably dangerous as all hell, and the third is definitely fatal. And we've only got three days to decide."

"We can't stop now," she said without hesitation. "I'll see that damned face in every window and every dark place forever and I want payback. Besides, I don't think either one of us could live our whole lives without knowing what the hell this is all about."

I had to laugh at that. There were a whole lot of things I'd go to my grave not knowing the answers to, including but not limited to the ultimate question of what, if anything, happens next, and all but that last one cost me no sleep at all. I could live without solving this one, too.

But, damn it, I couldn't live with not *trying* to find out when the possibility was there.

"Alex, what are you doing tomorrow night?"

"Depends on the weather, the number of homicides, how

many cars are in the accident that might happen, that kind of thing."

"Well, I think I can get your services for a while through the On Highs."

"Why? If you want me to drop you silently down on that pad on the back of that ship down there, then you're crazier than I think you are."

"No, I know that's impossible. Easy to spot. But night, day, general cloud cover—those aren't particularly serious factors in getting good pictures from positions like this, right?"

"You know they're not."

"Then I'm going to need some monitor. I'll be wired, live feeding at all times, and I'll swallow and wade in tracker shit. The best insurance I got is something like that. I've spent a night or two in jail before for trespassing, but I don't want to vanish and I don't want to lose whatever I find."

"Fair enough."

"Hey! What's this 'I' bit?" Karen wanted to know. "This is a 'we' operation, remember?"

"Not this time. One is better than two. Besides, I wouldn't want to be worrying about you. One of us needs to stick with this, and right now you're the only one who's been there from the beginning."

"No."

"It doesn't matter what you say, that's it. You're going to be my lifeline up here with Alex."

"It's not gonna happen, Chuck. Period. You better make up your mind, but no matter what, either I go in or we do. I don't care where *you* sit it out. I'm younger than you, I'm in much better physical shape, and much more likely to be able to hide if need be. You can't stop me. If I have to move out, resign, and go in with no backup, then that's the way it is."

I shrugged and sighed. "I'll think about it," I told her.

"Comm check."

"Got you loud and clear," Alex's voice came back to me. "Good visuals and good audio, and the parallel has you both lighting up like a searchlight. Hope they don't have the same monitors."

They probably didn't. While the place was gated, of course, the beach and riverfront area was effectively public and there weren't even any nasty dogs running around at night. True, they had this very high stone wall around the whole compound, with both sensing devices and razor-sharp stuff on top of it, but there were no routine grounds patrols, either. There was simply too much traffic here, particularly involving folks who were used to a level of security but not to threat of vicious attacks and the like. This really was, for the most part, a getaway for the old company and a jumping-off point for really secure regions.

The house and docks did have the usual visual surveillance and some automatic alarms, but these were pretty easy to see and, in fact, the alarms were mostly turned off at this point. There was very good reason for the lax security, too: they were clearly moving out of the place.

Even from the chopper you could see inside the drapes of the main building to certain rooms and they were bare or nearly so. Furniture trucks were moving out the expensive stuff and the place was up for sale by the bankruptcy court. Almost everything of value inside would have been on loan from private individuals, though, and thus not subject to seizure, and if they hadn't been long before the filing, they certainly were two minutes before it and backdated at least two years so tight the FBI couldn't prove otherwise.

This made things easier for us on several levels, but the most important one was that security was down on the house and grounds and there was unlikely to be anyone other than some workmen inside. Any people around would have moved to the much greater security of the big yacht. I assumed the small one either came with the house or would be disposed of separately, probably bought at auction by some Wall Street house that would prove to be partially owned or controlled by some of the principals in the late, unlamented Genetique.

Karen was impressed. "Jeez! *We* did all that?"

I grinned, even though it meant nothing in the darkness. *I did all that.* "Yes, we did, kid," I told her.

I probably could have stopped her from being here, but, what the hell, she did have a point in that she was smaller, faster, younger, and more agile than I was. *Other than that, Mrs. Lincoln, how was the play?*

In fact, I had no business being here at all. I was out of breath, feeling every one of my sinful excesses so thoroughly enjoyed up to this point, and for the few times some kind of breaking and entering had been required in the immediate past I'd usually recruited just such a younger person from the reporting staff or gotten a private detective to help out when I could get one on the company tab. It was just, well, this one was different. They had snatched my source right out from under me and roughed me up. I just had to be here.

We were both wearing black ultralight insulated wet suits that hugged our bodies with almost embarrassing fidelity but which could keep us alive and well in zero-degree water for a couple of hours if need be, including hoods, gloves, and rubber-soled boots. Our faces were blacked out with a synthetic makeup that wouldn't wash off but came off easily using a cheap solvent provided with the stuff. We also both wore all-purpose minigoggles that could shift to infrared and one lens of which was a V.R.D. so that we could actually call up anything, from the plans of the estate to instant information from any database in the world on anything we might encounter. The thing unnerved me and I kept mine turned off except for the little circle in the lower left "corner" of the virtual screen showing that it was on. It reacted almost to thought and controlled itself with cues from my eye movement and that was too spooky for me.

Each of us had been sprayed with a specific compound about which I understood less than I did the V.R.D. controls, but it seemed like you could mix it up into millions of slightly different combinations and it would show up only if your camera was tuned to that specific chemical "fingerprint." Since our mix was virtually random, the assumption was that

Alex's cameras from far off and on high could see and track us easily while it was unlikely that anything else would notice us. Sure, there were computer systems that went up and down all the known scales and registers in blinks of eyes, but those were where you put your topmost secrets and were monstrously expensive. This wasn't the kind of place for that; the Genetique headquarters and particularly its labs and computer systems were.

We had tiny cameras linked to the V.R.D. goggles in our clothing, so Alex and the others could see anything we could, maybe more and better. Finally, we had actually *swallowed* tiny capsules that contained microphones and locators, each of which had been tuned to eliminate our body sounds. So, not only could the bosses see us if we were anywhere in line of sight or via the goggles and such when we weren't, they could hear everything as well and always know just where we were.

We came in, separately but not far apart, along the far section of the private beach, as far away from the wharf and yachts as possible. There were some overhead lights, but these had shadows and were more for illumination than security; too bright would have involved all sorts of permits and notification on pilot charts so as to not fool boats going by. And, of course, the neighbors around here would be livid at stadium lighting.

Our goggle vision showed that the lights did have sensors on them to detect movement above the size of a small dog, and that these were turned on. If we broke one of those beams *then* there would be some illumination, but when you could see them it was pretty easy to keep out of their paths. It wasn't major security; for that, and in a place like this, you still couldn't beat dogs, and if they'd ever had them they were gone now.

The landscaper had created a nice floral shield between the river view and the main house; lots of trees, thick growth, even some fake rocks and growth just to fill in the natural gaps, particularly this time of year, when all but the evergreens and ferns were bare. Ironically, the twisting path through all this, lit by an occasional walkway light, had the least security, while dashing through the underbrush would have set off some alarms.

We went up to the house first, having agreed not to enter it unless there was a great and compelling reason to do so. When we reached the flagstone-and-marble patio leading inside I immediately ducked into the darkest shadow I could find and gestured for Karen to do the same.

The drapes weren't drawn; apparently they were pretty lax until you got down to the big ship, and we could see straight inside. This was the spectacular living room and indoor pool grotto that showed up on the old listings, and if anything it had been understated or improved. There wasn't much furniture left, and there was a lot of stuff just lying around or in crates and boxes, but you could still be impressed by it. It was the living room of my dreams, if, of course, I could manage to win three consecutive lotto jackpots in a row.

Standing just inside, talking animatedly to a guy I didn't know in one of those tailored suits, was Myra Ling Kelly herself. Of all the ones in the black-project business, she was always the one I was most scared of, and I couldn't explain it with any specifics. There was just something about somebody in that kind of business, who'd spent her first nearly thirty years on earth studying to be a coroner, that put a bad association in your mind. That and the fact that she was deep-down mean and nasty and almost anybody who was near her could feel it. It may be why she preferred corpses; they couldn't run.

"Well, there's another link to both Syzmanski and the government," I whispered, just loud enough for it to get picked up by Karen and by the controllers far away. "Got her own Black Squad now that poor Johnny's on the Most Wanted list."

"Take it easy, you two, with the likes of her!" Adam's voice came to me all the way from the managing editor's office in

Baltimore, where they were watching this with us. "Those squads have better technology than we do by half."

"But not here," Karen breathed. "They're moving out."

Karen only knew the Dragon Lady from my descriptions, but she'd figured out who we were looking at right away. As I said, there was something always odd about her, something you could feel even walking past her on the street. The bloodiest dictators in history could be real charmers, but there were some people who just couldn't keep the evil from coming out their pores any more than you could fart unnoticed in an elevator.

"Are they armed? I can't tell from here," Adam asked us.

"The Black Squads always pack something, usually needlers," I whispered. "Her—I doubt it. She doesn't need a gun."

I'd have liked to have a needler with me myself right about then, even if they weren't completely legal for the average person, at least not to use like the Feds did. They shot a dozen or more tiny little supersharp slivers at one trigger pull, and you could custom program the potency of each projectile. The stuff was another example of better dying through chemistry; artificial, lab cultured, it nonetheless was based on a now extinct South American rain-forest poison that could paralyze, knock you out, rot out a limb, or kill you, all depending on a computer dosimeter on the gun stock. And the needles dissolved in bodily fluids or of their own accord in a matter of minutes, making autopsies difficult.

I motioned to Karen to move around to the side of the house and keep out of the light; we were here to document, to see what we could see. We weren't here for an incident, not if we could help it. At least now I was finally breathing normally again, and probably would continue to do so until and unless I had to run for it, climb for it, or take some needles.

"If you could just both do a close-up fix on that water in the pool first," one of the Hopkins types we'd invited in on this said. "We see something unusual and we want to see if we can get some sort of analysis."

It always beat me how they could tell all that from a picture, but, then again, they were always telling us about the composition of faraway astronomical stuff and a lot of it was the same sort of technology.

The docs controlled the spot as each of our goggles sent out a thin, nearly invisible line of light, converging the two on the water even though we were hardly still figures.

"Thanks. Got it. Rather odd results. If I were you I wouldn't go too near that stuff, and I'd definitely avoid anybody who did. It sure isn't water but its registering one whale of a lot of life. A kind of artificial primordial soup. Just exactly what it is and what it is for I have no idea, but they will have a difficult time disposing of that without setting the place on fire or creating a toxic dump, and I don't think they want either."

"What a waste of a great pool," I sighed.

"What about the EPA?" Karen suggested. "Can we call 'em in on this evidence?"

"We'll tip them off but we can't call them in officially," Adam replied. "Remember, you two right now are trespassing. Still, it would be nice to get somebody in there and get a physical sample of it."

"Jeckyl Juice," Karen muttered. "I bet it's Jeckyl Juice."

"What the hell is Jeckyl Juice?" I asked her.

"You know, like in the Mr. Hyde thing. Jump in there, come out a monster, maybe?"

"You've been doing too much interactive video," I told her. "Jeckyl to Hyde may be possible now, but not you or me to our flying thing."

She, however, was convinced that we'd happened on the secret, and nothing like realistic science and natural laws were going to talk her out of it.

We moved as much around on the left side of the house as we could, avoiding the camera zones. Theoretically our little bath had the added property of making it very difficult for even infrared monitors to see us, but you couldn't count on things.

The place wasn't as empty as it looked from the outside, but it certainly was preparing to be. What windows we could see into tended to be piled high with boxes, crates, even old-fashioned steamer trunks. Furniture was mostly limited to folding chairs and cheap lawn furniture and such; we'd expected that. We circled back around and did the same tour on the right side of the place, but discovered little more.

Having surveyed and peered into as much as we dared without breaking in, and feeling by what we had discovered that there wasn't much point to getting in there unless we wanted to get caught, we moved back down the pathway toward the river.

This was going to be the harder part. Two guys with guns were wandering around in front of the wharf, looking uncomfortable in the cold but still very clearly guards. Beyond, the forklift was removing stuff from the back of a parked trailer and moving it into the wharf building and, apparently, from there into the big ship, which looked not only imposing but downright dramatic at this distance.

There were also guards on the decks of the big ship, maybe just one per upper deck on the superstructure, but they were in constant motion and you could see that they carried rifles over their shoulders. It would be interesting if we could find out what was being loaded so late at night, for even with the shadows there were a *lot* of people with firearms around.

I timed the forklift. It went up to the trailer, then one of the two guards went over and hopped in and started a small motor which brought another of the minicontainers close to the edge of the trailer lip where the forklift could snare it. Then it steadied it and drove into the warehouse. There wasn't any driver on the lift; either it was being remotely driven or it was strictly a utilitarian robot.

It took seven minutes, almost on the nose, before the forklift returned and the process was repeated. In that seven minutes, allowing for the thirty seconds or so for the guard to drop to the ground and walk away, and for maybe another

minute when it returned and the guard would be walking toward the trailer, you still had a good five minutes for
somebody to get inside there and maybe see what those containers held.

"You'll never make it," Karen told me. "You're too big and
too slow. I'll give it a try. You be ready to divert the guards if I
get trapped."

Before I could object she was gone into the shadows and
over to the far wall. I could see her, of course, with the special
viewing and the chemical coding, but I switched that off
mostly and switched it back on only to check her progress. I
wanted to see if she'd show up so the guards could see her.

Karen looked like she was so thin she'd break in a weak
wind, but actually she was a committed weight lifter and had
surprising upper-body strength for a woman. She just didn't
show it unless her arms were really flexed.

Now, as soon as the guard jumped down and the forklift
was turning with its new load, she pulled herself up onto the
lift from the far side and got into the trailer. My heart skipped
a beat; the guard was no more than a few meters away, but
continued to walk back toward the parking area. The lift and
its boomy echo as it went down the wharf masked any sound
and clearly he'd seen nothing.

I switched the V.R.D. to Karen's channel. The interior of
the trailer was very dark, and had a robot-controlled pack/
unpack system. Each container was about four meters across
by perhaps two meters square on the sides. It wasn't at all
clear what was in them; they all looked alike. Still, I could
hear one of the Hopkins guys say, "Zero in on the small
number written on the front, lower-right-hand corner usually.
This often tells you a code for the contents, along with an ID
stripe for machine sorting."

It was pretty much just that way, but the code, a long combination of numbers and letters, meant nothing to me.

"That's the code for Kaifin, a programmable endorphin re-
placement," the scientist commented. "Very good. So we can

be confident that these are medical supplies for the most part, and probably pharmaceuticals."

"So why the night loading?" somebody, maybe Adam, asked.

"This sort of stuff can be extremely dangerous in the wrong hands, and in those quantities is a controlled substance. Assuming the other containers are also packed with drugs, then they are shipping out industrial quantities of some very nasty stuff. Worth a ton on the international black market."

Kaifin, huh? Well, that fit. You mix it with a few other brain chemicals and program it to pretend it's a natural endorphin and it goes in, docks, and then delivers whatever you've added directly to the brain. A rather nice psychiatric tool, it was also one of the ultimate tools in brainwashing and worse. Give it enough times and the brain would be actually altered; it would begin making and reinforcing the pattern naturally. One of those ugly sidebars of progress, and just exactly what these folks would find most useful.

I couldn't help but think about poor Kate. If they had this kind of stuff, then their new "recruits" could become very dedicated very fast.

We'd started a counter on the side of the V.R.D. screen and it was now down to two minutes. Time for Karen to get out of there and she knew it. I peered out and saw no guard heading that way yet, but I could already hear the forklift slowly coming back from the cargo hold of the ship.

I was relieved when I saw her come to the edge of the trailer, look around, jump down, and become hidden against the big tires just as one of the guards started walking toward the trailer, grumbling.

The forklift emerged and came up to the trailer and the forks raised to the tailgate level. The guard pulled himself up, then just stood there as equipment within the trailer sent the container of Kaifin coming. Apparently the guard really didn't do anything, but for some reason they wanted somebody there to watch whenever a container was loaded. It puzzled me for a moment, then I guessed that it was because it *was* a totally robotic, rather than remotely run, operation. They just wanted to make sure that if anything was off-kilter somebody could push the big red "Stop" switch.

The container was on the forks, then balanced, then the lift slowly backed away as it lowered the container to about halfway down. As it did, the guard was already heading back to the relative warmth of a van in the lot while the other one was looking over the grounds even farther away.

I don't know if that was what made her do it or not, but suddenly I saw Karen come out from the shadows behind the big wheels and jump up on the forklift, which had a running-board-like step around it. She hugged it as it started inside the wharf building.

"Karen! What are you doing?" I said in a whisper so loud I was afraid I was getting picked up.

"Hitching a ride," she responded. "I want to see what's in here!"

Well, it was too late now, and I had to note that none of the bosses and experts back in Baltimore watching us had made the slightest protest. In fact, if she lived, she might even get a promotion and a raise for this, particularly if she found out something useful. There had always been a certain lack of heart for specific reporters in the news biz; the story was what counted.

Funny; all my professional life I believed exactly the same thing, and I wouldn't have been there if I didn't hang my own neck on it, but for maybe the first time in my life I didn't accept it for somebody else.

Well, at least the V.R.D. showed that there weren't any guards down the end of that warehouse; the forklift whirred along, turned about halfway down, and entered the opening in the ship's side leading to a dimly lit cargo hold big enough to drive a small truck into.

There was somebody in there, though, and Karen reacted quickly, sliding off the forklift and getting over behind some boxes while whoever it was had all his or her attention on the lift and its cargo.

Well, she was in. Now what?

I was just about to request some instructions for my own options when I heard Alex Montoya's voice in my ear.

"Everybody! Something's coming toward me. Much too big to be a bird, too small for a plane!" There was the sound of the chopper in motion and a slight cut in the audio, then, *"Mother of God!"* He had the foresight to put the forward tracking camera on. Although worried about Karen, I was mesmerized by the helicopter action and switched momentarily to his camera view.

Caught in the sudden narrow forward light of the helicopter was the human gargoyle of a creature that had been playing cat and mouse with me, and it was heading straight for the chopper's undercarriage.

NINE

I couldn't help but sense the absurdity of my position, which matched only my helplessness. Here I was in some bushes, trespassing on dangerous ground, with armed guards all around, and on the little miniature display in front of my eyeballs I was watching somebody I cared about prowl around a place that might get her killed in an instant while switching to a dramatic midair confrontation between a news helicopter and a monster from Hell.

The monster was extremely strong and remarkably agile, but it was no match blow-for-blow with a helicopter piloted by a frightened man who flew the thing as easily as he wore a suit of clothes.

It was clear that the intention of the creature was to grab on to the undercarriage, swing up, and then pull off the door to get to Alex and Mark, our producer up there, but as it closed in the chopper always managed to pull away or angle itself so that the thing kept missing. Finally, though, it did seem to latch on to one of the runners, and as it did Alex gunned it straight up. Modern helicopters could easily make twenty thousand feet and they could do it very quickly and in place; even with the drag of the flying creature, the powerful engines lifted the chopper ever higher. Alex and Mark were automatically pressurized as that happened; there was no such pressurization on the outside of the craft, and the undercarriage camera clearly showed that our flying fiend may have been built to do the impossible but not to breathe and function well six kilometers straight up.

I admit it gamely tried to hold on, and you could almost feel sorry for it as you saw the agony in its contorted, inhuman face, and saw the screams you couldn't hear.

It let go, spread out its wings and tried for a slow descent back down to more comfortable altitudes, but by now Alex wasn't scared anymore, he was incredibly pissed off. "Hold on!" he yelled to the producer, then swung around and descended rapidly while keeping a laser tracking beam on the creature. It took him almost no time to catch up with it.

No longer the aggressor, the gargoyle was far too slow and too clumsy to avoid or outmaneuver the chopper. The thing tried every way to shake him, but the game was on the other foot now, and with the rotor Alex was forcing the creature lower, ever lower, toward the river below.

I couldn't figure out what Alex was doing, then I realized finally that he was angling the rotor so the creature couldn't try a fancy maneuver and get under it. Still, he'd have to pull up before the river, and then things would be back on the earlier plane again.

"What do you want me to do, boss?" Alex asked, and I knew he wasn't talking to me or the producer.

"Kill it!" I heard a woman's voice say, a voice I knew from the media but hadn't heard in person before that night nor even realized was there.

Our esteemed publisher was in control.

"Kill it and track where it falls," she instructed her pilot. "I'll cover for you."

"Yes *ma'am*!" the pilot responded and pushed in almost at the last moment. The rotor cut into the creature as he gunned it to full power, cutting it in two. Almost immediately he had control trouble, as the bulk of the thing hitting the rotors caused some momentary losses, and suddenly he stalled out.

"Hang on!" Alex called. "We are going down in the Potomac but we should be okay!" With emergency descent on and main power lost, the computerized safety systems kicked in, sensed water below, and applied enough power to the rotor while simultaneously inflating a huge bottom float that the chopper struck quite softly.

Still, it wasn't going anywhere in the air again soon, and was probably slowly heading down to Point Lookout and the Chesapeake Bay.

Karen and I were now on our own, and it was at that moment that I remembered her and where she was and switched over to monitor her view.

Whether she knew about the helicopter or was strictly counting on me I didn't know; she could hardly speak where she was. She kept pushing her luck, though, and I started to have some heart pains just watching her through her own eyes.

She moved away from the action and the guard inside the ship and was searching around. There was a lot of stuff in there, quite a lot; if this was all the same kind of stuff we'd seen on that first container, they had enough psychochemicals here to take over a good-sized country.

There was a stairwell in the bulkhead to Karen's right, and I just knew she was going to take it. Damn it! This was somebody who thought she couldn't get caught! I knew better.

Although well lit, the well wasn't in direct line of sight with the loading operation and she was able to duck into it. A stair with rail went up at one of those shipboard-type impossible angles to a landing far above.

Damn it! With the Dragon Lady in charge and God knew who or what else on that ship, our luck just couldn't hold much longer.

The loss of the helicopter wasn't drastic, although I was happy nobody was hurt except the bat-man thing. I had to wonder, though, if that thing had been sent to down or disable the chopper, or whether, again, it was acting in its brutish mode entirely on its own. If it had been sent, then they at least suspected that we were here. Getting away was going to be tough enough as it was.

I could do nothing right now except continue to follow Karen's progress and get more and more nervous about it.

Fortunately, the chopper didn't take out our comm links; those were being relayed via our minitransmitters to a satellite uplink tower. What we had lost was backup, and the ability of the remote teams to see just where we were. We could each see and hear what the other was seeing and hearing and we could get audio from Baltimore, but our surroundings were no longer being monitored nor our security sensors tuned, and our video recording was dead. Basically, we'd been reduced to sneak thieves on the ground with an audio link out.

Karen came up on the lower passenger deck of the vessel. There was a sliding door forward leading to the deck and one to her right leading inside. With a guard patrolling the deck, she opted for the inside passage.

It was really nice in there, I had to admit. Ornate Oriental carpeting stretched in both directions while the bulkheads were a dark wood with insets in which there were paintings lighted like you'd find them in some art galleries. I had no appreciation or much knowledge of art, but I suspected that at least some of the paintings were originals I couldn't have afforded prints of.

Karen moved toward the stern of the ship since it was docked bow in; this would allow her to see what might be hidden from normal view, and also was an area less likely to have armed patrols.

There were some staterooms amidships, and a few voices could be heard, mostly female voices, but what they were saying or even what language they were speaking was impossible to pick out. The only thing that was certain was that they didn't sound like they were in any distress.

I could *feel* Karen's urge to find out who they were, but I also felt a lot of relief when she decided not to. She was already farther in than I thought she'd get, and if she got out now it would be a miracle.

There were more sounds of people just ahead of her, more boomy and echoing than before, and also sounds of splashing water. It didn't take much brains to figure out that there was a pool back there, and indeed she soon came to it and stopped. There was a barrier that appeared to be made of some kind of strips of material that you could walk through. It didn't block sound, but I bet that it contained humidity. Carefully, she stepped through the strips and then moved flat against the bulkhead and froze. There was little cover beyond where she was, and she was at pool level but below the diving board and such.

It looked almost like a mini–water park, complete with slides, diving board, and tubes, and on the next level up there was a wide area where people could sit and look down on the pool. The whole thing was covered by a translucent dome that I suspected could be retracted in warm, sunny weather; it looked hot in there even now. In fact, Karen's goggles began steaming up from the humidity that apparently the strips kept from the rest of the ship.

There was a man and two women back there, or so it seemed. Nobody else was in evidence, and they were paying attention only to one another. She focused on them and brought them into closer view using the telescopic properties of the goggles, and I could hear her give a slight gasp as she examined each of the three in turn. I had almost the same reaction.

All three were naked; no big deal in this day and age, and this was a private ship, anyway. And all three were those perfectly proportioned or maybe overly proportioned types that you expected from Genetique.

What she didn't expect was, well, the woman sitting on a stool near the pool was bright green, and quite uniformly so. It was a handsome, even pretty, bright green and it was unbroken by any sign of blemishes. The short hair was a darker green, as were the lips, brows, nipples, that sort of thing, but otherwise she was just a stunning amphibian green. Her hands and feet seemed pretty normal, but it did seem as if the fingers were slightly webbed. Hard to tell without getting too close. Even the pupils of the eyes seemed to reflect that same bright green color.

The thing was, I recognized her, or thought I did. Her general features closely matched the photos we had of Dr. Sandra McCall, but somehow the fact that she was green had not shown up in those pictures or other data.

The second woman had more African American facial features, but her skin was not the middle chocolate brown that she'd been born with; instead, it was mottled, blotched, making her look like she was infected with some terrible skin condition. There were brown areas, and areas that seemed more brilliant yellow, light and dark green, you name it. The best I can explain the look was maybe that she'd been painted by an expert in military camouflage.

The guy really didn't seem to have a skin problem, except that he was as white as I was and his balls and penis were a dark brown. Kind of a dramatic contrast to the winter pastiness the rest of us natural-color folks had. It wasn't until he turned his back for some reason that you could see a real difference; it was still minor but obviously in progress, but something was growing out of the guy's back, a kind of bony plate, and he was clearly growing a tail out of the base of his backbone just above the ass. The plate was only four or five centimeters so far but it was noticeable; the tail was maybe seven or eight centimeters long and looked rather stubby and strange, but it was clearly going to grow some more. Both were just enough to cause him real trouble with tailoring.

Well, now we knew what the damned things could do. What sort of charge could you induce with one or two large shots that would develop rapidly enough that you'd notice? How about skin color? That was an easy one, I suspected, knowing it probably would have won the Nobel when I was a kid. The guy I couldn't figure out; those plates would take a little while to grow, a lot longer than simply turning you green.

Was that what Kate had seen when they'd taken her back there at Genetique? Had Sandra McCall greeted her all bright green that day, and maybe with some associates who looked like the African American woman or even the guy?

It was still kind of weird, though. Why risk them being exposed here? One accident sailing out and they could easily be found out. What would happen then?

I felt a little guilty at that thought. We'd spent the past almost two weeks scaring the hell out of people with genetic monsters. These people might well be accomplices, but they were more likely victims who now went along because they feared exposure as freaks.

Of course, there was that shipment of Kaifin—one of the scariest mind control agents—in the hold. Maybe these people were happy as they now were because they were being made that way.

One thing was sure. I risked a whisper. "Karen, get the hell out of there now!"

She was ahead of my command, moving carefully back through the strip barrier and onto the inside corridor. Almost immediately one of the guards approached from the outside deck, not particularly looking inside but generally looking back and forth for anything out of the ordinary. She dropped below the windows and hugged the deck.

I don't know whether I moved involuntarily or made an inadvertent exclamation, but the next thing I knew a hand came down on me with incredible strength and threw me completely to the ground, then a knee held me there while the other hand ripped off my goggles, and thus my vision of what was happening aboard ship and my control of the whole package suddenly ceased.

Blinded as my eyes tried to adjust to the dimly lit beach area, I felt the pressure on my chest lessen and a very large man got off me and stood up. It hurt like hell, but I couldn't do very much; another guy not much smaller loomed even larger and stronger in my eyes because he was holding a needler and it was pointed directly at me.

This pair didn't seem to be the guards from the car or forklift areas; these were Suits, even if they did look like they'd just escaped from a wrestling arena.

"Get up!" one of them instructed, in one of those basso profundo voices you'd expect of somebody that size.

"I'm trying!" I gasped, then coughed and tried to catch my breath.

As I pulled myself painfully to my feet I could hear footsteps from the walkway running toward us, and I turned and saw, as I'd expected, the Dragon Lady coming at full speed.

Of all three, I feared her the worst, because these guys could only hurt or kill you.

Myra Ling Kelly looked ready for just about everybody and everything, but when she saw me and threw a flashlight beam on me, even through the black coating on my face she instantly recognized me, and she sounded more exasperated than angry.

"Just what we need! Vallone, what the hell are you doing here in that getup?"

"You wouldn't let me in the front door when I asked nice," I replied.

One of the big guys moved to teach me a lesson, but she waved him off, much to my relief.

"So that was your helicopter that went down off Piney Point, then," she said more than asked. "Producer and relay control. You're in the wrong business, Vallone. That's our kind of thing. Did anybody tell you how ridiculous a wet suit like that looks on a man with a pot belly?"

"There were some comments on that," I admitted, "but it had to be me. You understand that, I think."

"I give you points for guts, if not as much for brains," she responded. "Now the question is, what do we do with you?"

"I'm trespassing on private property. Call the cops."

She was not amused. "I think we can put that off for a bit." She looked at the goggles in one of the men's hand. "You! Take those out front and put them in the trunk of my car. Don't damage them. We may be able to analyze them and find out just what's gone out."

"You can read it in a few hours in the paper, or on the nets," I told her. "Just not as well written as if I were doing it."

"Smart-ass!" She turned to the other guy. "Have you checked to make sure he's alone?"

"We've done a sweep, yeah. Nobody but him," the deep-voiced guy replied.

She turned back to me and I didn't like the look or the expression. I braced myself for something very painful, but she suddenly stopped. "You're still wired, aren't you?" she muttered. "*That's* why you're your usual smarmy self!"

I gave her a weak shrug and sheepish grin.

"You want to tell us where it is or should I ask Morgan, here, to look?"

I definitely didn't want Morgan looking for anything on or in my body. "He's not my type. It's a capsule, Agent Myra Ling Kelly," I replied. "I demand to be arrested and read my rights!"

I could hear the sound of a distant siren and started to hope. "Guess my boss decided to double-cross me and turn me in," I commented, sounding more confident than I felt. This woman was not at all above going after the capsule anyway, although I suspected that once it was clear she was named and labeled as being in charge she'd toe the line. Unlike John Syzmanski, she was a federal agent, and in this atmosphere she couldn't depend on the usual level of protection she otherwise might have gotten.

Karen, too, had one of those horse-pill transmitters inside her, and I could only hope that whatever was going on aboard ship, if she got nabbed that might offer her a measure of protection as well.

To my great surprise the sirens *did* turn into Chathams Court and apparently breezed right past the gatehouse. Kelly looked like she was going to strangle a few chickens to improve her mood, but instead simply said, "Shit! Come on! Bring him!"

Westmoreland County's finest wasn't exactly used to this sort of job, but they didn't like getting guff from gatekeepers and they *particularly* didn't like getting guff from federal types. In fact, I don't believe they ever shut down the Good

Old Boy factory these guys came from, not since General Bobby Lee took over and they made Richmond the capital. And they were born and raised surrounded by, and used to, the Feds; it meant that an FBI badge and ID not only didn't impress them, it made them a little more belligerent.

"Now, just what right do y'all have to post anybody at the front?" Officer Patrick asked the gathering squad. "This here's been declared seized as part of a company bankruptcy and I served the papers myself. Now y'all show me the warrant or maybe we'll start callin' in the networks and some higher-ups. Got a state trooper on his way now." All of it was said in that soft but firm tidewater accent that pronounced *ou* like the Canadians—*oo*—but with a southern twist and also eliminating any letter *r* within a word.

Myra Ling Kelly did not get as far as she did without being smooth when she had to be.

"Officers, I'm sorry, but we've been frustrated here in our surveillance activity. We wanted to stop them but could do nothing legally. Then we discovered, inside the building, a toxic waste substance and we've had to post guards until the HAZMAT crew can come in here and clean it up."

"Yeah? So what were you puttin' under surveillance?" the other officer, whose badge said "Rawls," asked. "Pretty damn much of a circus here for anything like that, seems to me."

"That ship docked in the back and its loader and trailer, as well as the dock, are all leased to the Ratorangan Embassy. The road, dock, and ship have diplomatic immunity. We can't touch them. And the trailer is certified as diplomatic mail so we can't touch that, either. You have enough diplomatic types and retreats around here. You know the limits."

And they did, too. Patrick stroked his chin and thought. "Now, let me get this straight. The ship, dock, and truck, immunized, but the house and grounds are not?"

"That's about it. It's an arrangement with the former owners of the place and we knew nothing directly about it until the bankruptcy. That's when we came down here to monitor what might be going in and out. So far, we don't have much, but we did have permission from the bankruptcy judge to enter and use the house so long as we didn't trespass on the leased area. Since we couldn't stop them, we decided that the best way to limit things was to be as conspicuous as possible."

"And it's because you entered the house for this that you found the other stuff?" Rawls asked.

She nodded. "It's in the swimming pool, of all places. You can smell it. We don't dare go near it and we have no idea what's in it, but considering that the owner was a biochemical corporation we don't want to even try and test it out. We called in HAZMAT and they should be coming in tomorrow or the next day to clean it out, analyze, and disinfect the place."

Patrick looked over at me. "And I suppose you're the close-in surveillance guy? Or is it just a late Halloween?"

"Chuck Vallone, *Baltimore Sun*, Officer," I responded. "I was just doing some surveillance of my own on this business, and Agent Kelly's people and I just sort of ran into one another."

"Figures. You guys don't believe in any privacy at all. Still, you're the one we're here for."

"This man is in federal custody, Officers," Kelly insisted. "He is not free to leave."

"Ma'am? And what are you charging him with?"

"Trespassing. Interfering with federal officers in the performance of their duties."

"Well, ma'am, that second one could take a little explainin' before a judge, and that first one, well, unless you're claiming that this place isn't privately held and in bankruptcy foreclosure after all, which it is, then trespassing is a county crime, not a federal one. You got no more jurisdiction here than he does. In fact, I'm not even sure who the hell would prosecute him for trespassin' right at this point. Until I do, and with your statement as basis, I'm takin' him with us. He'll be placed before a county magistrate who gets paid to make decisions like that. In any case, you know who he is and where to find him. Don't seem like he's much of a threat to flee. His bosses'll just pay a big fine and spring him anyway. We see this all the time, too. Mr. Vallone, get in the rear of the patrol car now."

"Happy to, Officers," I told them, and I sure was.

Now, Kelly and her people could easily have overpowered the locals, but that was the last thing you wanted in a place like this and it would raise more stink than anything since, well, since Johnny Boy invaded the city room. Kelly's parents were academics now, basically; comfortable and connected but by no means a group of highly placed billionaires. Still, you could see that it griped her, and the rest of them, that these local yokels could take control here, and I could see her mind working furiously trying to figure out some way to keep me and get rid of them.

At that moment, though, the state police car pulled in, and she knew she'd lost. Now there were too many jurisdictions in the call—too many to use any leverage, at this time of night, in time to do anything meaningful.

"Oh, take him and welcome!" she snapped. The county cops looked a bit too smug, and the state trooper never even got out of his car. Instead, I was cuffed, thrown in the back of the county squad car, and both cops got in the front. Rawls put the car in gear. The state trooper followed.

Both cars pulled over about a mile down the road and Patrick got out. Rawls sprung the lock and Officer Patrick slid in beside me. "Turn around and I'll get them cuffs off."

I was even more delighted about that. I'd been handcuffed before in demos and such but this was the first time I'd had the slap-and-lock type they used on crooks, and these *hurt*.

As I rubbed my wrists, I asked, "What about my partner? Any word on her?"

"Nope. They said there might be a young woman dressed up like you, but there was no sign of her. Think she's still back there?"

I nodded. "But they don't know she's there, I'm sure of that. Thing is, she snuck on board that ship."

The trooper came over. "Any problems, Jimmy?"

"No, no, well in hand. We may still have a girl in there, though. If so, she better swim for it. I doubt if we can get her out as easy as we got Mr. Vallone here, and if she can't get off that ship then she's toast."

I didn't like that. "What do you mean?"

"Well, that federal woman, she's up to no good there, that was for sure, but she was right about one thing: That trailer, ship, and dock are leased and are diplomatic hands-off. If she's on that ship, only that embassy and State could get her off."

"You mean there *is* a country called Ratatouille or whatever?" I was appalled. How big could it be if I'd never even heard the name myself?

"Ratoranga. Yeah, it exists. Has a kind of mini-embassy in with a bunch of them other South Pacific little places over in D.C., but, hell, boy, we got some No Fishin' zones bigger'n the Vatican and *it* has an embassy, and so do they."

"Ratoranga," I repeated. "Where in hell is that?"

"Somebody told us it was near the Marshall Islands," Rawls said from the front. "Somewhere down where I'd like to be right now, in the South Pacific."

The Marshalls again. "Figures."

"We got to take you in like we said," Jimmy Patrick told me, sounding almost apologetic. "But we got a magistrate who'll set bond real quick. Your paper called and squared it already. We'll hold you a little so them Feds won't stalk the courthouse and wait for bail and snatch you on the way out. Your office is sendin' somebody in from Washington for you."

"Okay, thanks. Any news on the helicopter that crashed? It was part of this."

"They down that?"

"I think they might have had a hand in it, but I'm not sure," I told them honestly.

"Got word on it, but haven't updated. Let's go up to the courthouse now. We might be able to get some information on them from there, and maybe on your missing partner, too. Let's pray we can, anyway."

As far as Karen was concerned, prayer was all I had left.

It was almost four A.M. before Phil Strichter from the Washington Bureau arrived in a company car, but I was pretty depressed by then. Oh, they'd gotten to the helicopter fine, and everybody was okay, and after some refitting at a private field near Leonardtown it would be up and running again, maybe in just a couple of days. These days you just popped out the rotor, popped in a new one, and tested it.

Adam, of course, had called in the cops, who knew full well who I was and what the situation was before they ever got there. In fact, Rawls was pissed off I'd identified myself so completely, even though he could understand my nerves. They were hoping that Kelly would lie about me in front of them and give them probable cause to arrest the whole batch. That was why the trooper backup had been called in, and there were other units, both local and state, nearby just in case things got ugly.

Well, what the hell, I was an amateur, although I was learning fast in this business.

Maybe too fast. Maybe I was learning that while I always knew there could be a price to pay for this level of work, it never really occurred to me that it might be paid by somebody else.

On the phone, Adam would only say that it wasn't more than a couple of minutes after I had my own comm link torn from me that Karen was heard to give a soft groan, moan, or exclamation—even after I heard the recordings I had to admit I had no better words—and then her link went dead as well. Unlike mine, her audio link had gone dead at that same moment; after the exclamation there was nothing but static. Even killing her wouldn't have turned it off, but a lucky blow to the midsection might have, or it might have been deactivated with a high magnetic field by somebody who just assumed it was a good thing to do when you caught an intruder.

Either way, the operative word was *caught*.

County police put a small boat out on the river, watching the ship and even monitored it with an infrared camera, but nobody jumped into the river and swam away. Nobody jumped into the river at all, not that night.

Damn it! No woman should ever come near me again! I said to myself over and over. First Kate Marshall, now Karen Reedy.

The fact was, Kate's loss wasn't that big a deal, but Karen . . . Karen was something else. I had grown really fond of the little tiger. She was good at all facets of the job, and if she was a little too nerveless in the field, well, she'd still delivered one hell of a set of visuals before they'd gotten her. By six that morning the initial story was on the nets and in the paper, along with some stills from the goggle cameras that showed both the coloration and the unmistakable face of the missing Dr. Sandra McCall, identified by several of her former colleagues, all of whom were shocked at this.

Adam, without much if any prodding from me, put Karen's byline on it, too.

The journalistic community mobilized almost immediately as well, pulling in favors, kicking politician's asses, and putting superheat on State. The Embassy of the Kingdom of Ratoranga had, it seemed, only three people assigned to it, and as of the next morning they were nowhere to be found. We had no embassy there, just one consular officer, his wife, and their two kids, and it just so happened that they also covered a lot of other small island republics, kingdoms, and territories out there, but actually were based in Majuro (again!), a mere five hundred and fourteen kilometers from Ratoranga, the capital of, well, Ratoranga.

The small diplomatic mission may well have been missing in Washington, but their attorneys were not, and they were doozies—one of the biggest and most expensive firms in the capital, chock full of former secretaries of state, deputy secretaries, undersecretaries, you name it, and specializing in representing the legal interests of foreign embassies and consulates and their people. That meant enforcing the rules even when there wasn't a clear complainant, and standing there at Chathams Court at seven in the morning, before the sun was even up, with assertions of diplomatic immunity for the leased area and even a spokesman to decry this persecution of a poor island nation by a reckless press with their faked photos and tales out of science fiction. The FBI was merely attempting to tie poor little defenseless Ratoranga, a primitive paradise, to the most horrendous high-tech crimes (that were clearly somebody else's), and trying to smear the royal yacht, which was going off toward home to become the basis of a locally owned cruise line for the rich and famous, tying the Marshalls to Ratoranga. These smear tactics were designed to doom their attempts at starting a tourism industry in Ratoranga. They suggested that the Marshalls, long affiliated with the U.S. and defended by it, was behind it all.

In the meantime, the lone trailer was already empty, no more showed up, and some of the crew who'd been on leave, and none of whom seemed to have the slightest South Pacific blood in them, started showing up in motor launches and going on board directly. The ship was clearly preparing to sail, and the press was emphatically told that it was not welcome aboard because there was much work going on inside to convert it to a luxury cruise ship and it simply was not safe yet.

Nobody believed them, with those lawyers and diplomatic immunity. Nobody could get past the hired guards, either.

Trucks and crews from the EPA, or at least apparently the EPA, did indeed show up as well, and provided a nice means to keep the press back and off the property. I wasn't sure who'd sent them—they looked and acted far too military for an EPA team to me—but there was no question that they were for real and that, once they looked at the goop and tested it in their own mobile lab, they didn't get more lax about their protections but much, much stricter. You couldn't talk to them, but even from a distance you could see on their faces as they emerged from the decontamination van, or entered the suit-up van, that they were very, very worried and nervous about working with the shit.

We did everything we could, but international treaties required a certain notice before diplomatic immunity could be lifted even if we severed relations for cause, and that in itself, short of war, was a real can of legal worms, if you had good people arguing on both sides. It wouldn't matter. Even in war, the ship, being in civilian merchant service rather than military service, would have been given one opportunity to sail.

"Adam, we just can't let them go and do nothing!" I argued. "I mean, considering what they were loading they could have a class-one brain rewiring network on board, and God knows what else. They sail, and in a week or two it'll be old news. She doesn't have any more close relatives than the missing scientists, so there's not going to be a huge hue and cry lasting forever. Eventually somebody will show up from Ratoranga and say it was all a big mistake, they had nothing to do with that ship at all, that their staff was forced to cover it at gunpoint or something by some shady types, and by then it'll be long gone and maybe everything on it transferred."

"Don't you think we know that?" Adam sighed. "Damn it, Chuck, what can we do? They've got the diplomatic cover when it counts, and that also means that if we try putting anybody of our own aboard they can shoot at will or worse, and while State's been a champ in this, the old black gangs and Black Squads have been at work shutting down meaningful action. The Feds are in this, at least some of them, probably military and espionage as usual, right up to their noses, and they'd rather let it all go than risk exposing whatever they've been up to. You know the news public today. We have about the same credibility with them as the government does, and that's not much. Circuses, that's all they've wanted since the dawn of the electronic age. Maybe before. Didn't Pulitzer once brag he'd started the Spanish-American War and mean it? They've got the attention span of fleas and we're still mostly advertising-driven and that means circulations, hits, you name it. You know the score. They're not going to drop a

SEAL team on that ship and the marines aren't going to be storming the beaches of Ratoranga. Not unless they're caught doing it again. And they wouldn't have been caught at it *now* except for those sloppy murders!"

"Anything on the remains?"

"The Potomac's pretty fast there and about several kilometers wide," he reminded me. Just down a bit it goes into the Chesapeake, which becomes at that point almost sixty-five kilometers wide. Even so, things usually wash up, or get discovered in some marsh grass or something, but that's when everybody's on the same page. The Feds, I suspect, may well have found and removed what remained. And if the DNA left on the little bit that adhered to the blades and fuselage come up with a flying monster, well, we've got pictures already of that, and all it does is prove that the monster existed and we got it in self-defense. They'll pin Wasserman and the two cops on it, and case closed. So what the hell do you want me to do? You didn't make much of a commando, you know."

"True, but who knows what shape I might wind up in if I keep going on this thing?" I responded. "Maybe I'll have fangs and a tail before it's done. But I'm not going to stop, Adam. I owe her that. And I owe myself that. I want to know the story here. Every time we find something explained, no matter how unbelievable, we get something worse showing up that makes even less sense."

Adam sat back in his chair and finally said, rather quietly, "Mrs. Archer agrees with you, and so do the boys in L.A."

I sat up. "What are you up to?"

"No matter where that ship goes, we'll know," he said simply. "If anyone goes on or off, we'll know, and we'll follow them. Satellites and, if possible, on scene. You can't believe how much money they've committed to solving this. It'll be chicken feed to what the story will be worth when we break it first. Mercenary and detective teams are mobilizing all over as we speak. The ship sails tonight, but it won't be out of sight or mind. We feel we know where it's headed next. We're going to both follow it and meet it when it lands."

"I want to go."

"Not into action," he told me. "You write and report. Period. But you take orders from whoever is on the scene who's likely to be able to get in and out. If you go, it's as producer, not action star. Got it?"

I nodded. "When do I leave?"

"When they do, if you don't get too seasick. We can handle monitoring along with our Coast Guard contacts until they pass Florida; after that, we'll have to tail them, as it were, although it's pretty crowded down there. Unless they do something totally unexpected, in which case we're ready to move to cover it, we should be able to intercept them with our own craft going out of Freeport as they come close. After that, well, it'll be open ocean in a large, but hardly cruise-ship-style, vessel, and it could get rough."

"I'll risk it. I'd still rather follow them than try and anticipate them, at least at this point."

He nodded. "Okay, okay. Go home, pack light, and we'll have you on a plane out of B.W.I. to Freeport tomorrow morning." His face got suddenly very grim. "You realize, though, that she's almost certainly had some kind of their special treatment by now? That this might be a revenge assignment for you?"

"Yes, I think that's probably certain, but I'll go no matter what."

"You ever hear of Sainte Germaine?"

"Sure. Little island, top of big volcano. Went off years ago. Not enough left for anybody to come back to. Why?"

"It's private now, has been for years. It's off the beaten track for just about anybody, and the shoals and reefs that resulted from that explosion a couple of decades back left no decent anchorage. Never did have much of a population, and those who survived got off and stayed off. There was nothing left. Lava and dust flows even buried the graveyard of the single town to a depth of eighty meters. Well, about fifteen years ago, while it was still smoking, somebody up and offered to buy it."

"Huh? You can do that?"

"Wasn't much left, wasn't worth much of anything, and the surviving natives got a ton of money in compensation. So, yeah, this private nature group bought the thing and essentially had their own little country. Only the group's a shell. There's a private resort on there now, but you can't tell much about it. Distorted from satellites. Very high tech for a little nature group. You can get there only by private helicopter—no place to build an airstrip and, as I said, no harbor left, or, if there is one, it's uncharted. I suppose they got the makings of the resort or whatever it is there somehow. We've been trying to get somebody in there for years. So has everybody else. No luck. Whoever or whatever it is, is well heeled and very good. People who try and sneak in just don't come out. But governments never seem to be upset enough at this to do anything about it. Getting the picture?"

"Kind of a private version of those classic places of romance and intrigue from the old days, huh?"

"Something like that. Maybe more than that. Reporters and paparazzi have gone in there and never been seen again. In fact, we have only secondary sources as to what's there. Well, our ship's heading for Sainte Germaine, we're just about positive."

"But you said you can't make a landing there."

"No, but they'll put in offshore on the old still-intact high-cliff side, a chopper will come out from the island, land on that heliport deck area, and pick up folks and maybe drop off some. Bet on it. It's the first link in this chain, although until they filed course and destination with the international maritime agencies we hadn't linked them to this. To espionage central, to spooks of several nations, to organized crime, smuggling cartels, and others, yes, but not to this. Until now."

"Holy shit! This is one time when it might pay for Karen to be as flat-chested as she is. God knows they don't need Kaifin sessions for a place like that. Just stuff her full of pinks on the way and keep it going until it's too late. She's not like Kate or

McCall and the others. They need geneticists and other biology types, not reporters. She's just excess baggage to them. The only reason I don't think they've killed her is that some of these people wouldn't get off on that. Not unless they had to. Too easy and no fun at all. They get their kicks from their power with the injector and the psychochemicals and all that."

"I know." Adam sighed. "We're going to have to hope that what they can do to somebody physically we can figure out a way to undo—you know the syndicate will always cover that—but we can't undo the brain damage some of that stuff can cause. And as for being flat, well, if they can grow a fin and a tail or whatever they were on that fellow at the pool, I shouldn't think a big pair of tits would be any challenge at all."

"How much sailing time until they reach this island?"

He shrugged. "Depends on the weather and a lot more. At best, four, maybe five days. At worst, maybe seven. Call it two or three days after you intercept, tops."

Oddly enough, I hoped that they were fast. The more time they had at sea, the more damage they could do.

TEN

My yacht was not nearly as large, as luxurious, nor as comfortable as *The Songs of Sunset* but it almost certainly had a friendlier, less hostile crew.

It was called the *Prince of Anguilla* and was under B.W.I. registry, and it had been used for everything from short interisland cruises to carrying supplies, people, and cargo where they shouldn't have been. When the Moresby Agency got hold of it, it had been seized by the British Navy off Baruda with a considerable amount of Golden Triangle opium aboard. Sold at auction, the Bahamas-based Moresby Agency had bought it because it was just what they needed for the kinds of jobs they specialized in, like sneaking in and out of island nations and territories unobserved and staking out small harbors and yacht basins. What was interesting was that, while all three agency crew members were Caribbean natives who spoke with that distinctive island accent, none of them were Bahamian. George Samuels was a big, hulking black man with another of those melodic voices of doom and he was a native of Antigua; Rita Tompkins was a strikingly beautiful woman, chocolate brown in complexion, with shoulder-length straight hair, and she'd been born on Tobago. Roger Dees, a lithe, athletic man with a medium complexion, but more European—probably British—features, was from Grenada. At least, that's what they all told me. I had the impression that none of them were quite what they seemed to be, but that they were indeed all agents of the widest-ranging private detective agency in the English-speaking Caribbean and that this was their "retirement" from a related occupation not ever mentioned.

Still, I always wondered if I'd find the graves of a Roger Dees in Grenada somewhere, a Rita Tompkins on Tobago, and a George Samuels on Antigua. They were that kind of people.

Normally, stuck in a place like Freeport on an expense account with a nice resort, good weather, big casino, you name it, I would have been in heaven, but, the fact was, I hadn't enjoyed a moment of the time there. All I could think about was green and mottled people and a robotic Karen waiting on them, maybe while turning into something odd and exotic.

Even with just the basic fast boat, I was glad to be under way, and anxious to see a certain ship once again.

George, who was in charge of the boat and also the nominal leader of the pack, sat back in the exposed upper pilot's chair and relaxed as we cleared the harbor and he started gunning it. He knew just where he was going; we were connected to the nets and satellite links here as surely as if we were doing an automobile rally somewhere.

Rita came up top with the full-blown computer analyzer and pointed it at us. She then said, "Okay, you two. Everybody's clean, de boat is clean, and we got de t'ree routine bugs heading for Cuba, so relax and speak if you want to."

Samuels chuckled. "Dat's Rita. Always de joker. Planted dose transponders on a Cuban diplomatic boat. Won't take 'em long to see t'rough it, but by dat time we'll be well away. Den anybody wanna talk t'us, dey have to show up on our sensors."

"You think our opposition planted the bugs she found?" I asked, worriedly.

"Naw! Dey just be routine stuff. Everybody gets bugged down here now. It's almost a game. Don't do nobody no good, dough. I mean, we also all know about dem and we all know how to get rid of dem or fool dem. Hell, even de tourists are wise!" He laughed heartily.

"How long until we get within eyeshot of the *Songs of Sunset*?" I asked him.

"Oh, couple hours, maybe near sunset. Still no big deal. I don't need to see her. I only need her on de navigational computer."

I sighed. "So we follow her. We know where she's going, or we're supposed to. So what then? What happens when she anchors off the island?"

Rita came back up, having put away her gear, bringing three cold bottles of beer. She offered me one and I took it, thankfully, already feeling the heat of the tropical day after having just acclimated myself to cold and sleet back home. I liked this better, but it was tough enough finding a news job anywhere these days, and down here even more so.

"We been tryin' t'get inta dat damn island for years," she commented. "Maybe we get a better chance dis time."

"Surely after fifteen years all sorts of operatives have been in there," I said, frowning.

"Oh, it's easy to get *in*," she responded. "It just ain't so easy t'get *out*. Dey got de best high tech—shields and guards you ever see, and wit' just de one place dey know everybody down to de rats and sea snakes dat be on dere at any time. George, you got a satellite photo of de place from last week, right?"

Samuels rooted through some material in a weather-beaten portable file under his feet and brought out a large glossy, which he handed to me.

The island itself was rather clear in the photo; ugly, jagged cliffs, a volcanic nightmare frozen in ash and lava. I remembered the eruptions from years back, and it hadn't changed all that much. What was different was the center of the island, the whole center, from maybe a hundred meters in from any land. It was just a rippled, distorted mass, like bubbles boiling up in a pan on the hot stove. I had only seen that kind of distortion on this kind of picture in aerial photo attempts of military bases.

"That's grade-one aerial security. And nobody's been able to penetrate it? NSA, DIA, anybody?"

She shrugged. "Maybe dey do. Maybe it's de price dey get for settin' it up in de first place, ever t'ink of dat?"

I suddenly saw what she meant. Such a place as that was its own business and service. If, say, NSA set it up, then NSA could also unscramble and see the comings and goings of unfriendly types who might not realize it could be unscrambled like that. Most of them would still get away with things, or else they'd be suspicious, but if, say, some group were in a bad mood like that fanatical crew twenty years ago who actually managed to smuggle in and set up a half-dozen nuclear devices in New York, Philadelphia, Washington, and so on, well, wasn't it a miracle that by some accident one of them was stumbled on, alerting everybody else, just in time? Hmmmm . . .

Or maybe it was just so damned convenient even to our folks that we, or somebody equally technically proficient, had done it to ensure it could be used safely by whoever, including themselves. Hell, you could have a meeting between our people and little green men from Arcturus in a place like that and nobody would ever know. The government, *my* government, had to be in on it. Otherwise nobody in that paranoid bunch would have waited months, let alone years, before sending in the marines.

And, naturally, the staff would be altered, programmed, and be good, obedient slaves. They'd never leave, never talk, and never even think about what they saw and heard.

I'd seen and even been in high-security buildings and installations that had near absolute security, but nothing like this, where your staff simply never left and always obeyed. Their DNA fingerprints would be on file, and they'd be implanted with a unique tracker and put into a security computer that would be sealed away deep. Everything you said and did would be recorded, and if you ever said or did anything out of line you'd be flagged. The combination of robotic and human security and service would be nearly impossible to break.

"You've had people from your agency get in? And then nothing?"

"Dat's about it," George told me. "We suppose dey got interrogated and den joined de staff, as it were. De ones dat don't work out, well, dere's so much dust and still a lot of live spots around up dere dat it wouldn't be hard to make somebody part of de bedrock. Even if you can see some of de udder islands from up top dere and watch de boats like dis one and sails go past, you got to be as isolated up dere as any place on de Eart'."

"So what's the plan here? We want our person back, period. That's priority one. Then, and only then, do we want the rest of this story."

Rita sighed and finished off her beer, then lit a cigarette. They all smoked, which was something I wasn't at all used to. I mean, they banned the sale or possession of tobacco in the U.S. when I was still in school, and unlike pot or bathtub gin, you couldn't effectively raise, pick, select, cure, and process your own backyard tobacco. I could only academically grasp its appeal, but I realized that I'd better get used to it. We were going to be in close quarters for many days, and you couldn't pick your allies in this. Anyway, I probably had body odor as offensive to them as their smoke in the middle of an open sea was to me.

"If we can't get her before she gets on dat island," Rita said to me, "den we're gonna somehow hav'ta go in and get her."

"You just told me that was impossible."

She shrugged. "Maybe it is, but we're gonna try new t'ings each time until we find de weak link. Maybe it's dis one."

"So you do have things aboard for that!"

"Oh, sure. We're pretty sure we can do it dis time, wit' all dat nice new money from your people to get only de best."

"But, of course, we t'ought dat last time, too," George Samuels commented, and he wasn't laughing now.

* * *

"Well, dere's why your lady's transmitter stopped," Rita said, pointing to her large and elaborate computer control screen belowdecks.

We were barely within eyeshot of the *Songs of Sunset*; we could see her running lights in the distance and the navigational screens told us that we were indeed looking at what we thought. *So near and yet so far.* But the dock back on the Potomac had been even closer.

"What are you talking about?" I asked her.

"Dere's your ship," she told me, pointing to a ship outline on the screen, "and dere is de *Starship Atlantis*, one big muther of a cruise ship over dere. See it?"

I did. The cruise ship's outline was almost twice as large as the *Songs'*, and I thought *it* was large.

"Now see how many boats are in de same spot?"

I saw what she meant now. Our quarry had a double line all the way around it, the big cruise liner only one. "Double hulls?"

"Nope. Dey all got double hulls now. 'Cept us, of course. Dat second outline shows it's got a local distortion field. Almost like de island, but dey can't do it like dat wit' a ship 'cause you got to be able to see and identify it. But it means dat no transmission go outside de ship 'cept by dere own codings. Now look."

She punched some codes into the computer and the view of the yacht changed to a full-screen outline. It was stunning, and she could turn it for a side view, top view, or even peel off each deck and zero in on specific points on the ship.

"It looks like you have the blueprints!"

She laughed. "Blueprints! What good are dey 'cept to start t'ings? Dis ship she go t'rough quite a lot of changes over de past few years. We been workin' at breakin' deir system and so we have. Now let's see just who's aboard."

Her hands moved in midair as if conducting a symphony orchestra, and suddenly the diagram came alive with maybe a hundred or more dots, each with a number attached, and some were moving.

"Good!" she breathed. "Not too many people aboard. Dis may actually be doable. Now to find your girlfriend."

A few more hand manipulations, as if she were some voodoo priestess casting a spell, and one dot was suddenly double circled and blinking. "Ah! *Dere* she is!"

According to the computer screen and diagram, if that circle was Karen then she was in what represented a standard-sized cabin for that floating palace, a bit to the stern of amidships. Maybe ten meters from where I'd last seen her that night through my goggles, only this dot was not moving.

"That's a good sign," I noted. "If they have her confined to a room then she's still a potential escapee."

"Maybe, maybe not. Best not to hope too much," Rita responded. "She could be sleepin', or drugged, or who knows what. Well, we're just gonna hav'ta see, I suppose."

"Rita, where'd you get all this stuff to be able to do this? I mean, that thing's got to be top-of-the-line in security when it's fully enabled."

"Not so big, but we had a few problems wit' some codings, I admit. Some—old friends, old colleagues, shall we say, get dem for us. Until now we weren't sure dey were de right ones, but dere you are."

"But isolating *Karen*?"

"Oh, if de rest worked, den she was de easy part, since we had all de data on how you two was fixed up for dat raiding party of yours."

"So now what do we do?"

"*We* don't do nuttin'," she responded. "When it's dark enough, den Roger do a little bit of snoopin'. In de meantime we gonna hope and pray dat de transponder she swallowed stuck like it should and hasn't gone t'rough her. It should be good for a week or more. Yours is."

"Yeah, but we lost contact on it."

"You lost contact a little bit after dey found you in de grass, or so we're told. At dat point all dey needed to do was turn on de magnetic field to cut her off from de outside. But now we can get around dat. If we're lucky, and somet'in' aboard dere actually happens near her, we just might be close enough to filter out de interference and hear it. What do you t'ink of *dat*?"

"I'm impressed. So the Dragon Lady was working with them after all."

"Oh, de Kelly bitch? Yes, she's been several times to Sainte Germaine, and dere ain't dat many folks can say dat!"

There was the sound of a door rattling, then a small *ding!* sound, and then the sound of the door actually opening and someone coming into the cabin.

"Time to wake up, Karen. We've got to keep you on a very regular schedule," a woman's voice said. Then, apparently to someone else, "Pick her up and carry her down to Monitor One. I want to get started quickly on this." The voice had the trace of an accent, perhaps Near Eastern, perhaps Oriental, but it was crisp and professional.

"Yes, ma'am," a man's voice responded, and we could now see a second dot enter the room, and Karen's and the new one moved as one out into the corridor and then up a center stairwell and forward toward the bow of the ship. It was a large area just below the bridge and wasn't totally characterized on the drawing. It seemed to have been designed as a restaurant or lounge, but it clearly wasn't being used for that now.

"Put her in the chair and close the restraints," the woman's voice instructed. She was fussing with some sort of tools or glasses or somesuch as Karen gave a low moan and seemed to be struggling as she came to.

"Oh, good! You're coming around," the woman commented as if she were a nurse in a clinic, friendly but detached. "That will be all, Geoffrey. You may go. I can take it from here."

"Yes, ma'am," the man's voice said again, and that dot walked out and back down to the stateroom deck. Clearly the woman in charge felt no threat from Karen.

"Well, dear, how do you feel today?" she asked Karen.

"Lousy. You ought'a know. Sick to my stomach, I itch all over, and I got a splitting headache."

"Well, we're doing a lot in a little time. Accelerants always cause some discomfort, but it will go away, I promise. Now we're going to take some samples from a few places and run analyses to see if we need any corrections. Yes, there. Now, let's see . . ."

There was the sound of minor activity, lab type noises, and then a series of oddly pitched humming sounds.

There was nothing much more but the usual sounds of two people in a room for another minute or two, and then the woman said, "All right, let's see . . . Yes, quite nice, really. I do believe that your discomfort is pretty well over after this session. The only way it will hurt after that is if you continue to fight it. It will be futile to do so, since you will be fighting yourself, but you can cause yourself pain that way. Otherwise, simply accept it, embrace it even, and you will start to feel a little euphoric. First a series of injections, which will not hurt any more than the others."

"No—" Karen protested, but there was a series of dull popping sounds and it was clear that the injections had been administered by high-speed devices.

Karen cried out. It wasn't so much a scream but rather a series of low moans, and then there was a good deal of very deep breathing. The lab woman said nothing, essentially ignoring Karen, for several minutes. The worst thing about the sounds and the wait was being totally helpless to do anything to help the poor girl.

Now the woman said, but not to Karen, "Identity Foo Luck Kai, confirm."

"Genetic and cross-check identification confirmed. Good evening, Dr. Foo."

It was a very pleasant-sounding man's voice, but it was also very clearly a computer.

"Subject requires transponder monitoring chip implant, worker grade. Programmable level-one trainee."

"Subcarrier neural fluids good but not optimum. Program anyway?"

"Yes. It can't be helped. Proceed."

There was a terrible high-pitched whine that fed the imagination with images that were probably far worse than what was actually happening there, but even that was certainly bad enough. Damn it, Karen! No byline was ever worth this!

"Identity chip implanted. Placement optimal. Synchronizing with neural carrier. Synchronized. Continue and run level-one trainee program?"

"Yes, continue."

"Programming." Pause. "Verifying." Pause. "Program accepted." Pause. "Programming running."

"Thank you. Estimated life of program in subject?"

"It will take three days minimum for her body to expel the programming fluids. How long after that it would take to break mostly or completely free of the program is too individualized to predict. A reinforcing cycle would be advisable in twenty-four hours, then additional as warranted by behavior."

"Good. Are you getting a good signal from her transponder chip?"

"Yes."

"Fine, fine. Still, do a security monitor on us for the moment."

"Running."

"What about the genetic reprogram?"

"Since the desired changes were mild and generic, the body is adapting well considering the stress the accelerants place on it. The proper nutrition and exercise should provide a good program."

"I will give instructions that, when she eats, she is to have anything her body craves," the woman commented, as clinical as ever in tone. "As for the other, let's begin that now."

Steps as the woman went over to Karen, still presumably strapped in the chair. There was no sound of shoes, but it was unclear if she had bare feet or was wearing some kind of medical disposables. Still, you had to wonder, had Dr. Foo once been the subject, rather than the perpetrator, of a process like this?

There were clicking sounds and it was clear that all restraints were being removed.

"Karen, wake up."

"Umph." Slight groan. "I—I'm awake." Her voice sounded distant, even a bit confused.

"Karen, how do you feel?"

"I—I, uh, don't know. It's hard to feel *anything*."

"No pain?"

"No."

"Now listen to me. You will address anyone whose title you know by that title, as in 'Doctor,' 'Captain,' and so on. If you do not know, then all other women will be addressed as 'madam' and all men as 'sir.' There will be no exceptions, even if you know their name. Do you understand that?"

"Yes, Doctor."

"Good! Excellent! Now, get up from the chair. I want you to walk to that exercise machine over there and begin using it until I tell you to stop."

It was impossible to tell what the equipment was from hearing the sounds, but clearly it was designed to distribute any injections quickly to all parts of the body and maybe it also had other uses.

"Is she hypnotized by drugs?" I asked Rita as we continued to listen to the drama from our boat.

"I don't t'ink so. Dis is deeper den dat, but in anudder way not as bad. Dis be psychochemical programming. It's unbreakable, but, remember, anyt'ing dey program can be reprogrammed or canceled."

"My God! You mean we're to the point where we can just inject some drugs and hormones into the brain and then reprogram it? Who the hell is *safe*?" This was a story I wondered if I'd be permitted to print, but, if so, it was one of the greatest stories to break of all time. Hell, I was ready to throw away my sat phone and other conveniences right now and go join a monastery.

"Oh, it's not *dat* absolute," Rita assured me, smiling slightly. "See, dey be doin' it in the intelligence communities for maybe twenty years now. But it's not good for much. You can't keep de person de way she was and also turn her into a zombie. De brain's much too complicated for dat, at least so far. You remember your zombie stuff, right? No way dey was mistaken for the folks dey were. Dat's all dis is, only dey get to do it wit' a white girl from America and dat makes dem a big turn on. No practical value. I mean, where's de profit in makin' smart girls dumb? Just old sick power trips, dat's all. Turn a church-goin' saint into a mindless whore or a reporter into some kind of maid or waitress. See what I mean?"

I did see. It made me feel a little better, at least temporarily, for humanity, but not better about Karen. "Is she aware of what's happened? I mean, is she still there?"

"Sure. Nobody knows 'nuff 'bout how de brain stores t'ings to dare wipe it out. Dey just put dis stuff in de way so it don't matter. But you can only take so much. It got to have a bad effect, de longer you're like dat. Too long and if you take de program away you can't find de old person."

I could understand that.

"If we spring her, any way that we could get rid of it ourselves?"

"Oh, sure! Dey use dat kind of stuff for real limited t'ings, like on fat farms for rich folks and breakin' some other bad habits. Smaller ones are used for quick language learnin', single skill stuff, t'ings like dat. Most don't have de kind of computer to analyze and do what we just heard, but wit' some budget it's not dat hard, and your paper got de budget for it."

That was something of a relief.

Eventually Karen was given other basic behavioral orders, including instructions to exercise in private whenever practical, and to always smile when speaking to anybody.

The term *zombie* was apt. Oh, they didn't *look* like the walking dead, but they were, anyway.

Roger Dees stuck his head in the computer room. "So, what's de word?"

"Not good," Rita told him. "No problem penetrating and getting on de ship, but de girl, she's got de zombie program. Lots of folks awake and around her, too. I t'ink it's gonna be rough. Worse, dere's some indication here dat her comm pill is comin' loose and movin' to de ass end."

Having only just discovered that we both were still broadcasting, I now was concerned about it shutting off, at least in Karen's case. "So what happens?"

"We got to risk it, if we can't get her off easy," Roger told Rita.

"Hey! Hey! Hey! Wait a minute!" I interjected. "What's all this risk stuff about?"

"If we could get her out easy wid no risk, we'd do it," Roger explained. "I wish we could have tried it last night, but we didn't get de codes until dis afternoon. Dat's why dere was no hurry to close. Without dose, it didn't matter. And even when we got dem, it took Rita a while to get de signal. Dat means we fall back to Plan B 'cause it's no more risk than Plan A."

"Yes? And that is?"

"If dat link holds up," Rita told me, "den when dey go on de island tomorrow we'll get several implant codes as the security system on de island checks de ones dere and keeps monitoring. We just might be able to pick dem up on your girl's link. If we can, den we got a way past de main security on dat damn island!"

"I don't like this one bit! I thought this was a rescue mission, pure and simple," I protested.

Roger sighed. "Well, dey don't tell you all de stuff dey want from us, den, and a lot more."

"My sister is on that island somewhere," Roger said, his accent slipping just a teensy bit but the hatred in his eyes glowing. "Dis may be our best chance."

"If she don't crap it out first," Rita added. Turning to me, she said, "You don't t'ink any of us would be crazy enough to do dis job unless it was *personal*, do you?"

I should have been mad at Adam and the syndicate and I was. So much for don't spare the money to rescue one of our own; they were on the trail of what definitely appeared to be the story of the century, and in that reporters were necessary but also expendable. I could see them now, telling one another, *Oh, well, she can write a hell of a first-person story on 'I was a zombie slave!' and we wouldn't even have to juice it up.*

Of course, that was in the old tradition, but it wasn't the tradition I found reprehensible here. It was the dishonesty, particularly with me.

"What are the odds that her transponder will give out, or will be too weak to pick up the side transmissions you're counting on?" I asked them.

Rita smiled. "Glad you asked dat. Now, *we* don't t'ink dis is a job for tonight, but we don't want to stop you from anyt'ing if you want to try yourself. We'll get you up there, you can play commando again, only dis time you'll be armed, and we'll tell you just where she is. You get her and we'll recover. If she resists, you can shoot her wit' de needler and she'll sleep for hours and you can carry her. *But,* you also swallow a new, even more special transponder pill first. Den, if you're caught, we'll be sure to get what we want when dey take you over dere wit' her. Fair enough?"

I sat back and sighed. "You planned this, didn't you? All along. Or was it Adam and his bosses?"

"Oh, no, it just worked out dis way," Roger assured me. "If you don't want to do it, we'll find anudder way to make sure we get some kind of signal. But *dis* way we're all sure."

"Okay, say I do this and I get caught, and I do get carted onto the island. Want to explain to me how you're going to get me and Karen off?"

"Nope. What you don't know you can't tell. I wish you didn't have to know us, but dat's only a little bit of it, 'cause, of course, you *don't* know us. But you do have just a couple of hours to make your decision. Even in winter dawn comes early down here, and if we go we got much to do."

Okay, so everybody knew I would do it, even me. I think that was the plan from the beginning, but, the fact was, even though I had a bad feeling about all this, and particularly after hearing that intercept from the old transmitter inside Karen, there was no alternative.

The funny thing was, I was much more frightened of the mind-control stuff than I was of being turned bright yellow or polka dots or even being killed. I wasn't even doing it for the story, or for my still-insatiable curiosity, or for anything else other than getting Karen out of there. I didn't know if she or anybody would have done it for me, but that didn't matter. And if I managed to get her out of there and she turned into a female version of Quasimodo, I damned well wasn't going to abandon her.

There was no funny black makeup this time, but I did have a black pullover shirt and some swimming shorts for the occasion, and they did rub a bit of grease or something to darken the lighter parts of my skin, almost a pro forma prep for this kind of thing. What was new was a class-three needler, very small, easily hidden in a zippered compartment in the shirt. There were seven cartridges in the pistol, all knockout, not lethal grade, but if I needed more than a couple I was probably already in too much trouble.

The thing they had me swallow this time was even bigger than the horse pill I'd had to swallow back in Virginia, but I managed to get it down with some of that island beer. What I really needed was rum, unadulterated, and then a good doctor to plug the hole in my head, but with visions of lambs going to the slaughter I climbed down on Roger's small, fast mini-Zodiac and we were quickly off into the darkness, with the lights of a large ship looming on the horizon.

It wasn't lost on me that none of the three of them had tried to talk me out of it. Not one. They were all encouraging and enthusiastic, but I had the feeling that they really would prefer it if I got caught.

And I was a volunteer all the way down the line, with no family or close relatives back home to cry if I vanished "in the line of duty," as it were, another martyr to American journalism.

Trouble was, of all the hundreds or maybe more martyrs to American journalism, I couldn't think of the name of a single one. So much for fame and glory.

As we neared the ship and the silenced Zodiac engine seemed to throb as it slowed to match the big ship, I leaned over to Roger and asked, "Now, you're going to be here to pick me up, right?"

"Of course, old boy," he answered in a crisp and totally unexpected Oxford accent. "King and country, you know. Never go back on your word."

"Yeah, and always be truthful, loyal, brave, trustworthy, and all that, too," I responded.

We came along the port side and stopped amidships. I wondered how the hell I was going to get up there, but Roger was ready. He brought out and raised a section of ladder that looked too frail to hold anybody but had humongous suction cups on it and came out of a kind of black suctioned base. He attached the base to the ship and threw a couple of levers that hissed slightly, and then the ladder part started extending out of the base until it reached almost to the railing of the first weather deck. Then, setting another control on the base, big cups between the rungs of the ladder, maybe every three meters, extended and grabbed on.

"Now, don't hesitate to jump in the water if you must," he told me. "I'll know where you are and I'll pick you up."

I looked uncertainly at the ladder in the light of the crescent moon. "That will hold me?"

"Trust me! It's held George, and he's much heavier than you. Go! I don't want anyone looking over here and seeing me. I'm going to pull back to the darkness as soon as you're on your way up."

More nervous about the ladder than about what happened if I actually got aboard, I nonetheless reached out, held on tight, and uneasily began making my way up the perhaps twelve meters to the lowest exposed deck. As soon as I was a quarter of the way up, I looked back down and saw nothing but blackness. No matter what sort of idiot I was, I was committed now.

The funny thing was, even though the ladder didn't give me nearly enough clearance room and my arms started aching almost immediately from the climb, the damned thing actually held! After realizing that it wasn't going to come off the side and dump it and me into the ocean, I made it up to the top pretty quickly.

The ladder only went to just below where the deck itself started, and that meant getting within a couple of rungs of the top, grabbing on to the open area between the metal shield and the rail, and then pulling myself up. If anybody was on deck or looking my way at that point, well, that was it.

Nobody, though, was there, and that became even better news over the next several minutes as I found it next to impossible to haul myself up enough to really get over that rail. I finally did it, swinging one leg over and almost castrating myself, but not before almost falling back into the sea or screaming in pain.

All the pizzas and all the beer and all the jogging and lifting I never did came back to haunt me right then and there.

Once I took the luxury of several minutes to get my breath and then my bearings, I was as ready as I would ever be to play the action hero. I opened the zipper but didn't remove the needler from the pocket. No use in betraying a surprise before you had to, and people in my business, me included, weren't known for a fondness for taking and using firearms of any kind.

There wasn't much in the way of maps and diagrams that I could have taken with me to help; other than doing a quick study of Rita's computer diagrams, what I had was a tiny part of that thing I swallowed, which Rita apparently could program. It picked up Karen's signal, which was in fact getting weak and intermittent, and when I was facing the right direction I got a little whistle in my ear, or so it seemed to me. Turn away from her and it subsided. Rita promised me that she could turn this off remotely when I didn't need it anymore; I certainly hoped that was true. Otherwise the artificial tinnitus would drive me nuts.

Still, it was an effective locator. I really began to suspect that my three friends back in the smaller boat were veterans of a lot more black bag stuff and questionable activities, perhaps for king and country, and possessed the highest of technical skills. Unfortunately, being on my side didn't make them any less dangerous, either to others or to me.

I went up an outside stairway and on the next deck up I got the best signal when I was level and facing maybe sixty degrees left of me, so I knew she was most likely on this deck and inside either a cabin or some other room. Whether or not she was alone I couldn't tell; Rita had deliberately ensured that I couldn't pick up anything from Karen's failing transmitter except this carrier whine because it would interfere with what they needed from me.

Once I did have to duck in between lifeboat davits and crouch in the dark as two people walked by. Both looked relatively normal, both were large men with Mediterranean casts, and both were in the uniform of a ship's crew member. Beyond that and the fact that one had a beard I could tell nothing.

Once again, just when I reached an entry point to go toward the maximum whine, I had to duck and freeze as a woman in just a bikini bottom came out on deck for a minute and stretched and looked around. She, too, looked fairly normal if you overlooked the blue and white zebra stripes that covered her body up to the neck, and the half blue, half bright white that divided her face precisely in half. Even her hair seemed striped.

She apparently just wanted some air during a period when she felt free to come on deck without any real risk of being seen, but she didn't stay long and went back in. I gave her five minutes just so I wouldn't be likely to run into her in the corridor.

I then slid out and walked quietly to the sliding door, which had a touchpad that opened it when you pressed on it. I knew of a security system that tripped people up by checking their prints when they did that, but I used my elbow and no bells went off that I could hear.

I doubted they had the kind of security aboard that they'd have for a land-based installation; they hadn't even put cameras and sensors on the dock in Virginia or inside the trailer. With diplomatic immunity they probably didn't worry about it, and, if they feared that somebody might overlook that technicality, I was certain they had adequate defenses.

There was more noise of people talking and moving about than I expected, but it was much like what Karen had heard when first going aboard. It suddenly occurred to me that if you happened to be green or zebra-striped or something more serious then you'd tend to be more active at night in these waters than in the daytime. Still, there weren't a lot of people aboard nor were they all in this area.

I heard some conversation inside one or two cabins as I passed, but I saw no more people while following my little carrier beam, and after turning center and amidships down an internal corridor I hit the door to a fair-sized room, maybe eight meters square, and I looked inside.

There was a table on which were the remnants of a small feast offering more food than I could have managed even if starving, and on the other side were three standard exercise devices, one of which involved the oldest of all exercises, lifting weights. Karen was on it, working up a major sweat, and showing a physique I would not have guessed was there. They had given her short red hair, in a buzz cut so it needed no attention, and although she never had shaved herself when she was living at the apartment I could swear she had no hair at all from the neck down, although she had developed a nice tan and her complexion seemed almost shimmering as she sweated it out.

When I stepped in, she saw me and immediately stopped, putting the weights carefully back into their holders and pushing a stop button on the device. Her eyes widened, showing me that in back of whatever they were doing to her she recognized me, but the sweet smile she gave me wasn't the Karen I knew.

"Hello, Karen," I said softly. "I've come to get you off here."

"Hello, sir," she responded, keeping that damned smile, her voice sounding even lower and more asexual than I remembered.

"Come on. Let's go."

"I am sorry, sir, but I cannot leave this ship without permission. You should not have come, sir. You should leave if you still can."

My hand went to the needler. Roger had thought this might be a problem. Even with that bulk up, I could carry her at least to the rail.

But then what?

If I threw her unconscious into the ocean, it would be a miracle if Roger got in and got her before she drowned. She didn't even have those natural Mae Wests to keep her floating face-up. Damn! And it had gone so well so far.

"Aren't you supposed to follow orders if the orders harm no one?" I asked her, guessing at the basics of the program.

"Yes, sir, but not if I violate basic rules."

I was thinking furiously. "Very well, then can you make certain that I am not discovered and lead me back to the rail so I can safely jump overboard?"

Heck, I figured I could toss her overboard and then jump after her if I had to. Easier anyway.

"No, sir, I cannot do that. I am sorry, sir."

"Why not?"

"Because," said a woman's voice behind me, "you've already been discovered."

ELEVEN

So much for Plan A, I thought ruefully. At least I'd gotten farther than even I figured I might.

I gave a thought to the needler, but until I saw who was behind me and holding what, I felt it prudent not to make any sudden moves. I raised my hands kind of halfheartedly.

"I may say, Mr. Vallone, that you impressed us by doing this at all. None of us felt that you really had it in you, or, if you did, that you would risk it in such a gallantly futile quest."

I slowly made to turn around and see who I was talking to, and, hearing no objection, I continued.

I did not, however, expect to be talking to a humanoid frog.

She was maybe under a hundred and sixty centimeters, shorter than Karen, but there was a slight knee bow that perhaps distorted this a bit. She was the same bright green that we'd seen with Karen's monitor on Sandra McCall, and she had frogman's feet—you know, the kind of flippers you wear when diving, only these were really her feet. The hands, too, were oversized for the body and webbed, and also seemed to have some kind of suction cups at the fingertips. Her face was still human, sort of; green, of course, and with a couple of flaps at the nostril openings that seemed to pulsate as she breathed. The face was Oriental, right to the almond eyes, but there was no hair, not even brows, and I realized that those big almond eyes were blinking without shutting. Either her lids were transparent or she had two sets, one see-through and one not. She also retained a female humanoid torso, rather broad in shape and with two small but firm-looking breasts. So she wasn't an amphibian or reptile in that sense; I knew for a fact that somehow I was looking at a designer life-form. Oddly enough, the effect was not at all monstrous; it was quite attractive—in the way exotic animals are attractive.

She was so strange that at first I didn't even notice her companion, even though he was a head taller than me and almost too big to fit through the door, and even at rest his muscles had muscles. The only thing that stood out as bizarre, considering his companion, was that unless those briefs he was wearing were performing a miracle of miracles, there wasn't anything there to hide.

"I am Dr. Foo," the frog-woman told me, although I pretty much recognized the voice by now. "I am a medical doctor, not a Ph.D. like most of those you have come in contact with during your poking around into this business. Unlike your friend and a number of our guests here, I am present voluntarily. I don't usually leave my normal work, but we are coming to a critical stage and that requires some hands-on activity, as it were."

"You've been advertising," I responded. "When you advertise, expect all sorts of attention."

"It was—not intentional, but such things could not be helped. Now, if you would please place both your hands behind your back. Karen, please move in back of him and hold his arms back there."

"Yes, Doctor," Karen responded, and I felt a grip that Karen would never have been capable of before boarding this ship. In fact, I actually tried to break her rather casual hold and could not.

"Well," the frog woman sighed, "I suppose it was inevitable that we should have to deal with you. Geoffrey, please check him for weapons or other gadgets. We don't wish any more problems here."

"Yes, Doctor," he responded in that dull but deep voice, and then I got a frisking like no cop had ever given me. He got the needier, of course, and handed it to Dr. Foo, who examined it carefully.

"Not lethal, I hope? You don't seem to have that in you."

"No, at least the people who gave it to me swore that it wasn't. Fifty percent, a near instant knockout for several hours for a normal human constitution."

She gave a slight laugh. "Although my constitution, as you call it, no longer is quite the same as yours, it would certainly react to *that*. Oh, well, having drawn you here, I suppose we must run you through a lot of tests and, of course, completely deactivate Karen's and any other internal electronics."

"*Drawn* me here?"

"Certainly. You don't think we don't have satellites and such like yours, do you? Not to mention simple old radar that certainly showed your people pacing us. I knew *they* wouldn't board; they've been burned too much. I suspected they might wish to use you, but I wasn't at all certain that you had your companion's nerve. I had to lay it on pretty thick to see, or did you think I always had a dialogue with my medical computer, spelling out the obvious?"

I felt like one of those old cartoons where the principal turns into a sucker.

"So now what? You turn me into a sexless zombie like those two?"

Dr. Foo shrugged. "Karen, you may let him go now and come over to me." Instantly I felt my hands freed, and I brought them forward and rubbed them. Where did that kind of strength come from in so short a time?

"This may be only the start of Karen's journey with us," the frog-woman responded. "In the meantime, this state removes a threat, and she will have to be somewhat broken in, as it were, in order to come over to our point of view and work willingly with us. If she proves to be one of those who cannot be convinced otherwise, well, then, this at least provides some usefulness to us. I haven't really decided about you yet. Your age and poor conditioning make you less a candidate for radical work, yet you might well be useful at some point." She turned to Karen and said, "Karen, take this needler. Do you know how to use it?"

"Yes, Doctor," she responded with that now maddening smile.

"Very well. It is nonlethal, merely a sedative. Shoot Mr. Vallone with it."

I started. "Hey! Wait!"

Karen shot, I felt a series of stings in my chest, and then everything started fading to black.

Now, I'd always been told, never having experienced it before myself, that you didn't dream or have any sensation of time nor any thoughts or whatever when you were under that needler stuff. It was kind of like a strong general anesthetic. In truth, I can't say I had any real sensation of the passage of time, nor conversations, or the like, but I do have distinct memories of being moved none too gently over and over and vague memories of sounds and lights and even a burning sensation. I don't know if any of it was real, but I kind of think that they put me through the mill.

Still, I have to admit, I was surprised to wake up on a bed, in a normal-looking hotel-style room, and, at least apparently, thinking like myself.

They had stripped me of my clothes, and my skin seemed a bit whiter and more sensitive than it should have. Some kind of radiation or sterilization? I felt extremely hungry and thirsty, but I had the taste of bile in my throat and a sore ass. The odds were they'd pumped my stomach and given me the mother of all enemas, I guess to flush out anything I might have swallowed. There were fluids, which left sour tastes and burnings, that were used to flush out swallowed electronics, so I guessed that this was it.

I got up, unsteadily, and saw a small hotel-style refrigerator unit in the corner. I went over, opened it, and discovered that it had the usual alcoholic stuff which I definitely did not want right then, and also plastic bottles of various juices and even, wonder of wonders, some cookies and cheese and crackers in small containers. I decided that maybe a Coke would calm the stomach and feed me some needed sugar, but I took everything that looked edible and brought it over to a small table. It was only when I had opened everything and was consuming it much too fast that I realized the one thing the room lacked: any sort of window. There was a door with a thumb pad, but I suspected that it wouldn't open to *my* skin samples. Of course, even if it did, where was I going naked and exposed?

The edibles were not nearly enough but they helped drive down the pounding in my head and the sourness in my throat. Since there wasn't any more food evident—even luxury prisons, it seemed, understocked the overpriced bar—I explored the rest of the room.

It was a nice room, as prison cells went. The bathroom had a European-style toilet, basin, shower, and a spa bathtub, which under other circumstances would have been really tempting. Even the bathroom floor was carpeted—waterproof, I assumed—and slightly heated, or so it felt, as were the towels on the rack. Classy.

I looked at myself in the mirror above the wash basin. Somebody had given me the same kind of short buzz cut that appeared to be the rage among genetic mutants and their captives these days, and I'd also been shaved. This included my usually overabundant body hair, but I suspected that this was part of the treatment they'd given my whole skin. One thing did disturb me; there was a tiny circular Band-Aid on my forehead, about halfway between the bridge of my nose and my hairline. I tried to peel it off, but it was one of those "smart" bandages that wouldn't budge until it decided things were all healed up. Not wanting to tear a hole in my face, I decided to leave it there, but I sure wanted to know what the hell they'd done.

A self-inspection, or at least as much of one as I could manage, revealed a tiny rash area about the size of a quarter right in the center of my chest—good shooting for an editor—that was already healing but itched a little after I noticed it, and in my right buttock there were signs of a number of injections but nothing of the sort I'd seen on Kate. What they were,

I couldn't guess, but they didn't seem large enough or clustered enough to represent one of those genetic gangbangs. Maybe I was being inoculated against warts, I thought.

Otherwise, there wasn't much there, so I went back into the main room and inspected it, finding even less—not even a Gideon Bible. I knew I was almost certainly being watched, and that maybe there was a whole observation system in there, but, if there was, I couldn't find it, or, if I did, do much about it.

One thing was sure. This didn't look like even the most luxurious ship's cabin and it didn't feel like something floating, either. I was pretty certain that I was now on land, so that meant some significant time had passed since I was out. It also meant that Plan B had worked in part, only the odds that I still had anything inside me that could transmit or intercept security codes were unlikely. Oh, well, the fearsome trio would figure out another way with another sucker. It just wouldn't do Karen or me much good.

One other thing was missing. No phone, no wallscreen, no access console. In that sense this was a very basic room.

There was also no dresser-type furniture, which meant that I was expected to stay au naturel, although if they could stand it I could stand it. Interestingly, at the foot of the bed I discovered a pair of one-size-fits-all male sandals, so I wouldn't have to risk my tootsies, I guess, just my behind.

So, there was nothing left to do now except sit around and try to imagine that I was somewhere else and wait for something to happen.

I was still amazed by the frog-woman, even if she was no more unusual than our flying gargoyle in any real sense. Neither one should exist, and if either or both had started out "human" and become what we saw then things were a lot more advanced in genetic engineering than they were supposed to be.

There was also the question of *why*. I mean, assuming that the whole human genome thing was a public blind and that somebody, probably with a more secretive government agency, had cracked things a lot faster than we were told, and assuming as well that you could really do a major level of genetic redesign, why in hell would you make an attractive woman into a mutant version of an amphibian? What was the point?

I mean, the color thing I could see, if only to keep you from escaping once they had you, but that was also relatively simple to do genetically, or so I assumed. I mean, they'd redesigned small animals and were working on larger ones now, officially, but those would take years and years to mature. All this implied that somebody, somewhere, about twenty or twenty-five years earlier, had made some sort of quantum leap in technology in this area and had been starting way back then from where we were supposedly officially at now.

Hadn't Doc Foo said something about *choosing* her form? As opposed to what? A gargoyle? How many varieties of formerly people were there at this point, and what the hell were they for?

At that point the room and everything in it, including me, shook slightly, and there was a sense of a below-hearing-threshold rumbling. It didn't last very long, but it sure was unnerving, with no exit I could control. The lights flickered and the door made clicking and buzzing noises, but it stopped as suddenly as it began and the lights came back up full in a few seconds.

I wasn't sure what I feared more: dying in this place, or having my body discovered wearing only sandals in a subterranean motel room . . . alone.

After I caught my breath, though, I decided to go over and try the door. I didn't expect anything, but, hell, you never knew. There wasn't any knob or indent, but I put my shoulder to it and tried to move it one way or the other.

It buzzed at me but otherwise didn't budge much.

Well, it was a thought.

I had no sooner walked back to the bed to flop down again than suddenly the door buzzed much louder, there were three clicks, and it slid open. I was so startled that I just stood there for a moment, and in came a hotel tray on wheels pushed by Karen Reedy.

She saw me and said, "Hi, Chuck! Got some goodies for you here. Glad you weren't so shook up by that little quake. They get a couple a day here like that, no big deal."

I was shocked. Karen comes in with food and drink, acting like her old self and like she hadn't been a programmed zombie the last time I saw her!

"Karen?" was all I could manage.

"Sure. Who'd you expect? Dracula? They say our news-chopper nailed *him*. Is that right?"

I nodded, and sank back down, sitting on the side of the bed. She rolled the cart up to me, and I could smell the coffee in the fancy table thermos and as the server tops were removed I saw a major breakfast there—pancakes, eggs, sausage, bacon, ham, you name it, including fresh tropical fruit and grapefruit juice.

"Well, go ahead," she told me. "If they want to drug you, they just come up with some guy bigger than a mountain and stab you." She went over and sat down in the chair, watching me.

She was, like me, wearing nothing, not even sandals, but she had changed in a physical sense from even the last time I saw her. She was, well, chunky, and when she moved I could see that most of it appeared to be pure muscle. For somebody as small as she was, I suspected that any guy, no matter what his size, would be in for a rude surprise if they came up and tried to just stab her with much of anything. She was also tanned very dark, a demonstration that she'd not worn much of anything even outside for a while.

I had another series of questions and more mystery on my hands, but absolutely nothing could be solved if I didn't eat the breakfast and drink the juice and coffee, so I did.

"How do you like my new physique? Not bad for under ten days, or so they tell me," she went on. "I barely have to work at it to keep it. It does have some drawbacks, though. All these naked people around and I'm not turned on at all. Can't even turn *myself* on. The only thing that gives me that kind of rush is doing the heavy exercises, which I guess is the way they designed it. They say it's just temporary, the accelerated shit suppressing it, but I noticed a couple of their goons who used to be guys and now should be sopranos. These folks aren't real good at telling the truth. On the other hand, I'm eating like a horse now and it all turns into instant muscle. Weird, but I don't mind that part."

Even as I finished the eggs and juice and poured some coffee, I had to say something. "Um, Karen. Don't you remember knocking me cold?"

"Huh? Oh—that must have been during that floating part. I mean, they caught me on the ship and they stripped me, loaded me up with something, and after that I don't remember much. I do remember they woke me up when we were at sea and asked me all sorts of questions, apparently to match them with ones they'd asked under drugs, and then they put me on this stuff, I guess it was a drug series, that floated my brain off to Happy Land or something. The doc's got her own lab on board that ship; I think I was given their treatment up to this or that and more, but I don't remember much. Kinda bits and pieces, like old dreams."

"You were a zombie, following orders with a smile," I told her. "When did you come out of it?"

The truth was, I wasn't at all sure that she *had* come out of it, or, if she had, that it hadn't been after she'd broken. Once you've seen a flying bat-man and a toad-woman you get so you can't trust anybody or anything anymore.

"Here. In a room like this. Only they came and got me and more or less put me to work right away. There's not much staff here, it seems. Robotics mostly. With that volcano out there they can't do too much here. I get the impression that it's useful but not for anything long-term."

"And what have they had you doing?"

She shrugged. "Personal service, mostly. After all, the others are specialists, I'm a spying reporter. So are you. Like

I said, it's mostly robotics here, but there's some things they like people to do, including serving stuff like this, so that's me."

"And doing it doesn't bother you?"

"It doesn't bother me, no, but it's not what I'd prefer to be doing or even where I'd like to be. Still, they control everything from the exits to the kitchen, so I got a choice? This new 'me' has got to be doing something anyway. I just can't stay still."

I had finished off everything except the coffee by this point, and now I was working on that. "Karen," I asked between swallows, "just who are 'they' anyway?"

"I haven't the slightest idea," she responded, looking genuinely pained. "Some reporter, huh? Aside from a few staff people here that I really don't want to mess with, there's Doc Foo, two eunuchs who do everything she asks and otherwise couldn't add two plus two, eight scientists in various stages of, well, you know, including Kate, and a small staff here out of government central casting for running a spy hotel. Not many. Everything's really run by a machine. You can tell most of the prisoners from the players because nobody but staff is allowed to wear anything except sandals, and sometimes even staff, like Foo, don't. There's a ton of satellite stuff here, but that's in areas off-limits to me. You finished? If you're not too modest I'll show you around."

"You know I'm not modest, but I'm done." I got up and went toward the door.

"Better put the sandals on," she warned me. "Your feet aren't ready for some of this. There's a lot of uncomfortable areas, small rocks, that kind of thing, and where the sun hits it can get super hot."

She got up and looked over the tray, then put things back together and started pushing it out.

"You're barefoot," I pointed out.

"Yeah, but I don't feel anything anymore on the soles of my feet. Like hard calluses. It's along one side of both my hands, too. Makes 'em a little stiff for some uses, but it's like instant karate or whatever it is. Instead of pounding my feet and hands in sand for months or years, you oughta see how many boards or bricks I can break."

I took the hint, went back over, and slipped on the sandals. They were uncomfortable and I instantly hated wearing them, but I had a feeling I should keep them on for the moment.

The hallway was typical hotel as well, with perhaps a dozen rooms, six on each side, ending at a spiral staircase and a kind of shaftless elevator. The thing had only a floor, and sides a meter high; it went up and down on an exposed magnetic track system. It remained comfortable, though, with some cool air-conditioning blowing through, even though it definitely seemed open somewhere to the outside. Karen pushed the cart on the elevator but didn't get in herself. I started to get on but she stopped me and gestured to the stairs.

"You really don't want to be on that thing if the lava moves," she commented.

She was right. Suddenly I didn't want to ride it at all.

The elevator surprised me by descending into a black hole of sorts. I'd thought the dungeon floor was the basement, but apparently the computer stuff and many of the service areas were deeper still.

One floor above, things opened up into what looked very much like any Caribbean hotel lobby. The heat and humidity overpowered you almost immediately. It was a very wide area, open in the center to the outside, and with a kind of tile-and-board walkway going around that center under a semi-roof that pitched away. The central area had a lot of tropical plants in it, and a nice stream that ran through it and down a small cascade to an opening on the other side.

Unlike a hotel, there was no reception area or cashier, just some outdoor furniture.

I instantly knew that she was right about the sandals. I could feel the heat through them, and I couldn't resist spitting on the floor to see if it would bubble up and prove to be above the boiling point. It didn't and it wasn't, but I didn't want to sit down on it anyway.

The eeriest part was how deserted the whole place seemed to be; there were no sounds other than the rushing water and some tropical birds and bugs; no sense of being lived in, either.

We walked around to the other side, following the stream, and then over a small footbridge and suddenly things opened up onto a sculptured garden. Nature had been the sculptor, at least for much of it, but it was still impressive.

Spires and cones and all sorts of colors met in an alien fairyland of shapes and sizes, all shouting "Volcanic!" at you, with palm trees and tropical flowers and bushes all around to set it off. In the distance was the sheer cliff leading up, not that far, to the jagged cone that seemed to have some steam coming out of it.

"It's always steaming," Karen reassured me. "They say they have all sorts of monitors and such and that the whole thing will give warning if it ever wants to go off again and that, if it does, the odds are it'll go off in the opposite direction. I'm not so sure they can predict that, but they also say that it only goes off, according to the record, every two hundred years or so, so we've got a long time until the next one. Right or wrong, not much we can do. The only way off has a cliff down to the ocean that's *twice* that steep."

As I followed her down a well-sculpted path, not knowing where we were going to wind up, but starting to feel the heat and humidity more than I expected, I asked her, "Any others like your Dr. Foo? I mean, not quite human?"

She laughed. "Or, as the doc says, 'human plus'? Not exactly, although I think some of the folks passing through here are already being programmed or whatever you might call it to turn into some other things. You got to watch the doc, too, by the way. Those suction cups really do work; I've seen her walk straight up a wall, if slowly, and I think that, while she's basically still an air breather, she can breathe water through small gills in a pinch. Neat, if you don't mind the makeover."

"Might be hell getting dates, too," I commented.

"Maybe not. She can bend in directions nobody else ever dreamed."

I was beginning to wonder if they had everything as perfected as they wanted to make it appear. Maybe you could make a creature, even a practical one, out of somebody else or even from scratch for all I knew, but there was little evidence that the process didn't neuter you. If so, it had very limited appeal, and even less use if you were going to colonize Mars or whatever.

Maybe that was why they needed some fresh scientific blood. Or maybe they were dying out and getting desperate.

That still, of course, left the mystery of who "they" were and why "they" were doing all this.

We came upon a tree-shaded grotto sculpted from the volcanic landscape, and in the center was a gorgeous and not quite natural freshwater pool. It was very large, but nature didn't make kidney-shaped pools and around it were shaded lounges and tables and the like, as well as a bar area with one of the eunuchs tending it. On the far side were two openings going into the rock, both curiously circular and somewhat unnatural-looking, but I wasn't sure about them.

"Lava tubes," Karen told me, guessing my question. "Off-limits to us. Hard to say where they go or what they might keep in there, but I've never seen anybody go inside except the doc. I think she may live in one of them. It'll be a damn sight cooler and probably wet in there."

Speaking of unusual-looking people, there were all nine of them around the pool, although at the moment nobody was in it. The blue and white striped zebra-woman was there, along with a guy who looked like he got much the same treatment. With them were the green and amphibian-looking Sandra McCall and another frog-woman, clearly sharing her fate; the guy with the gray blue complexion and the growths; a woman I hadn't seen before with much the same type of coloration and growths; the mottled African American woman whose coloration was beginning to look more natural and who, it appeared, was growing fine straw-colored hair from her waist down while also having that part thicken up in a muscular way the same as Karen, although Karen showed no animal hybridization characteristics; a guy with very similar characteristics although his lower-body hair was a dark reddish-brown color; and Kate, gorgeous as ever, even if she did seem to be growing short but uniform strawberry-blond hair all over her body, except on her behind and breasts and palms and probably the soles of her feet. She also seemed a little off balance or something, but I couldn't really place what was wrong yet. Still, it was interesting that she was unique among the group, the rest of whom were paired up, even if both the froggies were female.

Most of them had the remnants of drinks or snacks nearby, and as soon as Karen got in among them she was going around asking them if she could get them anything, all that. She was open and friendly but it seemed to me that she was a bit too eager to wait on people and almost seemed to enjoy her role as waitress. I also had the feeling that she had no sense of having changed at all in the personality department, and that was worrisome. For all her new physical strength and the confidence that it brought, I got the impression that there was no longer any rebellion in her whatsoever. She could question but not dig for answers; she could dislike her job, but never consider not doing it.

I wondered if the others had been similarly treated. It seemed a good way to get technicians, but not the kind of people who'd work day and night to solve your problems with new and creative ideas.

I was oddly self-conscious that I wasn't anything or anybody but myself. I felt like a common crow in among a grouping of colorful macaws.

I went over close to Kathryn Marshall, who was relaxing in the shade, apparently dozing and unaware we'd come.

This close I could see that the process was working other changes, subtly, yet at an unbelievable speed if my sense of time was correct. Her arms seemed to be slightly longer than they should have been, and her feet were about halfway in their turn into apelike hands. It was kind of like looking at a museum exhibit of *Homo erectus*; not any kind of ape-human I'd ever seen in the flesh, but a definite step backward in physical evolution, or so it seemed.

"Hello, Kate," I said, wondering if it was worthwhile waking her.

She stirred a bit, then opened one eye, saw me, and then opened both in surprise. "Oh, my God! Chuck!" She sounded almost embarrassed and sat up, straddling the chaise lounge. It wasn't a particularly "natural" position from my point of view; the legs were almost at right angles to me, as if attached to the hip on ball joints, but it seemed so natural to her she hadn't even realized it.

"Sorry if I startled you. I assumed you knew they nabbed me."

"Um, yes, sort of. There was talk, but nobody'd seen anybody new, not even poor Karen."

I pulled over a chair and sat down, almost regretting it. It had pads, but it was still hot on a bare bottom. I survived.

"Why do you say 'poor Karen'?" I asked her.

"Well, surely you've noticed. She's sort of our personal servant. You want something, ask Karen. She can go places we can't, and get things we can't, because she's got the limits set inside her brain somewhere and other than that, well, her job is to make us comfortable. It's a lot easier than this, this— transformation, I guess is the best word. It's astonishing. I still can't believe somebody got this far this fast, and that nobody else knew."

Well, I'd confirmed one feeling. I still couldn't trust Kate, or any of the others, either, for much the same reason, but I suspected that their physical changes were more than sufficient to keep them in line. Where were they going to run now?

"I thought you told me that this was impossible. I even remember the term. Pleiotropy. Eighty-thousand-plus genes in the human body, change just a few and you change everything because the same genes work in different sequences to do different jobs."

She nodded. "That's the truth. Only someone *solved* it. I can't imagine who or how. Some of the finest minds on this planet worked on the problem and determined that the encoding sequences were too interrelated and too complex to ever get beyond a certain point. We could grow livers and kidneys and hearts, maybe, and that is tough enough and fails more than it works, but a whole human? Even a dog or cat? There's no mind in all of cryptography who could solve that, especially when it would be on a unique one-to-one basis, since all of us except identical twins are genetically distinct. And yet, here we are."

"And you still don't know how they did it, or who?"

"No. I've had some hints in talking with Foo and comparing notes with the others, but nothing has yet slipped out. I'm sure it's a government project, but whether it's our government or what, I don't know. But, Chuck, I told you, I was there when Chameleon was organized, when it met, and when it was disbanded. I swear to you that even if we'd gotten the go-ahead we couldn't possibly have done this in the time since. This wasn't *developed*. It's not from a program. It's the result of someone's single, probably accidental, breakthrough."

I nodded. She'd actually said the magic word, and it wasn't *genetics* or *adaptation* or *pleiotropy* or anything else. It was *cryptography*. That's what solving the DNA riddle had been in the first place. And the center of cryptological research for more than eighty years had been on land that once held the big Fort Meade army base. And programs and research on the fastest supercomputers were also right in that area, even if they did have a bunch of experts from Pittsburgh involved.

Had they been building the world's biggest, fastest, most truly awesome thinking machine there, and had somebody tried something brand-new in computer processing means and methods, and had they thrown it the human genome mapping just to run some theoretical problems and gotten more than they bargained for?

Yeah, it might have happened that way, and what if it did? How did it get from that point to this?

I looked around at the others, most of whom had noticed me and were pretending not to stare, but I knew that introductions were in order as soon as possible. Still, looking them over briefly, I turned back to Kate and asked, "Aside from the obvious servants here, have you seen any logic to these forms? Any consistency?"

She shook her head. "I'm not at all certain. The quasi-amphibians are interesting in that they are hermaphrodites. Both male and female. They're a kind of in-between life-form, a designer form that I keep thinking of as a bridge. They can breathe water, but with limitations, and they're basically air breathers. They retain the mammalian sexual characteristics, but have means to both impregnate and be impregnated. The gray ones are either male or female, but from the coloration and the cartilage developing on them as well as other emerging characteristics, I suspect they are going to be aquatic creatures of some kind, maybe dolphins with hands or something like that. The others—well, I'm watching them develop, like me, and trying to see where it goes. As for myself, I'm not only getting rather apelike, as you can't help but notice, but I'm starting to get urges to climb trees and other things."

I looked over at them. "All geneticists?"

"And medical researchers of one or another kind. Two M.D.s, a Ph.D. in pharmacology, another in sociology, and including myself, five geneticists from different backgrounds and types of research. And I can tell you, we geneticists feel like we're back in grade school seeing *this*."

"I can imagine. Well, might as well do introductions. At least until Herself shows up and decides what the hell she's going to do with me." I stopped a moment. "Unless she's already done the job on me and, like Karen, I just don't know it."

Kate shook her head. "No, I could tell. Dr. Foo is not terribly subtle in these matters, nor, I think, is she ever troubled by conscience. That's what worries me about those behind this. I keep being afraid that there's not a conscience in the group."

With that cheery thought, I finally got introduced around. The zebra-type couple were Lucille Baranof, a molecular biologist, and William Sandhill, an M.D. and medical researcher involved in developing new delivery systems for genetic treatments of humans. Other than the fact that they had really obvious coloration and, according to them, they felt increasingly younger, in better shape, and were also developing abnormally large sexual features, they seemed the least changed on the genetic level. Still, blowing at least part of my theory, the couple, who'd not known each other before being pretty much abducted here, found themselves, shall we say, overpoweringly physically attracted to each other.

The two blue gray ones who'd pretty much lost their hair and were developing more backbone than I'd think was useful were George Mecouri, a former professor of sociology at Harvard who had been on sabbatical working on a book, and Myra Zelkov, a geneticist specializing in creating pollution-resistant breeds of edible fish and shellfish. Mark Kolodny was the pharmacologist, and he was convinced that he was turning into some sort of Pan or satyrlike creature and he had no idea why. He did know that he was undergoing the same sort of sexual growth and interests as Sandhill was with Baranof, only the object of Kolodny's affection was Alice Thomas, the African American woman who seemed to be developing less a goatlike and more a catlike lower half, but she was also finding him, and maybe not just him, very attractive. That left Sandra McCall as frog-woman number one, and, to my surprise, Lawrence Kohl as frog-woman number two. I was startled to hear a male voice from someone with developing female characteristics, but then I remembered that Kate had said the race was hermaphroditic. Still, it was impressive that they could do this so quickly with two such genetically different people as an XX and an XY. Both of them were not only geneticists, they had both worked in the labs at Genetique.

I had hoped at least that somebody from that now accursed genetics lab might be able to tell me more information, but it wasn't to be.

"Yes, they did begin feeding us a great many experimental problems," McCall admitted, "but we never dreamed that anybody had gotten this far."

I frowned. "So what kind of problems? Don't spell them out—if somebody yells 'Doctor!' here I'm the only one who won't automatically turn around—but in general. How to build a mermaid? That kind of thing?"

"No, nothing like that. It was more like, 'Here's how we think a mermaid would be built, so test this sequence by developing stem cells for it and report the results.' "

"Did they develop into anything?"

"Most died or misfired, but a few, a very few, appeared to develop into something stable and predictable. That's the best I can give you, since looking at a cluster of cells from an organism you've either created or don't know the origins of doesn't tell you much about what they might be. You need much larger and more diverse tissue samples to even guess at it. We'd send off the results, and, after a while, something else would come down and we'd go again. We never knew who was sending them or from where, but Dr. Foo's name was on some of them. The first and, before this, the only time I ever heard it."

"Same here," Kohl agreed. "And then, well, they had this so-called accident. Now I know it was staged, but then it was just scary. A seam ripped, just a wee bit, in the lab e-suit while I was working on a sample. I was quarantined, of course, and the robotic monitoring systems took samples and injected me with stuff, I *thought* to treat and contain. Turns out it was doing *this* to me. Then Sandy had a similar thing happen, and we were put in adjacent containment sections. After we both turned green, as it were, we were offered positions with a project that would allow us some freedom in isolation on a Pacific research station, or so they said. We accepted. We were pretty scared and very naive, so what could we do?"

"And your families bought it?"

As it turned out, none of them really had families. Several were orphans who'd never married or had any lasting relationships, others were estranged from distant family members, that sort of thing. In no case, particularly if they got a Christmas card every year, would anybody really miss them except their coworkers, and they all knew about security clearances, and new and mysterious positions opening up and the like, and would be more curious than prying. So that deduction had been right on the money: these people weren't randomly selected, they were recruited without their knowledge. Recruited, then placed in positions where they just couldn't refuse.

One wondered what would happen, though, if one of them had refused. That answer proved easy.

"We'd be in quarantine for life," Zelkov said flatly. "It was part of the risk of the jobs we had. All except poor George, of course. Sociologists don't tend to wind up in anything more risky than some rioting mob or remote settlement."

"Not even that, most times," George Mecouri responded. "I was writing a book, actually. I wasn't even doing a ton of research—I had grad students do that over the past couple of years under me. I was just organizing and writing the damned thing."

I looked at him, wondering what the pattern was that was changing him into something bluish gray and bony, and asked, "What was it on, if I might ask?"

"The reasons why social organizations of different sorts developed for different high-order species, including us, of course. Why some things would work in some circumstances and not others."

"Any particularly dramatic creatures outside of us you focused on?"

"Actually, yes. Marine mammals." He paused, then added, almost like the relationship hadn't occurred to him, "Speaking of which, I have to get back into some water here, and so does Myra. This skin blisters really badly if it's allowed to dry out too much."

TWELVE

It appeared that all of them had gathered mostly on a tip that I'd be making an appearance, and most of them were curious to know "as what." The fact that I'd appeared as myself had everyone as puzzled as it had me, although I still had a feeling they weren't telling me everything, at least not yet.

Nobody could really trust anybody here, and that probably suited our keepers just fine, but it was hell on social relations.

The two bluish gray types spent most of their time in pools or tubs. They certainly didn't have any sense that they could breathe water, but not keeping themselves pretty well wet and exposing themselves to too much sunlight apparently was potentially very painful. I saw what Kate meant about them possibly turning into "dolphins with hands."

The pair who were turning into frog-type people, which, I discovered, Foo called Anurians, apparently after the scientific order frogs were in, didn't particularly feel like they needed to be in a pool but they very much liked being in the water; it felt natural and quite comfortable to them. However, so did moist, dark places, so you couldn't make any real judgments.

I couldn't help but notice that, while they were still far from turning into the complete sort of Anurian or whatever you wanted to call it that Foo was—although they were further along than any of the others by virtue of having started earlier—they were on the way to looking a lot like twins, even though they'd started out as different sexes with different body weights. Kate suggested that the only way to get these kinds of dramatic results this fast was to use some kind of template, some sort of genetic reprogramming system that would rely on creating a standard set of characteristics.

But that begged the question of why do it at all, particularly when just turning them green or striped or whatever would have been enough incentive. What was the hurry to "accelerate" their changeover, even at the cost of using uniform templates? Unless . . .

Unless all of them, even Karen, were experiments-in-progress.

But experiments to what end?

I also found myself a bit more popular in ways I hadn't expected, among a couple of them, anyway. It was kind of a weird position for me to be in there; both the overendowed, if striped, Lucy Baranof and the leopardish nymph that was developing as the new Alice Thomas didn't seem satisfied with just their existing male counterparts. They both came on to me whenever they could, and I got the idea that Kate was feeling a bit angry and maybe jealous about it even though we hadn't ever had anything but a professional relationship. Though my Italian ancestors had endowed me with equipment to maintain the ethnic reputation, I was extremely unused to being regarded by anybody, at any time, as a boy toy or sex stud.

Even more interesting was that their matched boyfriends didn't seem to mind it all that much, or accepted it as natural behavior. In a sense, that made it more awkward.

The only thing I could be thankful for was that neither the frog folks nor the water people seemed to share in this.

The "hotel" staff, however, wasn't immune from this, I discovered, although if any succumbed I never knew it. They were exactly the sort of folks I expected to be in charge here: humans, agent types, all business, no sense of humor, even if they did forgo their usual suits for shorts, sport shirts, and sunglasses.

I guessed there were maybe a dozen of them, half men and half women, but they tried not to be obviously there, and often went out of their way not to interact with any of us. I got the distinct impression that they wanted us out of there as quickly as possible if not yesterday, and that the guests, in particular, made them very uncomfortable.

I had to admit I had no such prejudice; if I could have figured out a way to do it with all three without getting anybody else upset I'd surely have done so. But I was discovering that horny scientists are still scientists; even as they got the urges they kept trying to figure out *why*. Something to do with the chemistry of sexual attraction and stimulation. I left that to them, particularly the pharmacologist, Kolodny.

Eating was kind of like it was on a cruise ship: when you were hungry, you told Karen and she got whatever you wanted, within reason. They did, after all, have to have it and be able to prepare it, and apparently the gourmet chef was off that week. Still, it wasn't bad, for hotel food.

My tastes hadn't changed, nor, indeed, had Karen's, but some of the others definitely were into diet shifting. The two water-types tended to go for raw fish and raw sea grains and grasses. I wondered how long it would be before they began eating the fish bones, heads and all, and, eventually, eating them still alive. The froggies tended to eat almost anything, literally, without much regard for it, but they ate a fair amount of stuff. Kate, who was now a vegetarian, hadn't much trouble with fruits and vegetables, although she found she no longer liked anything cooked or prepared. Coconuts, plantains, and bananas, citrus, even, as it turned out, a number of leaves from certain plants and trees, all of those were fine. The satyr and his cat-woman tended to like meat, extra rare or even raw, and the zebras tended to eat a lot of what the rest of us considered mostly grass.

Me, I started having weird dreams. They were sort of the same in one way, but never quite. Each time I'd dream that I woke up and I was changing into something or somebody else. Mostly these were creatures that I knew existed, including our late and apparently unlamented bat-man, but sometimes I'd be one of the eunuchs, or like Karen, or like one of the others. A few recurring ones were to wake up a member of the opposite sex, which probably said more about my psychological state of mind or self-image than anything, and, every once in a while, I'd become something I never saw, normally something monstrous, but occasionally I'd be something common, like a dog or cat or horse, that nobody could guess had ever been a human.

All of this was fed by boredom and uncertainty. And, of course, there was the ultimate paranoia, that little spot near the hairline in the top center of the forehead.

"We all got one," Karen told me. "Nobody knows what it is 'cause when the bandage falls off there's only that tiny dimpled bump. See mine? The medical docs here say it looks like the kind of thing left by a minute robot-directed brain catheter, but nobody knows what it might have done."

The idea of anything having drilled into my skull and then roamed around in that area, particularly that area, where thoughts and ideas got assembled and personality happened, was maybe the most unnerving idea of all. Foo had assured them all that it was just some kind of ID placed just inside the skull, but nobody believed that this kind of risk in that sort of place would be used for a mere identification chip. On the other hand, it seemed unlikely that it could plug into or do anything to the thinking process itself; holographic memory, on which I'd done more than one series of articles and a documentary, was much too tricky for that.

Still, was it any more tricky than manipulating eighty-thousand-to-the-eighty-thousandth genetic combinations and coming up with even a few like the ones we were seeing?

Mark Kolodny, the pharmacologist, had what may have been the most likely idea, although it, too, was unsettling. The introduction of a small amount of some chemical cocktail via that route was more than possible, it was somewhat common. And there were media that would remain there, which the body would not expel, and which could, in a pinch, transmit many basic commands to the rest of the brain through the connections to the frontal lobe. This method had been known for years, he told me, but was prohibited by international treaty and conventions since it was a very efficient way to control someone. Not that it could erase anything or convince you that you were someone you weren't or that kind of thing, but it could be used, with a good enough computer-program interconnect, to create a simple series of filters that would influence or block certain aspects of personality. Add genetic propensity toward these kinds of behaviors to their gene-treatment cocktails and you could quite easily create a very different personality without the subject even knowing it, or realizing that the change was taking place.

Clearly this was describing Karen, but it didn't have to be used the same way on the others. It could reduce or filter out your inhibitions to eating raw meat still dripping with blood, or reinforce a predisposition to dark, damp places, or give you an assist in learning different capabilities and senses of a changing body.

And I had it inside me, too. That was not a pleasant thought this early in my captivity.

And suddenly I realized that this was missing among all nine of them, or even ten counting me.

"There aren't any computer people," I noted to several, including Kate. "No repair types, no programmer or developmental types, zippo. You all use computers—we all do, in a world that would collapse without them—but where's the technicians, the maintenance people? If all this boils down to cryptography, whether genetics or pharmacology, then where's the tools to break and redo the codes? Who was creating those experiments for Genetique and, I bet, a hundred other such companies worldwide?"

There was no real answer to that, but one more deduction was clear: they weren't here because somebody didn't need them. They needed these people, for one or another purpose, but they didn't need computers. Had the old nightmare taken place? Were machines running this show? Was that why we couldn't figure anything out?

Speaking of running the show, Dr. Foo was not with us

much. She stayed down in those lava tubes a lot of the time, leading me to believe that there were other places you could go from them, but the couple of times I looked them over I saw that they didn't go too far in until they started to go very steeply down, and, not having suction-cup hands and feet, I wasn't about to try anything.

I did get the idea, as did the rest, that now and again one of our number was being taken someplace for some reason, but nobody ever remembered these sessions, just had vague half memories like you did after some general anesthetics.

After a couple of days, I took to using some of Karen's equipment and working out a bit. I was almost afraid at the impulse, since it was a foreign idea to me, but the fact was I found it as unpleasant and painful as I remembered and that thought never changed.

The only other thing it did was make me decide that long, slow walks were better for me than exercise machines, and they gave me a chance to explore the place, or as much of it as I was allowed. I knew I would never really be out of somebody's sight, and I wasn't trying to escape. Rather, I was trying to get the lay of this mystery installation.

Most frustrating was a place I named Heartbreak Overlook. It was through the dense jungle foliage and then maybe fifty meters forward at a distinctly lung-straining upward slope of barren basalt, but at the top you could look out and see the rest of the Caribbean.

There were always sailboats out there, which, I suspected, were fairly good-sized to be seen from this height, and occasional big ocean liners, cruise ships to various exotic ports of alleged romance at a thousand dollars a day. In the distance at least two other islands, probably much bigger ones, were visible; exactly which I wasn't sure, but we were in that area where the Dutch, English, and French used to harvest their cane and that now catered more to the rich and famous than the islands that were better known.

Also, if I dared get too close to the edge, I could see a mixed basalt and obsidian cliff that was sheer and at least a kilometer, perhaps more, down to a very tiny rocky reef below. Even the greatest diver was never going to try this one, and I wasn't sure even Foo's suction cups would be secure on that vertical, shiny, glasslike obsidian.

I wanted to be out there, though. Anywhere out there.

After a week on that rock, the only changes in myself that I could see were that I was suntanned almost to black all over, something I'd gotten genetically from the usual places, like my parents and other ancestors, and my paunch was definitely less. I wasn't sure if that was a program or simply the result of regular good diet and at least some regular exercise; probably the latter. Still, to have no painful spots or nonuniform browning even with no sunblock, and my getting sufficiently toughened on my feet to actually not use the sandals much anymore suggested some subtle changes. Not dramatic; by this time the rest of them had been green or hairy or gray blue or whatever.

"It's probably a protective for you delivered in your food," Kate Marshall told me. "That's the most common way to deliver things like that. I wouldn't fight that at all. In fact, you're looking years younger and in very good shape. If that's what they had done to any of us, I don't think we'd have complained, and everything I've seen so far in your changes has been within the technology I know."

My always-heavy body hair was growing back pretty much where it should and as thick as ever, but I was a newborn compared to Kate. Palms, soles, genitals, and ass, the ends of two very firm breasts, and areas of the face were the only parts of her not covered with a thick but very short reddish brown fur. Her feet had developed into mirror images of her hands, although a couple of sizes larger. Her legs were at least triple jointed; she could be sitting and scratch her head with either foot if she wanted to. The skin on her face had toughened, thickened, and darkened slightly, but it was still her face and it was still an attractive one. Walking on one's hands wasn't as natural as using feet, and when she walked she did so slightly bowlegged, not as extreme as a chimp but something like that, and her somewhat-elongated arms that looked fairly normal when she was sitting reached almost to the ground when she walked slowly bowed. She was painfully self-conscious of it, but I suspected she'd cried herself out on all of it before now.

"I've been practicing doing things with my feet," she told me. "They feel just like hands, too, but the soles are tough from being walked on, so they don't have the full dexterity of the palms. Other than that, no difference. It's very odd, but convenient."

I couldn't imagine what it must have felt like, but I knew that all of them were undergoing some sort of trauma, no matter how much the whatever-it-was in the brain lessened the strain. Maybe it kept you from killing yourself. Even I felt guilty as sin. I mean, here were all these nice folks, M.D.s and Ph.D.s and the like, going through all this, and me . . . all I was doing was feeling younger and getting better-looking.

The zebras now appeared to be growing a second set of arms in a slightly elongated torso and a second set of breasts to go with it, particularly overkill in Lucy's case, and they both also seemed to be growing thick but unremarkable-looking tails from the base of their spinal columns. The froggies continued to develop more and more into clones of Dr. Foo, only with a more uniform, and, frankly, more amphibian-like face. Kolodny was looking so much like the Greek god Pan, even to developing little horns on his head, that he was thinking of requesting a flute, while Alice was becoming a kind of leopard from the waist down, including growing a now stubby, but probably not for long, catlike tail, while her upper part was a camouflage-designed nymph. Our water pair seemed to be developing as Kate had guessed; their legs were already merging and their feet were turning to horizontal fins, and the bony stuff was developing into a slight bony ridge supporting a stabilizing fin. There were signs, too, that while their faces had changed least so far, a blowhole was developing along the back of the head. Interestingly, unlike the froggies, their hands were not webbed but were growing a bit oversized on thinner arms and the whole of the arms and hands could be held in tight against the body to produce streamlined swimming of a sort.

I couldn't figure out where I fit in all this. I couldn't even be the control; I mean, not with them slipping me skin protection and pot-belly remover in my salads and baked potatoes.

I had tried to stay close to Kate. She alone had no counterpart, no similarly changing individual with whom to commiserate, and she needed to feel like she was still herself. To go from such a good-looking fashion plate to the Missing Link had to be especially traumatic.

I will, however, call her game. She was trying to adjust, and if she had to be an ape, then she was going to find out what an ape could do. Using the long, strong arms and nearly identical legs and feet, she went up some of the tall trees in nothing flat, and found that jumping from one to another and judging distances and strengths of limbs and the like were automatic. And from the tops of those trees she could also see far more than I could from Heartbreak Overlook, not to mention the tops of the resort as well. With no animals about more serious than birds and insects, thanks to that volcano, she had little hesitation in moving around where, she thought, even "they" might not be able to fully see and track her.

I doubted that; if nothing else, this implant, or whatever it was, certainly was a coded tracer. My ace detectives (thanks for nothing, group!) had said that. Of course, they also said that Rita's brother or somesuch was a prisoner here, and, if he was, he sure wasn't with the help. The two eunuchs were both Caucasians, and while there were a couple of African ancestry types in the permanent party I hardly thought that they would be likely candidates for prisoners.

Still, Kate had something to do, something only she could do, and it helped her self-esteem no end while giving me information as well. She began exploring the forest of mini-satellite transmitters and receivers—and that was the term used, *forest*—over on a plateau that didn't appear to be accessible from the main resort, along with the two antennae of some kind, complete with aircraft warning lights, that appeared to sit right on the rim of the volcanic crater.

It wasn't like the old days where you needed big dishes to receive a ton of stuff; digital streams at light speed could be sent and received by rather small and hardly-dish-shaped devices now. To have a forest of them meant an enormous amount of information was being moved, and routinely. Hmmm . . . How many data streams to accommodate all the combinations of eighty thousand genes?

Kate was in the best mood I'd seen her in since this all started after doing these explorations. "There's such a sense of freedom when I'm up there," she told me. "I can't really explain how it feels."

"And you never were afraid of falling?"

"Never! It just doesn't enter your head. You just know, that's all." She grew a bit more serious. "You know, I'd never choose this form or this look. I'm not sure what I'd choose if they gave me the catalog. I'm sure there's more than we see here. But there's two of me, really. One's the human woman, always thought of as attractive and who knew it and liked it, and the other's the scientist, whose whole knowledge of the field has been reduced to the equivalent of first grade, but who's now getting a chance to experience, and maybe eventually practice, what she had thought was a century away. The others are going through similar soul searches. I think that's why they've left us here to develop and do little else. They need scientists, not robots. To get them, they need us to answer 'yes' to the question 'If this new nonhuman existence is the price of working at a level in your field you barely dreamed of, will you accept that?' "

"Well," I responded, "you're still human enough for me, if that makes a difference."

She looked at me. "It makes—a lot of difference, Chuck."

Okay, so I eventually succumbed to temptation. I heard the occasional whispers from the not-quite-out-of-sight staff about a "freak show" and "bestiality" and all that, but

I couldn't see most people that way, never could, and I definitely couldn't see any of these people, Kate in particular, as anything less than human. In fact, it was really more damage to my ego than anybody else's concern, since there was no way I could fully satisfy the kind of pent-up appetites these folks had. Still, I discovered that the friendly-but-distant manner all except Kate had had toward me vanished after that. I became a member of the club, so to speak, not because I looked the part but because it hadn't mattered. I thought it was kind of ironic that finally fitting in was due to my doing what I'd been suppressing as inappropriate up to now.

Much of the heavy weight on Kate's ego also seemed to lift after that; she became companion and not just friend, and she seemed to shed the last of her abhorrence for what she had been turned into and began embracing and exploring the capabilities it offered instead. Some of that worried me.

"You ought to have seen me up there today!" she said excitedly. "I climbed at least a quarter of the way up that nearly sheer face on the side opposite the antennae. I know I could have gone all the way. I was as sure on the rock as I am in the trees."

"You fall and that's it," I warned her. "Don't get overconfident. It hasn't been long enough to rely fully on any instinct they might have built into you!"

"Oh, stop worrying! I tell you it's no more of a problem to me than you walking back to your room from the pool. I bet I could get up to the caldera or all the way down to the beach if I wanted!"

I thought I should put a damper on this kind of thinking. "And then what?"

"Huh?"

"And then what? So you're down on the beach way below. You don't fall, you're fine. Then what?"

She sighed, seeing my point, and it really took something out of her. "I climb back up. You're right. Just what I want to do for the rest of my life. Appear on video freak shows as the monkey-girl."

"I'm sorry," I told her honestly. "I didn't want to disappoint you, but the fact is that rescue is not what we're after at the moment. Sure, I'd love to be able to contact the outside, to report things so far, but even I don't want to leave. I don't want to leave you, either, and I don't want to walk away without finding out the answer to all this."

She gave me a quick peck on the cheek. "How's it feel to have a monkey-girl falling in love with you?"

"A heck of a lot better than with my last ex," I told her. "There's a reason why a guy with a Pulitzer and production shares in some high-rated documentaries was living in a barely furnished one-bedroom apartment in Laurel."

She laughed, then remarked, "The thing is, we all have to get out of here. We have to move on somewhere. If we keep on here, with nothing to do, nothing to look forward to, nothing to explain anything, then we'll rot. I don't think they did this because they wanted to create an ape-woman. I think they wanted a geneticist who could climb and move like I can. I'm convinced of it. The Anurians are there because they need land-and-sea type creatures with certain capabilities. The Delphinides in the pool turning into a new kind of aquatic mammal, ditto."

"Yeah? So explain the four-armed zebras and the leopard-woman and the satyr," I responded. "They don't seem to have any major functions at all except to be what they appear to be. They can do their jobs, certainly, but they could do that without being those kinds of creatures. It still makes no sense."

She nodded. "You know, there was something in the original Chameleon think tanks about processes for developing complex working forms. I hadn't thought of it in years, since it was so far in the future I was sure it wasn't something I'd live to see, let alone be. There wasn't even enough computing power in the world to figure out half the angles. Still, the progression was to computer model, using combinations of humans and working higher animals. Mars and other biomes would require whole new life-forms, but the start would be to see if we could actually come up with working, functioning, hybrids. And that's what we all are, really—hybrids. A lot of the proposal and planning documents used Greco-Roman mythology because their creatures were mostly hybrids of one sort or another. Mermaids, flying horses, centaurs, satyrs—you see what I mean?"

I nodded. "Glad nobody put Medusa in there."

"I suspect the snakes for hair would have been more trouble than they were worth," she responded good-naturedly. "Still, who knows what else they've cooked up? After this I don't think I can be surprised much more."

As close as Kate and I were becoming, she was much more comfortable in daytime than I was, and I tended to use the late-night or early-morning hours to mostly cool off and relax. The nightmares didn't have me sleeping very well, and it gave me a chance to be just with my own thoughts and not have to worry about the harsh sun, although we did get quite regular doses of heavy rain squalls going through as well. Those tended to renew the vegetation and refresh the water and particularly the stream that went through the resort. Normally I didn't even bother to run for shelter when they came up, although when the thunder and lightning came around I tended to seek out plastic furniture on inlaid stone well away from the pool or the jungle areas.

It wasn't like that this night. In fact, while there'd been an evening shower the skies were now quite clear, with only an occasional puffy cloud here and there, and there was a nearly full moon that made negotiating the, by now, well-worn trail through the woods to Heartbreak Overlook easy.

Many times Karen would come with me and we'd talk. I supposed that the only thing worse than having your life hijacked and turned into service was knowing that things were so very different and yet being unable to really get a handle on how much of a change you'd been through. She no longer compulsively exercised; she didn't have to. Her forty-five kilos of youthful-but-slight figure was now seventy or seventy-five kilos of pure muscle and, once attained, it stayed that way, making her appear almost as though made of stone or cement—squat and, well, dense looking. The skin was also tough. I'd seen her accidentally step on a heavy upturned nail and it was the nail that had bent. I picked it up and tried to unbend it but couldn't, and I was getting in pretty fair shape myself. She was as much a remade creation as the others, only to less effect, all for having too much nerve and ambition while having taken the wrong college major.

This night, though, I was alone. The earlier rain just before sundown had cooled things down a bit without them having time to heat back up, so the Overlook was tolerable even to my bare bottom, and I could sit there near the edge and look out at the lights of the ships and boats and the glows from the nearby islands and dream a bit.

"Psssst!"

At first I wasn't even sure I'd heard anything.

"Psssst!"

I turned around and looked, puzzled, at where the hisses had come from. Suddenly I saw a dark, amorphous mass just beyond the tree line and well off the jungle path. More curious than afraid, I got up and cautiously approached the person or thing making the noise.

"Hey, mon!" a voice whispered low, "Just come ovah near de bushes and sit. We dunno what kind of watch dey got on you here."

I went straight for him. *The hell with this!* I thought. These guys never did *me* any real favors. "Roger?"

"Shhhh! You want to give de whole show away?"

"The odds are pretty good they got the bugs permanently inside me anyway," I told him. "So when you hailed me, you probably hailed them. Either that, or nothing's here and nothing's listening. Now, what the hell are you doing suddenly popping up here after all this time?"

"Experiment," he replied, going to at least a quiet tone rather than an outright whisper. "I'm outfitted wit' de new chip. If dey can't find me on deir machines, den I'm invisible to dem. And if I'm invisible to dem, we can come and go here as we please."

"How'd you get here in the first place?"

"Parasail. Dat's de easy part. It's gettin' *off* dat's always been de problem."

"How did you find me?" I asked him.

"Partly from you. Dey couldn't purge *all* dem little t'ings dat embedded demselves in your tummy and colon. Matched it up wit' some independent intelligence we got, and here I am. You're lookin' really good, by de way. I t'ought you'd be purple polka-dotted by now."

"Thanks a lot." Frankly, so had I, but I wasn't going to give him the satisfaction. "But what are you going to do here even if you get away with this?"

"Depends. If we can plant our intercepts in wit' deir transmitters and receivers we'll have a big coup. If we can come and go we can plant and retrieve intelligence no matter what."

"So what are you going to do?"

"Reconnoiter. Survey. Look around. No big chances, just poke here and dere. And den get out'ta here. If I can, den we got it made."

I frowned. "How in hell are you going to get off?"

"Same way I got on, mon. Put 'em on, run right off dat cliff dere. Got two spares for you and de girl. We can deprogram her easy enough."

Maybe they could, but they couldn't turn her back into the Karen that was, nor restore what was taken from her in other areas, either. I wasn't at all sure that a deprogrammed Karen could live comfortably with what Dr. Foo had done to her.

I shook my head. "No, she's too far gone and I'm not prepared to leave now that I'm inside, until I know the answer."

"But when you do you probably won't be able to leave," Roger pointed out.

I shrugged. How could I tell him that the only two people I currently cared much about were both here? "I have to take that chance. Besides, as you say, I'm looking real good. Why risk it?"

"Okay, but dey gonna be movin' you all pretty soon. Maybe way beyond any place we could get."

"The ship's preparing to leave?"

"The ship! Dat's been gone a long time. Stopped once in Suriname, den went through de canal. It's sout' of Hawaii 'bout now. No, I t'ink you're all goin' someplace else by air, or so we figure. Lots of good strips off de beaten pat' in dis region where some money dropped in de right places will guarantee privacy. We got rumbles, but we can't stop it and dere ain't nobody else would want to."

"Suits me. We've been dying of boredom here, really."

"Okay, den. Up to you. But I'll put de extra paras here just in case you change your mind. Dey ain't hard to figure out, and if you land anywhere near one of dem boats out dere de'll get you someplace where you can call home. In de meantime, even if I get caught, you didn't see me. And watch out for dat Dr. Foo."

This I was interested in. "Got stuff on her?"

"Medical license lifted in six countries. Dat's almost a record. All for illegal or unethical chemical experimentation on humans. She's actually a jail escapee. Broke out of de one in Singapore wit', it's said, some inside help. Wanted posters all over China and South Asia."

"Well, they'll never recognize her now."

"Ah, maybe not. But you know she's related to anudder big overseas Chinese family wit' lotsa money and influence dere in Singapore. De Lings. I t'ink you know her cousin."

One more puzzle piece was suddenly swinging into place. Too bad it was a ten-thousand-piece puzzle, and I'd yet to find the master piece that would connect all the others. Still, here at last was a connection.

"I'd better be getting back," I told him. "Good luck."

"You, too, Vallone. You ain't got much sense—den, neider do I or I wouldn't be here now—but you got real guts."

I kind of appreciated that, but I wasn't at all sure it was true. I had this deep feeling that the best way to explain my actions so far was "stubbornness."

I started to say something else, but suddenly realized that Roger was gone. It was a good idea to break things off, but I kind of thought he'd at least say good-bye and I could tell him good luck or something. Still, I moved to where he had been and, with not much effort, I was able to move a rather nicely done cap of logs and leaves and see the packed parasails.

Now, I had never parasailed in my life and wasn't even positive what the hell they were, and I really felt like I didn't have the guts to put on one of those, hope I'd gotten it right, and take a running jump off the cliff, but it was nice to know that they were there and that Roger had at least been truthful on this part.

I carefully replaced the covering and walked back toward the overlook, but it had lost some of its allure. Now that there *was* a way, even if risky as all hell, to get out of here, and I knew I wouldn't take it unless it was my life at stake right then and there, looking out and wishing I was on some real resort near the horizon lost a lot of its appeal. Stubbornness, affection, loyalty, curiosity, or even fear of flying may be excuses, but the choice had been freely made.

I went back to the resort and without much pause walked straight to my room and collapsed on the bed.

I didn't see Roger, or anyone else who shouldn't have been on that island, again during this phase. I did hear the sounds of some conventional firearms from somewhere far off toward the inaccessible part of the island but I never knew if that was Roger being nailed or the staff practicing or even somebody far away and down below, ignorant of us, shooting skeet off the back of a boat or something. I did wish I had counted the parasails in that hideaway, though. I did go back the next night and find that two of them were there, but I wasn't sure if it had only been two or if there'd been three. Except for Roger's health, it didn't matter. By the time they invaded this place, and they certainly would at some point, we'd all be long gone.

Two days after Roger's brief visit, the helicopter arrived.

They didn't keep the chopper on the island; it appeared to

be parked at an airstrip or maybe even a commercial airport on a neighboring island and called in when needed, the better to control any alternate means of escape I supposed, so when it showed up it was always noticed. It had occurred to me that they never brought in supplies with the thing, but nobody ever seemed to run short here. That implied that there was indeed some ocean-level access, perhaps totally automated, for that sort of thing, but while Karen and the two big eunuchs had vanished once for several hours together, when they came back she wasn't able to tell me where she'd been or what she'd been doing. They had some routine for just blanking out periods when they needed to, possibly related to that damned chip implant whatever it was. Even I had lost a few hours here and there.

When the helicopter came in and landed on the pad, it was always surrounded and greeted by staff with automatic weapons, and there were also automated guns on the heights around it, kind of just in case. It never stayed long, and I never saw evidence of a pilot. It was almost certainly flown remotely, or entirely by computer; another safeguard. Ten to one anybody approaching it on the field where it was based got nastily surprised, too.

This time Dr. Foo herself was down there, so I knew that whoever was inside was either a prisoner or somebody important or both. She had her big muscle with her, so there was also something heavy to move.

The door on the sleek craft slid back, and a figure got out that was at first hard to make out. It looked a lot like a large man wearing some kind of cloak or cape, and I wished I had binoculars to see him closer up. He turned his back to us—all but the duo in the pool were as close as we were allowed, there not being much other change in our routine of late—and he suddenly looked like a large and somewhat shiny oval on nearly invisible legs. The big eunuch approached and was handed a large trunk, followed by a smaller rectangular case that was put on top. Whatever was in them did weigh a bit; I'd never seen one of the big guys strain before.

Then the newcomer turned and started walking toward the resort, which meant toward us, while Foo, much smaller, waddled along next to him having constant conversation with the newcomer, who now looked like a tall man in a kind of suit, wearing something large, black, and oval-shaped on his back. It was a very odd appearance, and his walk seemed slightly stooped and every bit as unusual as Foo's legs and flippers made hers.

As they grew closer, it was Kate who gasped first and said, in a hushed tone, "Oh, my God! It's some kind of giant *bug!*"

And, indeed, the closer they came, the more she was proven right. It was as if a great German cockroach had grown to maybe one-and-three-quarters of a meter tall and in proportion, then developed thick hind legs that allowed it to walk bipedally, with the underside up. And embedded in that underside was the complete appearance of a human male in pants and jacket. The center set of legs were held close to the torso and, being the same color as the back shell, were almost unnoticeable until you looked for them, and the forelegs, which were the arms and hands of the "human," were lighter in color, matching the human face. And, in fact, not only they but the face itself was functional.

The giant cockroach was smoking a cigar and also using it as a pointer.

"I have the feeling the boss has finally arrived," I told the others.

"I agree," Mark Kolodny, the satyr, put in. "Look at how Foo defers to him. She's been giving him reports."

As they came within the residence area, the helicopter gave a high-pitched whine and took off, then turned and headed out to sea, back to where it came from.

Up close, I still wasn't sure if the human part was originally the newcomer or was part of the design. The face looked real enough, kind of a heavyset Polynesian man, and the mouth sure worked, but there was a mass of, well, *stuff*, above it that extended, including some very imposing tendrils and maybe some insectlike eyes. The face looked like a classical Polynesian statue whose mouth moved, and, real close up, the body and clothes looked far less natural and were clearly part of the creature itself. The hind legs that could support it bipedally, though, were very thick and almost dinosaur-like, though smooth and black. The hands were more like soft pincers, but they could hold that cigar or most anything else, I suspected, and the center pair of appendages, located at the "waist," were long enough to interact and work with the lighter-colored top pair if need be.

The thing looked scary and monstrous as all hell, even to the other monsters. This was not mere experimentation; this was out of the *other* lab, the one that made the gargoyle that had stood on my porch peering through my French doors.

But it sure did seem to be enjoying puffing on that cigar.

It stopped as it reached us, and we could all feel that we were being looked over with minute attention to detail, although by what, or even which eyes, it was impossible to say.

As we gaped at one another, the "clothing" look vanished like it was on some kind of computerized sign and was replaced by a simulacrum of a large Polynesian man's naked torso, complete with, I assumed, simulated male organ. In many Pacific societies, this guy would only have to show up to be an absolute god even in the twenty-first century.

"Good day, everyone," he said at last, in a voice that was surprisingly deep and cultured, with a trace of British accent. "I am Halohe Kahota, but to make it easy on everyone just call me 'Hal.' Since most of you and most of those with whom you will work are doctors of one sort or another, we tend to avoid titles. First names, last names, nicknames, your choice. I apologize for not being with you earlier, but there was much to do, and more, alas, since things this time out got so *messy*. You will all be pleased to know that your exile here is coming to an end, and we shall be leaving this place tomorrow."

There was almost a tendency to cheer at that, in spite of the unknowns ahead. Anything was better than rotting, or so we all hoped.

"In addition to having a schedule to keep, the security of this station appears to have been compromised and so it won't be useful anymore anyway. I haven't seen you all yet, or the detailed reports and readouts, but it appears that our next-stage efforts have paid off as well as we hoped. You have come along in a few weeks at a pace that used to take us a similar number of years. I will be meeting with you in small groups or individually this afternoon and this evening. At that time, perhaps I can give you some answers to certain of your countless questions. The rest will have to await our arrival at our final destination."

I noted Karen coming close to me. "That's the voice," she whispered to me.

I frowned. "What voice?" I whispered back.

"The one on the phone. The one that tried to call you through the City Desk from East Baltimore."

I sighed. So this was the one who had been pushing the human and creature pins all over since this began. And, hell, if he stuck to the dark and the poorer sections of cities, even a six-foot German cockroach would hardly attract attention.

Well, he had our attention now. The problem was, we also had his attention, and he was definitely in charge.

THIRTEEN

"So you're the man who did in poor Hugo," the creature who called himself Hal said to me.

He'd called in the others pretty much as pairs, and he hadn't yet spoken to Kate or Karen, but me he wanted to speak to man-to-bug, as it were.

"I never did anybody in, except with a computer, by words in a column or feature," I responded. "And I don't believe I've ever even met somebody named Hugo. To me it's a name for cartoons and the last name of a great novelist."

Hal paused a moment, then said, simply, "Hugo was the one who could fly."

There was one of those pregnant silences at that statement, said in such a matter-of-fact, yet somewhat sad and wistful tone. All I could think of, finally, to respond, was, "I didn't kill him. He attacked a helicopter and the pilot defended himself. You know that."

"Yes, indeed I do. I suppose it's some guilt on my part, too. I knew I should never have brought him with me, but he could fly and he promised me that he would obey me implicitly. He just wasn't ready for civilization, I suppose."

"He had a temper," I noted.

I never knew a giant cockroach could clear his throat, or that he even had one as such, but this one did. "Um, yes. But, you see, with all that strength, and size, and power, he was really only a child."

"Some child! He was bigger than me!"

"True, but size, as someone once said, isn't everything. He

243

was only ten years old, and perhaps younger emotionally. I don't even think he thought about the deaths as such. It was just a game to him."

Another puzzle piece. Our flying friend hadn't been transformed via the latest medical technology as others had been; he'd been *designed*. "I'm sure Wasserman and the two cops, let alone the families of said cops, would find that less than a mitigating factor," I noted. "What about *their* kids?"

"Nobody was supposed to be killed! Nobody except Wasserman, of course, and he was committing treason. The others were simply supposed to be stopped and the sample case taken. As I think you know, the mere sight of Hugo was enough to scare most people half to death. But they tried to run him down, and he lost his temper. Had I been there, it might have been different, but I was stuck picking up *our* samples back at Genetique. Hugo wasn't even supposed to go after them. He simply heard me shouting orders to the security team and decided he could please us by doing it himself. As I said, he was simply a young boy. Very sad."

"Any more at home like him?"

"He was the first one who could fly. I told you that. *I* was supposed to be able to fly. The computer models all say I can. Unfortunately, the amount of energy I have to expend to stay up is greater than the amount I can take in, at least for any meaningful distance, and my ability to steer aloft is even worse. The best we've been able to achieve has been a few gliders designed from the basic high-primate template, but they're extremely limited."

"Just who exactly are you?" I asked him, deciding on the direct approach.

He paused a moment, then replied, "I am your tax dollars at work. An alliance of government and industry, unfettered by so-called ethicists and alleged Luddites, who want to push the envelope on all facets of creation. We're the genie that escaped from the bottle that society and politicians decided should be shoved back in, only you can't shove something back in once it's out. There were seventeen nations involved in Project Chameleon, Vallone. Some of them were barely sociable then, but it was thought that if we all cooperated in space exploration and colonization then we'd evolve into one big happy peaceful family. A few of those nations are very unfriendly now, and they've got money and expertise. We built nine so-called neutral research installations beyond the usual snooper's range. That meant hidden behind Third World fronts or in nations you can't just pop into for a visit and travel around."

That much I'd figured out in advance. Now I knew that, no matter what poor Hugo was, this guy was no creature born in a lab. He either made himself this way, or was made this way, and not just recently.

"So, okay, you're run by the government and the program's got as much logic as the usual government program," I said. "But what the hell is going on now? And why are some people out there changing into creatures never seen on this planet before while folks like Wasserman and now me are kept pretty much as we had been?"

"For one thing, I like your work. Always did. As for Wasserman, well, we have to have somebody who doesn't walk and talk like a Fed interact with our suppliers, salespeople, pick up and deposit various samples, and so on. Ones like me would be rather obvious if we did that often enough, and I'm afraid some important people would recoil at having dinner with me."

"So Wasserman was kept, for want of a better term, human norm, because you needed some interactivity. Okay, that makes sense. But why kill him?"

"Because we had a bit of control over Dr. Wasserman. Inside him, a complex agent that could be triggered should he no longer prove useful to us as he was. But over the years he proved smarter than we thought he was, and he managed to fool the system and turn off his activation code. That meant we had no hold on him, and then he flew to the United States with the objective of selling us and the project out. We couldn't allow that. But he didn't know we'd discovered his secret. It cost him."

"I'll say it did. But you took as great a risk bringing Hugo and yourself to Washington, I'd say."

"There were . . . other factors. True, we could have had a Black Squad take care of him, but there were reasons against that as well. I don't believe we'll go there yet, Mr. Vallone, but you'll discover the reasons and more later, when you see my home and our final destination."

"Is this an island belonging to Ratoranga or is it somewhere in the Marshalls near Majuro?"

That seemed to startle him a bit. "You are very good. I am impressed. All one and the same, really. There is an island that the Ratorangans consider to be a part of the eastern Marshalls and that the eastern Marshalls consider Ratorangan. It's much more convenient that way. Even more convenient, the Ratorangan government is corrupt as all hell and the government of the Marshalls just knows it's the highest form of national security installation and so long as it isn't for atomic and hydrogen weapons it doesn't really want to know. Almost a century ago we ruined some of their islands with those bomb tests, you see. After them, there were all sorts of tales of horrible mutants created by radiation. Nonsense, of course. We don't need bombs to do that anymore . . ."

"Obviously." I sighed. "So what am I doing along for the ride other than that you like my stuff?"

"You're here because you invited yourself along," Hal reminded me. "We didn't want you, and we tried time and again to scare you off. You insisted. Very well, now you're inside. Now you may be useful in a way you can't imagine at present. In one sense, someone with your talents and contacts could be very handy in times to come. Until then, enjoy the ride. Just remember that *you* do *not* know your activation code, nor how to turn it off."

That was a jolt even though I should have seen it coming.

"So somebody can push a button and I turn into something? Like what?"

"That is not a matter for current discussion. Something that the still romantic Kate would not find easy to love, although I commend you on your own incredible tolerance. Your lack of revulsion and much of any inhibitions toward the others has been duly noted and has impressed those like myself who might have a say in your ultimate fate."

"Speaking of ultimate fates, Karen did a good deal of the work with me, and was a damned good field reporter until your people turned her into a muscle-bound cocktail waitress. She doesn't deserve that."

Surprisingly, he showed some anger. "And what does she deserve, Vallone? Like you, she invited herself! Her camera sent pictures of creatures our agencies are still trying to discredit! You're not in the United States anymore, nor is she. You're on another planet, or so you should think of it, from this point on! One that isn't at all a bad place to live, but it lives only because it controls its own links to the outside. There's no First Amendment in the new world you two invaded. Now you will have to get used to that!"

He suddenly seemed to calm down, but I had the feeling he'd embarrassed himself by losing control, even for a moment.

"Get some sleep," he told me. "We have a long day tomorrow."

I turned and started for the residence, and he suddenly added, in the most sorrowful of voices, "Hugo was supposed to be seen. There is a whole different and creative cover story for him that you partially heard yourself. The country could sleep safer after that . . ."

I sighed, but continued walking. Message received. I could see the campaign building now: insane researcher steals revolutionary new robotic suit, goes on rampage. Monster slain by brave helicopter pilot. Yeah, it sounds crazy and it takes a leap with some of that video, but you'd be surprised what you can sell. The message, though, wasn't about salesmanship and the press: I knew that one backwards and forwards, since I did it so well myself.

It was, rather, if he'd sacrifice one of his own, I was definitely a footnote.

I was quite surprised that they didn't knock me out or something when they flew me off that damned island. In fact, I actually asked dear old Hal why no precautions on me, since I didn't think he trusted me all that far, and he gestured to Geoffrey with one of his claws or whatever they were and the big eunuch produced a package and dumped it at my feet. I knew what it had to be: one state-of-the-art parasail.

"If you didn't leave before, you're not going to leave now" was all he replied after that, but he was right. I decided not to mention that I'd never parachuted in my life and wasn't about to do it the first time by walking off a cliff with a kilometer or two sheer drop.

The whole staff was involved in the evacuation, which required not just the usual helicopter but a much larger industrial one, obviously borrowed, rented, or commandeered for this operation. Our two increasingly water-bound subjects were taken in special containers like the kind used to transfer dolphins or sick whales; the rest were more or less crowded into a large cargo area, along with the two eunuchs and Hal. In fact, so many got on that for a minute I thought only Karen and I were left and that we'd be going on our own. At the last minute, though, the creepy Dr. Foo hopped out of the big chopper and came over and got into ours.

I had been right about the official chopper; while it could fit four rather large, er, people, there was no pilot, and only the three of us, although Foo insisted that at least one of us ride in a backseat to balance the load. I much preferred Karen as a seatmate to the doc, and the two of us got in back.

One of the staff men brought us packages which turned out to be some box lunches with drinks, and we lifted off. I wasn't sure if the staff was to stay there or get picked up; they sure looked like they were ready to leave as well.

We lifted off and immediately swung out and away from the island. I felt no regrets about leaving it, and more anticipation that I was heading toward answers than anxiety about what those answers might be.

From the sun, I could see that we were headed south, toward the mainland of South America. There were several countries there within range of the chopper, and I had no way of knowing which one was the destination, only that I sincerely hoped that we wouldn't have another long stay in a midway point.

Roger had said that the ship had docked at Suriname, but I doubted if that was our destination. We seemed to be headed a bit west, perhaps toward Guiana, where the French still basically ruled, or Guyana, which had lots of jungle airstrips and virtually unmapped interiors.

We were perhaps thirty minutes out and still well away from anything except islands below when Foo, who'd been silent except for routine comments, suddenly said, "Pilot, slow to hover and hold position."

That woke me up, but I knew it would be futile to ask questions, particularly now that I knew her family. You had to be a real skunk to have me wishing for the company of a giant cockroach.

The chopper stopped in midair, and I peered down and could see nothing special below.

"Turn one eighty and hold," the frog-woman instructed.

The helicopter slowly turned until it was looking back in the direction we'd come. Peering forward through the bubble, I still couldn't see anything unusual. Some islands off in the distance, some little white things in the water that could have been whitecaps or sailboats, that was about it.

Suddenly the sky in the distance, just over the horizon, turned dark and you could see a giant plume going upward from a spot beyond my vanishing point. A few seconds later the whole helicopter shook, and it was all I could do to hold on.

It was over in a few seconds, but not without the helicopter having to go through some fancy power-up moves to keep from turning over or falling too much in reaction to the shock wave. Recovering, which meant mostly disentangling Karen and myself, I managed to grab a front seat and get back to an upright position where I could see once more.

Everyone's seen the old historical footage of an atomic bomb. A big flash, then a monster sonic wave, and finally a gigantic mushroom-shaped cloud going up, up into the sky. Nobody'd seen one for real since the India-Pakistani War, which was before my active time, but that's what I was looking at in the distance, or so it seemed, as the whole horizon began to darken.

"My God! What did you do?" I asked Foo, appalled.

"Relax, Vallone!" the frog-woman responded, sounding quite pleased. "It's not an atom bomb, if that's what you're thinking. It was quite a bomb, I admit, but very conventional, no radiation or such. The geologic computations were perfect, though. It blew out the plug. I'd say from that smoke and ash that the island no longer exists, although it probably will again someday. Another Krakatoa, they'll call it. And the nice thing about magma is that it dissolves all the evidence of anything unnatural. We weren't quite sure it would work—it's never been done before—but it looks like, if you can work out the complexities of human DNA to the degree we have, that one was child's play."

I wondered about the staff. I wasn't going to lose a lot of sleep over those creeps, but, on the other hand, they were people, probably with families somewhere, if only brothers or sisters or whatever, and they didn't deserve to be vaporized no matter what they were in. Of course, the official line, if pressed, would be that they got picked up and taken out after we left, but I wouldn't have bet a fingernail clipping that it was true. They had seen us, and done their jobs, but they hadn't liked that job at all and they had been pretty clear on that to the folks undergoing changes.

Hal didn't like folks who thought he was a monster. And now, with the ship way off in the Pacific and Genetique completely shut down and the relevant Black Squad dispersed and possibly disbanded, that left a lot of holes but no witnesses and very little evidence that meant anything, and a cop named Monaghan scratching his head but going on to the hundreds of other homicides he was undoubtedly burdened with.

Roger and his inevitable camera would be about; they may not even know about Roger, I thought. Still, what the hell could he do? We were going far away from him, and, no matter how ex-MI5, or whoever he'd worked for before "retiring," he wouldn't have very much now that the island itself was blown.

A bit of solving that problem with compromised security, Hal?

"Pilot, resume previous course and speed," Dr. Foo instructed, and like that we turned back around and headed for South America once again.

I'll never know where the airstrip was that we ultimately arrived at, but I'm pretty sure it was on the continental mainland and well inland. We crossed over some fairly high mountains on the way, so it might be that we went farther west than I thought, but in any event it was in the middle of the jungle, with no obvious roads around.

The airport had an impressively long, paved runway for such an isolated place, and there was a small town perhaps five kilometers to the east, but clearly at this point the place had been rented and nobody was there except, parked on the tarmac, one of those very large high-speed cargo jets that's generally only used by military types. This one had serial numbers but no markings at all; not military, not national, not a private logo, nothing. All that meant was that it was probably registered as Bob's Air Cargo and somehow only did business with certain agencies of certain governments. Its tail was down, providing a ramp that could be used to drive a truck into it or tanks or almost anything else you wanted or needed. In this case it was a large electric flatbed with the end open, but with sides and a roof of some translucent plastic, fitted so busybodies wouldn't be able to easily see what it was carrying.

The big chopper had landed, but was still taxiing over to the flatbed, so I figured we weren't all that late. Apparently Hal also wanted to see the big bang bang.

We didn't set down, although there was loads of room for us to do so, but hovered until the big one had stopped and the engines were cut and the transfer of people began. The two big eunuchs helped load the water cases on, and I thought I saw some swatches of green move in as well, and then the flatbed moved almost silently away and over to the big plane, then up and in, the two big guys riding on either side of the cab.

About five minutes later, the thing came back out, the two eunuchs again holding on, and the process was repeated. I was quite surprised that it did this more than twice; certainly twice was enough to transfer ten people, no matter what the size and shape, but it was clear that more was being trans- ferred than that. Large containers, possibly some or all of those we'd seen in the truck back in Virginia loading onto the ship, were now being moved to the plane. I had no idea why they hadn't been kept on the ship if they were indeed the same ones, but it was hard to figure anything about this bunch.

Finally the big chopper was empty, and it immediately taxied away and then took off, flying northeast toward the dis- tant mountains.

We landed about where the big one had sat, and I saw now that the flatbed was on some kind of embedded track, probably magnetic, making the spot mandatory.

"Heck of a runway for such a remote spot," I commented, aloud but not really expecting a response.

"It is a tourist destination," Dr. Foo responded matter-of- factly. "They come in here in small jets and are picked up and taken to remote jungle sites, then flown out that afternoon, often linked to cruise ships and the like. There are hundreds of these along the northern sections of South America, and lengthening the runway a bit and contributing to its mainte- nance makes it very handy to use, since we can often arrange for an equipment breakdown of the dedicated jet so that the tourists are simply disappointed for a day. The locals do not mind, either; they will get a bit more money today for not working than they usually do for working."

Very neat, I thought.

The heat and humidity of the jungle strip, however, made me yearn for even the discomfort of the island; it hit you like somebody throwing a hot, soaked wool blanket over you. I was glad to see the flatbed headed our way, even though I was already sick of flying.

The little unit was strictly utilitarian; open at the front and back, walled on the sides and top. I didn't feel any hotter on its floor than I had by the pool on the island, but this was definitely not comfortable. We had no luggage, so as soon as we three were inside it started off, the breeze created by its open front and back welcome if inadequate relief.

We'd gone only a few meters when the island's chopper revved its engines, slowly backed off, and then rose up and went in the direction of its bigger brother. Now that it no longer had a destination to fly to regularly, I idly wondered what would become of it.

Silly question. There were always secret destinations, even in this day and age, when there was so little privacy. The fact that they'd managed to keep a project like this secret for twenty years was testament to what could be done. In all my years of reporting, I'd never once gotten a hint of it, and it had to cost billions a year and involve some of the highest of high-tech firms.

We kept going toward the cargo plane and it just kept getting bigger. I was beginning to wonder just how large that sucker was. Plenty big, as it turned out.

The flatbed finally reached the big aircraft, and as it went up the ramp I saw that the ramp, too, had an embedded dual track in it which continued the one in the runway. Clever. One uniform system, and you could carry your truck with you.

Once inside, the sensation was of being in a huge tunnel or the cargo hold of a gigantic ship. There were levels, and what looked like elevators along the sides to get to those levels.

The initial part was lots of catwalks and utilitarian cargo areas with the overhead track cranes to move, store, and stack it. The truck came to a halt in the middle of this, and Foo said, "Okay, everybody out."

Either there wasn't a lot of cargo in this one or it was so huge that a lot of cargo just didn't look like much. There were metallic bars and walks and cages and all that, like a big warehouse would have, and there was also what looked like netting all over the upper levels of the thing. I was startled to see that something, someone, no, quite a number of some-ones were moving up there, jumping casually from catwalks to netting to the tops of compartments and back again with total confidence and ease.

Well, now I know at least one thing the hominid types do, I thought, and not without a tinge of apprehension. There were maybe half a dozen of them up there, and some, at least one or two, were males.

We followed Dr. Foo forward, toward a huge wall that sealed off this section from the rest of the plane. At the end there were several sets of sliding doors, and when she reached one she put her palm, suckers and all, on an ID pad. It waited a moment, then decided it liked the taste of her and opened the doors.

The center section of the plane was quite different than the cargo area. In fact, it almost felt like we were back on the ship, with a broad corridor and lots of numbered doors and other corridors intersecting it. We turned down one of those corridors, and I was surprised to see a basic cargo elevator right in the middle of it. We took it up two flights—if the elevator wasn't mismarked there were five levels—and it opened on a medium-sized administrative office. There were a half-dozen or so people there, including two of the ever popular froggies, these with faces as individualistic as Foo's, two of the four-armed zebras, both women, proving that once you got the hang of it you could type with two hands and file with the other two, and two much more exotic-looking bug types. I didn't think these were female versions of Hal; they were varicolored, quite striking, but they had triangular, humanoid heads. Their upper limbs were chitinous, but at the ends they had exposed, soft hands, three long pointed fingers and an opposing clawlike thumb, and just the way they moved when they weren't holding anything or doing something suggested that they could be withdrawn into the arm for protection if need be.

It was, however, one of the zebra-women who came over to us. It was kind of unnerving to see them in their "finished" state, as it were; kind of like a picture of a plump but huge-breasted woman cut off above the breast and then pasted onto another photo of the same person only cut off below the breasts. Believe me, I barely noticed the striping or colors.

She took samples from both Karen and me, and then said, "All of you go up to the lounge and strap in. We will be taking off very shortly. We can do all the processing while you are relaxed, and we will notify you of what is needed."

Foo nodded and led us back to the elevator and up to the top level.

This indeed looked like a lounge, only the seats were designed for all sorts of shapes and sizes, including some I decided that I'd rather not think about right now. Our party was up there, except the two dolphinlike ones who, I suspected, were in some kind of watery equivalent. Hal, too, was there, strapped into the darnedest contraption I'd ever seen on a plane although it fit him well.

Karen and I were shown to a row of large, individual airline seats and when we sat down next to each other the belts and webbing automatically deployed. From the level of restraint, this was going to be some kind of ride.

I never liked hypersonic jets; they were too expensive, made you a little or a lot sick most of the time, and they were uncomfortable, noisy, and everything else travel should not be, which is why there were few commercial ones even though we'd had them for decades, but I also understood as a reporter that sometimes getting from New York to Tokyo in three hours was important to a breaking story.

This one was a hybrid, which would take off and land on shorter, mere three- or four-kilometer runways, but which could kick in well up in the stratosphere. I didn't want to think of what it cost to run one this size, even on fusion engines, but at least I was beyond paying right now.

Various alarms sounded, and one by one each area was being checked by the computers to ensure that there was nobody left not properly secured and strapped in, and no cargo loose to get banged about.

As soon as all systems were satisfied, there was a sudden huge shudder and a lot of lurches and a rushing sound that quickly rose to nearly unbearable levels.

We had started to move out.

I began to regret eating the box lunch.

Still, to take my mind off what was coming up, I tried to figure out what the hell this thing was doing here anyway. It could certainly carry perhaps a third as much as the ship could, so if they had use of it why not just carry everything fast and secure in this?

And, of course, the answers were too quick and too obvious. They needed both to carry whatever they were moving, and they clearly had this thing on loan for a very short period of time. The special seats for the folks with tails and the like didn't quite match the interior of the plane itself and were obviously add-ons, modules for this special period of use.

I looked over at Karen and she was shouting something to me, but it made no difference. We wouldn't be able to hear much of anything until this was well under way.

Then I felt the lurch and the g-force pushing me back into my seat. The big plane was rolling forward, and fast. I really began to wonder how the hell it was going to take off on a runway that short, and whether all this had been for nothing.

I felt the nose come up, and at that instant special thrusters kicked in and really slammed us against the back of our seats. I felt like a giant hand was suddenly pressing against my chest, and it seemed to last an eternity. I was literally gasping for air, listening to my heart strain even over the tremendous noise of the engines.

Then, suddenly, there was a sense of release and I could breathe again and even hear a bit. The engines throbbed but didn't overwhelm, and yet I could feel the plane angling and setting itself up for its next stage.

"Is that it?" Karen yelled at me. "Are we in space or something?"

"No, we're not even close," I replied loudly. "And hold on. There's a step that gets worse yet. They just need to be truly in the Pacific before they kick it in. Otherwise they might accidentally dig another canal."

"How much longer?"

"Depends on how high he is now, and his airspeed," I told her. "If he's high enough it may only be a few minutes. If he's not as high and fast as he needs, then it could be up to an hour."

It was tough to gauge how long it was, but just when I'd decided that the hour was the better guess, they suddenly sounded a buzzer alarm through the ship and then, just a few minutes later, they reached what hyperjockeys liked to call the jump point, even though it was hardly that exotic.

The effect was like the plane exploded; the noise was suddenly even greater than it had been, and the pushback into the chair was several times greater than you expected as you rapidly accelerated from about mach one to not quite escape velocity. And this one lasted for an eternity of ten or fifteen minutes before it cut off, and, when it did, it really cut off. There was suddenly almost no sound at all, and very little sensation of movement, vibration, whatever.

Of course, I was mostly deaf from the noise by that point, but it, and the headache that went with it, came slowly upon me.

A gong sounded, and then an unfamiliar male voice said over the speaker system, "We are going to release the netting, but please do not release the belts. The seats swivel three hundred and sixty degrees, can lock and recline, and also contain all that you need. The small screen that pops out on your right contains a list of choices for beverages, appropriate food, and so on. If you need to relieve yourself, push the red key and the appropriate conformation will be created so that you may safely and quickly do so. Hands may be sterilized in the two inserts on either side of you. We do this because we are currently in a weightless condition and you are not used to it, nor is the ship designed for neophytes. Also, there will be two periods when we will slam, rather suddenly, against the atmosphere during this trip. If you are not in a position to be secured by the netting, this would probably kill any of you. Thank you for your cooperation. Flight duration will be slightly over three hours."

"Jeez! We're in space and they won't even let us float once down the corridor?" Karen sounded disappointed.

"You'll see why when that first bang hits," I assured her. "It's disappointing, but what can you do?"

If it took three hours from Venezuela or Colombia or wherever we'd started, then we were either going to the Indian Ocean or they had a lot of braking to do and a lot of conventional flying to bring us in. Probably the latter, since I doubted that any airstrip in the South Pacific islands would be much more than the one we'd just left.

I tried to sleep and not eat during the trip, knowing how queasy you can feel, but just as I managed to drift off a giant hand grabbed the airplane and smashed it against a rock.

Okay, that's not what happened, but it sure felt like it, as we hit the atmosphere and bounced off, regaining speed. After that, and the burning sensation from the sudden netting and belt tightening on bare skins, there was little griping about not being able to move around.

If they had it timed and angled right, and since it was probably all computer flying, there was no reason to believe it wasn't, then the second slam would come at the midpoint. After that, maybe I could eat or sleep.

I was disappointed not to be close to or in line of sight with Kate. In fact, the only ones around me were Karen and some of the froggies, so it just wasn't worth doing much but trying to endure the flight.

Karen did manage to eat and hold it down; apparently she didn't get spacesick, either. Still, she was too keyed up by the flight to sleep, and too restless to sit idly even in the all-in-one wonder seat.

She felt a mixture of wonder and frustration when one of the frog-women with a face we didn't, know swam by. No, no kidding. She looked very much like a good amphibian in water, kicking and moving forward, only it was in midair and about a meter above the floor. She was certainly experienced in this sort of thing, and I suspected that perhaps we were only the last pickups. It was almost as if this huge plane and the ship were clearing out all of the operation from the Americas, both personnel and necessary data and equipment. This was far too grand a plane for taking a few of us to their central base; the elimination of the entire island only added to the impression.

They had kept themselves and their operations secret for maybe twenty years; they'd recruited and installed and built and maintained, albeit with black project support from government and industry, a vast operation without ever making a serious mistake during that whole time. And then, this time, they'd been reckless, exposed themselves . . .

Almost as if they didn't care anymore.

Was a similar operation pulling in the African and Eurasian divisions, assuming that they existed?

What are you doing, Hal? And do your sponsors know that you're doing it?

Dr. Moreau's beast-people had eventually rebelled against him, choosing to revert to their natural forms and overwhelm him and his work as abhorrent to God and nature. But that was fiction, and Victorian at that.

Suppose they couldn't revert? Suppose they hadn't wanted to revert? If that choice, the only choice they had ever faced in the madman's megalomaniac island empire, hadn't been available to them? Was there another choice? A point between human and beast?

Even as we had the warning, got the webbing, and hit for the second and last time on our journey, I could only wonder if perhaps I was going to get the answer to that.

FOURTEEN

I'll forgo the blow-by-blow, as it was indeed a reverse of getting on. Remote but overly long airstrip, tropical island, helicopters waiting. The only difference was that most of the cargo apparently went from the airstrip down to a landing and onto a barge rather than coming with us, and the fact that there were people there to help with the transfer process who looked neither strange nor overmuscled. They were, in fact, mostly Melanesians, the island relatives of the Australian Aborigines, whose DNA was so ancient and so removed from their African roots that it constituted a separate race. They were dressed in flowered or single-colored shirts and jeans, and were wearing tough workboots, and the only thing really odd about them was that they could clearly see and often assisted the new and strange-looking arrivals and didn't even blink. They spoke to each other in their native dialects, but I had the impression that they all knew English, and perhaps other languages, quite well.

One of them, a middle-aged man with one of those classical faces and just a trace of gray in his hair and neatly trimmed full beard, smiled at Karen and me and tossed each of us a parcel. We looked around, saw nobody paying much attention to us, opened them, and discovered T-shirts, shorts, and baseball caps. Interestingly, they fit, too, although it felt odd and a bit itchy to have things on after this amount of time wearing nothing at all. Still, there was something about feeling a bit more civilized—okay, *human*—with even this little bit on.

261

With the all-terrain trucks lined up, I figured that the workers would be there for a good day or two. We wouldn't; there was no lack of helicopters here, even though all were of the small type like the one that regularly had gone to and from Sainte Germaine when there had been a Sainte Germaine, and, like that one, they were either robotic or remote controlled.

The trip from the airstrip was not a long one now. As dead tired as I was, there was a kind of energy I felt as I was finally getting close to the end of the rainbow, even if that destination might turn out to be a circle of Hell.

In under half an hour we came upon the place, and it was, well, underwhelming. At first it looked like two crescent-shaped islands, but the water was so clear and blue and our approach was high enough initially that it was obvious that we were in fact landing on one wall of an ancient crater. I just hoped it didn't have a thin plug with a massive charge attached as well, but this didn't look like there had been much action in the region for maybe a few hundred thousand years.

One crescent appeared to be about four or five kilometers wide and no more than fifteen or twenty kilometers long. There was some jungle growth, but most of it looked to be fairly flat and sandy, on which were built a series of equally underwhelming buildings, all old-style government prefabs. Except for the cluster of transmission and jamming antennae and rods, and a stock radar dome, there appeared nothing out of the ordinary, and certainly this was not a place where you could house a lot of people or do a lot of basic research.

The other crescent was about half the size of the larger one, had a cluster of the same sort of buildings and some more antennae but nothing above two stories high and nothing very fancy, and it was just as flat as its counterpart and had virtually no jungle growth at all, just rocks and volcanic sand. A small covered flatbed barge and a couple of sailboats were tied up at the larger island's pier, and a sailboat and a small catamaran were moored at the smaller island. It was hard to see where a barge would even land on either one, let alone where you'd store that much stuff. Still, the larger of the two was where we were heading, and I could see the other chopper landing on the smaller island, kicking up some sand.

If any view deflated all my hopes and expectations it was this one. Either we weren't being taken where the operational headquarters and real work was going on, or this was one hell of a disguised installation.

As soon as we landed, Dr. Foo shouted, "Okay, everyone out! When you clear the aircraft, go to the large white painted building over there. Karen, you are to stay with Vallone until further notice. Now, go! We have much to do!"

I was feeling a little spacey from lack of sleep and not much to eat, but there wasn't anything to do but follow instructions. I just needed a bed at this point, though, preferably following a steak-and-eggs breakfast. I wasn't sure where we were but it was someplace in the South Pacific, and that probably meant that it was late in the morning of the next day, maybe twenty to twenty-two hours by the clock and calendar ahead of where we'd been four hours earlier. That was one of the curses of the hypersonic plane; you never did know what time it was.

The large white painted building was easy to locate; it looked kind of like the old pictures of Coast Guard stations, minus the lighthouse, that used to dot the east and west coasts of North America. Kind of a Victorian-style structure, red roofed, on pilings, with a big, wide porch all around, maybe two high stories tall, with a broad wooden staircase leading up to the main entrance. I couldn't help but notice that there was also a wide switchbacked wooden ramp to the first level as well, although I doubted that you could get to it in a wheelchair through the soft, gray volcanic sand. So it wasn't for the chair-bound, but most likely for those folks who couldn't handle stairs for other reasons.

Even Karen sounded disappointed after the buildup. "There's got to be more to it than this, doesn't there?"

"I'm not sure," I admitted. "I'm not sure about anything anymore."

We went up the stairs and into the structure, which looked inside even more period than I'd expected, with a varnished wooden floor and wall paneling of tropical mahogany and other real woods. There was another story, or at least half story, going around the top but not filling it in, and in the center of the place was a huge room with big, broad windows looking out over the island and with those enormous drop-down fans you see only in old period-piece movies providing some, but not much, relief from the heat.

There were a few of the multicolored bug people at consoles along the walls but they ignored us. In the center was a cylindrical structure with a bar, ringed by a series of colored zones etched into the flooring. It reminded me very much of the reception-center console at Genetique where we'd lost Kate, and, while not quite the same in shape and design, it was clearly from the same maker.

Since we were being ignored, I decided that the logical thing to do was to walk up to the console and break the plane of those zones and see what happened.

As soon as we hit the first one, a yellow zone, a holographic creature appeared in front of us. If they'd started with Mediterranean mythology, then its appearance made sense. It was in the form of a very large, muscular man, but with the head and horns of a really mean-looking bull. Still, in spite of that mouth, it could speak. Electronic creations are handy for doing things like that.

"Halt!" it said in the kind of voice-of-doom tone that we'd heard from the more human "guardian" at Genetique. "Please place both your hands palms out toward me."

I glanced at Karen; she shrugged, so we did it. The minotaur reached out and I felt a slight burning sensation as its huge hands "touched" mine. It then did the same with Karen.

"Identification acknowledged. Your chips are now registered with master security. This means that there is no place in our security zone where we will not know where you are at all times, and you may or may not be monitored or observed at any point. You will therefore observe, and not question but instantly obey, any security warnings, and will not attempt to go into areas where you are unauthorized. The punishment for this can be severe and painful. Do you understand?"

"Yes," we both answered, feeling a response was required. So what else was new? At least I figured out the system; whatever they'd stuck in our heads had a unique identifier and a specific band transmitter; when we'd "touched" the hologram some connection was made between our implants and the computerized security system, which I had to assume was the best that government money could buy.

If the late Dr. Wasserman figured out how to beat this system, he was an unrecognized supergenius.

"Please advance to the red zone," the minotaur said. At least he was programmed for politeness.

We stepped forward onto the red-tiled ring, which put us right up to the bar around the apparently wooden cylinder. The minotaur vanished, but his ghost was still hovering around.

"Please stand facing the bar," said the disembodied voice. "When instructed, walk forward."

Since we were flush against a pretty solid bar I wasn't sure how this was to be done, but I heard the sound of machinery in front of me, and, suddenly, an opening large enough for the two of us to enter simply appeared in the cylinder, and the bar rose until we could both easily walk under it and into the rather dark opening.

It was instantly clear that it was the cylinder that was the illusion and we were in a high-speed elevator which obligingly switched on an indirect light in the ceiling and then started dropping, and fast. As I felt my ears pop, I really hoped and prayed that the volcano was not merely dormant but dead, dead, dead.

We finally slowed, then came to a halt, somewhere very deep inside the crater, and the door used its dissolve effect and we walked out into a corridor that looked disappointingly like another hotel floor.

"Please proceed to room twelve," the voice instructed us.

"There you should eat and sleep. It will be necessary that you remain in the room for a period of time so that your bodies may become properly acclimated to the biome beyond this point. When we are satisfied that you have done so, you will be asked to proceed."

Well, okay. I'd figured we were already deep enough that we'd need to depressurize to go up top, but who knew how deep this might go? There were areas of the Pacific that were rumored to be deeper than Mount Everest was tall. Even though it was still pretty mundane, this was more like it. We hadn't been abandoned on a backwater after all; this was indeed Project Central.

The room was about the same as the one on Sainte Germaine, although it had twin beds, and, interestingly, it had both a comm module and a wallscreen, although no 3-D stuff or V.R. The comm module, however, was dead, or at least it was for us, and the wallscreen, instead of giving us anything entertaining, kept playing a tape in which they explained the pictorial meanings of the different security codes and colors and such until we got bored and turned it off. The room also had another door opposite the one we'd entered by, but that door was solidly locked.

The food was good, well prepared, and about the right amount. Not steak and eggs, but a big breakfast nonetheless.

After eating, it was pretty easy to peel off our sweaty new clothes and just zonk out on the beds. It didn't even occur to me until later that the juice or even the omelette might have been drugged, but what difference would it have made if we'd thought of it?

When I awoke, I got the feeling something was different but I wasn't sure what for a minute. Then I realized that the other door, the one that had been locked tight, was now open, leading to a well-lit, tubular-shaped corridor with a flat walkway laid from our door to an intersection maybe five meters away.

Karen had apparently been up for some time.

"Did you take a look out there?" I asked her.

She seemed a bit disconcerted by the question. "No. I was waiting for you. I got up maybe ten, fifteen minutes ago and found it just like this."

No curiosity? I wondered. Or was it that she'd been ordered to stay close to me and that was that?

"I think this one's for you," she said, holding something out that looked like a wristband or watch. She was wearing one herself, I noted.

I sat up, feeling remarkably wide-awake and quite energized, a state I never am in when things are normal, and looked at it.

Okay, it was a watch, apparently working on whatever local time they had here. Stock twenty-four-hour clock from the looks of it, in which case it was 0919. That implied that we'd slept the clock around, something I hoped wasn't true.

It seemed a rather basic watch, with just the time showing, but I put it on anyway.

Almost as soon as I did, the watch showed it wasn't a cereal-box premium after all. It buzzed, and I looked at it and said, "Huh?"

"Mr. Vallone," a tinny little voice said from the watch. "Would you and your companion like to join me for a late brunch?" It was an odd voice, neither quite male nor female, but not in the husky way Karen's voice was, and I thought I detected a trace of a French accent, although who could be sure with that little speaker?

"Um, sure. I don't seem to have any conflicting appointments," I responded.

The voice chuckled. "Fine, then. Just exit, and the watch will lead you to me. Don't gawk too much. I dislike eating alone but I *would* like to eat."

I got up, hit the bathroom, and when I was done Karen threw me a clean set of shorts and pullover shirt, both basic white. She already had hers on. I looked at her and shrugged. I hadn't the slightest idea how the watch would lead us anywhere, but there was, after all, only one direction to go.

At the end of the short exit corridor was another long tube, this going in both directions, but the watch beeped and an arrow showed on the floor pointing to the right. It was actually kind of neat, and I suspected it could be keyed to anybody if they had the watch. We headed down as directed, and soon reached the point where we shouldn't gawk.

We both gawked.

The tube opened into a vast complex of tubes, not only going in various directions but also up, via escalators, and down as well. What was startling was that it was all transparent, to a large degree, like glass or very heavy plastic, and it was definitely underwater.

The complex was circular and seemed to go around the rim of the sunken crater, with connecting tubes forming an X shape across and then the escalators up and down at all junctions. Only the center was solid, and it appeared to be a massive elevator whose shaft went up as far as I could see and down the same. It was unsettling.

The watch beeped and the floor showed an arrow leading to a down escalator, so we went over when we shook the vision free, and took it.

We weren't alone in the complex; all around us were creatures of the types we'd seen and many new ones, again mostly hybrids. Most striking were what Karen instantly dubbed the Puff Girls, rather amply endowed women with heads of long, flowing hair which met tails of matching long, flowing hair, both styled in often unique designer ways. Other than the tails, what set them apart was their skin colors: lavenders, pinks, oranges, greens, you name it, all pastels, with coordinating colors for hair and tail. For example, the pinks had a kind of metallic silvery hair color, the oranges a lighter palomino-type blond, the greens a metallic crimson, and so on. There were a lot of them in a lot of colors, but the pastel shades and metallic hair sheen was consistent. Several appeared pregnant, but we didn't see any male equivalents—another one of those mysteries, like what the heck they did here, where were they going, and so on.

Just as unsettling as those we passed while following the magic arrows were the creatures *outside* the tubes and thus in the water. They were easy to see; the water was well illuminated by whatever kept the tubes bright, and that meant most of the crater. It sure wasn't sunlight; I had the distinct impression we were very far down.

Still, out there, was a fair amount of life. Not all of it was humanoid, and some of it was probably more in the category of food-chain stuff, but in the humanoid varieties we saw finished Delphinides. I was surprised that they could survive the pressure that surely must be crushing out there, but equally mysterious was where they were getting air. I doubted that even they could hold their breaths long enough to work this low with such uncaring ease. And they were not only uncaring, they were busy, maneuvering various equipment and inspecting and checking various areas of the structure. Clearly this particular group was part of the maintenance force that kept the crushing pressure and water out there and not in here.

Others clearly didn't need to go up top or find an air supply. These creatures were bizarrely humanoid, but had major gills and no evident alternative way of breathing. They had skins like lizards and were colored a stippled green-gray-yellow-orange which probably provided nice camouflage if needed. The eyes were deeply set but overly large, and they had mean looks and webbed, clawed hands and feet. I couldn't tell one from another, but I suspected that these, too, had either been created from existing people or bred in a lab, although there were enough of them to suggest that they could indeed reproduce.

"Creepy," Karen commented, staring at them. "Like out of some old monster videos."

The arrows finally took us to the crater wall three levels up, and down one of those darker tubes like the one we'd exited by. I wondered just how huge this complex could be, and I didn't want to think about the answer.

We finally entered a large room that was clearly designed

as a cafeteria for people like us. A pink Puff Girl with really silvery hair and tail saw us and came over to us. I suspected this was not the guy from the watch. Her face had the look of Central America about it, a mixed Latin and Indian cast.

"Hello," she said in a rather pleasant soprano that did seem to have a trace of a Spanish accent. "I'm Tigua. You are Chuck and Karen, is that right?"

I never argued when somebody built like that wanted to be on a first-name basis with me, even if she was pastel pink. "Yes."

"The Director was called away on an urgent matter, but he will be back as soon as he can. In the meantime, he told me to meet you and tell you that you should get breakfast here and wait. While we are here, I should point out the yellow decor."

We both nodded. It wasn't high design, but it was utilitarian enough.

"Well," she continued, "make sure that you only eat in dining areas of this color. You would not like some of the things served in dining areas of other colors."

"Understood." I had already seen what the froggies liked to eat and I'd discovered that the zebras developed a knack for eating anything that wouldn't eat them first, so long as it was animal or vegetable once, so this was a tip I was not about to ignore.

It did appear that, while the basic recipes were done by people who knew cooking enough to be called "chefs," the food operation appeared to be almost totally automated. I decided not to think too much on where the meat might be from in a genetics Disneyland like this, and so long as it looked and tasted right, I tried to not imagine that they couldn't keep cows or pigs or chickens around somewhere.

This was clearly a place for at least middle management; I couldn't imagine any other reason why they'd offer not only the usuals but also Bloody Marys and light wines at a brunch.

Our companion didn't stick with us but went back to her own group, meaning we couldn't pump her with questions. Still, I got the feeling from their conversation that they were technicians who did the basic and boring stuff for all the Ph.D.s and M.D.s around. Apparently the hair and some quality in the skin somehow protected them from a lot of dangers. I couldn't imagine a sterile suit that they would fit into without all that hair getting tangled, but for basic stuff they seemed to be able to just step into a sterilizer, out, and then reverse when leaving and it was deemed safe.

There were lots of accents and lots of different races and nationalities in the faces, but the common language, at least around here, was English of one kind or another, and that made communication, at least, not a big problem.

We finished eating and then continued to wait there, since there seemed nothing else we could do. Finally, through the door came what appeared to be a very young man, perhaps no more than early teens, in a wheelchair. His torso was covered with a white pullover short-sleeve shirt and his legs were hidden in a hard metallic case.

The young man, who seemed rather androgynous, like his voice, appeared to be East Indian or Pakistani, with coal black hair and a very dark complexion. He was, in fact, quite a good-looking fellow, although, considering this place, I had no idea what lay below that covering.

He immediately spied us and came over. "My apologies for not being here sooner," he told us, confirming my impression of a light French accent. "Minor things are always coming up and wasting my time. I am Jerry Neherwali, and most people here call me 'the Director,' which is fine since that is basically what I do."

I figured he knew more about us than we did, so I didn't return with identification or even try and shake his hand. Instead I asked, "Indian?"

"Quebecois, actually. I was born in a small town just north of Quebec City. My grandparents were from the old country, of course, but I never even got the chance to visit there. Busy, busy, and then this place."

"Well, you look young enough that it may happen yet," I noted.

He smiled slightly. "I am seventy-eight years old, sir. This appearance, both the good and the bad of it, is the result of experimentation and accident combined over the years. Like all great leaps in technology, the ones we have made in this one have both the potential to do great-and-good things, and great-and-evil ones, and even a number of banal ones, I'm afraid. Come, both of you. I shall try and fill you in while we go for a little demonstration, in the thought that one picture is worth a thousand words at least. No offense, sir. I know you are a writer."

"Yes, and we still put the big photo on page one," I responded. "No offense taken."

He turned, and the wheelchair silently glided out at a pace we could comfortably match with a walk. I noticed that he was not guiding the thing in any way that I could see; most of the time his hands were folded, except when he was pointing out something. I also wasn't sure what was holding the wheelchair up; it was a wheelchair in name only; a seat, yes, but barely off the floor and with no visible wheels or treads of any sort.

"We are now almost two hundred and thirty meters below the Pacific," he told us as we went. "The water pressure outside would crush us in an instant, but these tubes are designed and, in fact, more or less grown for this environment."

"Pardon me? *Grown?*"

"Indeed. We can use the technology here to produce a large variety of things we need. The tubes are relatively simple and the power comes from a chemical reaction with the saltwater, thus 'feeding' them, as it were, on the purest basis. The elevators and walkways, of course, were fabricated, but only the elevators and their power plant were imported from the outside world. The heat and power for the place comes from geothermal sources sunk deep down, and this includes the vast amount of energy we must expend on keeping the air circulating and fresh inside. Fruits and vegetables we cultivate here in our own hydroponics levels, and the meat is basically cloned using a process that eliminates the need to keep importing parents for them or raising lots of animals. In a sense, hundreds of people having been eating the same cow, pig, and so on for years."

"That's your commercial side, I take it? You develop these processes and then they're fed to dummy companies up top who patent and then manufacture them in exchange for your nearly inexhaustible line of credit?"

"Something like that. I knew you were above average in such matters. I have read a great many of your columns, all four of your popular-science books, and I have seen the shows you and others have done based upon your work. I was quite impressed."

I looked around at this complex, and at the only seventy-eight-year-old teenager I had ever met. "Kind of pales in comparison to this."

He chuckled. "Oh, do not give me credit for this. In fact, most of it was done in ways that nobody here can quite follow even when it's explained to us. We've passed beyond the stage of those kinds of breakthroughs, I think. But I did pretty much develop the means of creation, as it were. Kind of a Zen concept. I am not behind all this, but I may be the *that* behind All That. Or, then again, maybe I just think I am."

No way was I going down that path. "You said 'hundreds' of people here. I would have said 'thousands,' maybe many thousands."

"Actually, I haven't any idea of the exact count, but I can get it if I need it. It's not as high as you think, though, nor nearly as many as it was earlier in this project." His voice turned dark, perhaps a little bitter. "Many of the original people, no longer necessary, are out there, in the cold and dark waters, in a substantial settlement dug out of the side of the trench. There's quite a civilization developing there now, the first nonhuman civilization in effect, and I suspect that the more time that passes and the older it gets the less human it will become. As a young man I never believed that Atlantis existed, and certainly not Lemuria. I know they both exist now."

"You don't sound too pleased by that," I noted. "I thought that was the original idea behind Project Chameleon. Sounds like you did it, and found a most practical way to test it out. Three-fifths of the world's surface and we know so little."

"That's true, in one sense," he agreed, gliding onto one of the escalators. Although his base was just barely narrow enough to fit and the steps themselves were not big enough, he held straight anyway. I didn't believe in antigravity, so it had to be something with magnets or other technology that didn't require the wheel. "However, most of them were not volunteers. Oh, the core people were, but most were not. The most knowledgeable, and dangerous, were put out there. They couldn't be trusted if they were ever permitted to return to the mainstream world, you see. And that, of course, eventually led to the policy where just about everybody was altered, even if in a stupid and inane way, simply to create bizarre mutants who would not be able to go back. That, and the remoteness of this and other such places, and the darker advances we've made into personal security on the biological level have kept us apart. Those few who must be our human bridge from here to there and back are actually little different from those here except that their cellular reprogramming is dormant. They need to *keep* it dormant by periodic connection to certain security equipment when outside, though, or they, too, will turn, and what they become is intended as much as punishment and example as it is something that makes sense for us or our work. The few over the years who have chanced it anyway, well, they've been . . . stopped, by whatever means."

"I saw what was left of Samuel Wasserman," I told him.

"Indeed. Somehow he'd found a way to turn them completely off. I understand that all that got him was an ugly death. Pity. Ah, we turn out of the crater here, and go all the way to the end. At that point, I will show you the ultimate secret of this place, and what we can really do, particularly after the last of the new lab equipment arrives in a few days and can be installed and checked out. They have never permitted us to have the full range of software and hardware to check and grow our own test samples. They were too frightened of the potential of that ownership to allow it. Now we'll have it, and a few people who can teach us how it all works."

"*Hmph!* So you could play God designing anything you wanted, but you could only do computer-model testing? Kind of like being a gun designer but you're not allowed to assemble one or given the ammo."

"An imperfect but adequate analogy," the Director responded. "But now, thanks to a lot of planning and some very big risks, we will soon have it, and a handful of top geneticists to set it up. Eventually, of course, it, too, will be automated, in preparation for our final-stage objective."

"Your what?"

"Never mind. That will come later. For now, let's go through the double doors ahead. I think you will find this place more than interesting."

The room was surprisingly small, perhaps a dozen meters across, circular, with two semicircular benches around the wall. Then a level down, kind of theater-style, there were banks of computer screens, and, finally, a raised dais in the center with a figure eight–shaped perimeter. The left section of the dais had two rods stuck in the floor, almost like canes with a kind of handlebar top, and above, a kind of tube partly retracted into the ceiling. The other section had a smooth floor and, on top of that, a rounded lens of some kind. I didn't like the look of either area.

Jerry Neherwali glided in, past us, and down to the readout level. I noted that there were no seats at that level, nor, apparently, any real input system, either. This place could be run by one person, if they knew what the hell they were doing.

Karen and I slid onto the soft top bench to the left of the entrance. There didn't seem anything else to do.

"Good morning, Circe," said the Director, and definitely not to us.

"Good morning, Jerry," responded the sexiest female voice I thought I'd ever heard, coming from everywhere and nowhere at the same time. I found myself jumping when "she" spoke.

Jerry turned and said, "Karen, please come down here and get up on the leftmost platform there in the middle, would you, please?"

Like she had a choice. She got up and went down and I saw that there was a small stair in back leading up onto the platform.

"Now please remove all clothing, anything inorganic at all," Jerry instructed. "You can toss the clothing on the floor in front of the platform. Thank you."

Karen was quickly nude, which wasn't unusual anymore, tossing even the new watch off the side, and she was now standing there, curious but obedient.

"Now please take one grip in each hand. Here—Circe, please place the grips in the proper position for Karen."

"Certainly, Jerry," came the ghostly woman's response, and the two poles lowered until the grips were just at where her hands could get around them comfortably.

"Now, Karen, grip both, one with each hand, and stay perfectly still," the Director instructed. Then, to Circe, wherever she was, he said, "Circe, you may commence full scan."

The tube I'd seen mostly recessed in the ceiling now descended and surrounded Karen, who looked uncertain but who wasn't about to move. Invisible when not in use, there appeared to be a circular channel to meet the tube in the base, so that it could descend to just a bit below her feet.

"Chuck—I hope I may call you that, we're quite informal here—do not worry about your companion. Nothing you will see has any real sensation. It's basically no different than the three-dimensional scanners used by hospitals, just much more sophisticated and detailed."

"Not much more you could do to her, I guess. You've put her under control as a virtual slave since the outset."

"Well, we had to. She was potentially dangerous. Anyone who would sneak aboard our ship like that and poke around had more guts than brains, you see. I have read the reports and the accounts. Do you think she would have used one of those parasails if she were her old self?"

"Particularly with those muscles," I responded. "Sure."

"And if we'd turned her into one of those hybrids as we did the others? Would she still have escaped to report?"

I thought it over. "I think she just might," I admitted.

"Case closed."

"But then, why didn't you do it with me?" I asked, then realized the answer to my own question. "Oh."

I *didn't* use the parasail and I had the chance to do it. In fact, I came in for the rescue but then stayed, refusing all help. The fact was, I did stupidly board the ship in a kind of romantic rescue idea that was too stupid for a man of my age and experience, but, let's face it, I would never have ridden that robot in as Karen did. I wasn't a risk. Kate alone, not to mention Karen, would ensure I wouldn't be a risk.

I felt like the whole evolutionary line of newspaper reporters had died out with me. The old guys from the early days wouldn't have chickened out, even for friends and loved ones. They stormed the beaches in wars armed with carrier pigeons and typewriters. They climbed into volcanoes with the volcanologists, and they went to revolutions in dark jungles in unknown lands. *My* generation accumulated facts and presented them, but we didn't actually risk our hides.

My attention was suddenly drawn to Karen inside that tube. She didn't seem to be in any discomfort, but there were all sorts of circles of light and energy pulsing up and down and reflecting off her naked body. Even the floor was pulsing with light, and overhead a series of multicolored rays sprayed her top to bottom as well. It took only three or four minutes, but what was "it"?

"We hope to cut the timing for this down to under a minute per person," the Director told me. "We have hopes that some new scanning techniques will allow this. But, of course, our ultimate hope is that we can dispense with the laboratories entirely and simply do it directly. Until we lick problems in this process, though—most of all, the introduction of chaos products—the rest will have to wait. Ah! There! It's done!"

The light show stopped, and the tube lifted off Karen. "Tickled," was all she said.

The screens on the instrument circle below me were going nuts with figures and weird shapes and symbols and all sorts of stuff. Meant nothing to me, and it seemed to be much too fast to be interpreted even by an observer who knew his or her business. The Director wasn't even glancing at them, so I knew this was a purely automated process.

"The computer as a tool of business started as a database storage and retrieval system," Jerry said, sounding now like a university lecturer. "However, it didn't move out of its cocoon of solving mathematical puzzles and processing databases until someone invented what the world really needed: a spreadsheet. You are familiar with what a spreadsheet is, Chuck?"

"Sure. A grid into which you put information."

"No, that can be a database. A spreadsheet is a device where you can *manipulate* data in any way permitted by mathematical modeling. That's what this is, Chuck. A spreadsheet program. A gigantic spreadsheet program with impossible power. Now let's take a look." He paused a moment, then said, "Circe, display Karen."

On the other platform next to Karen appeared, well, *Karen*. It was so real, so utterly solid and convincing, I had to look at both of them and shake my head. Karen, too, looked over and seemed a bit startled. "I really look like *that* now?"

"Yes, but not necessarily forever," the Director responded. "Circe, base measures ninety-two, sixty-one, ninety-two, keep ratio proportional, height not to exceed one hundred eighty. Process."

"Processing," came the response, and I watched as Karen's other self morphed instantly and effortlessly into an extremely tall, still-athletic young woman with near-perfect proportions, yet it still had Karen's face and coloring.

"Wow!" Karen breathed. "I *want* that!"

"The tip of the iceberg," the Director responded. "We can do almost anything in the model here, and we don't even need to be that precise. I just did that because it was easy and routine. We also have a number of prefabricated programs, as it were. Circe, default."

The figure morphed back instantly into a twin of the real Karen.

"Shit," Karen muttered.

"Circe, powder puff, blue with metallic violet."

Again, the figure on the right morphed instantly into one of the Puff Girls, only it was still very definitely Karen behind that pastel blue skin and big breasts and lots and lots of strikingly violet-colored shiny hair.

"Because we've got every molecule scanned, and we have the matrix of her genetic code from the countless tests performed during the examination, we can do just about anything and make it merge with Karen's own natural self," the Director explained. "Like a spreadsheet, if we change any factor, all the other factors that need to be changed, such as better back support for larger breasts or muscle development in another area for, say, tail support, will change automatically. Circe, default."

"Default," the voice, which I now determined with some disappointment to be a computer's voice, responded.

"Let me just show you that this isn't merely a graphics toy or game," the Director said to me. "Circe, simplified internal, please."

The Karen hologram was no longer easy to look at. In fact, it was Karen with the skin and much of the surface tissue removed or overlaid transparently. It was a gruesome sight.

"Circe, please put up the first model, per my original measurements, keeping this view. Side rotate, transparent skin."

The image morphed again, but this time the result was anything but sexy or attractive. Still, it was that photographer's model version, now turned to the left, only you could see all the internal organs and skeletal structure. I suddenly was startled to notice something.

"It's moving!" I exclaimed. "It's breathing and all that."

"Indeed. Wouldn't be a good simulation otherwise. Now, I'm going to create a gross distortion. Watch what happens. Circe, enlarge breasts to one-two-two centimeters."

The figure was now extremely forward, and, as he said, the balance was off. I'd liked to have seen the example fleshed in, as it were, but I wondered what the point was.

"Note that she's still standing straight. In a normal structure, to have this much weight at the top front would cause pains and eventual curvature of the spine," the Director explained. "However, when I changed that one thing, other changes automatically happened as well. The backbone is thicker, the rib structure is firmer, the muscular support for the upper body is shifted and the center of gravity is thus adjusted. No ordinary woman would stand this for long; they'd get a reduction. But this woman would find it no problem at all because everything else is adjusted to make the distortion work."

He ran it in slow motion, and I could see how the bones and muscles did in fact change, and, indeed, she was a bit shorter and slightly wider as well but this wasn't noticeable because of, well, the prominent part.

"This is how we do it," Jerry said with some pride. "Or, rather, how Circe does it. She is quite a remarkable computer. The amount of information she must hold, comprehend, mathematically balance, and manipulate in order to do this is greater than the capacity of most of the computers running the world's governments and economies put together. There is nothing like her anywhere else."

"I'm impressed, but it's still just a three-dimensional graphics computer to me," I told him. "The kind of thing you use on a Saturday night for escapism if it has a good plot."

"Entertainment!" the Director snorted. "This is far more than imagery and illusion. We can run any physiology, any simulation, inside and out, with full knowledge of who and what we're dealing with. Circe, default."

"Default," the computer responded, and Karen was back to being twins.

"In that one scan, we can pick up any genetic mutations and malformations already there and eliminate them. Flush all the veins and arteries. Renew the cells to a state they hadn't been in since true youth. We can alter the chemistry of brain and body as well, or anything else we choose. One last example. Circe, male pattern interpolation, basic."

"Running. Interpolated. Completed."

And Karen's psychic twin morphed again, but this time in a very different way. The whole body structure changed; the skin coarsened, there was a very different cast to her, and even the hips and rear end altered a great deal.

Standing there was a very convincing "what if " showing what Karen would have looked like had she been born a man.

Karen stared at it, kind of amazed. It wasn't any kind of playact or dress up or even the usual fun computer game. No, this was convincing. I really could believe that, had she been male, she'd look pretty much like that.

"Couldn't you have at least made me bigger between the thighs?" she asked.

"We can do most anything," the Director reminded her. "What this is, however, is an attempt at accuracy. We took the less dominant of the two X chromosomes in your body, retained what would be common to X and Y, added the Y instruction set that was not present before, and threw out most of the rest of the X chromosome since the Y is such a wimp, you might say, compared to the X. That is what resulted. I have no way of knowing which X was from your father and which from your mother, but that's as good a modeling as any."

He turned to me. "Now, Chuck, would you like to see what you might become?"

I hadn't any choice, he was obviously enjoying himself, and I had nowhere else to go, so I humored him.

Most of the results were predictable. Better looking, younger, lots more muscle, and a few examples of what I'd look like as some of their creatures. It *was* kind of fun, but I still really wasn't impressed with it yet as more than a parlor game that might be played by major Hollywood-simulation stories—you know, the kind where you walk in and interact as a character and get to do all those things you never could in the real world? Even so, I had an idea that we weren't being run through this processor just for fun, and that there was a lot more to this computer than entertainment.

And, of course, he did me as a woman by reversing the process, adding to the common information interpolation of what the rest of it should look like if I were consistently female. What he came up with startled and impressed me; the resulting image looked one hell of a lot like pictures of my mother in her early twenties. That kind of bothered me, too, because you're not supposed to see your mother nude and in her prime.

Finally, I stepped down and dressed and went back up to my seat, while the strange old kid in the wheelless wheelchair turned to face us. *Here it comes,* I thought, and it did.

"Now, inside Circe, is all that information about you. At any time, I can turn to this machine and create out of it any variation or hybrid I wish. Then, when I'm totally satisfied, I simply instruct Circe to create a program and she does. The program becomes a complex series of memory cubes which we tag and collect. If we want to just check and see if the program is valid, we send instructions for a tissue sample and then it is mixed in a biotech lab off-site and allowed to grow to a certain point to test viability and integrity. If we're just doing what we did here, using templates of variations and hybrids we know to be true, then we could send this program directly to a pharmacology lab and out would come a proper genetic stew, as it were. Then all we need is to either deliver it to you, and only you, in some form, and it will begin to work because it will recognize you and no one else. In our case we use our own semiorganic nanomachines. One large injection and then they will go into the body and lie dormant until a program is introduced, then they will reproduce to whatever quantity and types they need and begin the changes, cell by cell."

I had a funny feeling about that.

"And those little machines are already inside me, aren't they?"

"And Karen, yes. Sleeping in both cases, waiting to be told to wake up and do something. Karen's initial makeover, shall we say, was rather basic and done with psychochemicals and a very small retrovirus-delivered program, kind of stock. The less you change, the faster and easier it is and the fewer complications you have. The others in your party also had generic programs, initially retro, then reinforced with better but still generic ones during your island stay. Speed was essential. You two, we can do more customizable work with now because we have you specifically on file. Circe knows you."

"But why?" I asked him. "Okay, I can see the deep-water breathers—the implications are enormous there, and God knows we've got ocean. I can even see some of the others, for specific types of work. But what's the purpose to the "powder puff ladies"? To the four-armed, four-breasted zebras, or the satyrs or the cat-women?"

"*I* didn't make or dictate that policy," he responded, suddenly sounding angry once again. "*Your* people did that. 'Security,' they said at first. 'We have to make them permanent because they'll all know too much to be let back into the world.' Then they started playing with forms, and sorting people by jobs. The 'powder puff ladies,' as you call them, are all laboratory assistants of one sort or another. Their internal biochemistry is quite unusual; they can work in environments that none of us could."

"But those tails!"

"Stupid, vain, and get in the way, don't they? Yes. So do the large breasts and pixie-type looks. Practicality was an afterthought with those people. But they worked, and they were reproduceable. Secretarial and administrative are all of another form, as much insect as human, as I'm sure you've seen. The hominids are basically loadmasters and maintenance, keeping watch over the self-repairing robots and occasionally doing things on their own. In each case there are a few scientists among them, except your powder puffs, to monitor and run research on the forms. They're quite important, those forms, as well as the gill people and the Delphinides and the Anurians, because they can all reproduce. Some senior scientists have unique forms, and are essentially just marked as freaks and monsters. Most cannot reproduce. Reproduction is, in fact, the most difficult thing we have to deal with. I know you've met Halohe Kahota, a very bright man, one of our best."

"Yes, I know him."

"He was here in the very early days. He created the Karrals—the colorful insect administrators—early on. They can eat virtually anything, you see, and thus have very low costs to maintain. He created the form he is today and has been for many, many years, but he did not realize that he would be the prototype."

Poetic justice, I thought. It was hard to feel sorry for a guy who obviously felt that turning secretaries into insects was a practical and cost-effective move when he gets turned the same way, only bigger and uglier.

"So he's one of your chief designers, then?" I asked him.

"Oh, yes. Invaluable. I am not a biologist, you see, let alone a geneticist. I am in fact a physicist."

"And a computer designer and engineer, I suspect. Your creation is Circe, isn't it?"

He looked up at me and slowly shook his head from side to side. "No, Chuck, I did not design Circe, and I did not design the current quasi-organic nanomachines nor indeed can I fully make out what they are doing. I am but what I look like to them now—a mere boy. I designed Circe's grandmother, as it were, back when I was working at the National Security Agency. The grandmother designed her father, a concept so radical that it took us years just to understand *why* it worked, let alone *how*. And the father designed Circe, whose entire being is unfathomable. I don't know how she works. I don't know how she *can* work. I certainly don't understand how she can store that much and manipulate that many variables in *any* time, let alone in the time you saw. And she's only one of the computers here, dedicated to just that sort of work, and monitoring the results of her work. Other siblings, equally unfathomable, self-maintain this entire complex, and four others around the world, and cover other impossibilities. One of them designed the tube system here. All I do is run the place. *They* do the real work."

"Are you sure you run them and that they don't run you?" I asked him.

He shrugged. "Who knows? They are so far beyond me, yet in many ways they are like my children, too. They don't know how to be dishonest or sly. I suppose that will come, if not with them then in a few more generations, but they are content to do what they were designed to do. No, they haven't become our masters yet. *Our* masters are off in the likes of Washington and New York and Los Angeles, not to mention São Paulo, Caracas, Johannesburg, Berlin, London, Paris, Rome, Tokyo . . . At least, for now."

FIFTEEN

We didn't see much of the Director over the next few weeks, but we did see an awful lot of the operation that was at once impressive and worrying. It was particularly worrying when the ship arrived, and we discovered that the central elevator was just right for sending some containers to the various levels, while others were going outside, to help set up and run a whole new wing and convert a level from administration to labs.

We weren't prohibited from very many places, although we could not access the freight elevator in the center, nor were we permitted on the extreme upper and lower levels, which were accessed by special elevators only and those were embedded in the rock wall, not the crater. If we ever decided to push it and overstep into a prohibited area, somebody would show up with astonishing speed, even if nobody had been around, and gently but firmly suggest we go elsewhere. It would have helped if I could have dispatched Karen elsewhere or used her as a diversion, but we were stuck together tighter than a marriage of Siamese twins.

Karen was also changing again; I had the idea that when we went to sleep we sometimes were being given something to put us completely out and games were being played. From the stocky, sexless, muscle-bound character she had been, she was now softening appreciably. At first I'd been concerned that they were just inaugurating her into their mutant system and she was about to turn purple or something, but instead the old Karen was starting to emerge, and maybe a bit more than the old one. Softer, sexier, shapelier, and, to her amazement, she was also developing noticeable breasts. Coming with this, of course, was not only the return of her period but an increasingly ferocious period; apparently the hormones were really beginning to flow, and she was seriously beginning to wonder if the price was worth the obvious cosmetic improvements. I was beginning to wonder what urges were eventually going to come with those changes; she already was having some problems with rapid mood shifts and, worse, she didn't seem to notice.

Not that I was immune to change. While not turning into any romantic Hollywood star, I was definitely in the best shape I'd ever been without working much for it, and, more, there was no question that I was somehow growing younger. When you're over fifty, gray and balding and paunchy and then, slowly, you start to see it all peel away so that you look pretty much, not the way you looked twenty or thirty years earlier, but how you *should* have looked, you can't ignore it. We were definitely being reworked into younger and far sexier versions of our old selves, but not mutated into other creatures. The mystery seemed to be compounding again.

I tried to locate Kate but was told that she was on an upper level, had settled in, and it was probably for the best that we not meet for a while. By the same token, I was happy not to see old Superbug or Jerry or Madam Froggie, although I did see a bunch of the Anurians around.

Our one contact and occasional social companion was the pink powder puff girl, Tigua, who, I gathered, worked for a genetics design team headed by Dr. Antonio Vargas and his wife, Dr. Juanita Vargas, the first husband-and-wife team I knew of here. I got the idea that she was a zebra and he was one of the Pan types, but that this hadn't influenced their relationship. I had wondered why distractions like Tigua hadn't disrupted relationships, but then I discovered that there were no male puff girls; they had a male organ somewhere under that tail that came from just above the ass. They could reproduce, and although they had to get permission from whoever they worked for, in general they were encouraged to do so. That was another hermaphroditic race that could reproduce, then, like the amphibians. The Karrals, those colorful humanoid insectlike creatures who did the routine paperwork and such, were a third. The fish faces who lived on the sea floor were reproducing bisexual types, as were the Delphinides and the zebras. The hominids I couldn't find out much about; they seemed a bisexual race, but who could be sure?

The others, including the satyrs, our giant cockroach-man Halohe Kahota, whose title turned out to be a euphemism for chief of internal security, and a number of others that we saw along the way, could not reproduce, at least not for now, and I gathered that this attribute was lacking more than it was present in any template, and this was the one mystery that still drove them nuts. The satyrs couldn't reproduce only because so far nobody had created a female counterpart, although it was said that several failed attempts had been made.

There were computer stations all over the place, all keyed to your security broadcast code and operated by voice. If you could figure out what question to ask, you could look up practically anything, and I do mean anything. You never got a denial or a "classified" sticker, but from the way some queries simply went nowhere I got the idea that these were simply built into whatever security code you might have. It was frustrating, since you never knew what you weren't being told because it never actually refused to answer a question. It just occasionally ran you in circles.

Rather quickly, though, I got up to speed on the true history of this place and some of its work.

The origins, indeed, had been with Project Chameleon almost a quarter of a century earlier. When the heat went on and it was clear that Chameleon was going to become an unfunded political football for the paranoid of the nation, a decision was made to keep it going using the security services, where money and specifics could be buried, diverted, or expenditures faked as going for a different project. The major labs for what was believed to be "defensive" work against biochemical sabotage from enemies elsewhere was spread around to certain key senatorial and congressional districts so the pork barrel flowed enough that they couldn't afford to either expose it or closely question it. In fact, if any of them really got too interested, they discovered that the cover company that generated all those jobs and such in their states and districts would dry up and blow away, and some more cooperative and pliant rival would get the goodies. This and a lot of covert flag-waving was generally enough to keep the politicians off their backs and the money coming one way or another.

The companies tended to be owned, controlled, or otherwise managed by top banks and investment corporations whose boards tended to be a *Who's Who* of science and industry. It sounded a lot like Genetique, but it also wound up being just about every other major "private" DNA and forensic-research lab in the Western Hemisphere. These folks tended to be the mover-and-shaker types who had tremendous political influence not just in the U.S. but allied nations as well. It had more and tighter control than the original Manhattan Project of atomic-bomb legend, all the more because fewer people knew exactly what was going on than in any past major project and also because the major work was being done offshore, as it were, by people who couldn't go home again, cutting off a major potential source of leaks. Only major specialists and their immediate assistants, who had no real family and who could even be "killed" in various accidents and thus never be missed, were selected—with a few exceptions. Those were brought in the hard way, as the nine I'd seen had been.

That much I had already surmised, but there was a second group that got involved that made the first part possible. In the new Project Regen Lizard, for regeneration and, of course, chameleon, there wasn't sufficient computing power to do the job. There wasn't that kind of power anywhere, really, except down the road from Washington at the NSA. There, the agency that had been reading everybody's mail and listening to everybody's calls for generations and which did it by always having the most incredibly advanced state-of-the-art computer systems with the highest degree of artificial intelligence to sort out the gold from the garbage in the mass of voices, there was a computer that could do it. The designer of that computer at that time was one of the great geniuses the world produces from time to time, but, unlike Newton and Einstein and the like, few knew his name. He had chosen anonymity in exchange for being able to design and build whatever he wanted without regard to budget or boards of naysayers. If it worked, he would not be questioned. And it always worked.

Dr. Jeruwahl Neherwali found himself the anonymous emperor of the computing world. Now he was called upon to build a second such computer, or even the next generation, and he could not refuse. With his money coming from the NSA on the basis that anything he developed would be shared between the agency and the project, he didn't even increase the Regen Lizard budget all that much.

But old Jerry didn't duplicate the NSA supercomputer, he built a bigger and grander and smarter one here. And, when that proved inadequate for their needs, he took the step of having his new computer design its successor. Or, rather, successors, since Circe was the big one just for biological computer modeling, but there were engineering ones and maintenance ones and all sorts of computers here now, most amazingly small, amazingly fast, and more intelligent than anybody would like to believe.

Still, it was clear that the revolt of the robots was not upon us; at least, not so long as Jerry was alive and reasonably well, anyway.

It was Karen, always the better researcher, who found Jerry's dream project, and the fact that some work had been done on it but that it had not succeeded. His dream was to create a kind of matter-to-energy-to-matter device that would allow Circe to literally disassemble and reassemble somebody as easily as she, or it, now did with the holograms. Jerry had not abandoned the dream, but for now it had been put aside. It seems that the old bugaboo, chaos, kept getting in the way. No matter how hard you tried, with such a complex operation the reassembly was never quite what it should be, but often just a wee bit off. A wee bit off on a human being, though, could be death, dismemberment, or other horrors. They had never totally banished it from the models, so the hard part, the matter-to-energy-to-matter part, wasn't even attempted. Not yet.

I could see it, though, now that the problem was stated: somebody, at some time, somewhere, would solve it. Then you could dial whatever you wanted to be. Or whatever "Authority" decided it needed you to be.

That was the ultimate worry, and, I suspected, the ultimate aim of those folks, not all shadowy, who had launched and nurtured and maintained and protected this project for over two decades. In the meantime, they were creating races when that was useful, and creating monsters to maintain absolute security.

Until Wasserman had found a way to beat the system. How? The guy was a Ph.D., certainly, and he absolutely would be the kind of headhunter who could locate perfect candidates to fill vacancies in places like this, but everybody agreed that, as a scientist and thinker, he was basically a journeyman, a technician. He had no background in cryptography, mathematics, or security, and he hadn't spent a lot of time in the labs on theory when he'd been here. How could he beat this kind of system?

Of course, the obvious answer was that he couldn't. Somebody else had beaten it, somebody who almost certainly was in literally no shape to take advantage of the discovery. Still, why would that somebody take a chance on the likes of Wasserman? Why now, or at least why last fall?

Wasserman had walked out, with samples and an altered

but valid genetic mutational program on computer disk, with his own little nanotechnicians deactivated somehow, and headed for Washington where, instead of discussing all this with colleagues gathered at the AAAS convention he'd proceeded to check out the nine soon-to-be victims and conveyed their IDs somehow, maybe as simply as by phoning good old Hal who was hanging out in the deep recesses of Genetique, or maybe Syzmanski's Black Squad, and . . .

And calling me for an appointment.

He wanted it out there under the aegis of somebody who would be believed and by an institution like the *Sun* that had some credibility. My science-writing Pulitzer, it seems, put me a leg up on the *Post* and *New York Times*, I guess. When you were talking things this huge and this outrageous, you needed both evidence and credibility. I should have been flattered, but look where it got me, I thought, and, even worse, where it got Wasserman.

I still didn't know what he would have told me. About all this? Yes? And then what? The big cover-up and he'd have an accident someplace and that would be that. He had to know the odds were against him staying alive, particularly in the den of all who had a real stake in this project. Noble or not, something had to scare him and the person who made it possible for him to escape security measures—scare him enough to put his neck in the guillotine to get the word out and stop . . . what?

It was right there, in front of me. I knew it, I could almost reach out and grab it, but it kept turning its back and scurrying away to hide. What was going on that would be worth risking the most unpleasant of deaths? Or trusting whoever it was who solved the immediate security problems to allow him to do it?

I knew that that mysterious someone had to be here somewhere, but in all these levels, and in the levels I could not access, there were a lot of candidates. Maybe they'd been caught and that's how Wasserman got nailed. Maybe, but somehow I thought that anybody who could outsmart this level of security wasn't going to be found that easily. If not, though, why hadn't they contacted me somehow, at least indirectly?

Karen. Of course, it was because of Karen. Not only my friend, companion, and assistant, but also my security shadow.

Okay, so that left the other half of the puzzle. What was different now than a year ago right here?

Answer: the new lab and new section. The ability to test and manufacture as well as model. They'd actually gone into the lion's den, potentially exposed themselves, and at the same time they'd discredited and disbanded Syzmanski and his Black Squad, turned over D.C. security operations to Foo's dear relative, gotten Genetique shut down and its laboratories dismantled and shipped here, blown up their getaway island, and . . .

Wait a minute. *I* was the one who got Genetique shut down, and *Karen* was more or less responsible for Syzmanski's effective demise. And yet, and yet, it had all worked out in their favor and they even had a good-sized ship and cargo-loading operation to take on the Genetique equipment and supplies. Good God! Were they really that smart?

Of course they were. They'd hidden all this for twenty years. And what was spooking an old lonely science writer and a young, inexperienced City Desk editor compared to turning human beings into creatures? *Damn,* I hated being used! And what bill of goods did they sell Syzmanski to panic him like they did? Still, he got to play the heavy and probably even took the fall for the flying gargoyle and the murders. I hadn't seen how they'd handled it but Foo had been confident that it was handled well, and I could easily see how I would do it.

Over the next few days I continued to work out my deductions until I ran into the stone wall that only lack of data could cause.

They had managed to put their own people in the security loop and consolidate all needed operations for making more mutants in their own hands, under Circe and Jerry's control.

And, one day, on the Island of Dr. Moreau, the beast-men had rebelled and refused to take their medicines, refused to obey and serve the Father. They reverted more and more to the ignorant beasts they once had been, and that was the end of the experiment.

But here the beasts were Ph.D.s with great computers, lacking up until now the means to take over and run the experiment. Here Dr. Moreau was the beast, and all the beasts, and he was neither ignorant nor savage.

The beasts were running the island, and not even the ones who created it for their own purposes realized that fact.

Okay, Vallone, so now what?

Huh?

Now that they're running the whole show, what are they going to do? I mean, eventually, somebody out there is going to figure it out. Figure it out and, if need be, trigger the inevitable doomsday ending. A new volcano, perhaps, or just blow up the air system. How long would it take a well-coordinated team of marines and maybe SEAL specialists to take and destroy everything above the waterline? Hours? Minutes?

Jerry, Hal, even their supersmart-ass computers have to have figured that out. So, now that you've got control of the experiment, what do you do to make sure you keep it? You can't sit because eventually you're on ground zero; you can't move because it's too damned huge and permanent. With Myra Ling Kelly doing the blocking, aided by the overconfident Black Squad snotheads, you can buy some time, keep giving them what they want, but only for a little while. They're going to figure this out. They're busy men and women, but eventually some smart-ass on their team is going to put it together just like I was now.

It was now so obvious to me that I could only hope and pray that I had overlooked something, that there wasn't a serious flaw in my reasoning. Still, it was becoming very clear.

If the beasts know that the marines must come, then what do they do? Sit there and get hit? They can't move, at least not transfer their work elsewhere with ease. Among other things, they aren't really human anymore.

Back in medieval Europe, the Black Death had killed more people than all the wars up to that point, and that was a mere bacterium. Back in 1918, a simple but supermutant influenza virus had killed more people than died in all of World War I, raging at the time. Just a few decades ago AIDS threatened to wipe out the entire population of sub-Saharan Africa, and it was less than ten years since an Ebola strain wiped out Haiti and the Dominican Republic and threatened much of the West before they found a way to kill it. And, as always, other diseases were threatening now. Every time you wiped one out, two more showed up that were worse.

So how do you administer these DNA mutations?

Nanomachines were the best way, I'd been told, but in many cases, particularly when curing specific genetic diseases and defects, a retrovirus was often used.

AIDS, hepatitis, and a number of other nasty diseases we knew were retroviruses. Microscopic creatures who could reverse the usual way of nature, and use RNA to make DNA that would incorporate itself into the invaded cell's own DNA and create, well, a mutant that was the perfect retrovirus host.

My God! *Could they really mutate the whole world using their proven generic templates and some superviruses?*

"Tigua, what are the Vargas's working on? Do you know? Can you tell me?"

"Of course, Chuck. They have been in the new section since it was completed, testing their models of new viral carriers for modeling programs."

They were going to do it. Somebody here had figured that out or even been taken into the plot and had been appalled by the idea. Wasserman was supposed to get the whole thing to me, along with proofs. Saving humanity can assuage a lot of guilt over picking scientists for permanent exile as mutants.

That was why Hal had to go himself. Why he couldn't trust anybody on the "human" side directly to deal with this problem. And why he risked taking poor Hugo along, even though Hugo was hard to control.

Hugo was the only one who could fly . . .

Good lord! With the aid of being here and the research on the computers and all my experiences I'd actually managed to put it together! All except why I was here and still human, and I was sure the answer to that would not be pleasant.

Okay, Chuck, you've got it all. So now what? You're hundreds of meters below the Pacific, with no easy way out, no apparent allies, and no hard evidence even if you could get out. And they're probably messing with your mind as well, and how can you know when the only ones who can see changes are changing themselves? So now what the hell do you do?

What you do is survive and pray for an opening.

As it happened, the two most dramatic developments in an otherwise dull existence converged to make something happen.

Even as Karen and I were using the vast data resources of the computers, as well as going through an excellent scientific library to learn as much as we could (understanding that we weren't scientists, and there were limits even to grasping explanations from the scientists-in-residence), our own physiological changes were threatening to overpower us.

Karen was becoming, well, voluptuous, even as I was now physiologically down in the mid to low twenties, hard and buff with minimal work, a real young Italian stud. Even my old self had never had a problem getting sex and I was often sexually involved because, frankly, size really did matter to a lot of women, and even that was enhanced. Hell, my vision was 20/20, my hair was full and coal black and I had a lot of it all over my body. The two teeth I'd lost and never replaced because they were in the back and couldn't be seen grew back. A ton of scars, even the appendix scar and the scar I'd had since being knifed in a riot I was covering in Rangoon early in my career—gone. With Karen turning just as perfect, just as young, but a buxom Irish lass, and the both of us together twenty-four hours a day, it shouldn't be hard to figure out that we eventually found a way to pass the time.

There wasn't any approach to it; it just happened and then it kept happening for a very long and very intense time, and after that it happened a lot. It wasn't safe sex, either; it was raw and animal and it was the best I ever had.

Still, they must have had me shooting blanks or her eggs had been affected by the near-eunuch stage because she got her ferocious period right on time, and this time it was so heavy and so painful that Medical actually sent down some pills that allowed her to kind of space out, and all she wanted to do was recline in a tub full of hot water under the influence of these pills and let it pass.

For the first time, even though I didn't actually want to by that point, I found myself outside, wandering around the complex, without Karen.

I decided to go up and pay a visit to the Drs. Vargas.

It was quite a complex, and not one that easily permitted visitors even if visitors had been permitted, if you know what I mean. There was more equipment than room to move around in, and all sorts of mysterious things going on, and, most ominously, a double-airlocked chamber that could be accessed only with an environmental suit or via "waldos" set into the transparent glasslike window openings. Just to get to that point you had to go through a high-level decontamination both going in and coming out, so I opted to remain outside the secure zone and pretty much try and use what knowledge I had and what knowledge I'd gained to figure out what was going on.

I could see Juanita Vargas in there supervising some varicolored Puff Girls at the waldo window, but the great man himself wasn't to be seen.

Tigua, always my ambassador and my line to others in the complex, saw me and emerged from an office area outside the lab. "Chuck! What a pleasant surprise! I haven't seen you in quite a while!" She looked at me from head to foot. "*Oooo!*

They've been doing a wonderful job on you!" She looked around. "But where is Karen?"

"The increasingly voluptuous Karen pays a price for the new attributes," I told her. "She's in a hot tub trying to survive her period."

Tigua frowned. "I remember those. Ugh! I sympathize with her. We still have cycles in this form but it's nothing we can't shrug off. It doesn't even particularly bother the ones of us who used to be guys. So what brings you up here?"

"Curiosity. I didn't think there was much left to know about retroviruses."

"Oh, they're still very tough to deal with because they can mutate so fast. It was the Vargases, you know, who found the one protein that exploded the Ebola Two virus a number of years ago. That was a big payoff for this place. It silenced a lot of folks who wanted to cut the budget."

I kind of suspected that that miraculous stuff had come out of here but this was a confirmation. "So have they got something else they're trying to talk into committing suicide?" I asked her.

She laughed. "What an interesting way of putting it. No, there's no earth-shattering crisis like that right now. In fact, they're trying to engineer an incredibly complex but *programmable* retro strain. Imagine being able to deliver a cure to a disease outbreak simply by spraying, or even putting it in the water or the like. A kind of reverse Ebola Two, where it could survive in air or any other medium but instead of making you sick, it would make you well!"

I thought about that. It sounded good, on the one hand, but on the other it also sounded like the ultimate terrorist weapon. I wondered whether scientists of the Vargases' class, who must have felt almost godlike beating one of the deadliest diseases in history and curing millions and saving perhaps billions, didn't think that all those folks they saved were somehow theirs now.

Hal, and Foo, and probably Jerry as well, thought like that, or were well on the way to thinking like that.

I know I was thinking totally paranoid, but these people had all acted very much that way, and if they'd saved all those lives, they'd also kidnapped and turned people into all sorts of things, many of them useless and/or senseless.

"Have you seen our zoo?" Tigua asked me pleasantly.

"Your what?"

"Our zoo. We need some pure-strain research animals here from time to time, as must be obvious, now that we have the ability to do our own biochemical work. Come on, I'll show you!"

We went up one level and had to pass a restricted security check that she was able to get through and authorize me as a guest.

It was indeed more of a zoo than a collection of lab animals. At least the "cages" were spacious, clean, and the animals seemed quite at home there. In some cages there were several of a species, whether it was rat, frog, iguana, you name it, and in two different cases, chimps and orangutans, they were almost like small zoo exhibits, with the animals able to run free and play on ropes and tires and such. Some were isolated in comfortable ape roomettes; I assumed they were ones with some kind of experiment running. The rest, though, seemed quite at home, although none of them were very active at the time we were there.

The long-armed reddish comical orangutans were essentially extinct in the wild now; zoos and their cousins, the preserves, were all that kept them from complete oblivion even though they were as close relatives to humans as chimps. For that reason, I found them quite fascinating; I didn't remember ever seeing one up close, and I wasn't fond of zoos in general before this. Still, in many ways they reminded me of the hominid class like Kate had turned into. Kind of like the next step in orangutan evolution, had it kept going instead of dead-ending.

"I have to go back now," Tigua said to me. "I don't think there would be any harm if you wanted to stay a bit, or even come up here with Karen when she's feeling better. Just don't go beyond the orange door down there. That one won't open for you anyway, but even trying will bring security. Otherwise, enjoy."

"Thanks," I told her, wondering how she got the buzz to come on down and suspecting that it was built into her little crystal somehow. I did stay a bit, though, dividing my time between the two ape species, wondering whether or not these guys might have stuck just long enough to become our inheritors after we started mucking around with monster building.

It seemed that, just as I could see them, they could see me. There wasn't any one-way glass here, and I found myself the object of some attention. One of the orangutans, a big orange character that also looked strong as an ox, ambled over to the glass and shaded his eyes as if looking up and down the corridor.

"Only me, pal," I said, knowing my voice couldn't carry through there since I couldn't hear them as anything more than an occasional dull sound.

And then the big fellow breathed hard on the inside of the window until he'd fogged up a fair area, and with his finger he actually wrote something. The action startled me, and I tried to make out what it said. It was backwards, of course, but block printed well enough that this wasn't a big problem.

VALONE HELP, it said.

As soon as it was clear that I'd read it, maybe from the way I gasped slightly and took a step back, he erased it.

Okay, so he left one *L* out of my name. What did you expect from an orangutan?

I had a really eerie feeling about this. I didn't want to try his trick since I wasn't sure I could manage it properly, so I got close enough to look straight into the ape's suddenly all too intelligent eyes and mouthed, "Who are you?"

He tried the same trick again on another portion of the glass and wrote, J SYZ.

There was only one way I could take that, and I wasn't sure whether to pity the poor creature or laugh uproariously. I stifled the laugh, but it was tough.

They hadn't spirited old John Singleton Syzmanski off to some millionaire's retreat to wait it out. Instead, they'd made a monkey out of him.

Well, if he could read my lips, probably an old security skill, then at least I had an easier time. I stared at him again and asked, "What do you think I can do for you?"

He huffed and puffed and got enough room to write, NO ME U CARYR.

What the hell did he mean? "No me" was clear enough—he felt he was beyond help. "U"—"you," perhaps? And "Caryr." Car year? Ca ryr? Cary R? *Carrier!*

Carrier of what? I was beginning to wish he could speak even though voices wouldn't carry; at least that ape's huge jaw would be able to mouth words. I was no slouch at lip reading myself, but I couldn't read those lips.

At that point a red and white zebra male entered and saw me. "Who are you and what are you doing here?" he asked me.

"I was brought up as a guest of Tigua, one of Vargas's assistants. I'm Chuck Vallone."

He stared at me. "Yes, I've heard of you. Those Vargas girls are always coming up here and treating this like an entertainment complex." He sighed. "All right, I suppose there's no harm done."

"I was just wondering . . ."

"Yes?"

"Are all of these purebreds? Not mutations?"

"There are experiments running in the ones in separated enclosures," he responded. "All of those in the large general enclosures are lab purebreds, though, yes. Why?"

"Nothing. Just wondering." *You liar,* I added to myself.

I thanked him, apologized if I'd gotten in his way, and left the place regretfully.

Now I had some extra information, and I couldn't help but wonder if all of those apes in there, or at least the orangutans, anyway, weren't mutants created out of people for whom they had no further use but who otherwise might be dangerous to them. I suspected that I had at least seen the fate of any who'd tried sneaking into the island group without permission, and maybe, who knows, some famous and not-so-famous disappearances as well.

I remembered somebody saying that those higher apes had the brains of two- or three-year-olds at best, although some gorillas had managed to prove that they were a lot more advanced by using sign language. Still kids, though. The fact that Syzmanski had recognized me and communicated in such a way that I felt sure no interloper had figured out we were doing it was an indication that he'd retained his intelligence and memories. Maybe that was because they just might need to ask him some questions on security and the like. Certainly if he'd had them he could have written with pencil or marker on paper.

Damn it, I needed a quick course in sign language and fast. If what he implied were true, then Karen and I weren't just being left "human" to see how young and sexy we could become; we were to be the canons in a very nasty first strike, and what we were to shoot was even now being refined and tested in the Vargas labs.

SIXTEEN

"You know, this really sucks."

Since Karen's naked body was still pressed into mine, I took that as something of an insult.

"No, no, I don't mean *this*," she pouted, rolling a bit to place us more side by side on the bed. "I mean this whole existence. Surrounded by people and we really are the only two humans on a desert island. And what are we doin'? Nothin', that's what. Nothin' but fucking. As fun as that is, and, believe me, since it came back I've been enjoying the hell out of it more than ever, it's nothin' the animals don't do. All the other types here do it, too, only then they get to go and do work. What do we do? I mean, we eat, we work out some, we once in a while look up stuff in the computers or get something to read or we find some old video from fifty years ago and watch it for the ninety-third time, and we sleep a lot."

"What would you have us do?" I asked her. I was still getting used to her voice. The hormonal changes had raised it an octave without removing her old throaty quality which made even "Good morning" sound sexy as hell.

She sat up and grabbed her very large breasts. "You know how long I dreamed of havin' even an A-cup version of these? Now I got 'em, finally, big enough that I can't see my toes standing up, and what's the good? And the rest of the body, it's to die for, and without doin' much of anything to make it, either, and who sees it? I want to show it off! I want to walk down any street and have heads turn. I want to go to the ball in a slinky, skintight designer gown, I want men to be fallin' all

303

over themselves and women envious as all hell. I spent my whole life lookin' like a fifteen-year-old boy, and now that I got what I always dreamed of I want to flaunt it, and if that's not what I'm supposed to be thinkin', fuck 'em. Jeez, I want to walk down the street on your arm, the way you are now, and have 'em eat their hearts out. That's what I want."

"Tough doing investigative reporting looking like that," I pointed out.

She made a face. "So what? So I get producers who do it and I stand there at the scene of the crime and I read the copy and do the rewrite before delivery and they pay me a jillion dollars. We'd be the anchor team to die for."

That was a tempting fantasy. Still, "So how do you propose we get out of here?"

"There's got to be a way. I know there is."

I sat up and shook my head and sighed. "I have to admit that sometimes I really still miss the old Karen, the *original* Karen," I told her.

She looked at me like I was nuts. "You didn't even want to sleep with the old Karen."

"Yes I did," I told her truthfully. "I just didn't want to be ditched one more time."

That got her for a moment. Then she said, "Yeah, okay, but what's the difference on that score now? You're sure the same gloomy Gus you always were. I'm still the same, deep down, only now I look like I always wanted to look. I guess Jerry figured that he'd take the best extremes for both of us, but that's just the outside."

I stared right into her sparkling green eyes. "Because I could *trust* the original Karen, even if she did make some boneheaded moves for ambition. I don't believe you're aware of the change, but I can't trust you anymore. Not since that first night on the ship. You have no idea how tough it is to need somebody, really need them, and have them around all day and all night, and still not fully be able to trust them."

Her expression was an interesting mix of hurt and being somehow touched. "You really need me?"

She got behind me and started massaging my neck and shoulders, and, as she did so, she started giving me little romantic kisses. Her head closed on my left ear, and she licked it erotically, then whispered, "But I love you. Tomboy Karen fell for fat, smelly, middle-aged Chuck way back in those times at your apartment. I'd do anything for you. I climbed on that robot not out of guts but just to impress you, the big-shot superreporter."

I nodded, a bit sadly. "But we're not really ourselves anymore. We're who Jerry and Hal and Doc Foo and the others in charge want us to be for their own purposes. And love doesn't mean trust. People do nutty things for love. They betray the lover to save him or her. Or they go on board a hostile and secure ship in international waters to try and save the other and then refuse escape when it's offered."

She stopped dead. "What are you saying? That you came after me because you . . . *loved* me?"

"Yes, I'm saying that, as old-fashioned and romantic as it sounds. I've been there a couple of times before and it wasn't real. Know how I know it wasn't? Because I wouldn't have stupidly put myself in that much danger for either of 'em."

"But—why didn't you say something, do something, back when you had the chance, before I went charging into trouble?"

"Because I didn't realize it myself, until after it was too late," I told her. "And then they turned you into a sexless blob who sounded like Karen but had no initiative and who aimed to carry out with a smile any orders given her."

"But—I thought—Kate . . ."

"She's a nice lady, a friend, probably has double my IQ, and if she'd invited me I'd have gone to bed with her but even if she didn't that was okay. But I was never in love with her, no. I still worry about her, but I don't lust after her. Never did."

Karen got up and started mildly pacing, finger on her lip, like she was chewing on the nail although I knew it was just a habit. She'd done that even in the first days of this when she got to thinking, but it just looked sexier now. Everything about her did. I looked at her present body and its inability to make a nonsuggestive move and wondered just how deeply she thought about things anymore. She was as smart as ever, but she was not an initiator, or at least she hadn't been. Now she seemed to have figured out whatever was puzzling her, and she climbed back in bed and came up close to my ear again. This time no rub, no lick.

"How about this?" she whispered very softly. "I know why you visit the animals, and I never told anybody."

That was a shock. Immediately I realized that I either had to accept that she was telling me the absolute truth as she knew it or my remaining secrets had been blown. Since there was no hope in thinking the latter, I preferred to believe the former and got excited.

She sat back up and leaned against the wall. "You know I went to Georgetown?"

"I remember you saying that once, yes."

"Well, one semester I had several schedule conflicts and I wound up with a big open spot and nothing much to take. So I decided to take something just for me, just for the hell of it and because it might be handy if I wound up teaching instead of getting a journalism job. It was taught by a Jesuit priest, but he didn't teach at Georgetown. He just came over and gave this one course.

"Most of the time, he was a professor across town at Gallaudet."

I grabbed her and kissed her so hard that we almost started in again, back upright.

I had been frustrated up to this point in my efforts to get more than a few sentences worth of exchange between Syzmanski and me using the basics of that first encounter. It was even tougher because people were always in and out, and not all of them were fond of me coming in, even if Tigua had gotten me clearance from the Vargases to watch the animals. Even when I had the time, there were only occasional instances where I could separate from Karen and get in there without her, mostly by forgoing sleep or waking early.

Time would still tell if I could trust Karen again, but she'd aced two semesters of sign language for the deaf and hard-of-hearing from a professor at the first university for the deaf in the whole world.

I knew that Johnny Boy would know the basics of signing just as he knew how to read lips; not because he or anybody in his immediate family was deaf, but because such skills were pure gold when you had somebody under surveillance and they knew it.

Karen had visited the animals with me a few times, but for some reason the chimps in particular raised something of a ruckus every time she'd been there so she had gotten used to talking to the Vargas Puff Girls and killing time for a few minutes. The chimps again started screaming and acting up, but this time we ignored them.

It was tough setting up a system like this when you never knew when your conversation was being monitored, recorded, and evaluated for potential problems, but I figured that security had to know that I'd figured out the secret of some of these animals by now but what the hell good did it do me? Now I had a different method, a more efficient one, but it would still depend a lot on Karen. We could only whisper so much, although today I was happy that the chimps were so loud because it would help mask any conversation.

Old John saw us and ambled over, glancing at Karen with a quizzical look. At least I thought it meant that; he might well still have a little cross-species ape lust, too.

He immediately spotted her reassuring sign-on, as it were, and looked over at me. I nodded, he shrugged a very human shrug, and, by asking very short and direct questions and allowing him as much leeway as he needed for the answer, we finally got some more key information.

"Are you the only one to be turned into an ape now?"

"No," he signed back. "Most of them, maybe all of them.

Chimps, too. This is what they turn you into if they cannot trust you or no longer need you."

"Is this the latent program they can trigger in us?"

"Probably," Syzmanski answered. "Be a waste if it happens."

We kind of appreciated the comment, even though I knew he was talking about Karen.

"Do they just let you rot here?"

"No. We are lab animals. This batch is being used to test how quick we can give sickness to others, how fast a change might be, so on. Both us and chimps are very close to humans. When it's all ready, they will make carriers of you two and a few others who still stay human."

"So few?"

"They can make more if they have to. Only took a few to spread AIDS to whole world. Three for Ebola Two. They know how to spread disease from so many years of fighting it."

That, unfortunately, made a lot of sense. And, of course, who would the world's health organizations come to, to stop the new outbreak? The folks who'd stopped E-2 just short of the Americas, that's who.

"What will it do to people? Wipe out the world?"

"No. Some will die. Generic formulas, chaos, so on. Most will mutate. Randomly. Lots more varieties than just here. Don't know how it works. Tropics may get their apes back. Others look like mythic types. They have lots they can't sustain in this place."

"Why are they doing this?"

"Took over the experiment. We never knew. They stopped working for us, had us working for them. Smart computers. Smart, scared mutants."

"But the armies will start wiping out those who get it by the millions!"

"Maybe, but only until *they* start to change. *Then* who will they point their guns at?"

It was a sobering thought. And it would almost guarantee

the safety of this place, which might even pretend that it was as surprised and shocked as they were. Wouldn't matter. If they invaded and destroyed this place it would be too late, and they would be taking out perhaps the only people and machines capable of stopping or reversing the plague. Nobody else had gotten *close* to E-2. Only here.

"How close are they to executing the plan?"

"There are some bugs, but if they had to for some reason, they could start it now. It would be a little slower and more dangerous but it's that far along. As to how much time before they have it just right, ask Vargas. Man, not wife. Man is also working on antidote. Tried to get early work out by Wasserman. Hal let the truth slip to me. That was why I was after you. Not to nail you but to get the Vargas files and convince my family so they could be used where they might do some good. Hal caught on. You can guess the rest."

I sure could. That program was still in storage in a lot of hidden places, but it would be many months old, maybe more, by now. It was impossible to tell how long we'd been here even though we had watches and calendars and the like. Things seemed to work on their own basis here, and time chunks were often missing.

"Watch out for female Vargas," Syzmanski warned. "She makes Foo seem nice. Likes playing with people's shapes, minds. A whip in all four hands. She does not know her husband is working both sides."

It was a good tip.

"Is there anything we can do for you?"

"Like to breathe fresh air, even as ape. Failing that, shoot Foo, female Vargas, and Myra Ling Kelly if you get the chance. Or make a monkey out of her."

We had to go. We'd already stayed too long to avoid somebody getting curious, but what the hell could I do?

I was suddenly aware that there was a near deathly silence in the place. The chimps had stopped all the ruckus and indeed many of them were now crowded at the window.

We moved casually over to their side and their eyes followed us. "Ask 'em if any of them sign," I whispered to Karen, who did so. Unfortunately, what we got back were sad shakings of heads.

We would have to figure out something. It would really help to know who all those apes really were.

It was time to take a few more risks and see if we could somehow make contact in the same sort of clandestine manner with Antonio Vargas.

Getting to Antonio Vargas was something of a problem, since he appeared to be a driven workaholic who did a lot of stuff on his own in sealed-off chambers or in the supermodeling rooms we were prohibited from even approaching. The few times we could find him in the lab section, it was generally with Señora Vargas lurking about, and just from her looks I got the idea that she saw little difference between me and the chimps.

Neither of us thought we could trust any of the Puff Girls, not even Tigua, as friendly as she seemed, since they all worked mostly with the señora. And it had been Tigua, after all, whom Jerry had appointed as his stand-in when we'd first arrived.

Still, even Karen argued that they had to know why we were so interested in the apes, and they didn't seem bothered by it which bothered us no end. As it turned out, though, before we could find a way to get to Vargas in private, he found us.

Antonio Vargas must have been a handsome man in his prime, and even in his current state he looked almost like a statue of a saint, albeit a small one, barely Karen's height. His finely chiseled, dark face was crowned by two small goat's horns and, from the waist down, he was more goat than human, right to a small tail that seemed to have a mind of its own. How he balanced on those small hooves I didn't know, but I figured that if Circe could find a way for Karen to have supermammaries without a backache or a center-of-gravity problem then a satyr was probably a cinch.

We were going up for perhaps one more try at breaking through to the chimps when he emerged from a nearby off-limits room and almost walked into us. I could see that a mental undressing of Karen and some appreciation of the result was first on his mind, but that quickly passed, or was forced to the background.

"Ah! Señor Vallone and his beautiful assistant! I have seen you around here many times. I am Antonio Vargas."

Karen beat me to the punch in replying, which was, in retrospect, a good idea. "We are honored to meet you, Dr. Vargas. It is not every day that one meets the man who saved the world."

Vargas was a bit taken aback, both publicly humble and privately, but obviously pleased as all hell.

"Antonio, please. If you say 'Dr. Vargas' around here they will not know which one you mean! I am not sure how to react to the compliment, however. I assume you refer to the Ebola Two business of years past, yes? Well, it was not just me, it was a whole team, many of us, working night and day without rest." He paused a moment, then added, "Come! I would be honored if the two of you would join me in a drink. I have been working hard once again, and my wife and colleagues urge me to take more breaks. Do not refuse me, please!"

We were hardly going to do that.

Vargas was wearing no clothing save what might be called one gigantic codpiece, but that codpiece was suspended from a thin belt. Clipped to the belt was a small intercom/pager, and he removed it and said into it, "Vargas, A., on Level Seven Two, short break. Comlink will remain on."

There was an indecipherable short response and he reclipped the link on his thin belt, then gestured for us to follow him.

He led us into a small anteroom where, of all things, there were glasses and bottles of wine. The vintages and brands were impressive, even for somebody like me who rarely drank wine and then drank mostly the very moderate stuff; these were definitely imports of the highest quality, set in a device where you could choose one and it would fill a glass without otherwise breaking its seal.

He handed each of us a goblet of chablis and touched our glasses. I started to sip it, and he seemed to take offense. "Oh, no, no, my friends! A great wine you sniff, then swirl around the palate, and then you drink." He demonstrated the system, and we both followed suit. I wasn't too much on the sniffing and swirling, but the stuff tasted as good as any wine I'd ever had.

We discovered that we were in for a short wine-tasting lesson with "no" unacceptable as an answer. Each vintage was as good as the last, only different, but I was beginning to worry about how my body, which hadn't had any alcoholic beverages since before it was worth preserving, and Karen, ditto, would hold up. I began to feel a bit light-headed.

Finally, he stopped. "You both feel a bit tipsy, no?"

"Yes," we managed at once. I yearned for a chair.

"Good. I believe the mixture is sufficient to block any audio pickups from internal implants, and this room has its own special security. A light head is not too big a price to pay for true privacy, is it? There is so little in this place."

We both got the drift of what he was saying. "It's your move, Doc . . . Antonio," I responded.

"I am sorry I have not been able to speak to you earlier, but I needed much more information first. I tried to help you by steering you to the apes and allowing you unfettered access. I must confess I had not considered that the lovely señorita here might know signing, let alone that one or more of the apes would as well! How much of this have you found out and from that what have you deduced so far? Come! Impress me."

I saw no reason not to tell him, considering the circumstances, even if it did mean also trusting John Syzmanski, something I knew I should never do no matter what he looked like. Vargas was a good listener, and waited until I was done and Karen had filled in some of the holes I'd neglected. Finally he said, "This is most impressive. I can see why Samuel took the added risk to reach you."

"Then it's true?"

He sighed and nodded. "Pretty much, yes, although it is even more comprehensive than you know. And it is virtually finished. We are on the final stages of testing now. These computers, they are amazing, but frightening, like an alien species. They *think*, they truly think, but in ways so alien that we cannot imagine it. Only Jerry has any grasp of their universe, and it is limited by the ability of even his great mind to absorb and interpret data. I am never certain who or what I am dealing with when I speak with him these days. Not since he mated himself to his machines, his 'children' as he calls them."

Karen gasped. "He's merged his mind with the computer?"

"In a sense, yes, but only in a sense. Their ability, through him, to experience some of our plane of existence has helped them fine-tune their biological programs to an amazing degree. He, on the other hand, can experience only fleeting glimpses of their very different plane of existence. Still, there is no question that, no matter what his limits, they consider him more than their father, perhaps even their god. They assume that the limits they see are simply as far as they can go into our plane with comprehension, just as he is limited in theirs. They think of some of the rest of us as demigods, I suppose, even though we do not directly interface with them. Everyone, everything else, you two included, I fear, they see as nothing more than laboratory animals."

"You mean Jerry and his 'children' are plotting a takeover of the world?" That was always my thought, but Vargas immediately dismissed it.

"No, no! You do not understand! Why should they want to take control of and rule our physical universe? Theirs is so much grander, and, to them, more comprehensible. We use laboratory rats all the time, but do we wish to rule and reign over all of them? They don't care about domination. They do the work we have because the problems intrigue them, or challenge them. They don't really care how they actually apply here. That is for us few demigods to understand."

"Then why do it?" I asked him. "Why change the world into . . . ?"

"Monsters?" he concluded, smiling grimly. "Yes, monsters. Some very pretty, certainly, some very practical, others utter nonsense, but monsters all to purebred humans of any stripe. There are other words. English, which steals whatever words are useful from all the other tongues of the world, is quite useful in this. *Freaks. Creatures. Monstrosity* or merely *curiosity*? Also *defective, deformed,* and grossly *abnormal.* One who brings forth *horror, disgust,* and *fear.* Do you see how we would look to the bulk of the world? Some would worship us, of course, but most would stone us, or pen us up in reservations and put us on display."

When they'd originally set up Project Regen Lizard, it had been an alliance between what seemed to be farsighted government, university, and business leaders. Four separate labs in four different regions of the world, all under nominal control of some tiny and easily bought-off nation, had been set up, each with a different part of the project. For a while, little was produced, although they did find some major antiviral agents and sufficient DNA-based cures for genetic defects and diseases and for the enhancement of plants and animals to feed an ever more populous world that in fact paid their budget and more. And then Jerry had come up with Ariel, parent of Caliban, one of whose offspring was Circe, using a revolutionary new process for memory storage and holographic memory retrieval that was unlike anything anyone had ever seen. With Ariel, built into the bedrock of an island in the South Pacific, they managed to produce their first true changelings.

"All of it was modeling, of course," he told us. "We had no idea that they were actually synthesizing these new sequences in labs across the known world. And testing them, first on animals, then on human beings who were not always volunteers, all away from everything else. We should have known, because one of the first things we worked on was a virtual Fountain of Youth program, one that would not only stop aging but actually reverse it genetically. The program was unbelievably complex; I do not think that any of us, even today, could follow it. And yet, it was child's play for Ariel, since it involved nothing more than mutating key stem cells and then sending them into a bloodstream to reverse-engineer youth, as it were. You two have experienced the results. So have most of us. And, of course, to one degree or another, our remote masters. When one of them died, do not think that they were in their coffins! Few were. Most were undergoing treatment to become lovers and tennis pros in Aruba."

Oy! I thought. A whole world of Syzmanskis.

"That didn't last long, partly because they could not afford to have this revolutionary discovery announced to the world, for obvious reasons, and also because many of us decided to rotate back to our corporate or government or university positions, not to mention the staff, but they did manage to hold on to us for another year or so because of the *first* Ebola Two crisis, the one that seemed to die out but frightened everyone. By the time we'd developed a treatment for it, they effectively sealed us off, and it was becoming clear that we were all becoming freaks and monsters. Only Jerry didn't give a damn. By that time Ariel had designed a radical new computer, Caliban, along with satellite systems to handle just about all maintenance and self-repair. All he cared about was that he be given the chance to build it, out here, in the middle of nowhere, just the way he dreamed."

"Why not give it to the world?" Karen asked him, wide-eyed. "Jeez! It's the dream of humankind!"

He gave a wry chuckle. "Oh, no, my pretty one. We have far too many people to feed in this world now, and we long ago decided that it was too expensive to colonize Mars or create orbiting colonies. So now we have mass extinctions of animals, food riots, starvations, more local wars, and unbelievable misery. We have always looked only at the short term, we materialists of the world. It is always next quarter's profits, and the executive or politician who invests heavily in the long term instead of the quick fix for the short term is turned out by his board or his electors. The Ebola was free. The great diseases yet to come are free. The decision to let everything just go along, *that* has great cost. And you wish to make it so everyone is suddenly young again? All you will do is increase the slaughter and misery."

"But—it's so unfair to keep such a discovery secret!"

"My dear," he responded sadly, "you would be astonished at the discoveries you know nothing about, many of which are older than you."

It had taken the better part of that year's delayed departure to begin the process that would give them the leg up next time to save the world, while slowly they had begun to change— though not nearly as slow as security hoped these smart folks would be at figuring out what had been done to them. There was some violence, some vandalism, and several attempted and a few successful suicides, but by that time the project's security teams had gotten control and subjected the trouble-makers to psychochemical changes of mind, where they'd become cheery, cooperative, and compliant, if not very creative. The high-end creative teams like the Vargases got the message. And in constant satellite communication with his beloved Ariel, Jerry built Caliban here to "her" exact specifications, using revolutionary new means of constructing and synthesizing what was needed.

And Caliban, in turn, built a direct interface just for Jerry, to Jerry's delight, and Jerry, who Antonio described as a kind of worm or snake hybrid we hadn't seen yet, fitted into that case and that case sent thousands of tiny tendrils into his spinal column and nervous system and they've been mated ever since.

"So what are you going to do?" I asked him. "Thin out the population?"

"Not me, no. All I would need for that would be to have done nothing when the Ebola mutation crossed the Atlantic. There *were* immunes, you know. One in eight recovered. One in forty never got it. Bad odds for maintaining a civilization, but because we are already in the age of robotics and thinking machines, humanity would barely survive. It is how nature prunes us, you see. We've been stopping that process for the past two hundred and fifty years or so. The grave population problems of India were caused by the British. No, do not look at me that way, I am serious! The Indian culture married young, the women began having children at fourteen and kept having them until they died, usually in their forties or younger. Most of the children died, of course, but the healthiest, most resistant ones survived and followed in their parents' tradition. Then the British took over. They built sewers, purified the water, brought in inoculations and all the rest of modern medicine. The Indian culture had been unchanged for thousands of years, so it did not change. Only now most of the children survived. In no time at all, in historical terms, India was suddenly nothing but human bodies."

"What a choice," Karen muttered.

"The point is, Jerry doesn't care, and neither do the computers. Ask them how to solve the population problem and they will say first to eliminate two-thirds of the population and then to colonize in space before the problem resurfaces. They also suggest changing the cultures, as if that were an option. Jerry does not care much, but, unlike many others, such as my wife, he is not full of hate. He does not want blood, revenge for a long imprisonment. He simply wants to be free to do as he wishes and without fear that he and his beloved computers will be blown to bits. My wife and many others want not only revenge, but to go home, to walk down streets in fresh air and rain and snow, to have a real life. Could she, four-armed and colorfully striped, have a life? Could I, in fact? Or what about Tigua?"

The question, of course, was rhetorical.

"What about the gill people and the Delphinides?" I asked him. "They couldn't do it even if acceptance was guaranteed."

"True, but they, and others about which you know little

or nothing, would not have to hide, or fear discovery. In a sense, they already have what we crave, since fish and other aquatic life are amazingly nonjudgmental. You're either edible or to be avoided. Period. They own three-fifths of the earth if they aren't murdered before they get everything secure. I just want a small, comfortable place, overlooking a bit of woods, with perhaps a lake in view, with fresh air and some real sunshine."

"And this new agent will give that to you?" I asked him.

"Probably not. Almost certainly not. Where I come from, there are two ancient tribal groups. Call them subcultures, call them asterisks, it's not important. I cannot tell who is who. I cannot tell until they tell me which they belong to. Yet they still hate each other, and feud with each other, and even kill each other. I once worked in a place in eastern Europe where all the people were Slavs. Some were Orthodox Christians, nominally, others were Roman Catholics, nominally, and still others were Moslems, at least nominally. They looked the same, spoke the same, had the same history, traditions, atrocious sauces, and bad wines. They lived in the same sorts of houses in identical-looking towns and villages doing much the same things in the same way. Except, every once in a while, they'd start killing one of the other groups, without hesitation, with enormous ferocity. Similar activities can be found everywhere on the globe. Hindu and Tamil, Orange Irish and Green Irish, Watusi and Hutu—everywhere. Think of the people who would have thrown Einstein in an oven because his parents were nominally Jewish."

"We get your point," I told him.

"I think not. You must take it a step further. Now imagine that everyone, everywhere, could instantly see and tell which primary tribal group or ancestral type you were. Because your people have four arms and are striped, and others have goatlike hindquarters, and others are hermaphroditic pastel-colored female shapes with tails, or half cat, or snake, or hairy ape, or so on. You see where I am going?"

And we did see. After the panic, after the now very rapid

changes, after the rioting and whatever that would come from the changeling plague, there would eventually emerge a dozen, maybe a lot more, different and distinct races. *Kill the horned goats! They caused this! They're demons!* And *No! Away with that race of rainbow-colored fornicators!* You could see each side having its own attitudes from existing cultures as well as all new ones, and all the time the last humans would be paranoid, always examining themselves, ready to slaughter all the freaks.

It was an uglier scenario than the one he'd painted for the world as it existed now.

"I do not know what our present future holds, or if it is destined to be as bleak as it appears," he said sadly. "But I can see Jerry's future, as clearly as if it had already happened." He looked at his watch and frowned. "Now, you two, you must go. We will speak again, and soon, I promise."

We both started to say something, but then didn't. He was calling the shots here, and he knew the system better than anybody, probably, except Jerry.

I looked at Karen, she nodded, and we both headed for the door.

"Señor Vallone," he called. "One more word, for your ear only."

Karen frowned, but looked resigned. I bent down and he whispered, "She is safe now. She is crazy in love with you. It is the kind of error they can never understand. Her devotion to you overrides anything they might tell her to do against your interests."

I nodded and smiled at him. "Thank you, Señor Vargas," I responded, turned, and left, with Karen waiting for me just outside with That Look on her face.

"Okay, so what was that about?" she asked crossly.

I leaned down and whispered, "He said not to worry about you. That you would not betray me."

"Yeah, right," she muttered, but let it lie.

So much for the truth, I thought. But, then again, what was the truth? The most famous guy to ask that question had first declared his prisoner innocent, then nailed him to a cross.

What did Vargas really want? And how did he expect to get it without getting himself, and probably us, either killed or made into monkeys?

At least it wouldn't be much longer before we knew. A few weeks, he said. Anything we could do, and it didn't look like much, we'd better do pretty damned quickly. I wondered about my nerve again, even after all this boredom.

Well, one way or another, we were destined to be the tools of a possibly mad genius.

Some choice.

SEVENTEEN

When we started seeing Dr. Foo Luck Kai and her gigantic servant Geoffrey around the levels, we knew things were not that long from popping.

With so many Anurians coming and going it may seem odd that both of us could instantly pick out Dr. Foo from a bit of distance, but it wasn't hard at all. I doubted if we would ever forget her, or not be able to almost sense her presence. If John Singleton Syzmanski deserved to be a great hairy ape, Foo deserved to be a mosquito.

I would have said "cockroach," only Hal, too, showed up. They seemed to be in frantic meetings with the Vargases and others at the higher levels of the complex. It certainly meant that we were in the endgame, but it also meant that Karen and I were not about to go up to the new level, not even to visit the apes. We had no choice but to wait it out and hope that Antonio would pull something out of his figurative hat.

Coming from the cafeteria, we ran into Tigua, who was carrying a flat panel of some kind. When she saw us, she stopped us and said in a low tone, "I was asked to give you this. Once you open and read it, the message will disappear. I do not know the contents and can answer no questions about it." With that, she handed it to me and continued on past.

By now we pretty well knew where the security monitors were; it was fairly simple to go over to a point where we'd be facing the rock wall, so no reflection, and angle it at such a point that we could read the thing but no overlooker could.

With Karen looking over my shoulder, I opened it, expecting some kind of visual image or voice. Instead, it was a small body of text in fairly large type, and all it said was, "When you are signaled, go immediately to airlock Seven Six. Trust who you find there. Do not delay. A." That was it. As we watched, the letters faded away, one by one, in the order they'd been input, until we were staring at a blank slate.

I closed it, wishing it had said a little more. The numbers of the levels, and the corresponding airlocks, were the approximate depth indicators. Level Seven Six, on which our living quarters were located, meant we were seventy-six meters straight down. That was a lot of water, and there was no way that I knew of that we could get out without a very long time in a decompression chamber.

The airlocks were used by both the fish faces and the Delphinides to deliver cargo modules too bulky or risky for the central elevator. Delphinides, who didn't seem to be much bothered by decompression and who could tolerate a maximum depth of about a hundred meters, or so it seemed, were operating here near the limits of their ability to handle the pressure and perhaps their ability to hold their breaths, although there were emergency oxygen feeds built into the external tube area for any in trouble.

The intent of the message was clear. We were being offered an escape route of some sort, while a diversion was created to aid us. Apparently Vargas had friends among the water people; he'd certainly spoken of them with some respect and perhaps envy. We even knew two, sort of, from our kidnapped band of scientists, but where they were now was anybody's guess.

Karen was thrilled by the message, and couldn't understand why I was so glum. "It means we're gonna get *out!*" she whispered excitedly. "What's your problem? Don't you want out of here?"

"Nothing more than that," I assured her. "But do we dare do it?"

"Huh?"

"We don't know that the message was really from Vargas, and we have only that one conversation and the dubious word of John Syzmanski that he's reliable. Isn't this the plot? You, me, and any other remaining humans, having been given our reward of our dream physique and the restoration of our youth, escape from the big, bad mutants. What if we're all carrying this new superbug? Everybody we meet, all those we come in contact with, will get it and pass it on. With a reasonable latency period and today's hypersonic travel, it'll be all over in weeks. And, being such drop-dead gorgeous humans, the newly mutated mobs will rip us to shreds."

She stared at me. "Are you telling me we don't dare get rescued?"

"Morally, it's pretty dicey, and I do mean we'll be targeted."

"Well, we might as well go anyway," she said flatly. "No, don't look at me like that! Consider—we're not the only ones, right? And we can't do anything to the complex or people here doing this, right?"

"Okay, so . . . ?"

"Well, then, we can't stop it, if you're right. We can just choose whether or not to run and maybe make it in spite of the odds, or stay here and join the chimp brigade. *It's gonna happen anyway,* no matter *what* we do. So, let's *do*."

"It's hard to argue with logic like that," I told her. "Of course, if, somehow, it's not just a plot to put us in play, it's going to be risky as hell. Security will wonder why we're heading for the lock, and if anything's there it's sure gonna be one hell of a slow-rising target."

"You were the one with the guts," I pointed out to her, "and look where it got you."

"Well, after a side trip, it got me tits and ass, even if I always dreamed of a C cup and I got at least an H here."

"I suspect Jerry measured your reactions, or mine. Okay, then, it's decided. The only questions now are what's the signal and how long until we get it? Hours? Days?"

"I think we'll know it when it happens," she assured me.

"Besides, there's gotta be something sittin' at the lock, right? And there's another question. If we are carriers, will there be enough latency for a full church wedding?"

I laughed. "Wouldn't matter anyway, baby. Sorry. Got multiple divorces but never got the first one annulled. The second was civil both ways."

She looked crestfallen. "You know, there was a time not long ago when just about nobody got married, and *you* had to take up the slack! Now that it's in again, I got to settle for a judge. It's not fair!"

I shrugged. "What can I say? I'm an old-fashioned guy."

The argument was loud and eavesdropping wasn't a major problem for the bunch of us, and not just Karen and myself, who tried unsuccessfully to be inconspicuous in the corridor area where the meeting was taking place. Everybody deep down knew what was at stake here, no matter what their feelings about it. It was sometimes hard to hear every word, but we could pretty well fill in the blanks.

"But it's done, right?" Jerry's voice asked loudly.

"Of course it's finished!" an unfamiliar female voice responded, but one whose Spanish accent suggested who she was. "It's been finished, tested, checked, and double checked for weeks! He's just been manufacturing delay after delay!"

"Well, Antonio, what about it? Is this true?" Jerry asked the legendary geneticist.

"I had hoped against hope, to this very moment, that I could persuade you not to do this thing," Antonio Vargas responded, sounding both sad and tired. "What you would have us do is more monstrous than anything done to us, more monstrous than anything we have done to our unwilling associates and conscripts here. Not because of the absurdist mutations, although it is impossible for me to reconcile something as right and just when we ourselves resent and hate it having been done to us. It is the massive death toll of the innocent, and, perhaps even more serious, the direct alteration of evolution without any concept at all of what it will do for our races' common future."

"We've been all through this," Hal's smooth, polished baritone came through clearly. "It is useless to keep rehashing the morals and ethics of this business when none of our business is moral or ethical nor has it ever really been."

The male Vargas wasn't accepting that. "Countless cures for misery, corrections of horrible genetic mutations that have plagued humankind for thousands of years? And halting an outbreak that killed fourteen million people and could have killed ninety percent of the world is not moral nor ethical?"

"Grow up and stiffen that goat's backbone of yours if you have one!" Hal responded contemptuously. "Holier than thou, the brave savior of the world. And you are brilliant, I must admit, within your lab and your computers and your models. But do you really believe you could have stopped Ebola Two in so short a period without that exacting data on the virus? You never even questioned where that data came from, did you, savior of the world? *It came from the lab experts and the computers who made that damnable virus in the first place!*"

There was a sharp, stunned silence, and I could see in my mind's eye the effect this had on that noble face. Finally, in a voice choking with emotion, he asked, "Jerry, is this true?"

"Yes, of course," he replied. Jerry sounded nice and human but behind it was the ruthless and amoral logic of the great machines. "They had a weapon. They had to know how to contain it. We did not create the virus ourselves, although Ariel had some part in it in the early stages, but we were presented with a problem that I felt only you and Caliban could solve. And you did."

"Fourteen million people . . . And the risk! Did you know about this? Did you?"

"Not when they did it, no," his wife responded. "But I knew when they brought it here that they either had done this or would do this unless we found a way to stop them. I was never certain of the chronology. But it only reinforces our point! Look at what they have done with our work! Not just us, our work! Look at you! You are fine, noble, and what did they do? They used you to control their terror weapons! And they tested it on a huge island of the very poor, including in Santo Domingo some of our own cousins. Now they will come for us if we do not come for them! They are stronger than the governments they supposedly serve! They finance themselves by betting on plagues and famines and shortages *they* create! That *we* help them create! Now let *them* live forever in filtered air in holes in the ground, or turn into what we are or worse! In the end, fewer perhaps will die by our actions than by theirs as they use their terror diseases to thin out the overpopulation, as if the whole world were laboratory rats! Do you not see? We are not attacking the world, we are taking it back!"

Good lord! I thought. *I'm almost on* her *side!* The trouble was, even if we got out clean, we couldn't print a word of this. The only evidence we would have is ourselves, and we could be explained away far easier than a flying gargoyle and they'd gotten away with that.

"There are other ways to deal with such evil men," Antonio Vargas said, although we could barely hear him. He sounded a broken man.

"There is no way to deal with them and survive," Hal responded. "Jerry has run the equations through Caliban. The only reason they haven't already taken us all out is that they haven't yet figured how to get past Jerry's security firewalls without triggering a mass destruction of data. But Jerry is not the only brilliant mind left in this rotten world. They came within a whisker of taking control of Ariel only a few days ago. They will eventually succeed. We are out of time, Antonio. Join us in attempting to create a better world out of the pieces that will be left. It sure as hell can't be any worse."

Karen tapped me on the shoulder. "I think we should go down to Level Seven Six, and quick," she whispered.

I turned and looked at her. "Why?"

"Because there's suddenly a large container at every air-lock along the core that I can see."

I turned and looked back at the central elevator. Just to the left of it was the airlock for this level, and, sure enough, there was something large and gray parked there, and I could see shadowy shapes in the water around it. Looking up through the complex, I could see several more in place.

"I cannot agree to this," Antonio Vargas was saying.

"You can do nothing about it," Hal responded. "You can participate or watch, but you cannot stop it."

"I believe I can," responded the scientist.

"Let's get out of here," I said, and Karen and I took the down escalator two steps at a time.

We had just reached Seven Six when a series of explosions above us went off. They weren't huge explosions, but they were definitely a coordinated series of bangs. At the same instant, our watches both went off with a sound I had never heard before but could not mistake. It was almost a siren's wail.

Interestingly, we two weren't the only ones with this alarm. We heard a lot of them above us, so the other chambers were for other people, probably not as human as we, but innocent enough.

There was a screech, almost a scream of panic and despair, echoing from above, so loud that it penetrated even the cacophony around us.

"Antonio! *What have you done?* WHAT HAVE YOU DONE?"

The problem was, we didn't know what Antonio had done, either.

Something came down the tube wall in front of us from above, about as fast as I'd ever seen anything that big go. Just before we could make the corridor leading to the airlock, it dropped in front of us and we stopped, dead.

"I don't think so," Dr. Foo said, breathing hard. "I don't know what is going on here, but I have the strong feeling that you two are very much in the middle of it. If you think you are getting out while we are trapped, forget it."

I was conscious of several others in back of us, and I turned to see if we were being sandwiched or what. It turned out to be several different kinds of mutants, including some of the Puff Girls with infants, all of whom also had watches that were wailing.

Foo unclipped one of those high-pressure syringes from her belt. "Karen, listen to my voice," she said in her most commanding tone. "You will come here, take this syringe, and you will plunge it into yourself, then stand with me."

Karen stopped for a moment, seemingly transfixed, as if fighting with herself. She could neither approach Foo nor do much else.

All of a sudden I realized the import of Antonio's reassurance to me. "Fight her, Karen! *If you love me, reject her!*"

Karen seemed to come out of it. "Fuck you, frog. You don't own me anymore, and you can't keep all of us from passing!"

I saw Foo's powerful legs tense, and I realized that she might not be able to keep us from rushing her but she could nail one of us with that thing.

A fraction of a second before she would have propelled herself into either Karen or me, syringe ready, two hairy— hands? no—*feet* closed firmly around her neck. Her legs, instead of leaping her forward into us, sprung out in front of her and she thrashed as she was effectively hanging by the neck, held by the twin handlike feet of a great orange orangutan. Foo's hands came up, trying to pry off the grip, and as they did the syringe fell to the floor.

Everybody behind us suddenly charged right at the Anurian, essentially right into her body, and we heard something snap. The orangutan swung Foo out and flung her onto the floor away from the tube entrance, where she lay twitching wildly.

Four other orangutans dropped to the floor as did the main assailant, and we didn't wait to see who was who. We all, Karen, me, and the apes, headed for the airlock, went through, and crowded into the already packed container. None of us minded; the airlock closed and hissed behind us, and then so did the inner seal, and within a minute we felt ourselves pulled away from the lock.

The next couple of hours were among the most nerve-wracking of my entire life, and that includes everything in this business that had gone before. And, no, it wasn't because we all discovered that orangutans really stink in close quarters, or the use of one lousy little chemical toilet.

The chamber had no windows, and while it had a series of color-coded indicators, it had no guide to what those indicators represented. We knew we were free floating, but if Jerry and Caliban and the others had any means to get to us, then there was absolutely nothing we could do about it except eventually drown. The oxygen appeared to be recycling, so we'd drown or starve or die of thirst before we'd asphyxiate, if that was a good point. Of course, they hadn't figured on five added primates, I suspected.

There wasn't a whole lot of conversation, either, although we did talk with the others just enough to determine that nobody seemed to know more than we did. It seems that the siren warning was quite old, and was something everybody (except us, apparently) had drilled into them in Indoctrination 101. It was the emergency signal, and everybody knew just where they were immediately supposed to proceed to, and just how much time they had to do it in. It supposedly sounded only if there was a catastrophic failure of the life-support systems inside the tubes and rooms.

It had certainly worked, for what it was worth.

Crammed inside the dive chamber, though, it was Karen and I who felt the aliens. Above, we'd be the ones who could interact with the world, while all of these strange mutants faced a very uncertain future.

In truth, I think the whole raising and depressurization took only an hour or two at most, but it seemed like an eternity, particularly when you were waiting to drop six or seven kilometers into the deep or suffer some equally nerve-wracking fate.

We recognized a couple of the Puff Girls as ones who either had quarters near ours or who'd worked in the new lab section with the Vargases, but they weren't any that we had more than a smile-and-nod acquaintance with. If all of them were to be believed, none had any idea that this was coming.

I assumed that our savior, as it were, the big male orangutan, was John Syzmanski, but he didn't try any sort of communication with us and all orangutans look alike to me. Still, there was one larger and obvious male, and four females, so it was entirely in character. I wondered why they'd opted to get out; if the future was uncertain for the other mutants, it was downright bleak for the apes, who at best would wind up in zoos, probably split up, or at worst would simply be left stranded.

Well, that was the most frustrating thing about all this business. Except for coming after Karen and then deciding to stick instead of parachuting out back at the island, all this had really gone on all around me, rather than due to any action or inaction of mine. Karen's decision to ride that robot into the superyacht was her only serious and conscious action, too. We'd been victims to an extent, and observers, but we hadn't really done anything. And now, with the biggest story of our lives, we were going to have to convince a ton of editors against the opposition of a massive conspiracy of silence, and whether we'd even have the evidence we were riding with (hopefully) to the surface was unknown. After all, what was up top except two small tropical islands and a lot of ocean?

And then, suddenly, we were on the surface, bobbing around, and being tossed against each other. Only the fact that we were so tightly packed kept us from serious harm.

A gong sounded and there was a bright green light on the airlock that we could all accept as an all clear. Our blood wasn't going to be filled with killer nitrogen bubbles, and we weren't going to be stuck at the bottom of a Pacific trench.

"Hold on!" I shouted to everyone as something grabbed, steadied, and then started moving us laterally. "Sit down for a moment! We're not quite done yet!"

"But the airlock's green!" protested one of the two zebra-women with us.

"Yeah, but we're still moving. Let's give it a little. I'd rather walk than swim."

It didn't take long before there was a sharp shock through the chamber, and then it was obvious that we were no longer in any sort of motion. I was nearest the airlock door, so I made the decision, spinning the wheel until there was a loud hissing and then an opening. Extremely hot, humid air came in and wrapped around us. None of us had been out of climate-controlled atmospheres for months, some for years, and it was quite a shock.

I swung the door away and looked around, seeing only wet sand, so I made my way out, then helped Karen, and, in turn, we all made it out of the chamber.

We were on the larger of the two islands, pretty much where we'd come in, but well down from the buildings, toward the forested part. Looking back toward the buildings, I could see three or four chambers identical to ours on the beach, and signs that others had been pushed up once and then dragged back into the sea. Way across on the other shore, I could see signs of similar events on the smaller island, although it was pretty far away and my eyes were already hurting from the brightness.

There were a lot of mutants milling about, and here and there were a few people, all couples, who were more like us. Young, sexy looking, but apparently "human." Some of the other carriers, no doubt. Some Orientals, two brown-skinned couples, one Indian or Pakistani couple, but we appeared to be the only ones of European ancestry—and the ones most vulnerable to the terribly hot sun. Both Karen and I were pale as ghosts after being underwater and we had no pigment or fat layers to help protect us, so I suggested that, until we found a gallon of sunscreen, we might be better off finding some shade. She agreed, although doubting that even the sun could hurt us much.

"I think they wanted us totally healthy and immune to most

things they could think of," she asserted, not for the first time. She may have been right; what would be the use of prepping your carriers only to have them die of sunstroke or the flu as soon as they were released?

My southern Italian ancestry had given me a more olive complexion, heightened by the youthful turn, and I'd never really gotten sunburned as such, but Karen was mostly Irish Celt and I knew damned well they fried in the tropics.

Still, we did have shorts and T-shirts on, so eventually I got antsy and decided I had to find out if anybody we actually knew was on the island. There had to be one or two, other than Syzmanski the Ape, and that meant Karen came, too. Not only was she never leaving my side, I didn't want her out of my sight, not after this. By God, we might not have actually done anything, but we were one hell of a team!

We walked toward the buildings, and Karen suddenly pointed at a pastel pink and metallic silver–haired Puff Girl. "That's Tigua! I'm sure of it! *Hey! Tigua! Over here!*"

The pink girl with the silver hair and tail stopped, looked around, then shaded her eyes. She was carrying something, but I couldn't see what, and when she saw us she broke into a run, then hugged both Karen and me. "Oh, I am so happy you made it out! That awful woman, she was going to stop you!"

"She almost did," Karen and I both said, almost in unison, then we laughed and I nodded to her.

"Do you know what happened?" Karen asked her.

"Not—*exactly*," the Puff Girl replied. "But I knew that a lot of things were in the works, as you say. Dr. Antonio, he spent a lot of time back and forth with the water people. They set this up between them. It was the water people who were key to this, you see. Both the ones who breathe air and, particularly, the ones who breathe water. We could not act until they had independent sources of power, and were confident that they could be self-sufficient. They did not help for us, but they are truly liberated, you see. We must still deal with the world, as we are, but they are now free. Free of the project, free of the land world. I do not know what will come of it, but I think that anyone who fishes the seas or comes into their domain now, and particularly in the future, will find that they are on someone else's planet, and that someone has more control than they. Dr. Antonio fulfilled his end of the bargain, cutting their cord as it were, and they fulfilled theirs, for we are here. I do not think we will hear from them again soon, unless our masters push it."

Our masters . . . From the standpoint of most of these people, and maybe even us, that was probably the way to put it.

"Tigua, are Jerry, and Hal, and the Vargases, and all that work, that big computer—are they all dead?" I couldn't help but ask it.

"I do not know. Some of them—but not Jerry—might have gotten in the escape pods. Or they may be still down there, but work out a different way. Levels Twenty through Thirty-six were completely flooded and destroyed, this I know. And it will eat its way down to the bottom anchor positions eventually, but it may take days or weeks or longer. And it will eventually work its way up, too."

"It?"

She nodded. "Dr. Antonio, he synthesized more than one virus. You know that the tubes are organic? They were designed by Circe and actually grow, sort of like hollow worms. The entire sequence was well known. Dr. Antonio, he was—*is*—as much a genius in his field as Jerry is in computers. Dr. Antonio, he engineered a minor organism that infects and breaks down the tube cells. Then he planted it in the center of the levels that are used for storage and backup, but that do not have any permanent people there. It spreads. When it finally broke down, it triggered the emergency system, which had been partly rewired so that important areas, links to the computer and to the outside, would blow up, see? And here we are."

I was impressed. "You mean Antonio did this all by himself?"

"Oh, no. He had the help of many very smart ones of the

water people for those areas where he did not know how to do something, and a few others who knew such skills. Most important were the apes."

My eyebrows went up. "The apes?"

"Yes. I hope most of them got here. Dr. Antonio, he only told me this morning, when he wanted to make sure they had a chance to get out. The apes, they may look normal, but they are as changed as I am, as you know. Some, like your Mr. Johnny, knew how to rewire alarms and spy systems and rig explosives—he was not a volunteer, but he had a very strong desire for revenge. Others who helped *were* volunteers in many fields. Not Hal, not even Jerry suspected that the apes were doing modeling, running theory, testing alternatives. They drug us in our sleep, they drag us in, they know what we know, so we were to know nothing that Dr. Antonio felt was harmful. But nobody, *nobody* thinks about the apes."

All I could manage was "Well, I'll be damned!" Karen's jaw had dropped too far for her usual exclamations.

Tigua finally brought forward the small boxlike object she'd been carrying. "Dr. Antonio, just before he went into that loud meeting, he gave me this. He told me to give it to you, Señor Chuck, the next time I see you. He said not to worry if I lost it or had it taken, that only you could use it."

I took it, curious, and saw that it was a small memo recorder. I put my right thumb on the indentation, a little green light went on, and we could hear Antonio Vargas's voice.

"Señor Vallone, by the time you hear this, if you do, I shall most likely be dead. If I am not, then I am trapped below in a self-contained underwater complex that may or may not have serious potential troublemaking power in the future, but not for a very long while. In any event, it, and even the great computer, are totally dependent on the good faith and will of the *Icthyo sapiens*, as I tend to call them, instead of the other way around. If Caliban is not dead, he is tamed.

"There will be a period after this when things may be difficult for you, but please trust that it will work out. The one thing a good scientist has is a mathematical mind which produces a careful experimental sequence. You will know what I mean in good time, but be patient.

"In the meantime, please try to help all the good people who I hope escaped with you. Perhaps they cannot go home again, but with the aid of a good press and one who can command public attention, perhaps you can make them into sympathetic victims rather than terrible threats, and find somewhere where they could live free and productive lives again.

"Over time, a great deal of evidence will be available, and come out at varying intervals. You will see why as time passes.

"Everyone will be picked up and taken to at least temporary shelter and safety over the next day and night. It is arranged. After that, you and your beautiful lady will have much to do. Hold on to her. You are quite literally made for each other.

"I do not know if we will meet again, or if we could, but I will wish you the very unscientific blessings of a God who *must* exist because we got away with this. *Vaya con Dios,* and name the first child after an old man."

The light turned red, and I could hear a slight whine, which, I knew from experience, meant that the little bugger had erased itself.

I looked over at Karen. "*Literally* made for each other, huh?"

She didn't care. "He said we could have *babies*!" she muttered.

"Maybe we can," I responded, holding her tight, "but we've got a lot of work to do first."

Within hours, and well before sunset, the first in a flotilla of small- and medium-sized power and sailboats began coming in. They appeared to be mostly island boats, crewed by Melanesians and flying mostly Marshall Island flags, but one of the first, a motor launch of the kind you generally see in tropical ports that's used for harbor tours and dinner cruises, was a bit different. It pulled up to the big dock, and a couple of crew jumped off with ropes and tied it off.

The door to the cabin opened, and a figure walked over to the upper rail and looked across the whole bunch of strange-looking creatures crowding the beach.

"Hey, mates!" he called out in what sounded very much like an Australian accent. "Anybody seen a bloke named Chuck Vallone?"

"Here!" I yelled back, surprised to hear my name as topic number one.

"Well, come aboard!" he called. "Got some messages for you!"

Curious as hell, we walked out on the dock and jumped the small distance from the pier to the removed rail section down below. Looking around, Karen spotted the stairs, and she and I made our way up to the pilot house deck.

Roger Dees stared at us and frowned. "Well, now, you ain't Chuck Vallone, mate! Vallone's an old bloke with a beer belly!"

"How would you know?" I retorted. "The last time he saw you, you were practically singing calypso, *mon.*"

Roger laughed. "Wrong ocean, mate. Next thing you'll be tellin' ol' Roger is that this gorgeous beauty is Karen Reedy."

"Genetic mutation isn't all bad," I told him.

He let out a huge laugh. "Well, glad to have you back in the world! George is about in another of these tubs. Rita's back home at the moment, dealing with setting up where things go from here. Besides, somebody's got to mind the bloomin' store."

Karen just stared. "You know him?"

"One of him. He's got multiple personalities, you see."

Roger laughed again. "Well, let's see if we can get this lot sorted out. We've got food on board for forty who can eat what we eat, and it's about four hours' sail."

"The pastels with the tails," I told him. "And the zebra stripers. They pretty much eat what we do. And the orangutans."

"The what?"

"The orangutans. Apes, Roger. They're people. Without them we wouldn't be here, and without them the part below could never have been pulled off. And you'll never guess who the big male is."

When I told him, his laugh was so loud and uncontrollable he scared some of the people on the beach and every seabird on both islands.

EIGHTEEN

There's a lot more to tell, but some of it continues to unfold, so there's no way we can know when it's finally really over.

Quite naturally, project security was waiting for us when we landed on a remote American military base in the eastern Marshalls, but also waiting was a three-star admiral, a two-star marine general, and a lot of marines who greatly outnumbered any Black Squad and various agency members there. And there was no pulling official Washington rank on the military brass; these guys knew as much as the project cover-up people and they were by no means pleased. In fact, when a couple of the intelligence types started trying to throw their weight around, I witnessed the most withering response I'd ever seen or heard from a military officer, particularly since they were usually so deferential.

"Son, you fuckin' assholes been out of your own goddam' loop! You fucked up worse than a two-dollar whore and as far as we're concerned you're all lower than whale shit and that's at the bottom of the ocean! You got no protection on this fuckup. None. Zero. Nada. Because of your fuckups the whole damned human race was within a mouse's tit of being history, and it was no thanks to any of us that we got out of this scrape! And if you kiss my ass and suck my sergeant's dick I might, *might,* allow you to sit in on some selected debriefings!"

And that was the mildest of the tirade.

We weren't under any illusions that we wouldn't wind up

talking to all the suits at some point, but before that a bunch of Roger's people had done a ton of debriefing and confirmation from as many refugees as possible, and it would be very unlikely that anybody would be able to completely sit on this, even though, Lord knows, they'd try. With over eight hundred refugees, representing eleven reproducing and about twenty nonreproducing mutant races, short of mass murder this could not be covered up, only smoothed over, and there wasn't any inclination to mass murder by most of the military and political types nor the project kingpins in their offices and boardrooms, because these people were the technicians and specialists who were at this point the only keys to understanding the technological breakthroughs Regen Lizard produced. They wouldn't recover a lot of it, of course, but they had Circe, divorced from Jerry and sealed off from Caliban, but still a tremendously powerful computer with much of the technology still inside its memory, if you only knew how to get it out.

And only the mutants, the scientists and technicians, knew how to get it out.

It wasn't, in fact, until we were back home and in interrogations with the suits, in this case mostly surrounded by and protected by the best Washington legal talent the Sunpapers and the L.A. syndicate owners could buy, that we learned that the Delphinides were the key and communications conduit between Vargas, the gill people, and Roger's organization and the navy just over the horizon from the project. And it wasn't until we were well back that Karen finally told me what Syzmanski had told her that she hadn't passed on.

"Chuck, Kate is one of the big red apes."

"What!"

She nodded. "She volunteered. She had the kind of up-to-the-moment knowledge of the latest in genetic modeling that Vargas needed, and she agreed to do it. It was an easier transition than most, anyway."

"Good lord! And she's stuck like that?"

"She's accepted it. She's learning to sign, and they're

gonna give her a kind of minilab with nonverbal computers wherever they settle the apes. She'd rather be human and back home, but even John says she's adapted better than most. I'm sorry."

I sighed. "There are a lot of good people victimized in this business," I told her. "I hope to God everybody learned something, but I doubt it. Even Antonio believed we kept making the same mistakes. They still are arguing over whether it's worthwhile to reestablish and fund a full-scale Chameleon, even though, God knows, we have to expand or it's all going to happen, one nightmare or the other."

She kissed me. "I hope they have learned. If not for us, for the future."

It was a while before we could have our church wedding; annulments take forever even when the boss is paying and there's no contest. Still, it's not everybody who gets a private civil marriage presided over by an associate justice of the Supreme Court. And, although it was considered old-fashioned and downright strange among middle- and upper-class folks these days, Karen insisted on taking my last name. She said it would be easier on the kids, and, besides, it makes a double byline fit nice across a three-column head. And working for one of the very few newspapers left in the country was pretty old-fashioned anyway.

Boy, did we get that byline and more, first in our own electronic and print editions, and then worldwide. It made us instant celebrities, which had its price, but it also made us safe from any retaliation, and we left out things that would really cause some nice people pain, while sticking it to whoever we could without getting sued.

The South Pacific complex over Ariel and a few other habitable and comfortable islands were also made available to the refugees, and, with a sympathetic press, some positive documentaries, and in exchange for a moratorium of some years, which we're just now breaking here, no mention of what almost happened to us all.

We have no idea about Jerry and Caliban, or the Vargases,

or any of the others left down there, but Antonio was awarded the Nobel in biology, and may now win the Peace Prize once it's known just what he did. He deserves it, wherever he is. The water people won't say, and they don't speak to us much unless they need something or want to register a complaint, but the zone around the old project is off-limits. Attempts to sneak even a robot sub into there have met with failure, and the navy's undersea listening posts in that area are dead. The only thing we can do, and we must accept them at their word, is maintain a basic contact. They have promised that if anything dangerous emerges from the depths they will tell us, but, of course, they only mean from any surviving elements of Regen Lizard. Even so, I suspect we'll all be long dead before they decide that three-fifths of the earth isn't enough.

In the meantime, much work has been done to hush up the one genetic plague that appears to have been loosed upon the world, although it was months before we knew about it. Even then, we agreed to keep it secret, but if you go to your local zoo and notice a remarkable increase in high-order apes after reading this, you might just consider that the one thing Jerry had in his computers was a DNA sample of every single mover and shaker at the top of Regen Lizard and every official or member of any Black Squad who needed security authorization.

Somehow, it seems, an otherwise benign but incredibly complex viral organism, that has since been found in our blood and in the blood and bodies of everybody we or the other refugees have come in contact with, and which can be transmitted by air as well as any other means, has slowly turned an awful lot of people all over the world into chimpanzees. When they're discovered, the Hot Zone squads, who are organized to contain dangerous new viruses, spring into action and the infected person is quickly isolated on a tropical island reserve off the coast of southern Africa that also has, and is essentially run by, the most secret of mutant strains— an incredibly intelligent group of orangutans.

You might think that, because of this mysterious plague,

we never again met Myra Ling Kelly or anybody in the Syzmanski clan again, but that's not really the case. In fact, now
and again, when we both take off for the summer from our
network anchor jobs, we work in a visit to that island, which
is off-limits to most people. We like to drop in on some old
Simian friends, and, even with the best satellite technology,
we remain solidly old-fashioned.

There's just no substitute for being there.

Except a pair of *really* good reporters.

✑ FREE DRINKS ✑

Take the Del Rey® survey and get a free newsletter! Answer the questions below and we will send you complimentary copies of the DRINK (Del Rey® Ink) newsletter free for one year. Here's where you will find out all about upcoming books, read articles by top authors, artists, and editors, and get the inside scoop on your favorite books.

Age _____ Sex ❑ M ❑ F

Highest education level: ❑ high school ❑ college ❑ graduate degree

Annual income: ❑ $0-30,000 ❑ $30,001-60,000 ❑ over $60,000

Number of books you read per month: ❑ 0-2 ❑ 3-5 ❑ 6 or more

Preference: ❑ fantasy ❑ science fiction ❑ horror ❑ other fiction ❑ nonfiction

I buy books in hardcover: ❑ frequently ❑ sometimes ❑ rarely

I buy books at: ❑ superstores ❑ mall bookstores ❑ independent bookstores
    ❑ mail order

I read books by new authors: ❑ frequently ❑ sometimes ❑ rarely

I read comic books: ❑ frequently ❑ sometimes ❑ rarely

I watch the Sci-Fi cable TV channel: ❑ frequently ❑ sometimes ❑ rarely

I am interested in collector editions (signed by the author or illustrated):
    ❑ yes ❑ no ❑ maybe

I read Star Wars novels: ❑ frequently ❑ sometimes ❑ rarely

I read Star Trek novels: ❑ frequently ❑ sometimes ❑ rarely

I read the following newspapers and magazines:

❑ *Analog*	❑ *Locus*	❑ *Popular Science*
❑ *Asimov*	❑ *Wired*	❑ *USA Today*
❑ *SF Universe*	❑ *Realms of Fantasy*	❑ *The New York Times*

Check the box if you do not want your name and address shared with qualified vendors ❑

Name _____
Address _____
City/State/Zip _____
E-mail _____

chalker

PLEASE SEND TO: DEL REY®/The DRINK
201 EAST 50TH STREET NEW YORK NY 10022
OR FAX TO THE ATTENTION OF DEL REY PUBLICITY 212/572-2676

DEL REY® ONLINE!

The Del Rey Internet Newsletter...

A monthly electronic publication e-mailed to subscribers and posted on the rec.arts.sf.written Usenet newsgroup and on our Del Rey Books Web site (www.randomhouse.com/delrey/). It features hype-free descriptions of books that are new in the stores, a list of our upcoming books, special promotional programs and offers, announcements and news, a signing/reading/convention-attendance calendar for Del Rey authors and editors, "In Depth" essays in which professionals in the field (authors, artists, cover designers, salespeople, etc.) talk about their jobs in science fiction, a question-and-answer section, and more!

Subscribe to the DRIN: send a blank message to
join-drin-dist@list.randomhouse.com

The Del Rey Books Web Site!

We make a lot of information available on our Web site at
www.randomhouse.com/delrey/

- all back issues and the current issue of the Del Rey Internet Newsletter
- sample chapters of almost every new book
- detailed interactive features for some of our books
- special features on various authors and SF/F worlds
- reader reviews of some upcoming books
- news and announcements
- our Works in Progress report, detailing the doings of our most popular authors
- and more!

If You're Not on the Web...

You can subscribe to the DRIN via e-mail (send a blank message to join-drin-dist@list.randomhouse.com) or read it on the rec.arts.sf.written Usenet newsgroup the first few days of every month. We also have editors and other representatives who participate in America Online and CompuServe SF/F forums and rec.arts.sf.written, making contact and sharing information with SF/F readers.

Questions? E-mail us...

at delrey@randomhouse.com (though it sometimes takes us a little while to answer).